Purgatorium

a Novel

J.H. Carnathan

PURGATORIUM
By J.H. Carnathan

Copyright © 2018 Jaymes Carnathan

Published by:
Jaymes H. Carnathan

Dust Jacket and title design: MadariStudio
Map and demon illustration: Alison Schofield.
Book cover design: Travis Unangst and Aleksandar Radivojevic

Paperback: ISBN: 978-0-692-89192-6
ebook: ISBN: 978-0-692-72533-7
eBook Cover Design - Red Sugar Studio
Manuscript Layout design- Bhavnish Kumar

"When the unclean spirit is gone out of a man, he walketh through dry places, seeking rest, and findeth none.

Then he saith, I will return into my house from whence I came out; and when he is come, he findeth it empty, swept, and garnished.

Then goeth he, and taketh with himself seven other spirits more wicked than himself, and they enter in and dwell there: and the last state of that man is worse than the first. Even so shall it be also unto this wicked generation."

—Matthew 12:43-45

THE A-SIDE

open my eyes. It's cold, and flakes of snow float gently around me. Where am I? Slowly, I rise and stabilize myself. My fine black suit is tattered and torn. A Jack of Hearts protrudes from my breast pocket. Why am I on the rooftop? I shiver.

The aurora borealis glows above the horizon, green ribbons dancing across the night sky. An hourglass, about a foot in height, stands on the ledge, steadily transferring sand to its bulbous lower half. The city is white, covered in a fresh layer of snow. I hear a beeping sound. Looking at my wrist, I see a watch that wasn't there before. I look closer, already dreading what it will tell me.

Fifty-five minutes.

I let out a groan, knowing I was correct. Inspecting my surroundings more clearly, I find a snow globe beside me. I pick it up and rest it comfortably in my palm. Inside is a miniature city skyline, an exact replica of the cityscape I see from the rooftop. I shake the globe, watching the tiny fake snowflakes float in precisely the same hypnotic pattern as the snow falling around me.

I remember how I got here. *How could have I been so careless?*

The sound of slithering sand grows louder with every grain. And a distant screeching weaves into the cacophony.

The screeching grows louder. Large, dark, ominous figures fill the sky.

The hourglass drops its last grain of sand. I look over the ledge. More dark figures glide up the sides of the high rise. They are about halfway up the fifty-story building. The white of their skeletal hands contrasts starkly with their inky black robes.

I am powerless.

The creatures flood toward me like a wave, blocking out any glimmer of light I can possibly see. I am surrounded, swallowed in a sea of blackness. But my hunger for vengeance is stronger than my fear. I have earned my fate.

A bony hand emerges from the darkness and touches my head. My memories, past and present, will be erased, the darkness spreading like a cancer through my cerebellum, leaving nothing but my soul.

Everything I know will be taken from me.

My hatred for the one who put me here will no longer exist. I will be a wandering soul, alone, trapped in a world of ignorance. I will be…content. I already feel my reality slipping away. *I need to fight it! I can't let them win!*

And just like clockwork, here comes the pain.

It is unbearable. My head feels like it's going to explode. My eyes burn as if on fire.

I close them tightly. Memories pour into the darkness as I try to hold on to…anything. I can't fight it. I need to remember something simple.

My name! My name is…My name is…. My name is?

In anger, I let out a big scream and listen as my voice escapes me along with the rest of my memories. My heartfelt cry withers down to a squeak, then to nothing at all. They suck every memory I ever had, leaving me only one. Always leaving only one. The only one I don't want to remember.

♣ ♠ ♦ ♥

Freezing wind numbs my face as I struggle to unlock the car door. I can feel the cold through the loose knit of my gloves. The key finally turns, and I pull up on the handle. The door is either frozen or just stubborn, unmoving as if clinging to the past. I yank harder, and it finally gives way. I jump inside and slam the door against the weather.

Dark, circled eyes stare back at me from the rearview mirror. I've seen better days.

The passenger door opens and closes. The rush of cold air hits me like a freight train.

I have to keep moving.

There's a whisky bottle in a bag on the floor. I start the car, trying to forget the reason I left it there in the first place.

The engine purrs. The dash illuminates. A rush of air from the heater hits my face. Everything comes to life at once.

I take off my necklace and place it around the rearview mirror. Tied at the bottom of the necklace is a golden coin pendant that has a Celtic hourglass carved into it. It's my number one treasure. My good luck coin. I internally beg it to guide me through this snow storm.

A thick layer of white obscures my view of the road, and I switch on the wipers. They are slightly reluctant beneath the weight of accumulated snow. My headlamps flood fifteen yards down the ice-packed shoulder. Tree limbs hang over the road like spindly fingers.

I turn the heater up and listen to the sound of the wiper blades for a moment. *Whirr, thwack, whirr, thwack, whirr, thwack.* A familiar sound interrupts- a buzzing in my ear like an alarm clock going off in my head. I turn my head toward the sound, and everything goes black.

SATURDAY

I jolt awake, the alarm clock still blaring insistently. I quickly turn it off.

A simple but elegant desk rests between my bed and a grand picture window. The cloudy day slips in between the heavy curtains.

Was I having a nightmare? I don't remember much.

A black, leather-bound Bible and a watch rests at the base of a chic lamp on the bedside table. The book takes me back in an uneasy way.

This doesn't belong here.

I shove the Bible into the drawer where it belongs and relax.

I snatch my watch and wrap it around my wrist, snapping it in place. Its case is stainless steel with carbon-titanium coating. Around the edge, white numbers mark every five minutes, stark against the watch's black face. It has only two hands, the long, thin second hand and the fatter minute hand. I wipe sweat from my brow. The display to my alarm clock changes to that of a stopwatch. 00:01…00:02…00:03…00:04.

The second hand on my watch is ticking, matching the seconds flipping on my alarm clock. The count has begun. Time to start my day. I edge to the side of the bed. The room's furnishings are stylish, modern, and expensive. The room is massive, with dark hardwood floors and ornate moldings accenting the sterile white walls.

There's a hatchet mounted in a glass case on the wall. It is worn and beat-up, used, like a tomahawk. Brutal by juxtaposition against the upscale decor.

I slide out of the bed and rest my feet on the smooth, gleaming floor. I pause and release a sigh of contentment. Opposite my bed hangs a life-size portrait of me. Behind the slight droop in my eyes, long nose, and soft jaw is a certain confidence, pride. My mousy brown hair is styled to perfection, and my overall appearance, in tandem with the lavish tuxedo painted onto the canvas, looks like something from the cover of *GQ*.

I force myself to stand and trudge past my desk to the window as the curtains fully retract. The sky is dark and cloudy. That seems right.

I look at the crystal-clear pane, focused not on the cityscape but on my own reflection.

To the left of the window is a brown Victoria Palace leather chaise with soft curves and a button-tufted design. I straighten my posture, roll my shoulders back, and raise my chin a little higher.

I turn from the skyline and look back to my desk. Something is off. A new object is lying on it. I go over to inspect this misplaced item. It's a snow globe.

Where did this come from?

Its interior is exactly the same as the city skyline outside my window. As I shake it, the miniature falling snow is mesmerizing.

An image floods my consciousness. Me, holding the snow globe, in the middle of the night.

My heart races. My head hurts. I thrust the globe back onto the desk.

I look out again at my city. I take a couple of slow breaths. My body relaxes, my pulse subsides. I am content.

I glance at the clock. 01:00. Four minutes to finish my morning routine and walk out the door.

I walk past the hatchet and into the living room.

Everything in this spacious apartment is of the highest quality, masculine and immaculate. Everything is in its place. Clean. Neat. Perfect.

My book collection populates the ceiling built-in case. Each book is meticulously placed one-and-a-half inches from the front edge of its shelf, every volume flush with the next. Inexplicably, I turn away to prepare myself for the day.

There's a deadline to meet. Three-and-a-half minutes to go.

Rapid pushups to get my heart pumping. Thirty. My breathing is heavy. Hasty pull-ups in the doorframe. Fifteen and done.

The bathroom is marble-tiled—a rich, clean interior space, just as immaculate as the living room. I stride toward the shower, admiring my muscular, toned body in the mirror. Perfection. My deep green eyes give me pause.

In the shower, I turn the polished faucet handles. There's a clanking in the pipes, followed by a chunky brown liquid pouring from the shower head. I turn it off and step out. I go to the basin and lather up, removing a straight razor from the medicine cabinet, but there's no water here, either.

Same clanking, same disgusting brown liquid.

I unfold the cut-throat and start to shave very carefully without water. There's something sinister in my reflection, an evil glint in my glowing green eyes. I bring the blade to my neck and press firmly, but the man in the mirror takes a different action.

My reflection slits its throat.

I drop the razor. Blood droplets ring the sink around the blade.

I nicked myself. In the mirror, everything is back to normal. I move my hand, and my reflection follows.

I must be tired. Nothing supernatural, just lack of sleep. I relax back into contentment.

I pick up the blade. It feels good in my hand. I am quite adept with a straight razor—a perfectionist, a running machine that never makes mistakes. But blood drips down my neck. I'm imperfect. I look at the tiny cut, but feel nothing. No pain. I finish shaving without another problem.

I wipe the blood from my neck and comb my hair back.

My watch shows three minutes, ten seconds.

Music begins to play in the living room. The smooth, beautiful tones rise and fall. It sends a tremble down my spine. Pain and death enter my thoughts for a fraction of a second.

In a dark corner of the living room, I find a Yamaha Grand Disklavier. The keys on the player piano move on their own. There's an amplifier console under the keyboard that sends the music throughout the entire apartment.

The haunting melody strikes me as pure, yet in some way terrible. I listen till the last key plays.

I need to get back on track. Keep to the deadline. One minute, thirty seconds to go.

In the bedroom closet are long rows of finely tailored, handcrafted dark suits and crisp, trim-fit designer shirts. Ties hang to the side above rows of gleaming Italian leather loafers. The racks and drawers extend the full length of the room.

I get dressed with a sense of calm urgency. I button my suit vest and jacket and pull something from my handkerchief pocket. A playing card. Jack of Hearts. The colors are different, though, the reds replaced with cyan, the whites with black.

With no time to waste, I shove the card back into place. I retrieve some leather gloves, a pair of platinum cufflinks, and a shearling dress coat.

A cabinet in the back corner of the closet houses shelves full of neatly stacked cash, sorted by denomination. I remove a single bill from each stack. In a smaller drawer is a leather wallet. I put in the cash and take out a business card.

Peter J. Cameron, Music Producer

Why do I have this card? I slide it back into the wallet and into my coat. I come out with an engraved, steel flask from the same pocket.

Après moi, le déluge

I'm not sure where this came from or why I have it, but I put it back into my coat, as well.

4:50. I half smile; I am content.

I look out at the city one last time.

I grab an apple from the fridge and step out my front door.

My watch beeps.

Five minutes.

The hallway outside my apartment is a mixture of earth tones. The walls are painted a light beige, and the apartment doors are creamy-white. Outlining the plush carpet is a strip of creamy-white, which matches the doors. The rest of the carpet is composed of muted brown, green, and mauve behind a white Japanese flower design.

Just outside my door are three transparent stacks of gum. Inside, each stick is packaged in a silver and white wrapper labeled, "Tredstones."

Across the hallway, a woman exits her apartment. She appears to be in her late twenties. Her wavy dark brown hair flows over her shoulders along her well-formed curves and ends at her petite waist. Her innocent green eyes hold my gaze from under her brow-length bangs. She has a pale, creamy complexion that contrasts with her cherry red lip gloss. She's in a housekeeping dress—a snug black and white number. Sharp, white collar, sheer mesh sweetheart neckline, and matching white cuffs. Long, slender legs extend from under the uniform's pencil skirt.

She nods and walks out the stairway door.

Before I can ask her about the gum, the door closes and she's gone. I drop the stacks in the trash chute and walk to the elevator.

The elevator doors slide open. I see a young man, probably mid-thirties, standing inside. What catches my eye first is the clerical collar around his neck. I have never seen a priest dress like this before. Instead of the normal everyday black suit priests typically wear, he seems to be in good money, judging by his expensive-looking midnight blue suit and polished black shoes. His hair is neatly cut and brushed back, creating a subtle wave on one side. In his breast pocket is a playing card, the King of Spades and just behind it is a yellow pocket square. The brilliant cyan and black of the card make a pleasing contrast with the yellow backdrop. He smiles, genuine, suggestive, and full of promise all at once. The dimple in his chin deepens. His confidence is almost contagious. His bright green eyes meet mine.

"Going down?" he asks. "Or somewhere in between?"

I press the Lobby button and the elevator doors shut us in.

He holds out his hand to me. "Name's Barachiel."

I look at him in silence and back away, not wanting to shake it. He lowers it again. His necklace catches my eye. It's a golden coin pendant with a Celtic hourglass carved into it.

Have I seen that before?

"I must confess, I've read your books, old sport." Barachiel laughs a little to himself. "Me confessing. That's new! I hear you're having trouble with your latest and greatest. If you want I can come and help..."

I turn to face the painting at the back of the compartment. The electric blue runs across the canvas, following its singular path from light to dark. In the center is a cross. Not a wooden cross, but a cross made of light, almost an electric blue. It seems to glow off the canvas. But even more interesting are the seven demons surrounding the cross, latching themselves to its top, arms, body, and legs, each one displaying a different color.

He turns to face the painting with me.

"Most people would say it is a battle between heaven and hell, but I believe it is much more human than that. To me, it is about holding on to the light inside one's soul. But the tricky part is this: demons are attracted to the light. The purple demon at the very top is Pride, clouding the head with thoughts of misperceived grandeur and an inflated sense of oneself. The red demon by the neckline is Wrath, strangling the light, suffocating it from ever having a clear conscious mind. The yellow demon, Greed, and the green demon, Envy, are on separate sides, playing tug of war, pulling one's arms in every direction apart from the right one. The orange demon below it is Gluttony. It fills one's belly with doubt and fear of doing anything productive. Then the darker shade of blue demon is Lust, who is driven by unbridled desires near the crotch region. And lastly the sky blue colored demon you see there at the very bottom is Sloth, clinging to one's legs, thinks unconsciousness is bliss. It forces one to stay down, forebearing one's achievements."

I stand there, still silent. There's nothing I want to say to this strange fellow.

I keep an eye on my watch. The minute hand rests on the seventh notch while the second hand steadily makes its circuit. 15...16 ...17.

Could the elevator possibly move any slower?

I try not to keep eye contact with him, hoping he will just stop talking.

The elevator light glimmers on the pendant around his neck. I can now make out a set of wings behind the hourglass engraved on its face. My mind calms as I get lost in its shimmering glow. Almost as if it were calling to me.

He turns to me, "It really makes one question on what to believe in. How about you?"

His eyes stop at my breast pocket. I shift my focus back to the elevator doors. The priest reaches into my breast pocket and pulls the Jack of Hearts halfway up, so that it protrudes like a pocket square, like his King of Spades does.

"What do you believe in?"

The wrinkle between his brows deepens as he offers a smile.

The elevator doors open, and I lunge forward, away from this maniac.

"God be with you," he says.

The doors slide shut on Barachiel's tanned, smiling face.

My watch indicates 7:35. I exit through the revolving glass doors to the street.

Cars are zipping up and down the street, and people are walking around like they have a purpose in their step. They stream down the streets, heads bowed as if in prayer, each of them mesmerized by what's on their phones.

Parked across the street is my beautiful 1987 Ferrari Testarossa. It's like a thinly disguised race car wrapped in gorgeous sheet metal. Its jet-black coating glistens beneath the streetlights. My pulse is steady as I open the door and get in. The feel of the cold leather seat underneath me is somewhat calming. My watch beeps again.

Ten minutes.

The radio is all static, as usual. I turn on the car and put it in drive. As I gently push on the gas, the car seems not to move. I look at my rearview mirror and notice a boot on the back of my left tire.

I get out and look at my watch. I can't be late.

Luckily, a bus pulls up to my building, and I quickly get on.

The door shuts directly behind me, and the bus driver already has his foot on the gas. We speed onto the interstate. I look around to find that every seat is taken except for the first seat. Almost everyone is playing on their phones. I continue to stand, watching the bus weave through traffic. When finally I go to sit down to look out the window, I spot a steel-black sedan passing on the right with a LBYRNTH plate. After that, a truck passes. It carries a cargo of window glass. My reflection stares back at me, almost sinister-looking.

My mind is playing tricks on me again.

The bus pulls off on the first exit and pulls into a run-down strip mall. *I need coffee.*

A warm feeling comes over me. Something good once happened here, but I can't remember what it was.

My watch beeps. Right on time.

Fifteen minutes.

At the far end of the strip is a little coffee shop. Its pink neon-lit sign can be seen from a mile away. It reads: "The Haberdashery."

The bus stops, and I walk out.

From the look of it, a long line is already in waiting status.

Stepping into the line, I begin to zone out. Minutes pass as I continue stepping one foot in front of the other, drawing ever closer to the register. The people in front of me are all on their phones in silence.

My watch beeps again.

Twenty minutes.

I can't wait any longer. I grab a newspaper from the rack next to me and head outside.

I cross the street and wander up a hill into the park. I stare at the green grass that fills the park. A distant Ferris wheel turns slowly on its own, the eerie sound of rusted metal echoing across the park.

People around the park are all walking like they are on a mission to be somewhere important, each one with a phone in hand.

A pair of cream-colored shoes and white pant legs invade my vision a few feet ahead. I startle. There's a man sitting on my bench, his short, graying brown hair parted on the side. He wears an all white suit and a green vest that heavily distracts from the rest of his attire.

His suit is just as stylish as the priest's suit—what was his name again, Barachiel? And just like Barachiel, there isn't a flaw anywhere on him.

His face is much longer, his skin a bit lighter, and he has a large, toothy grin on his face as if he were listening to a favorite niece telling a story. Oddly, he's sipping tea with a bone china teacup in one hand and a saucer in the other.

There's an Ace of Spades card protruding from his breast pocket. Barachiel had displayed the King of Spades. Is this really a style of some sort?

The scent of bergamot tea, still steaming, permeates the air. I take a seat on the other end of the bench and lay my newspaper next to me.

"If I may say, you're acting quite the lost soul," he says to me in an impeccable British accent. He tilts his head up, causing his horn-rimmed glasses to deflect a blinding glare in my immediate direction. "Pleased to meet you. My name is Sealtiel." I can see that he notices my ill comfort, and he moves his head away from the light. His big frames bring out the green in his eyes. I get completely lost in them for a second. "It is quite pleasant out today," he continues, snapping me out of my trance. "Quieted down, as well. Makes you wonder why everything is so silent."

I look around, suddenly overwhelmed by the quiet.

"It's particularly interesting, I think, eh?" He enunciates every syllable of *particularly* with that crisp British accent of his.

The silence is strange, but I'm not sure I want to encourage this man, either. I give a slight nod.

"You seem slightly out-of-sorts," Sealtiel continues, his green eyes curious. He looks at my watch. "Exquisite timepiece. May I examine it?"

I'm about to refuse, when he puts a finger on my lips and says, "Don't say anything that will get you into trouble later."

He places his china on the bench and takes off my watch as I sit there, frozen. I don't want any trouble.

Sealtiel seems excited, almost childlike, while he handles my watch. He plays with the display before returning it to its original settings. He turns the piece over to look at the back and smirks.

"It is a powerful thing, love," he says. "It can never be taken, only given, much like this watch. To other people, acts of love may seem quite meaningless, but to the recipient? Love is everything. That, my friend, is more valuable than gold."

What exactly is he talking about? He hands the watch back to me as if he is hesitant to do so and takes my newspaper from where it sits on the bench, finding the crossword section.

"I'm quite keen on these!" Sealtiel says. He studies the clues for a moment. "You wouldn't happen to know a nine-letter word for *A Season in* blank by Dominick Dunne, would you?"

Annoyed by Sealtiel's strange behavior, I ignore the question. The ace in Sealtiel's pocket adds a splash of cyan to his otherwise colorless suit. What is the deal with the playing cards? Fashion trend, maybe?

"The five-hundred-and-fifty-foot High Roller is the tallest Ferris wheel in the world," Sealtiel says. "It has twenty-eight glass-enclosed, air-conditioned gondolas that can each hold up to forty people." His t's are all very sharp and distinct. "A full revolution just takes a few minutes, too. Simply fantastic."

I look up at the Ferris wheel. I hadn't noticed how tall it was.

"You cut yourself?"

I look down to see him staring at my neckline where I had nipped myself this morning. I don't answer. Instead, I use my collar to hide my minor imperfection away from his sight.

"Never thought of you as one who makes mistakes. Particularly interesting."

I shift back and forth in my seat and scan the Ferris wheel again. I don't make mistakes. And this random stranger certainly doesn't need to be thinking I do. I give him a sour look so he'll quit talking to me.

"Make no friendship with an angry man; and with a furious man thou shalt not go, lest thou learn his ways, and get a snare to thy soul." Sealtiel laughs giddily for a moment, then replaces the paper with his cup and saucer and takes another sip of tea.

I look across the brown expanse of the park, trying to clear my head of this loony tune.

A gust of wind interrupts the calm of the moment, and the newspaper blows away, its pages scattering. Two sections are caught against a huge, lifeless tree with a hollow in its base about the size of a large dog.

The wind calms. I look over, and Sealtiel is holding on to the same newspaper. Not a paper in sight against the tree.

How did he do that? I must be seeing things.

He takes his pen and goes back to the crossword puzzle. "Purgatory," he says triumphantly, the last syllable sounding like *tree* instead of *tory*. "Nine letters!" He grins like he just won a million dollars.

I look up at the large, desolate tree. Its black, naked limbs seem to ensnare the wind as if nothing can escape its eerie frame, the empty cavity in its trunk a portal to unknown darkness.

As if reading my mind, Sealtiel warns, "Some might say that is a door that leads to hell. But not what your mummy and daddy told you as a little tyke, no. Your own personal hell"—he lowers his voice—"where a fellow's personal demons lurk."

Sealtiel suddenly breaks into song. "Where your fears and sins collide into one, and your demons play tricks till your soul is done."

He flashes a broad smile then takes a long sip of tea. The sound is cloying.

"Ah. Now that's a nice cuppa. Course, these are only ghost stories. Demon stories, rather. Not afraid of demons, are we? Or are you the kind of fellow who wrestles with them daily? On occasion, they do get the best of you, eh? Well, that's what second chances are for, I suppose. You believe in second chances, eh?"

Wind blows across my face, frigid. It chills me to the bone. Sealtiel is tipping his teacup toward his mouth with a satisfied look. But no tea meets his lips. He turns the cup sideways over the saucer, and a small disc of frozen tea drops onto the saucer with a tink.

"It's about 'time' to be off, I think." He lets loose a high-pitched giggle.

My alarm hasn't gone off. My watch shows 26:05. I'm late! This crazy nut messed with my watch!

I break into a dead run in the direction of my office building. *I am content. I am content. I am content.*

I hurry down the hill and across the open space, past a life-size marble statue of a nude man. Its muscles are chiseled to perfection, and its face is flawlessly symmetrical. In its extended hand is a glass box, approximately a foot cubed.

As soon as I pass it, the wind dies down, and the temperature returns to normal. I turn away from the statue and look over to the other side of the park, where my publishing building stands, thirty stories high. I begin making my way toward it, all the while wondering to myself if I'm dreaming. I pinch my arm and don't feel it. My heart begins to pound at a faster rate. An indescribable feeling overwhelms my senses. Something new. Almost painful but also exhilarating. It gives me a strange rush I never felt before. I think I feel afraid. Feeling this way is very unnatural. I can't be dreaming. But if I'm not dreaming then…*what is happening to me?*

y private glass elevator runs along the side of the building, making its way down to greet me. Inside the building are two public elevators, available for clients and employees.

After boarding the elevator, I watch the park get smaller while more of it comes into view. The people become more like ants the farther I climb.

The elevator doors open into a massive room filled with busy people walking in and out of doors. The place runs like a Wall Street stock exchange. Phones are ringing off the hook, as people are too busy to even pick up. My watch beeps as I enter my office.

Thirty minutes.

My office is cavernous. There's a full bar, leather sofa, and treadmill. A long hallway in the far corner leads to a small kitchenette. My bookcase, with all the works I have published under my name, stands opposite the wall of windows. My legacy is in this bookcase. My only treasures in life. A large evergreen stands in the corner, adorned with twinkling red, green, and white lights.

I head over to an enormous mahogany desk. A glass case at the end of it holds two flintlock pistols pointing toward each other, as if held by invisible duelists.

The gun on the left features a dark-stained wooden stock, engraved lock, and a simulated blunderbuss barrel with a silver lamb engraved into the butt plate. The gun on the right is almost identical, except its butt plate displays a golden lion. Behind the desk is an old phonograph sitting next to a grandfather clock. The ticking of the clock is the only sound to be heard.

I gaze out over the city. Seconds pass, and time reverberates through my bones, echoing in my heart. 31:07.

I close my eyes, the events of the last half-hour racing through my mind. Both the refined man in the elevator and the Brit in the park were exceedingly weird. I force myself to take deep, slow breaths to calm my mind.

The sound of the grandfather clock eventually penetrates my meditation, letting me know that I need to get to work.

A black man, late forties, wearing a dark violet, perfectly tailored suit saunters in. "Tick tock, tick tock, tick tock goes the clock." A Ten of Spades protrudes from his breast pocket. His hair is cut close to his scalp, and he has a well-kept goatee.

The man swaggers to the grandfather clock, his shoulders back and head held high. Even through the thick fabric of his violet suit, his sculpted muscles bulge with every move. He snatches the grandfather clock into the air and shatters it against the floor. Then he puts a cigar in his mouth and holds it there while he pulls a matchbook from his pocket. The matchbook is elegant, silver filigree against a gold backdrop. He lights a match and touches it to the end of the cigar.

I lean away from him. My watch reads thirty one minutes, thirty seconds. I don't have time for this guy.

15

"You late, brother," he says, blowing smoke in my face. His voice is cool, calm, and collected. "I take pride in the work that I do. You know why?"

The man takes another pull and walks to the window. He gazes out over the city.

I am about to say something when his bright green eyes lock onto mine.

"Because I'm good at what I do. I'm Raphael, your new boss."

He laughs heartily, his green eyes trained intensely on mine. Then he grows serious. "If you show up late again, I will have to choke-slam your tail right out that damn window."

Raphael takes his cigar out of his mouth and puts it out on my desk. "I bought your company out today with cash money, paid in full. This publishing company needs a restart. Needs a name. Who ever heard of a multi-billion-dollar company not having a name? But I digress; where was I? Ah! A refresher course on what works and what don't, you feel me, my boy?"

He's supposed to be my new boss?

Raphael takes his finger and grazes my shaving scar. "Something off with you, but I ain't figured it out just yet. How about I think about it while you pull up the book you working on?"

Unsure where to look, I try to remain calm as I flip through the folders on my desk for anything. Grabbing one, I hand it to Raphael.

"This must be what 'pretty well' got you, huh?" Raphael says, opening the folder. He pulls out a blank page. "Still waiting," he says, handing the folder back to me.

I begin flipping through the other pages, looking for anything resembling a body of work. This has to be a joke.

Raphael leans against the desk, uncomfortably close, and pulls out another cigar. "All the long hours—I mean minutes—spent scribbling over what? Your garbage sees more action than you do."

I look over at the plentiful amount of crumpled-up paper in my overflowing garbage can.

He lights the second cigar of his visit and blows smoke in my face. Again. "What you even do here? Write books, right? Like these on your shelves here?"

He walks to my bookshelf. "These yours, right?"

I nod.

He opens each one of them, turns one page, and immediately tosses them to the floor. "This a joke?"

He hands a book to me. I flip it open to find it blank. Madly, I tear through the empty pages, wondering where all my words went. "Every book is completely blank. You got any words to say about that? 'Cause apparently you ain't got none to write."

He takes a book off the floor. "You remember what this one called?" He slams the book onto my desk. "Or how about this one?"

He picks up another and slaps it onto my desk. "Or this one, or this one, or this one." He stacks my desk with all my books. All the while, I can't seem to remember any of their titles.

Without giving me time to speak my mind, he starts up again.

"I see you only work five minutes a day. How much you get paid for that? Five thousand dollars a minute?" He laughs. "I mean, it got to be close to that to afford those nice expensive clothes, that sports car, and that bachelor pad. How do you find this job gratifying enough to stay?"

He blows smoke in my face yet again. I try waving it away.

"Excuse me." He snickers. "But have you even so much as coughed once since I been here blowin' smoke in your face? Even better, do you remember the last time you was really coughing?"

Oh. He's right. I haven't been coughing. What's he trying to get at?

Raphael takes out a book from his suitcase, flips to the last page, and slides it over to me.

"Do something useful. Tell me what you think of this?"

I look down at the long, developed page, not sure how much he wanted me to read too.

"Hurry up now, I'll tell you when to stop," he says with a puff of his cigar.

I recognize the writing is my own. *Did I write this?*

I start at the top and begin to read:

It seems like forever ago when I first arrived here. I've had my memories erased so many times that I forget how long it's been but I do clearly remember the feeling of nothingness. Stuck in a deathlike trance. Trapped in a void of darkness where everything just felt cold. A frozen face to a world that was beyond my control. Reapers on guard judging my every move, all waiting for me to get out of line so they could feast on my memories. Even as a cruel joke, this prison used my desires against me, plaguing me with money and independence, yet no time to enjoy all the fortune, no thanks to the specifically structured schedule made to keep me in check.

The time zones were never the difficult part of my day, it was the countdown up to the last second. Filling every drawing minute to sixty with agonizing pain. Every moment I had my eyes closed would make me relive that dreadful car accident over again, watching Madi lay there almost lifeless while Anna screamed out for me, just to wake back up to repeat the whole day again.

I get ready to turn the last page, eagerly wanting to read more when Raphael yells, "That's enough for today!"

Raphael grabs the book out of my hands, rips out the last paper, and throws the book into the trash can beside my desk.

I don't remember writing that.

I watch as Raphael folds up the torn paper and places it in his back pocket.

"I bet none of that got through to you?"

I look at him blankly.

"It will soon enough. Until then you needs to get your head back on straight."

He reaches in and pulls out one of the crumpled sheets, flicks another match, and sets the page on fire.

"What I'm saying is, you a conformist in a rule-bound society living by the seconds of time you been dealt. You a slave. And I am here to set you free, my man."

I feel a shock run through my entire body. I've been able to control my reactions until now, but what he is saying is starting to make sense. *A slave?* My obsession with my watch has consumed my life. There's nothing more important to me than being where I need to be when I need to be there. Is that slavery? If so, who's doing the enslaving?

My head hurts.

"You see! This is what this place do. Emotionless. Passionless. I would say soulless but that is maybe the only thing you do have. You are a prisoner inside your own mind and I'm the man with the skills of helping you get out. It's just up to you if you want to get out or not. How about it?"

Raphael's cigar has gone out. He lights it again, using the burning piece of paper.

"Time's up, but I'mma do you one proper; I in a good mood today. I'll give you a second chance if you think you deserve it." He pauses and waits for me to respond.

What do I say? What do I do? My pulse is pounding. I need to think.

"Write me a short story. No wait! Even better, write a name for our company. A simple name. Go crazy, for all I care. Start naming mascots and add *company* at the end of it, whatever floats your boat! You like sports, right? Anything that pops in your head. Go!"

I don't respond. He hands me a blank piece of paper and a pen.

"Go on. Really, I ain't got all day!"

I try to think, but the words don't come. I am content. I am content. I am content. Why don't I feel content? Why can't I think of a simple title? My heart races, my forehead sweats, and my body stiffens. What is happening to me?

"Let me guess. Writer's block?" Raphael slams his hands on the desk and shoves his face close to mine. I can almost feel the coarse black hairs of his goatee on my nose. "You feeling content now?"

I freeze.

Raphael throws the smoldering piece of paper in the trash. It ignites the rest of the used papers, and he laughs sadistically as smoke fills the room.

His words still ring in my head. *You feeling content now?* The elevator doors open.

The smoke makes it hard to see even Raphael's loud violet suit. This is my chance to get out of here.

I leave the office and notice no one caring or showing any emotion over the fact that my office is burning down. They oddly keep going about their business as if nothing's wrong.

I rush to the elevator and dive in. The elevator doors close with no sign of Raphael.

I take a few breaths, waiting till the doors open to the lobby. Then I rush out, trying to get my head focused.

I leave the building and cross the empty street toward a restaurant with a lighthouse facade.

The sound of an engine roars through the street. I turn toward it, and my body slams against the hood and windshield of a bright red Dodge Viper. I tumble across the rough asphalt, finally coming to a stop on my back.

I'm still alive. I feel my head, chest, legs. All there. Nothing seems amiss. My suit isn't even torn. The Viper door opens, and a hairy, sandy-colored foot plants itself on the road, followed by another.

It's a man, late thirties, with a long, dirty-blond ponytail and a closely-trimmed jawline beard. His flawless skin and friendly smile are oddly disarming. He's wearing a navy blue tie with a charcoal suit of the latest fashion. Who would've guessed bare feet would complement the ensemble so well?

The song "I Wanna Dance With Somebody" blares from inside the car. He sings along while looking at the dented hood of his car and lays his hand on it gently. Then he kisses it, lowers his head, and shakes it slowly.

More amazed than angry, I rise from the pavement to confront the driver, but I don't know what to say. He has a King of Diamonds protruding from his breast pocket. Instead of a red and white theme, it's inverted with cyan, like mine. Reminds me of a photographic negative. He looks back at me, repeatedly twisting what appears to be a wedding ring on his left hand. I brush myself off.

"I'm Uriel." His *I'm* sounds more like *oim,* and he keeps his mouth mostly closed, forming a thick Australian accent. "Hope I didn't ruin that beautiful suit you're wearing."

This guy hits me with his car and he's wondering about my suit? He could have killed me!

He walks toward me. His movements are polished, almost as if he's modeling the dark gray suit on a runway.

I stand up about to say something, and he puts his finger over my lips.

"May I?" His *may* sounds more like *moi.* He runs two fingers over the fabric of my suit. "Gucci. You're a man who knows style. I admire that."

I step out of his reach just as a car rounds the corner and barrels in our direction. We jump out of the way. "Doesn't anyone know how to drive anymore?"

"So where were we?" He points at his damaged car. "Now, who is going to pay for this? Not I, says the mocking bird. By the look of that handsome face of yours, you don't seem to concur? I'm going to need to speak to a witness." I look around at all the people just playing with their phones, not one of them gawking at our situation.

"Isn't that just typical. Not a single soul around when you need them."

I point at a random person walking, showing him proof of life.

"I dare you to go touch his face and prove a point for me," Uriel suggests.

I stand my ground, thinking he's absurd.

Uriel takes out a roll of cash. "I will bet you ten thousand. All you need to do is get somebody to pay attention to you. Bonus!

If you can get someone to talk to you, I will buy you any car you desire!" He sticks the cash deep inside my pants pocket.

He is actually serious. I go up to a random woman playing on her phone and stand in front of her. She doesn't stop and, at the last second, walks around me. I turn around, and she is gone. What just happened?

"Mindless drooling de-animated human husks. They're as much zombies to you as you are to them. Though they only exist because you are allowing them to exist." Uriel gets in my confused face.

"Now back to what's important. How in the hell didn't you see me? I mean, the fiery red body? The chrome detailing?" Uriel looks at the passing cars. "'Especially since my vehicle is the only one with a driver actually in it—at least for the time being." Uriel pauses while I look at all the passing cars with drivers inside, talking on their phones.

In the blink of an eye, they seem to have disappeared from their vehicles. I shake it off. I begin to react when he puts his finger on my lips again.

"You're not much of a talker. Good. I prefer shy people." He leaves off his *r*'s and pronounces *shy* like *shoi*.

He smirks and rubs my lips with his fingers. "You still see them, don't ya? Don't worry; all in good time. At least now your brain is on the fritz. Just a few more tune-ups required, and you will be as good as you again."

He stops when he sees I'm starting to get pissed. Uriel shrugs.

"A simple apology would suffice," he continues in his diphthongal accent. "Saying you're sorry is powerful, y'know? And I'm a big believer in second chances." Uriel's gaze drags my eyes to his. Green, just like mine, just like all the rest.

"What about you?"

This is the fourth time today someone's talked to me about second chances. That can't be coincidence. I am about to say something when Uriel slaps me across the face. "Now we're even. I think that was a fair trade."

Before I can reflect further, a silver Porsche Carrera convertible pulls up beside us, driverless.

"Not bad," Uriel drawls, "not bad at all." He drags his hand over the car door, turns to me with a smirk, and hops in. "It's been real nice chattin' with ya—keep the Viper. It's about time I got a new ride, anyway!" The engine roars. "Have a nice day, Gucci!" Uriel shouts, then laughs.

I watch in stunned silence as the car speeds away.

I look over at the Lighthouse restaurant across the street. There's a black spiral staircase making its way around the white exterior walls. My watch beeps insistently for a moment.

Thirty-five minutes.

I brush the dirt off my pants and make my way inside, not to be late for my appointment.

I enter the restaurant and find people all eating quietly, playing with their phones. A fire crackles in the small fireplace to the left of the back windows. A gold chandelier hangs from a lofty, pearl-colored ceiling. The walls are crimson with gold accents. High-backed booths of deep blood-red line the edges of the room. Tables fill the rest of the interior, displaying crystal stemware and fine porcelain place settings for two. Each table has its own linen tablecloth and matching origami napkins. I stride across the cherry-wood floor and take a seat at a center table. Above the bar hang five masks. Each mask is painted with the representation of a playing card. Ace of Hearts, King of Hearts, Queen of Hearts, Jack of Hearts, and Ten of Hearts.

They each have a pearl white backdrop, except for two. The Ace of Hearts is jet-black, and the Ten of Hearts' color is split down the middle, with jet-black on its left and pure white on its right. Each mask has a heart displayed in a different location. The Jack's heart is on the upper left hand side, while the Ten's heart is on its right. The Queen's heart is placed on the right cheek. The King's heart is lying behind its left eye, and the Ace's heart is covering its right eye almost like an eye patch.

Stay focused.

A menu sits next to my place setting. There are no prices listed, and all the items are written in French. A door swings open, and a waitress walks out with a bottle of red wine and a covered platter. She glides across the floor with poise, her black pencil skirt not making a sound. Her uniform's white collar and cuffs are ironed to perfection. Her waist-length brunette hair has been pinned back under a white headpiece. It's the woman I saw in the hall. She pours a glass of wine and removes the silver platter cover, revealing veal medallions in raspberry truffle sauce, along with sea scallops with puréed artichoke hearts.

She averts her gaze and hurries away into the kitchen.

A few seconds later, a man stumbles out of the kitchen—mid-thirties, wearing light blue suspenders over a crisp white shirt, swank dress pants, and a black fedora. Tucked into the ribbon of the fedora is a Queen of Spades card. He's carrying a bucket of water with soapy green foam on top. He trips over his own foot and drops the bucket. It lands upright, but some of the green contents slosh onto the cherry-wood floors. He rights himself and carries the bucket to my table.

His close-cropped hair makes his prominent nose and ears even more noticeable, and his lanky body exudes a certain awkward charm.

"It's all in your mind!" His voice is high, bright, and full of a sense of glee. He taps my forehead and softens his voice. "It's all in your mind."

He begins to sing, horrendously out of tune. "Humpty Dumpty went to sleep. Humpty Dumpty sleeps twenty weeks. From all of the places to all of his sins, he can't bring his memories back again."

He falls silent and unscrews the lid of my saltshaker, pouring the white crystals onto the tablecloth. He pulls four small tinfoil balls out of his pocket, puts them into the shaker, fills it up with the green liquid from the bucket, and screws the lid back on. He covers the holes with his thumb and shakes it vigorously, looking at me all the while with a stupid grin on his face.

The shaker slips from his grasp and flies into the air. I stand up, knocking my chair backward, and jump out of the way. The shaker hits the floor and explodes. Green liquid and shards of glass pelt both of us. My jacket is ruined. No wonder he'd already removed his.

"Needs water to dilute it, but it's hard to find water in a waterless place," he says. His white shirt is now speckled with green, which seems more befitting of his odd, lanky charm. "They call me Jehudiel. What do they call you?" He takes a drink of wine straight from the bottle on the table.

I am about to say my name when, for the life of me, I can't remember it.

Before I can answer, he sneezes the wine all over my face.

"Just releasing that ole demon," he says. "Don't bless me." He laughs. "Salem witch joke."

He throws me a napkin, and I start to dab my face.

"Not for your face, silly. You're bleeding." He points to my neck.

I touch my neck and come away with blood. "Got lost in Wonderland again, haven't we, Alice?"

Great, another weirdo on this weirdest of days. I'd welcome the strange solitude again if it meant getting rid of this waste of time.

I'm about to speak my mind when he stops me once again. "Have you seen my silver? I've misplaced it. Can't have gone too far."

He then goes around to every table, asking everyone about his so-called silver. When he finally comes back to me, he says, "Nobody seems to know. Sorry. Got sidetracked again…Wait. What was your name again?"

I finally open my mouth to respond, but for some reason I can't speak. I try again, anything to make a sound but—nothing.

Why can't I speak? What's wrong with me?

"Cat got yer tongue? Don't worry your little head about it. We all don't know our real names either! Never was strong enough to remember. Once the demon goes up, no more memories to remember. Name goes bye bye."

This odd man has had either too much to drink or is completely insane.

"I was lost for a long time. Then I found friends that wanted to save souls from being lost like me. They even gave me a new name. Jehudiel. Told me I was a part of the seven archangels. That's our gang name."

Jehudiel grabs a bottle from the bar and a corkscrew from his pocket. He pulls the cork and starts chugging the wine, all while seriously eyeing me over that big nose of his. He downs the entire bottle, takes a breath, and looks totally satisfied.

"I know your name by the way. You figured it out months ago and told me. I guess you don't remember again."

I wait eagerly wanting to hear if he actually knew my name.

"It's very simple, sir. Simple to find, that is."

Just what I thought. He is just a drunk man wanting attention.

"Oh, how that hole is vast and deep, white rabbit," Jehudiel says, his face becoming serious again. "White? Envious was the man in white."

He pauses for a few seconds before he slaps himself.

I look at the time. It reads 39:20. I want to leave, but something inside my head is forcing me to stay. I must keep to the time. I adjust myself.

Jehudiel bangs on the table, tearing me from my reverie. "Let's play a game!"

I remain silent.

Jehudiel continues, "My silver is as priceless to me as a person's name. You find my silver and, as a token of my appreciation, I will tell you your name. Deal?"

Jehudiel wildly shakes my hand and leaves through the door to the kitchen.

My watch beeps.

Forty minutes.

The temperature of the room plummets.

"Time's up, Alice!" Jehudiel shouts, smashing the table with his hand. "But I will give you a second chance if you find my silver. Then, after the exchange, out of your head you go!"

I jump up. What is he going on about? I can't believe I listened to this crackpot for so long. I've got to get out of here. Now.

"It's all in your mind! Do you get it, Alice? Everything! This table, this spoon, this empty bottle, me, you! All these mindless people! It's all in your mind!"

I head for the door, Jehudiel laughing insanely behind me.

I pull my jacket tighter around me, dash to the subway, and rush down the stairs.

The ticket booth is unmanned, but I swipe my MTA card anyway. I wait with a group of people on the platform. The train arrives, and we flood in. As the doors to the empty car close behind me, my watch beeps once more.

Forty minutes.

In the window opposite my seat, the reflection of a skinny little girl stares back at me. I look back in her direction, but she is gone.

I stare dreamily out the window into the darkened walls of the subway tunnel, then gaze upon my reflection. The green in my eyes captivates my full attention.

Releasing myself from the reflection's hold on me, I blink several times. What was I thinking about?

There's movement to my right, in my peripheral vision. A well-groomed man walks toward me. He looks to be in his mid-thirties and has a square forehead and pointed chin. His dark hair is stylishly messy. He's wearing an expensive-looking black leather vest over a black dress shirt with a brilliant red skinny tie.

He walks closer. An inverted cyan King of Clubs is sticking out of his vest pocket.

He looks at me intensely from deeply shadowed eyes. The darkness mutes the bright green of his irises, and they appear to simmer with something like fury. He is carrying an old 1980's Polaroid camera in his left hand.

He lifts it and snaps a picture of me, which slides out the front of the camera. He pulls it out, waves it back and forth, and blows on it intermittently. He looks at it and grins.

"A picture is worth a thousand words, so they say. The name's Michael."

Michael pockets the photo and pulls out a butterfly knife. He deftly performs a reverse twirl, a backhand opening, and an aerial with the knife. In a flash of movement, he stabs the knife into the car just beside my head.

The people sitting around me don't react.

"They will not help you. The more you start to unwind the less they will exist. They are merely disposable ornaments."

He twirls the knife again and jerks toward me. Then he straightens and says, as calm as ever, "It's grand; you can sit down." He grabs my shoulder and forces me back down into my seat.

He puts the blade back inside and slides into the seat opposite where I'm sitting.

I remain immobile.

"Almost lost my head there." He laughs. "Fear before pain. Fear before pain," he repeats softly to himself. "Sorry. I'm learning self-control. I just have to remember that fear is the easiest emotion to tackle first." Michael grazes my neck with the blade and curiously notices my shaving scar. Then he presses the blade hard up against the shaving wound.

"You see, because fear can be used to interrupt the balance of the everyday routine. Fear of the unknown is always a good emotional ice breaker to SNAP..." Michael retracts the blade. "...you back to life again. Sorry if I brought you any discomfort. I'm supposed to bring you discomfort later on, but NOT today. Fear before pain."

Michael looks off in the distance and speaks to himself, "It's almost time."

A little girl appears as if from thin air and walks past us. She's a skinny little thing with brilliant green eyes, shoulder-length brown hair, wispy bangs, and light-brown skin. I take a second look. No. I don't think I've seen her before.

"Mannequins walkin'," Michael says, and takes a picture. After the flash goes off, the girl is gone. I bend down to see if she ducked under one of the seats, but there's no trace of her.

"It's okay if you're afraid with all the stuff that's happened or is happenin' to ya."

I rub my brow. My head hurts from trying to process the strange happenings I've had to put up with today. I just want it to end.

"Don't you fret. We'll get you to fear right quick. You almost are kind of giving off a sense of panic in yer eyes as we speak. If so, we can move right along to pain if you really want? Blink if you are afraid and want to move on to pain."

I try not to blink but do the opposite by mistake. With a grin, Michael flips back open his knife.

"Heaven itself will bring it to your recollection," he says. "First, you will come to the sirens that enchant all who venture near." He rips open his vest and shirt, exposing tattoos of elegant crosses, ornate shamrocks, and Gaelic writings across his tanned, muscular torso and neck.

What is he talking about? I need to get away from him before he snaps. I rise from my seat, but he holds up his knife to greet me. I sit down instead and rub my temples.

Michael grips my forearms and squeezes them tightly. "Listen to the sirens!" he screams, his shadowed eyes wide. "Get lost in their melody!"

A horrendous screech—like a needle across a vinyl record—echoes through my head.

My watch indicates 42:02. No one else seems bothered by it.

I cover my ears to block it out. Michael rips my hands away from my head. "That noise yer hearing is music. Can you hear the melody? A tune from long ago, maybe?" I am in agony, wrestling to put my hands over my ears again, but Michael is too strong.

He continues preaching. "You have to fight through the noise, fight through the pain. Find the melody hidden deep inside the void."

What is he talking about? It's just a loud noise! Nothing else!

I squeeze my eyes tight. I cannot take any more of this abuse. I just want to escape. I cover my ears, focusing on the sound of my own heart beating.

"Let your heart feel it! Let the melody take ya in!"

Suddenly, I feel like I'm back in my nightmare. I can imagine the snow melting on the glass, wiper blades flicking it away, headlights flashing in front of me.

But I can't see anything. I'm blinded!

I hear Michael in the back of my thoughts, whispering, "Listen."

My body spins out of control like a car has hit me or something.

Michael whispers again, "The pitch. Tempo. Meter. Articulation. The art form whose medium is sound and silence. It's all there! Open your ears to it."

I focus, using my ears to pick up anything out of the ordinary.

Slowly, the loud static in the background transforms into instrumental harmonies. Soft piano music plays. The cadence of the music resonates in my bones. It's familiar and exquisite, beautifully painful.

Michael appears beside me. He slaps me hard across the face, and it's as if he's knocked something back into place. I can see again. I am back on the train. I look around me, and every living person is magically gone except for Michael.

I can still hear that same soft melody. Bells tinkling just out of sight.

The heavenly instrument collapses an emotional barrier in my mind, and I let them guide me where they will.

The music is louder, right next to me. I open my eyes to see where it's coming from. Instead, the train car, the floor, the lights, Michael, the seat I'm sitting on, and finally, myself, all break away like puzzle pieces.

A pink neon sign on the roof of a small-town coffee shop shines over the city block. Within its pink glow, it reads, "The Haberdashery." The windowpanes are cold, frosted over on the outside from the recent burst of bad weather. The interior has been decorated for Christmas, with twinkling lights around the menu board, a Christmas tree set on the counter beside the sign advertising specials, and yuletide music playing on the stereo. In early December, holiday cheer is inevitable.

I look in the window of the coffee shop and see reflected a young twenty-year-old me. *How is this possible?*

Music seeps through the walls.

I've heard this music before.

Violins, piano, and harps haunt the air and beckon to me as I stumble in. A tiny bell rings from above the door, announcing to the employees that a new customer has arrived. I notice a jukebox in the corner that is playing the soft melody from before.

I know what it is! The melody is the same piano music I heard on the subway.

There are six people inside. An elderly man talks and laughs with what appears to be his teenage granddaughter in a booth lining the walls. At one of the tables near the door is a brunette woman with smooth, light-brown skin and softly arched brows. She's wearing a dark green sweater. Near the back, two gentlemen, still wearing their coats, converse as if they've just met up. They are partially blocking a woman seated in the back corner. Only her dark hair, pulled into a tight bun, is visible. I was just in the subway car. How am I now in this coffee shop?

I take a step toward the counter, as if on autopilot. There's a vending machine to my left. I look back at the entrance. A newspaper rack is located next to the door. It's my coffee shop! The one I go to every morning. A newspaper lies on the counter to my right. The date is 1991. That's changed. The song on the jukebox permeates my mind, trying to dredge up old memories.

Am I dreaming? I try to move, to speak, but I am powerless. My stress level rises. What's happening? I must be dreaming—a mere observer, forced to watch. The thought maddens me, but the soft melody overpowers the feeling.

I remember…I remember why I am here in the first place: a blind date. The girl I'm meeting loves horses, baking, and, surprisingly, action flicks. She's not sure she's ready for anything too serious, but she's definitely ready to see what's out there. Her profile made her sound like a fun night out. I'm always up for someone new and surprising.

Without my prompting, my eyes scan the room. That dark-haired woman in the back corner, whose face I can barely see…is that her?

I walk toward her. I pass the first table and the brunette in the green sweater pops up from below with a highlighter she apparently dropped. Or is this my date? I am about to lean in when she takes out a book. It is bound with worn, black leather, with two rotary dials placed over locked latches. She puts in a code and it unlocks. I glimpse further and to my surprise it's hand written musical notes that are drawn inside.

"You're late," Green Sweater says, sounding unhappy, without looking up from her book.

Still observing rather than in control of myself, I smile.

Words force their way from my mouth. "Am I?"

"And I see you didn't bring it." Her voice turns dour.

What's she talking about? "Bring what?" I find myself replying.

Our eyes meet. Hers light up, chestnuts over a brilliant flame, as she looks at me.

She's got liquid brown eyes, and her bangs are swept back from her flawless, light brown skin. My attention is now completely focused on her.

"I sent you an email," she continues. "And in it, I told you my favorite flower. I asked you to bring one, so I'd know who you were." I heave a sigh of relief. This was just about a flower?

"Sorry," I find myself saying. I grin. I have no recollection of such an email or any conversation about a favorite flower. "I guess I didn't get it. What's your favorite flower?"

"Sunflower."

I can't stop myself from laughing. "Unusual. I took you more for a lily kind of gal. It's refreshing to be around someone who is out of the ordinary. You're not like most girls."

"Well," she says coyly, "I can already tell that you're like most guys." She nods, closing her book and folding her arms on top of it.

"I may not have any flowers but I do have some gum though!"

I present a pack of 'Tredstones' gum. She waves it away.

"Your loss. This gum is really hard to come by these days. This is the only place who still carries it. I live across the street and come by here at least every other day to grab a pack, knowing sadly that one day they will be discontinued."

I put the gum back in my pocket, deflated.

She looks out the window. "You live across the street?"

Sadly, my apartment building looks even more run down up close. I'm quickly embarrassed.

Why did I tell her that? So stupid! Think of something to say.

"Yeah, but I'm in the process of moving."

The music continues to play, and we sit in silence for a moment.

A server approaches. As if dreaming, I sit down and ask for a cup of coffee, black.

Then I look over at someone coming out from behind a curtain in the far back.

Looking at the waiter, I say, "What's back there?"

"Isn't this your favorite place?" she says, almost surprised.

I shake my head. "I just come by to get the gum. I don't even know what a Haberdashery is"

The waiter chuckles. "Think of this as something between a coffee shop and a highway service station shop. You would be surprised how many people leave out of here with a good cup of joe in one hand and a pair of track shoes in the other."

"Clever." The waiter gets called by another table. We smile, letting him know he is okay to go.

I turn to her and say, "Would you like to go check it out?"

"Sure?" She says in a confused tone.

We stand up and walk toward the curtain. I lift it up for her to go in first. The confusion on her face subsides when she looks down at my neckline. "What's that pendant mean?"

I tuck it under my shirt, out of her sight. "It's nothing special," I find myself answering.

Looking over the curtain, I gaze at all the miscellaneous items sprawled out all over the place. It resembles something I would see at a yard sale. We walk through each of the lanes, looking at the random junk on each of the tables. I pick up a pair of track shoes, grazing my fingers across the spikes at the bottom.

"Are you a runner?"

I look down at the shoes. "A long time ago." I look up and put them back on the table. "I was a half-marathon runner. A lot of other people were very good. I left it behind."

"Do you still run?"

"No. Not anymore."

I pick up a snow globe from next to the shoes and shake it.

She looks at it as if she has seen it somewhere before.

"I had a snow globe just like that once."

She takes it out of my hand and studies the city buildings inside. She turns the crank at the bottom, and soft piano music begins to play.

"My mom bought me an old, secondhand snow globe when I was real young. Inside was a city that lit up just exactly like this one. My mom would always say we would go to a city like that when the time was right. The globe was also a music box. Inside sung a beautiful piano melody just like this one. I would play it when I wanted to feel safe, as if my life was different than it was."

She wipes her eyes, trying not to smear her mascara.

I slide my thumbs across her cheeks, smoothing the moisture away. If it's possible, she's even more beautiful when she cries.

"I loved that snow globe. It even had a secret compartment to hide treasure in."

The music stops, and we find no secret compartment. She sighs and puts the snow globe back.

"What was your hidden treasure?"

She takes a few seconds to respond. She looks back at me, happy for a moment. "It was a picture of my mom and me when I was a baby."

Her expression makes me think there is something more to her story, but I don't push it.

A whisper from somewhere inside my head says, '*Be prideful.*'

She scans the room and shifts from foot to foot.

'*Be prideful,*' the voice whispers again.

I square my shoulders and sit a little taller. I lean forward and nudge her forearm with my elbow. "Don't worry. By the end of things, I'm sure I will be your next treasure."

She looks at me in a way that seems displeased. I quickly change the subject.

"What happened to it?"

"Jacob." Her voice frosts over. "He broke it one afternoon in a drug-fueled rage because I wouldn't hand him the remote." She stands a little taller and pushes her shoulders back.

"Who's Jacob?"

Laying the snow globe back on the shelf, she says, "I'm sorry. This was a bad idea."

She walks out through the curtain as I follow her.

"Wow. Normally I have to be naked to disappoint someone this quickly."

She laughs a soft, genuine laugh. She sits back down, gathering her stuff into her book bag. "No. It's not you. I'm sure you're great, it's just—"

The waiter comes back to deliver my black coffee. It gives me the opportunity to sit with her again. "Go on."

"It's just, I'm not really comfortable with dating electronically. My friends kind of made me fill out the questionnaire..."

"I'm not an axe murderer, I promise." I sip my coffee and lean back, trying to appear funny.

"I'm sure you're not."

"I prefer a knife. Less cleanup."

She laughs again. "It's not that, though I did bring bear mace with me in case you're not joking. It's just...I want the serendipity! Like I'm Meg Ryan in one of those cheesy movies or something."

As the piano music from the jukebox continues to play, she moves her hands in the air as if she were playing on the piano keys.

She turns to me and blushes. The dark green of her sweater is a perfect complement to her light-brown skin and her now-pink cheeks.

"I'm guessing you're the one guilty of the song choice."

Still with roses in her cheeks, she says, "It's my favorite part. Have you heard this song before?"

I shake my head and say, "Do you play professionally?"

"No. Lately I've been making my own music."

"You've written your own music sheets? That's amazing! Do you write them all in there?"

I nod toward her black leather-bound book.

"What makes you say that?"

She leans over and holds it.

"I took a guess. An encrypted lock book either means you're a C.I.A agent or it's something that holds high importance that's near and dear to you."

She laughs. "Good guess. It's what gets me through most days," she says, placing her hand on it. "What about you? What gets you through most days?"

"Well, I like to write too." I try to swallow my words, to take them back.

"Oh!" she says, the smile returning. "What do you like to write about?"

"I don't know. So far, I've just been dabbling."

"Dabbling is the start of something."

We both look at each other, and, for a moment, I get lost in her brilliant smile. I could start and end my day with that smile.

"What were you looking for when you agreed to this blind date?" she asks. "I mean, you had no idea what I might look like."

"That's true."

"I could have been repulsive."

"Well, thank God that wasn't the case."

She blushes again and looks at her hands.

"But not to sound too self-indulgent, I want a girl that can surprise me."

She looks up. "What would be a good surprise for you, then?"

I take another sip of coffee. "If I knew that, it wouldn't be a surprise."

"That's pretty sad. You have to go on a blind date to find someone like that?"

I shrug sheepishly. "What were you looking for?"

She focuses on something far away and remains silent. A few seconds go by, and then, "I don't really know." Her eyes move back and meet mine. "Ever since I was young, I've always dreamed that I'd meet this super-amazing guy out of fate. Like how my parents met."

"How did they meet?"

"At a carnival. He won her a snow globe."

"Let me guess. The very same snow globe she gave to you."

She nods.

I finish my coffee. "So...you want the fairy tale. I bet you're the kind of girl who wants a big church wedding."

She sits back and shakes her head. "Just the opposite! I had a dream about my wedding when I was a little girl. It's going to be really small, outside, with an amazing view, an assortment of beautiful lights scattered everywhere, and—" She stops.

She zips up her bag and downs the rest of her tea.

"And what?"

"And ..." She turns toward the window, that faraway look back in her eyes. "And...there's fireworks. It's silly! I know. You really are sweet. Don't get me wrong, but I just—"

"Can't." I smile, maintaining my pride.

"Man! I wish we had met, like, on top of a volcano or something."

"A volcano?"

"I dunno. Just something random. So it felt like providence. Like it was meant to be." We look deeply into one another's eyes for a moment.

The jukebox finishes the song, and the shop goes quiet.

She offers a small, closed-lipped smile and rises from her seat. "I think I could have really liked you."

"I think you could have really liked me, too."

She smiles intimately. Her pager dings. She checks it. "I'm so sorry for this."

I help her into her camel peacoat and walk her to the exit, not wanting her to go, but knowing I have no choice. We stop at the door, and our eyes meet once again. I can only think of one thing to say, "I hope you get your providence."

She takes a few steps away before turning back. "And I hope you get the surprise you deserve."

And just like that, she is gone.

I return to my chair and casually lean back. I am so frustrated that I'd been powerless to stop what came out of my mouth. I wish I could have intervened instead of just observing.

But, deep down, I know it would have ended the same way.

Her leather-bound book is still lying on the table. Did she leave it there on purpose? I open it to the inside cover.

Property of Madi.

Wait. My blind date is not named Madi. Who is Madi? A sister? A friend? She seemed like the kind of girl who might frequent the Goodwill store just because it's the right thing to do. Maybe she picked it up there.

I run a hand though my hair and tilt my head back. The tiny bell rings from the entrance door, making me snap my head back up. I'm depressed to find that it's not Madi but a man instead. He looks to be in his mid-thirties, his dark hair stylishly messy. He has a square forehead and pointed chin. Green tattoo ink peeks out from under his collar. He's holding a bouquet of sunflowers.

"Get you another cup?"

I hadn't noticed the server standing in front of me with a coffee urn. I shake my head quickly as the man walks past me and approaches the woman still sitting in the back-corner booth, reading a book. His position blocks her face from view.

"Sorry I'm so late. I believe you asked for this," he says warmly as he hands her the bouquet of sunflowers. "Madi, is it?"

Madi?

The woman closes her book, and her bun shakes from side to side.

"You're kidding, right?" the man says, laughing nervously.

"Madi? That's not me, sorry."

The man slumps his shoulders and walks to the bar close to where I am sitting. He slowly puts the bouquet down on the bar counter. "I can't believe it. I got stood up," he mutters to himself.

I look back down at the book. *Property of Madi.*

I jump out of the chair, grab the book, and rush out of the coffee shop. Bundled pedestrians hurry by. Cars move along with their beams casting long shadows. My heart pounds. She's nowhere in sight. I run across the street to the snow-blanketed park. No sign of her camel-colored peacoat. The chance that I'll ever find her again is slim to none.

I slowly turn and walk back to the coffee shop, holding her book tightly in my hand. Maybe she will return for it. Or maybe... she'll return just for me. Wouldn't that be a surprise? I smile.

Obnoxious beeping sounds in the distance, getting louder by the second. The coffee shop breaks away into puzzle pieces, and my consciousness plunges back into darkness.

rakes squeal on the train rails. The sound of my watch beeping is still going off. I open my eyes. I'm sweating. My watch reads forty-five minutes.

A metal grill comes into focus. The train grinds to a stop as light from the station streams in through the windows. I get to my feet, brushing myself off.

What was that?

Above me is a dirty, cushioned seat, then the broken window of the train car. Looking up, I don't see any of the passengers who were previously on here. The doors to the car slide open. Michael leans over, grips my hand, and pulls me up.

I clamber to my feet. I'm in control again. I'm no longer watching myself act out a script.

"Looks like someone got lost in nostalgia," observes Michael. His lifting voice mocks me.

Did I just go back in time? Is this train a time machine of some sort?

"Ha! This isn't '*Back to the future*', kid."

I try to speak but can't make a sound. My head starts to spin.

"The voice leaves as the memory fades away. That's a shame, lad. But you'll get it back soon enough. The first time leaves ya a bit dizzy, so don't make any sudden movements."

Did he slip me a drug or something? But it felt so real. In either case, I need to get away from him. I quickly jump through the sliding doors just as they start to close, leaving Michael inside.

I climb the stairs out of the subway and look up. The sky is glowing with ribbons of green. My blood pressure falls back to normal, and my breathing regulates itself.

Streetlights flicker on, illuminating the empty roads. I walk toward an empty old traffic bridge, its iron expanse deserted and grim in spite of the hanging lanterns along its span. I suddenly find it odd that there isn't anyone on the bridge. Where did everyone go?

There is a billboard lit up on the other side, displaying a woman's face. Her brown eyes smile at me from beneath soft, windswept bangs. Her smooth, light-brown skin is flawless. The word "Madi" appears beneath her face. It's the same girl from my dream!

She appears to be a famous pianist, and the billboard is advertising her new, eponymous solo album.

I recall my conversation in the coffee shop with Madi. Was I dreaming, or have I really met her?

The aurora borealis glows in the night sky. Its colors accompany me all the way back to my apartment building. My watch indicates 46:30. I must keep moving.

I walk on, lost in thought, over the bridge and into my apartment building. I step into the elevator and press the button for the roof.

Fifty minutes.

The entire elevator ride, I am fixated on and vexed by my vision of Madi in the coffee shop.

The doors open, and I'm not surprised to see an Asian man standing beside a dining table set for two—two bowls of soup, two plates with steak on them, and two glasses of wine. He appears to be in his late forties, with jaw-length, black hair parted down the middle. He's wearing dark sunglasses, a black sports coat, and a light gray V-neck shirt.

The features of the inverted Jack of Spades sticking out of his jacket's breast pocket are strikingly similar to his own refined nose and square jawline.

Only his bright orange socks throw the ensemble off balance. With the limited time left in my day, I don't have any reserved for one more fool. I walk across the roof to the ledge, looking out at the aurora borealis dancing on the horizon. The city lies dark and silent below. I look over to the ledge where the tall hourglass is laid. Its sand moves constant to the bottom half of the glass. It consumes my vision, but I quickly restrain and focus my attention back to the roof.

Among the tables and chairs scattered around the roof is a telescope pointing toward the sky. I gaze through its eyepiece but see only darkness.

"Do you still feel content?" he asks.

I turn to him.

He sits down. "First and foremost, I'm Gabriel. And you? Well, you're just screwed up in the head, aren't you? But you already knew that after a day like today. Which I must apologize. We found it best to ease you in first. Took us numerous times to get it just right to where you wouldn't run from us. That was key. Keeping you in the time zones while trying to open your eyes to the world before you was extremely tricky. But we will talk about time zones at a later date. Let's stick to the routine for now. Speaking of routine. Have you started to realize yet that your life is set on repeat yet?"

Repeat? What is this loon going on about now?

"You're doing exactly the same thing, day in, day out, in five minute intervals. You're a slave to time... Maybe you can answer these questions for me. Why does your day only last sixty minutes and not twenty four hours? Why aren't you able to express emotions? What does your job entail? What happens if you get sick? Can you get sick? When's the last time you remember being sick? What's the last thing you can remember before this morning?! What's your name?! Go ahead, tell me your name. Just open your mouth and say it."

I try once again to speak and nothing comes out.

Gabriel cuts a piece of steak, lifts it to his mouth, and stops. He puts the fork down, sticks his hand into his pocket, and pulls out a silver and white wrapper.

"What was that? I can't hear you. Probably because you can't speak. Yeah, that's definitely it. You would need to achieve full contentment within yourself in order to get your voice back. But I always found it difficult to remember the name part. That's not an easy thing to do. None of my team, myself included, can remember our birth names. I want to say I was a Chris? Christopher? Christoph? Christy?"

He takes a chewed piece of gum from his mouth and folds it neatly into the wrapper.

"That would have been bad," he says.

The name on the wrapper is "Tredstones." Did he leave the sack of gum at my door this morning?

He offers me the seat opposite him with a wide gesture. I walk hesitantly toward him, stop near the table, and sit down.

"If you don't eat or drink, then you'll make the host—me—feel very unappreciated and obliged to withhold any dinner talk." His pale skin contrasts with his black hair.

Better to appease him than to waste too much more time. I take a bite of the steak, chewing it slowly. It is tasteless. I take another bite—still no flavor.

Gabriel takes another bite and savors it. If I could see his eyes, I would guess they were closed in ecstasy.

Gabriel sticks the last piece of steak into his mouth, crosses his silverware on his plate, and uses his napkin to clean off his lips. "Now, how should I begin?" He leans forward, enlarging my reflection in his dark glasses. "Let's start with you being in an accident."

I sit motionless.

"Did you hear what I said? You were in an accident, and I am not talking about your little shaving accident." He motions toward my neck. "It's not like you to make mistakes, is it?"

I continue too look at him as if waiting for the punch line.

He cocks his head. "You're acting strange. You're usually a bit more animated by this point." He straightens and pushes his empty plate away. "Well, change can be good. Moving on! Let's start off small and work our way up. You see, there are two types of souls that exist here: a lost soul and a soul survivor. A soul survivor is someone willing to fight for a second chance at life. To be either, you must be half-dead, which, I'm sorry to say, you are."

That's enough. I stand up to walk away, but Gabriel appears in front of me.

I look back at his empty chair. How did he do that?

"You're neither asleep nor dead. Merely a hollow shell of a man. Do you get it now? That's right, my boy, you're a comatose patient at St. Vincent's Hospital, room five-oh-five, where you're fed through a tube."

I push Gabriel aside and make a run for it.

He screams from behind me, "You have eight days to live!"

I stop.

"Eight days! Eight hours, to be exact, till your life plug gets officially pulled. In the final minutes leading up to that eighth hour, you may face either your rapture or your despair, depending on what you do at this very moment."

I turn to look at him. He's working his jaw like he really cares what I'm about to do. There's no way any of this could be true, is there? I take a couple steps toward him.

"We'll get to how you got here at a later date. Let me try and explain what this place is, though."

Gabriel takes out an unwrapped candy bar from his coat pocket and bites into it.

"My personal attempt at describing said place would be that it's a soul-made reality inside the mental workplace of the mind. Its purpose and function is to give a soul the opportunity to earn a second chance at life by testing his willingness to survive. We call it Purgatorium."

Purgatorium?

"Let me break it down for you slower, like a child. Purgatorium can't be described without understanding the full details of its existence and how it works. It all starts with you and when I say you, I mean your soul. The soul, as the life essence of the body, and it is removed either at time of physical death or by comatose. If by comatose, then the soul can be locked away inside their own human mind. Do you understand what I'm telling you? You are a prisoner inside your own mind."

This guy is completely nuts, but I can't help but feel entertained by his fictional story.

Gabriel goes over to the ledge, reaches his hand out, and wraps his fingers around the hourglass.

"Now, you're wondering who I might be. Let me oblige you, then." He starts walking toward me again. "Remember when I said that there are two types of souls? A soul survivor and a....?"

He waits for me to say it but he knows I can't speak.

"A lost soul is someone who has given up on life and chooses to stay here rather than face reality. I am a lost soul, sadly."

He grins, licks his lips, and moves his tongue around his mouth to check for any pieces of food before swallowing. He takes his used gum out of the Tredstones wrapper and puts it back into his mouth.

What is he talking about? I take a step back. Now the elevator's only nineteen steps away.

Gabriel shakes his head and yells. "Why did the reapers have to go and erase *all* your memories? They could have at least left the ones from this soul-made reality so we wouldn't have to re-teach you everything again for the billionth time!"

He is insane.

I take another step back, aiming my body more toward the elevator.

"A lost soul is nothing to be afraid of. At least not me and my group. We consider ourselves more like soul protectors! You also already met other soul protectors today. I enlisted each of them to help souls like you get back home. You'll see them again in time. We like to call ourselves 'The Archangels!'"

He strikes a Superman pose and stops. "We named ourselves after each of the seven Archangels, mainly because none of us remembered our names and there were seven of us. So why not? Besides they sounded cool. Sorry! I forget we are on the clock!"

He smacks his gum harder as if it were a nervous tick.

"We had flesh and bone just like you did. We walked on the same dirt, drank from the same water, and paid our never-ending taxes. The difference between us is that I was too weak. I know this now, but you still have time to make the right choice."

I turn my head to the elevator, but Gabriel is miraculously now standing in front of me.

"Pay attention! You need to understand what this place is. At some point a lot of coma victims end up like you. In a place like this. To put it bluntly, this is all one big action sport competition event. And just like all athletic games there are rules on how to play. This place will give you three challenges that you will have to accomplish to succeed. Challenges that will test your mind, body, and soul. The mind challenge will be finding the *key* to why you're here. The body challenge will be a trial you must compete in. The very last challenge is a duel to make your soul whole again. This task is the most important because there aren't any redos with this one. You lose the fight you lose your life. You accomplish all three and you get your life back. It's kinda like *Legends of the Hidden Temple* meets *Nickelodeon Guts*. But not really. I just love those shows. I would have never gotten past the crag mountain part with all that glitter spraying everywhere. You know what I'm talking about right?"

He waits for a response but I'm too baffled by his looniness to even gather an intellectual thought.

Gabriel looks at my watch and speeds up the rest of his crazy ramblings.

"Remember what I said about losing the last challenge? I am a soul that lost. Ergo why my type are officially named lost souls."

I stop listening, letting him continue to jabber on about how they all initially met as I try to make my way around him. He quickly pulls me back into frame.

"Sorry, got side tracked! Time is a ticking. You see we are different than other lost souls. We have come to terms with our mistakes and choose to help soul survivors, like yourself, earn back their life." Gabriel does a few karate hand motions. "Each one of us has a specific purpose... to teach souls, like you, how to pass your trial. We would have told you the truth about us from the get-go, but, in our experience, that never turns out well. We have been trying a new approach, easing you into all of this one day at a time. Each day we break you, layer by layer, till you can think straight again. We have almost gotten it down to a science. It has been working much better, considering..."

I make a run for it and head to the elevator. I press the button and the doors open.

"We are here to detox your soul!" he shouts as I board.

Gabriel grabs my collar and drags me to the edge of the rooftop. I try to scream, but I can't.

I stare at my reflection looming large in his black lenses. He says in a placid voice, "I'm afraid I'm going to need your full attention."

The street looks painfully solid over the edge of the high-rise, and I imagine what my body will look like after it splats on the pavement. I squirm and try to get free from his grip.

"Listen, damn you! We are here to help you! This is our last attempt to help you out. Do you understand me?! You have only eight days left! Or else!"

Or else what?! I die? Give me a break, wacko.

I stop squirming, and Gabriel takes off his sunglasses, revealing his glaring green eyes. "I know it's hard to understand but in eight days, next Sunday, the day of the Sabbath, your life support will get pulled, your heart will be pumping its last beat, and you'll be pushing up daises, biting the dust, giving up the ghost, and my personal favorite, cashing in your chips. Do you feel me? No more redo's. No more retrying. No more restarts. This is your last chance to live again, and time is not on our side."

Let's say what he says is even true. How would he even know that they were going to pull the plug on me?

I try to get loose again, but he tightens his hold on me.

"Once you're a lost soul, places like this gives off a certain frequency to the outside world. We can sometimes hear what's going on up there. So, when I hear a doctor say that you have eight days left before he pulls the plug then that's something not to take lightly."

Did he hear what I was thinking?

"We've done this many, many times, you and I. I've gone through this speech in numerous ways and it always seems to bring us back here. With your memories being reaped and me going through the motions once more. I can be a bit pushy. That's on me. But this time we have to get it right. We must!"

I try to push him off of me, but I can't move.

"As per usual, the hard way, it is."

He pushes me off the rooftop. I try to scream as the air charges past my ears. My body strikes the pavement, and my watch beeps.

Fifty-five minutes.

I lie there, seemingly intact. I don't feel any parts of me oozing onto the street. I pat down my arms and legs. Nothing is broken or even cut. My earlier run-in with that bare-footed hippie flashes before my eyes. I wasn't hurt then, either. Gabriel is standing right beside me now, his eyes focused intently into the distance.

"I told you I was pushy. But that didn't hurt at all now did it?"

He takes out a half-eaten chocolate candy bar, wrapped in an orange wrapper, out of his back pocket. He takes a bite, relishing the flavor for a few seconds.

"That hits the spot! Tell me, what are you still holding on to? Your wealth? Independence? It's all fake. Your job is useless. Day in and day out working on your same novel never being able to write a conclusion. Let me tell you what happens at work for you tomorrow. You will continue sitting in your office chair, staring at that same single white sheet of paper, and you'll leave in hopes the next day will bring you fresh ideas, but that paper will stay white. It will always stay white. You understand? That's the joke. You're the joke. All the wealth and independence you posses are meaningless. How about tomorrow you let us help you take back your life instead? Become a soul survivor!"

The air around me turns frigid.

He shifts his focus back to me. "Feeling numb? Out of breath? Like you've been dropped from the *Titanic* into the North Atlantic? That's what they do when they're close. They make you feel it. This isn't one of your silly nightmares; this is what's really coming for you right now. This isn't fire-breathing fiction I am spreading to you. This is cold-hearted truth, and their truth will not set you free."

Each breath becomes a thick vapor in the cold air. There's a screeching noise from somewhere behind me. Black, hooded creatures, vaguely human in shape, fly toward us from about three hundred yards away. Their faces are obscured in darkness.

What the hell are those?

White, bony fingers peek out from the black sleeves of their robes. Everything they pass becomes covered in frost.

Gabriel looks to me and says, "You are not where you need to be right now. That forces them to correct the situation, meaning they are on their way here to snatch you and your memories away. Poof!" He throws his hands apart. "Like everything you just learned today never happened."

I want to run, to scream, but my body is not responding to any of my brain signals. Gabriel tries to pull me up, but I am rigid and unyielding.

He forces my head around in the direction of the bridge and the billboard with Madi's image.

"What if I told you what you saw in the coffee shop was real? It was just one of many classic memories you have yet to see. The music you heard just before you entered that little coffee shop will play again, and with it will come more of your memories. Don't you wanna know what happens next? Spoiler alert! You do see her again, and all you have to do is run back to your over-sized bed before your watch hits sixty. Once you do that, it will reset the order of things, and they will leave you alone."

Gabriel lets me go and quietly waits.

Is he telling the truth? Should I believe him? This day has completely gotten out of hand. *How do I regain control?* But that's just it. Maybe I was never in control. Maybe time has always been controlling me. *Maybe he is right.* Or maybe all of this is just a dream. But what if…I look over at the billboard again.

The dark creatures have advanced a couple hundred yards. Even if he's lying, running from these hideous apparitions is better than being fish bait.

I spring into action and sprint toward the apartment building.

"Finally! Let the games begin!" Gabriel shouts behind me. "Again!"

Frost crystals spread over the metal handle of the door as I pull it open. The elevator doors are closed. There's no time to wait for them to open. I head for the stairs instead.

The lobby air temperature has dropped another twenty degrees by the time I'm in the stairwell. I slam the door behind me and run up the stairs two at a time. My legs are burning by the time I reach the second-floor landing. The stairwell door creaks open below. I peek over the railing. The dark shadows advance up the stairs, preceded by frost crystals.

Somehow, I manage to reach the sixth floor. I throw open the door and stumble through. I run left, down the long hallway toward my apartment. I pull my keys from my pocket and hear loud screeching from behind me. My breath hangs in the air. They're too close, and my hands shake. The keys slip from my hands onto the floor and freeze over on impact. No time to stop and retrieve them. I propel myself onward. My heart is beating so fast that I find it almost exhilarating in a weird way.

The stairwell door bursts open behind me. One of the creatures glides down the hallway, reaching out with its skeletal fingers. It's close enough for me to catch a glimpse of white skull beneath its cowl.

I'm not going to make it!

My apartment's just ahead on the left. I shift my body right to gain momentum. Ice crystals race up and across the surface of the door.

Hardly breathing, I slingshot myself and slam my shoulder into the frozen door. It swings open. Shards of ice break off from the hinges. I fall to the floor and slam the door shut with my leg. It shatters like a broken window.

I'm in! I'm in! Need to hurry.

Frost spreads across the hardwood floor and up the walls, beautiful and deadly.

I scramble across the frozen floor. What can I use to defend myself?

The reaper is at the door now. It floats through. It must know that it has me pinned.

My books are the only things within reach. I throw them at the creature's face. They freeze over on impact.

My watch ticks away the seconds: 59:50…51…52…

I run to my bedroom. What I am supposed to do? 53…54…55… I snatch the snow globe from my nightstand. The miniature city holds my gaze momentarily. I can't destroy this.

The reaper is at my bedroom door now. It doesn't seem to be in a hurry now that I'm cornered.

I inch away, hitting my calf on the bed. The bed! Gabriel said something about the bed! I fall backward and instinctively pull myself into the fetal position. My watch ticks…. 59:59…60:00.

I close my eyes, and everything goes black.

♣ ♠ ♦ ♥

I'm shivering, and warm, dry air blows onto my face. The windshield wipers move at an alarming rate. *Whirr, thwack, whirr, thwack, whirr, thwack!* I should count to see how many times they move side to side. Is the speed constant? If it isn't, I can't be sure of getting an accurate count. My vision swims, dizziness overtaking me. It all seems impossible. And what would it prove, anyway, even if the count were accurate?

"You're being irrational," I say. "You're not making sense. Get yourself together." I breathe deeply, and a sense of control returns.

I refocus on the road. The snow is now falling slowly enough that my headlights reflect off of ice-coated tree branches while casting long shadows.

My coin pendant dangles from the rearview mirror, the same place it's always been. But in this moment, for some reason, it cannot seem more foreign.

I remove my glove with my teeth and bring the cold, metal disc to my lips, kiss it, and sigh.

A loud crack from outside in the darkness makes me flinch. I lower my head and immediately look around for the source.

It sounded like a pistol, or rather an echo of a pistol, as though from another realm.

My heart pounds. Sweat beads on my forehead and under my arms. My chest tightens.

The snow falls more heavily, the visibility worsening. Ahead is an exit sign. I floor the gas pedal and careen onto the off-ramp.

Remain focused. It's too late to turn back now.

Once off the highway, I make a hard, fast right onto a country road, my tires squealing. I take a deep breath, and my pulse slows. The car lurches around the road's twists and turns. The engine roars and purrs as I alternate pressure on the gas pedal. The crunch of the slush and snow on the road is barely audible through the car's sound insulation.

My apartment shouldn't be much farther.

The snow is blowing ferociously across the front of the car now. It catches the light from the headlights and obscures my view. A low, guttural echo sounds outside of the car. My heart is pounding again.

My grip on the steering wheel tightens, and my hands sweat profusely.

Keep your eyes on the road! I am not far from home now. But I'm wracked with doubt and a feeling of fated tragedy. Warm fingers lightly touch my right hand. Madi smiles softly at me from the passenger seat.

I reach out to touch her arm, and a strange sound is heard inside my ears.

The *beep, beep, beep* of my alarm once again blares.

MICHAEL

SUNDAY

FIVE

I slowly open my eyes. Was it all a nightmare? I'm drenched in sweat. I push the off button on my alarm. It begins ticking the seconds once again. My American flag is hung by the door. I count the stars, from left to right, on the flag to get my vision in order. My breathing regulates.

The Bible is once again on the nightstand next to my watch. I quickly tuck the Bible in the drawer.

How did it get out? I remember shoving it in the drawer. Maybe yesterday was just a dream.

Images flash in my mind: dark skeletal creatures and the books I threw at one of them.

I leap out of my bed and run into the living room. All the books are back in their proper positions. Also, the floor is neither frozen nor wet on my bare feet.

The apartment is silent. No shrieking sounds. Nothing. I run to the front door. I put my ear to the door but receive only silence. Everything seems to be normal. I turn the lock and slowly, carefully, pull the door open just a crack. The hallway is quiet and reassuringly warm.

I make my way back to the bedroom and pick up the snow globe.

Out of the corner of my eye, a glint catches my attention. Snow globe in hand, I walk toward the window.

The trees are tinged with gold and amber, the city littered with scuttling leaves. As I take in the brilliant colors, I breathe deeply. The season has changed, and autumn offers a relief from the usual gray.

It was all just a dream. The coffee shop, Madi, the bizarre strangers. My imagination has reached a whole new level. I should write a book about this.

I smile at myself in the reflection of the snow globe. I set it down and start my routine. Everything is going to be fine.

I walk to the bathroom and begin my workout. Thirty pushups, fifteen pull-ups, and then I make my way to the mirror. The stubble around my face has grown out a little more than usual. My sideburns now have a connecting strip to my jawline. I pick up the barber knife and begin with my neck.

There's no scab, but yesterday's nick seems far too real in my mind. I stop and take extra care to not cut myself. I shave away each layer slowly until it's all clean, then wipe away the rest of the cream. Once again, my neck has a tiny cut. What am I doing wrong?

I walk into the closet and select one of my dark, hand-crafted suits and its matching accessories. I exit the closet, holding my shoes.

The piano in the living room begins to play, letting me know it's 3:10. It's the same melody as the day before. Or I mean in my dream. Or has it always played this same song and I never realized it? I need to get my head back on straight. Stay the course.

I look back at my bedroom and notice the lights going in and out. I walk in as the lights illuminate hundreds of Polaroid photos covering the walls of my bedroom. I drop my shoes on the floor in a heap. The pictures are all of me—moments inside this in-between place of life and death. They are from before my memories were erased. And each one resurrects another memory as I piece together the time I've spent here. Most of them capture me looking like a bum, and I am either passed out, drinking, reading, or writing in a book.

My beard grows longer in each successive photo, and there are more and more empty bottles around me. The last few photos show all the ways I have tried to kill myself.

I rip the photos from the wall from as high as I can reach and claw my way to a standing position to tear the rest of them down. The blood from my right hand smears over the walls and photos. As I rend them in half one by one, I throw them in the air and let them drift to the tiled floor. My frustration and rage only become more uncontrollable. I hit the wall over and over with my bloody hand, trying to feel pain, to feel anything that will erase my desperation.

In my haste to remove the photos, I bump the light switch, and the bedroom is bathed in darkness. My watch ticks steadily.

Suddenly, it feels as if someone is watching me. I turn around, and a flash of light obscures my vision.

My eyes soon adjust back to normal, as the blurred object in front of me begins to take shape. The man's bright red tie comes into focus first, letting me know right away it was the knife wielding psychopath from the subway.

Michael, holding a Polaroid camera, takes another photo.

"You be a lion or a lamb?"

This startles me, and I leap up off the floor. Anger still simmers from his shadowed eyes. Those eyes, coupled with his sharp chin and squared forehead, are not the features I would imagine an angelic, peace-filled being to have. The inverted, cyan King of Clubs still peeks from his vest pocket, contrasting against the brilliant red of his tie. Michael takes the photo out of the camera.

"There're superstitions that talk about how a simple photograph can steal a person's soul, imprison it in its amalgam of polyester, celluloid, salts, and gelatin, leaving it trapped with nowhere to go." The minerals sound odd in his Irish-accented voice.

He rips the photo in half, "Each picture hanging is of you. Many versions of you. Some of them before and some after you got your mind erased."

I stand completely still and speechless. It was all real. The eccentric strangers, Madi, the dark creatures. Somehow, it wasn't a dream. But if this is real…am I really in a coma?

Michael walks closer to me. His collar shifts to reveal part of a Celtic cross splayed across his neck in dark green ink. He snaps a photo of my bedroom window. "Today we are no longer their prey. Today we study our hunters. Their weakness. Their strength. Find out what makes them tick." He pulls the photo out of the front of the camera and waves it back and forth. He walks to the bathroom and looks at the mirror. What is he staring at? Whatever it is, he snaps a photo of it, and the ancient machine whirs as it spits out the image. He looks at the picture and smirks.

The clock by my bed says 04:05. Less than a minute before I leave my apartment.

He saunters toward me, reaches into his jacket pocket, and pulls out the balisong knife. Then he flips it around in trebuchet style again. "To be a lion, you have to be ready for your prey." He takes my right hand and places the knife in it.

With adrenaline shooting through my veins, I drop the knife and run for the door. But Michael now stands in the doorway with the knife in the palm of his hand. I pull up short and fall butt-first to the floor.

"No need to be afraid anymore," Michael says, offering his hand to help me up. I don't take it and remain where I've fallen.

"Don't be thinking of us as every other lost soul. We were just like you once and now we're all ya have if you're lookin' to get out of this place." He looks at me with a gloriously smug smile on his face.

"We might've come at ya a bit strong there the other day. But in fairness, it was the only way for you to see the full picture of what's become of ya in this place."

Michael pushes his hand even further toward me. I look past it to his bright green eyes and his spade-shaped nose. *What did I do to deserve any of this?*

"You've grown accustomed to a world that has forced ya to go by a set system of rules. It's put a barrier around your humanity. Till yesterday, it's made ya numb and emotionless toward everything around ya. Ever since we awakened fear in ya, pieces of that barrier are gettin' chipped away, making ya feel less numb and more likely to interact socially. In layman's terms, we used scare tactics to jolt out your emotions. Before, it was like you were in a trance. Humans have done a load of studies on this usin' heavy sleepers as subjects. You see, fear is a strong emotional response. It's the one thing that'd instantly wake ya from a deep sleep. It's actually amazin' how humans are so easily frightened. To say we didn't mean to frighten ya would be misleadin'. Please be acceptin' our sincerest apologies for yesterday." Michael extends his hand even closer to my face, almost touching my nose.

I leap up and turn. There's no other way to escape. I turn back, but Michael has disappeared. I check the bathroom. Nothing. I run to the kitchen. Nothing. *Am I going out of my mind?* I'm drenched in sweat again, but I've got to get out of here fast. I stop in the kitchen to grab a towel for my face. Lying inside my towel drawer is Michael's knife. I back away and bump into something. Michael is standing there, arms crossed, green eyes blazing.

"Right. Pleasantries are over. Let the hunted now become the hunter."

He stretches out on the brocade settee in the living room.

"You might want to get a good stretch in. These creatures are very limber."

I creep to the door, passing Michael's disappointed gaze. My hand hovers over the doorknob just as my watch goes off.

Five minutes.

I open the door to find Michael magically standing there. He punches me so hard in the face that I slide back into my room. He walks in and closes the door.

The air turns brisk, and the temperature drops by the second. I turn back. Michael is splayed across the sofa, watching me with a blank expression.

"The reapers'll be here any second, don't ya worry. Just wait here a couple seconds more."

I turn back to the door. It can't be true. I am simply in some long, horrible dream. I'll wake up at any moment.

I turn again and walk toward the kitchen. The cold air gets stronger with every step I take.

"Just remember now. Don't let them touch you. Ya'll forget all about yesterday, me, the other lost souls, feelin' any kind of new emotion, and even...Madi."

I stop.

Madi?

I turn around, and Michael is gone again. I stand in the kitchen, puffing warm vapor into the icy air. Madi's innocent brown eyes appear in my mind. Could I ever explore the depth behind them?

The front door is only a second away. Fear tackles me. My heart pumps a mile a minute. My breathing is erratic. I rush into the hall and slam the door behind me.

Instantly, the temperature is back to normal. There are three clear stacks at my feet, filled with gum wrapped in silver and white, and labeled "Tredstones." The waitress exits her apartment and looks down. I follow her gaze to my naked feet.

I forgot to put my shoes and socks on.

She smiles at me with those cherry-red lips. She strolls to the stairway door, her hips swaying in a calming back-and-forth rhythm.

I walk to the elevator and press the button. When the doors open, Michael is inside, holding a pair of running shoes. He throws the shoes at me. "Put these on. Ya'll need them."

They are sleek and aerodynamic, black and white with bright blue stripes from the top to the toe. I stare at them for a moment.

He grabs my arm and pulls me into the elevator. He presses the button for the roof.

The elevator quickly ascends. I sputter and cough. What is Michael trying to pull now? "Why are we going up? That's the wrong way!"

"You don't need to be afraid anymore. We're past all that. Fear before pain, remember? Now, hurry up and get them on before I beat you half to death with them. Okay? Great!"

I quickly shove the shoes onto my feet. They feel heavier than they look, as if there's extra weight in the bottoms.

"Nice tread, no? Those are cross-fit X shoes. They were made for extreme cross-country marathon runners. The unique design was created to withstand hazardous climate change. They might seem a bit heavy on the legs initially, but the longer ya wear them, the lighter they'll be."

I lift my feet one at a time. It's like I'm walking across metal in a pair of magnets. Bare feet would allow me to run faster than these cumbersome things.

"When reapers accelerate while flyin', they form a solid layer of ice under their cloaks, which makes these babies come in real handy. They've a built-in sensor for detectin' icy terrain. They'll auto-eject spikes from the treads, so you'll have stability on any icy surface that ya decide to clamp yourself onto. This'll give ya traction, so ya won't be fallin' or slippin'. Once ya detach yourself, the spikes'll retract."

I walk around, each step feeling lighter than the one before.

"Last chance to get a good stretch in. These reapers are all bones. All they need is one good grab."

I look at him, horror-stricken.

"You may remember them from last night. Dark hoods, skeletal masks, cold. They're the timekeepers. They bring balance to everything that's goin' on around here. If you were a puppet, they'd be your puppeteers, and the strings attachin' you to them would be time. They'll do whatever it takes for you to adhere to the rules that you've lived by for so long."

He nods at my watch.

"Your brain is controlled by time. When ya leave and where ya go are based on certain timed sequences that you've been forced to comply with, I'm afraid. If you leave before the specific time or long after, they'll know. You witnessed it firsthand just a few minutes ago out in the apartment. Got cold pretty fast, yeah? That's their signature."

I cringe. I can still feel the cold, like knives prodding my skin.

"The cold air is like their own personal cologne."

He straightens and leans in close to me.

"The good news is that you escaped before they could pluck your memories away again! I really don't think your mind can handle another memory wipe. Each time it happens, it just gets worse for ya. Takes you longer to remember who ya are, and when you do start to pick up the pieces, ya normally never quite get all of them back."

He grips my palm, and I come away with the butterfly knife.

Michael lunges toward me. His nose is almost touching mine. "Right. I want ya to listen and listen well. No actin' about. Next Sunday, your heart monitor's gonna stop. The machine keepin' ya half alive'll be unplugged. Your soul'll cease to exist here, and you'll be sent to the devil's playground for the rest of your soulless existence. So, if I were you, I'd start mannin' up now."

Michael smiles at me, but it's too sharp, too predatory, too steeped in the promise of violence. It's almost a threat—bared teeth rather than an expression of joy.

I try to speak, but I still can't. I try again. No words come out, and my mouth doesn't even move. I glare at Michael.

"When ya finally know the truth about yourself, only then will your voice be heard," Michael says, looking down at me. "And the only way to see the truth is for you to man the hell up."

I grip the handle of the knife. How did this happen to me? What did I do to deserve this? I want answers! *Who am I?*

Michael looks at me as if he is reading my mind. "Sad that the reapers take more out of ya than just your memories. Must be hard to be mute. The power to speak…ah, it's a shame, really. So many people take it for granted—just like a name. Ya see, a name to some people is just a name. But a name…a name is the identity of the soul. We all know your true name, but good luck if ya think we're gonna share it. You, and only you, can figure out your name and discover its importance. I never even remembered my name."

Can he hear my thoughts? I try to clear my mind, offer him only a blank slate.

My warning alarm sounds. I've got only ten seconds to make it downstairs and to my car. I whip around and charge back toward the elevator.

Michael stands in front of me. "This is what I mean when I say to ya to get your mind straight. Did ya just see yourself there? Once your warning went off, ya shut down on me. Ya completely resorted back to what ya were before. A hypnotized little drone following the system's antiquated protocols. D'ya see your strings now, Pinocchio?"

He is right. I had been moving as if I didn't have any control over myself. My body continues to move around Michael toward the elevator door. There's not much I can do.

"I know what'll make ya stop." Michael back-steps to get in front of me again. "I'll tell ya a story. A telling of a story distracts the brain's primary functions."

Michael strikes my throat, and I gasp and fall to the floor.

Above me, Michael gazes at the painting as if seeing something beyond it. His eyes refocus, and he snaps his head in my direction.

A shiver runs through my back. My watch shows nine minutes, fifty-seven seconds. My stress level rises with each elevator floor ding. My watch alarm goes off.

Ten minutes.

"Each year that passes here my memories tend to fade. I remember I loved the color red. The smell of pumpkins in the fall. You see, I was once a man followin' the American dream."

I look at him, knowing he is trying to calm me and it's working. My curiosity of who he once was has my full attention.

"I fell in love when I was young and got married, but I thought it was more important to make my mark in the world. Though I hadn't intended to have a baby with my wife, I let my wife know every day how I regretted her havin' the child. I fell deep into this rabbit hole, and my life and thoughts became darker and darker. But no matter what I did or said, my wife stayed with me in my darkness. Her love was strong, but I never valued her love. I went so far down that hole that when I hit the bottom, I thought I was finally free from all the pain, but God had other thoughts in mind for me. Death wouldn't be my fate. Instead, I was given a second chance. A place that showed me things I had done in my darkest moments—my sins, which haunted me every day without ceasin'. A place that ultimately locked my soul away. I could never understand that where there's a lock..."

Michael points at a strange card slot above the button panel. "...there'll always be a key. I was just too late in finding it first. I don't even remember their names anymore."

He bends his head down and I almost feel pity for the guy.

I snap my wrist up. It's 11:00!

Adrenaline charges through my body. Every muscle springs into flight mode.

"I can see ya still don't quite understand what I'm on about. That's grand, I get ya. It's always hard to take in the complexity of a place like this and figure out which parts we all have to play."

Frost is now forming around the elevator doors. Ice crystals spread across the carpeted floor underneath me.

Michael looks at the developed photo, each puff of his breath adding to our mutual steam cloud.

"The reapers are comin' to bring us pain; we have to bring them chaos."

A screech echoes through the air. I shudder. The sound is close. He tightens the gloves over his hands.

Michael chuckles dryly as if this brought him a hidden thrill. Another shriek, this one even closer, shakes my resolve.

The elevator opens, and a reaper storms through. Michael stands firm. The dark cloaked figure screeches. The sound knocks me off balance, and I tumble out the door to the floor. The reaper's skeleton mask leers at me from under its inky cowl. Michael yanks off its hood.

"Don't give them the chance to get their legs on solid ground," Michael advises. "The minute they touch somethin', it and everything near it turns to solid ice."

Then Michael jumps over me while yelling, "Down hood and strike!"

The reaper screams and lunges at me. I try to flip the knife open, but it falls out of my hand. I lose my balance again and land hard on my right shoulder. My face follows and slaps the frozen hardwood.

"Throw me the knife!" Michael screams.

I hurl the knife to him. Miraculously, he manages to catch the handle, whip out the blade, and drive it into the reaper's skull all in one motion.

The reaper lies on the floor and begins to steam, liquifying the layer of frost that blankets the elevator floor.

Michael walks out of the elevator, carefully tiptoeing around the liquid. "I'd try not to touch a reaper's remains in any kind of way. Unless ya feel like sticking around."

I lie on my back for a moment.

Michael offers me a hand, and I take it this time.

"Ya need to learn to defend yourself," he taunts. "Ya acted like a child. I can't keep saving ya forever. Ya need to learn how to save yourself." He helps me back up.

Michael closes the knife and places it in my right hand.

I tumble to the PVC roof surfacing and curl up to protect my vital organs.

My watch indicates 13:20. I've got to get to the coffee shop.

I flail my arms and legs, trying to drag myself away from Michael. I break from his grip and stumble to the edge of the roof.

As I stare at the ant-like cars and dots of trees, an icy breeze sweeps through.

Michael cackles. "Looks like the little maggots have regrouped! 'Bout time."

There's no way I can make it to the coffee shop before those monsters appear. And I'm in no shape to put up any more of a fight than I just did. *Perhaps I could outrun them...*

I turn back toward the elevator, but Michael grabs my arm and whirls me back around. "Where do you think you're going? It's time I teach you about learning how to hitchhike." A blow to my back sends me flying over the edge. Michael looks down and cracks his knuckles while the space between us expands. "Was that too much?!" he yells. "Oh well!"

A reaper appears over his shoulder. He spins, throws his arm around the reaper's neck, and forces them both off the ledge.

As they accelerate, a sheet of ice forms under the reaper's cloak and creates a frozen trail in midair. Their descent slows as the layer of ice takes on their weight. Michael takes his knife and stabs the reaper's skull. "Not enough to kill it, but enough to control it!" he yells. He works the knife like a joystick, controlling the reaper and steering it toward me.

I adjust my body the other way and notice my car is in plain sight almost a mile below me. *I might just make it out of this.*

Michael swiftly plunges between me and the streets below. I fall onto the layer of ice they've left behind. The surface is rough, with shallow pits and peaks. My face skids across it, leaving skin and beard behind.

My hip hits hard, and I roll onto my shoulder, then onto my knees. The edge of the icy surface is dangerously close.

My feet slide across the ice, and spikes eject from my shoes. The auto-cooling sensor must have kicked in.

I try to use my cleats to dig into the icy structure but fail. I reach the edge and topple over. I crash myself right into the hood of my car, completely wrecking it on impact.

I jump down, just about to touch on land, when Michael scoops me back up.

"Wasn't that your car?! You need to be more careful! Cars like that don't grow on trees!"

He thinks he's funny. I insultingly throw him a look of displeasure. As he steers the reaper toward the interstate, another reaper comes shooting out from below me.

The reaper kicks in a new gear and forms its own icy sheet underneath me.

"Okay, this time...don't fall off!"

Michael purposely lets me go, and I become completely terrified. I land on this new slab of ice, lose my balance, and slide toward the edge. At the last second, I stomp my right foot, burying my cleat into the ice. I take my other foot and dig in, making another stronghold.

The reaper looks back at me. It turns around and heads straight toward me. The ice starts to fracture, and I jump off. The reaper reaches its skeletal hand toward me as I fall. Its finger is only inches from my head when Michael swoops in and stabs it in the head.

Falling through the air, I look back as the reaper freezes over into death.

Still in control of the first reaper, Michael has managed to form a sheet of ice under me once again. I dig my cleats into the icy slide. The spikes hurl ice shards in their tiny wakes. I stabilize my descent and look in front of me to find that Michael is steering us straight ahead.

I see the highway below me as Michael gets closer to the truck with the glass windows in the back. He takes a picture of it.

Just up ahead is the coffee shop.

Michael jabs the rest of his knife down into the first reaper's skull. The ice slide underneath me soon fractures from Michael's actions. The two of us crash through the coffee shop doors.

I land hard. The cold has chilled me to the bone now, and white-hot pain shoots through my torso and limbs. I can't lie here, though. That horror is in the room with us. Pushing through the agony, I get to my feet. As my shoes touch the floor, the cleats retract.

The dead reaper lies steaming atop the espresso machine.

Another reaper shows up at the window. My watch beeps.

Fifteen minutes.

"That's what we like to call a mulligan."

Michael takes a picture of the reaper outside the coffee shop window and the reaper floats away.

Why did it just float away?

Outside, the snow has stopped. The wooden floorboards crunch under my feet. There's no trace of anything remotely covered in snow, like it all just evaporated into thin air. I am horrified of what I just experienced and in complete and utter shock when Michael screams, "Y'wanna go again?"

We walk into the Haberdashery and Michael begins pushing me to the back of the room. "I wish you and Madi could have met at a snow lodge or a hardware store. Would have helped shape this place up a bit. But it could be worse." He pushes a curtain to the side, and I see a whole new undiscovered area of the room. I look at all the miscellaneous goods —hardware supplies, school supplies, cooking supplies, clothing, and more.

I guess this is how I built my fancy shoes.

"Here is where ya can build any oddments ya might need for surviving from reaper attacks."

"The thing to know about reapers are that they are attracted to heat. Reapers can read a soul's heat temperature. That's how they always know how to find ya. But heat can be generated in another way."

Michael grabs a purple book off the shelf and hands it to me. The cover of the book reads, *Physical Science*.

"Things like fire and flares are a good distraction. Draws them in quick. Holds their attention. Gives you an extra few seconds if done right."

Michael takes a cart and begins dropping random items in. A metal-encased marker, six sparklers, paper, scissors, straw, aluminum foil, and some lollipop sticks.

"These items may look random to the untrained eye, but put together, ya get some pretty wicked flare sticks."

My watch beeps. Twenty minutes.

Michael, in anger, tips the cart over. "There's just never enough time!" He takes out the butterfly knife and whirls it around as if he is calming himself back down. "It helps get your mind back focused. Try it." He hands me the knife and pushes me out. "I need a minute!"

I begin playing with the knife as I walk out of the shop, making my way to the park.

A wind blows, catching and lifting the autumn leaves. Brilliant yellows, oranges, and reds swirl through the park and scuttle across the ground. The Ferris wheel rotates faster as the wind intensifies.

There's a picnic set up by the gaping, dead tree. Apparitions of Madi and me flash across my memory. We laugh. The leaves swirl lightly in the wind and settle all around us. Madi is gathering a pile of leaves. She runs over and drops it on my head before turning and running away. I blow the leaves out of my face and chase her. She approaches the tree, looks back at me, and runs inside it.

The images fade. I sit on the park bench, fumbling with the knife, and throw it to the ground in frustration.

Michael appears in front of me. He seizes the knife from the ground and sits down. "I'll tell ya another story. The Lord instructed a prophet to say to another man, 'Strike me!' The prophet refused. Then the wrathful God said unto him, 'Because thou hast not obeyed the voice of Jehovah, behold, as soon as thou art departed from me, a lion shall slay thee.' And as soon as he was departed from him, a lion found him and slew him. Now, I'm no Jehovah, but when I say 'stab,' ya do it. Ya get me?" His eyes simmer with dark rage.

Do I get him? He pops into my life, my apartment, as though he has a right to be there. He tells me I'm in a coma and I have to trust him to survive. He almost gets me killed by those appalling creatures, and now he expects me to do what he says as if he's God?

"I see you're startin' to feel it burnin' inside of ya. The feelin' of anger is an emotion that is very freein'. Everythin' that's been bottlin' up inside of ya wants to come out. Ya really should release the tension before ya explode."

Pressure builds deep in my chest. My skin surrounds my body like the crust of the earth before a volcano erupts. I could kill him. I could kill him, and every one of his cohorts with him! This all can't be real! If I am in a coma, this whole world, these lost souls, the dark creatures, are all a figment of my imagination. A result of a brain doped up on pain killers. And Madi...

I close my eyes tightly. If there's any chance she might be real, perhaps I should placate Michael for now.

"The more ya begin to break away from your chains, the more ya begin to see." He raises his eyebrows ever so slightly. I'm still not sure I can trust those shadowed green eyes. I feel trapped. And I desperately want answers.

"Hold that thought," Michael says. He walks to the nude marble statue at the bottom of the hill. He takes a picture of the glass box in the statue's outstretched hand. The picture develops, and he puts it in his pocket. He walks back up the hill and gets in my face. "Ya wanna feel anger, but you've no idea what real anger is. To feel anger, or any feelin' for that matter, ya must first acknowledge your fear and surrender to it."

I push him away and ease over toward the big dead tree. As I get closer, the shadows shift and reveal a black door recessed within the gaping hole. It appears to be at least a hundred years old. Carved into its ebony surface are angels and heaven on one side, fighting a great battle with demons, and hell on the other. A tiny square mirror lies right in the middle. Michael joins me and takes a picture of it.

"Careful how ya play your cards when you've a queen already in your hand," he says in a low voice.

"There're two types of pain ya must endure to survive here. One being physical, the other being mental. Inside that door," —he nods at it— "lies the mental aspect portion. The things you'll see and hear are somethin' that can't ever be trained on, only learned from. It tests the true part of your soul."

He seizes my chin and looks deep into my eyes.

"Inside there lies the pain that dominates your dreams every night, that darkness you never let in when you're awake. It's as if there're no seconds, minutes, or hours inside this door."

I step closer to the door. I do want to understand what is going on in this place, who I am, why I am being stalked by these strange men, and why I keep remembering only fragments of my life. Still, who knows what lies inside? And can I really trust Michael?

I reach for the gnarled doorknob. Foreboding sweeps through me as if carried by the wind. I step back.

"Ya aren't going to do it. You know how I know? I've lived this Sunday a hundred times with ya, and not once have ya ever been—"

With a trembling hand, I grasp the twisted handle and push through. I'm engulfed in darkness.

Behind me I can hear Michael say, "Right. Well, that's new."

he darkness fades, and I am in an immaculate, black-tiled, multi-stalled bathroom. I'm wearing a full-black tuxedo, and a glance in the mirror reveals that I appear much older than I did at the coffee shop. I am unable to control my movements and feel totally disconnected from my body, as if watching from inside a shell.

A newspaper lying on the red upholstered bench displays the date: 1999. *How did I get here?* Where was I just a second ago? And why am I wearing a tux? I rub the fabric of the tuxedo between my fingers.

Explanatory images fill my mind. I stole this tuxedo from the adjacent checkroom. The attendant shouldn't have left his post. He was just asking for someone to take the expensive-looking ensemble. I'd made it back to the bathroom before the attendant returned, and I'll be leaving out the opposite exit. Should be good as gold. No way is the owner of this tux out there, or he'd be wearing the thing himself.

Doesn't look half bad. I turn from side to side in the mirror. Everything is black—the dress shirt, jacket, tie, socks, shoes. It fits as if it were tailored for me. A King of Spades sticks out of my breast pocket. It's black where a normal card is white, and brilliant cyan instead of red. Must be a high-end fashion trend.

I step into the hallway. It echoes with the sounds of slot machines, roulette tables, chatter, people calling and bidding, and cards being dealt. The haze of cigarette smoke is saturated with equal parts cologne and perfume. I turn the corner into a gaming room with all its electric, exciting splendor.

I make my way through the different gaming stations and find myself staring at the roulette table. I sit down and purchase a stack of blue chips. After a few minutes, I'm tripling what I put in. My hot streak is blowing up, and a crowd of elegantly dressed patrons swarm around my table, cheering me on.

"All of it on six," I say as I eye my stack of blue chips. The crowd around me hushes.

"The player bets his lot on the number six," the dealer replies, holding the ball up for the room to see before spinning the wheel and dropping the ball into the groove.

I lean back. A waitress sidles in beside me, leans over, and puts a tumbler of what looks like bourbon or scotch in front of me. She lingers in that position for a moment. She's got big eyes with long lashes and full, wet lips. Her blonde hair is loose around her shoulders and glistens in the colorful lights. The dress she's wearing hugs her curvy body and leaves little to the imagination. She glances down at my left hand and looks back up at my face. I slide my left hand into my pocket to conceal the ring. She raises her eyebrows ever so slightly and smiles.

I turn back to the table, and the ball rolls slower and slower. To my right, an amber-haired woman in an indigo dress that looks like it cost more than my salary gazes at me. She's got smooth, ivory skin, a petite nose, and dimples when she smiles. Her pouty lower lip is caught between her teeth.

The dealer rakes his stack of chips across the table. My breath shortens to almost a standstill. The ball, rolling more slowly now, begins to bounce, finally settling into place.

"Yes!" I yell, pumping my fist in the air.

"Number six it is!" the dealer shouts.

I breathe out deeply, look around, and straighten my jacket. The crowd is cheering and clapping. The dealer begins counting my winnings. People across the room turn to look and approach the table, trying to see what's happening.

"Nine thousand to the fancy-pants man to my right!" the dealer says.

He stacks chips in front of me. Nine thousand! That's five times more than I've ever won before.

"You must be feeling good, sir," the dealer says, pushing the chips across the table toward me.

To the house, this is small potatoes. I need to get a lot more money.

"Indeed, I am." I smile at Dimples on my right. She smiles back, her long lashes framing deep blue eyes.

Someone reaches over my shoulder, drops a napkin in front of me, and sets a drink down on it. I turn around to find a cocktail waitress. She smiles and points to a woman at the bar before moving on. The woman rises, her sparkly red dress catching and reflecting the light like a crimson mirror ball and walks toward me. She gracefully maneuvers her slender body through the crowd and nestles in sideways between Dimples and me. Her dress exposes her nearest shoulder, smooth and cream-colored.

"My name is Lisa. I see you've been on a winning streak."

She nods at the King of Spades sticking out of my breast pocket.

"I'm holding my own. But my name isn't—" She puts her finger on my lips.

"Follow me to the big boy's game." She takes a step away and looks back at me to follow. Her straight, chin-length amber hair sways across her large hoop earrings.

I turn back to the roulette table and cash in my chips. I tuck the money into a black velvet coin purse and slide it into my pocket. Lisa is waiting for me in a far corner of the room. I make my way toward her, and as I near, she passes through a set of burgundy velour curtains.

I ease through as she rolls apart a set of sliding wooden doors. Inside, there is a narrow, white hallway with an identical set of doors at the far end. She closes the doors behind us, and we proceed down the hall.

There is an array of avant-garde paintings hanging on the right side of the hallway, almost as if we are walking through a small art museum. The first five paintings are of a single, shadowed porcelain mask against a white backdrop. Cracks penetrate the porcelain, and each mask has a band of color across the top, resembling a different high card from a deck of playing cards.

I think aloud, "The Jack, the Queen, the King, the Ten, and the Ace."

Lisa follows my eyes. "I see the royal flush family has caught your eye."

"Why do all the masks seem as if they were withering to pieces? What's the artist trying to convey?"

From behind me, Lisa says, "I like to think that we are like the face cards and the deck is our universe. We might be the highest in the suit, feeling as if we were eternal, but our cracks, our flaws, show that we are still vulnerable, still only human."

I stop in front of the Jack mask. Its pearl-white skin with its blue mustache and eyebrows resembles the playing card. Even the red crown attached to the top is a nice touch. But what really draws me in are those black rectangular eyes. It almost has a sinister quality look to it. "I have never seen these paintings before. Who's the artist?"

Lisa steps next to me and faces the paintings. "Jacques Philippe Dawid. He was a thirteenth-century undiscovered French artist, well-mastered in the art of oil painting." She sweeps her hand from left to right. "He only painted these six. The five pieces here are named: *Vernal, Estival, Autumnal, Serotinal,* and *Hibernate,* after seasonal climates, due to his finishing each one in a season's time. They're worth at least fifty thousand a piece. The man responsible for this little card game is a big fan of his work. A real big fan."

We proceed down the hallway, and when I get to the fifth painting, I stop again. The portrayal of a cross surrounded by demons is markedly different from the other four paintings. The cross is painted in hues of electric blue and looks as if it's made of light and energy. Surrounding it are seven different colored, impish demons. Their long claws anchor them to the light, and their gaping mouths drip black sludge.

"His *Mona Lisa.*" Lisa admires it with me. "Set at around one hundred thousand dollars."

I'm drawn into the light of the cross, and the room around me fades as the electric blue consumes my gaze.

"The reason it's so expensive is because it was his last. Remarkable story about Jacques is that he never even picked up a paint brush until after he awoke from his coma."

"Coma? How did that happen?"

"Not too sure. I just know his coma lasted four months. When he awoke, he was said to be a different man. Started wasting his hard-earned money away on gambling and overly priced auction items. Once all his money went bye-bye, he joined the monastery in Bandouille, France, and spent the rest of his days creating these paintings. He was mentally unstable, which is why his paintings reflect so much broken creativity. But this one was his masterpiece. He called it, *Matthew Twelve Forty-Three Forty-Five.*"

On the cross's left arm, a bat-like yellow demon strains against the light as if in a tug-of-war. Something is different about this one, compared to the rest. It has one eye that seems to be completely made in gold. I become immediately hypnotized by it.

"The eye of greed. That's real gold by the way."

"Real gold?"

"He stole it from some very bad men just so he could place it right there."

"Why?"

"He believed that greed was the smartest sin out of them all. He wanted to embrace its importance more visually. Ironically, it was that same sin which lead him to his bitter end."

"How did he die?"

"Remember those bad men I told you about?"

I can picture the ending being a bloody one. I make a cringing look toward her to where she gets the picture to not continue any further.

"Now are you going to stare at it all day, or do you want to go make enough money to take it home with you?"

The word *money* tears me away from the original art piece.

We move on to the second set of sliding doors, but before we go through, Lisa opens the top drawer of a dresser to the right. She reaches in, takes out a white hard resin mask, and hands it to me. From the inside, the mask has a small symbol of a face clock drawn in the upper region, and inside are sprawled playing card suits. A cyan heart at the twelve, red diamond at the three, black clover at the six, and the black spade on the nine. The outside resembles the Jack of Hearts, identical to the painting.

"I told you he was a fan," she says. "Put it on, Jack."

"Why am I wearing this?"

"They don't like cheaters. So, to make it fair, everyone has to hide their face. No expressions, no way of players signaling to each other or the dealer what they might have. No cheating…And I guess they think it looks cool."

Lisa takes out my playing card from my jacket pocket. She turns and slides it in a card slot connected to the door panel. The slot inside turns green.

I drape the mask over my face.

"You called me Jack? Why?"

She turns to me and laughs. Her steel gray eyes sparkle behind long, thick lashes. "Funny and cute, I think you will fit right in."

She puts the playing card back in my jacket pocket, fixing it to where it sticks out again.

"Welcome to the Labyrinth Club."

The doors slide open, and in front of us stands a man wearing the Ace version of the mask. Except his is the only one that is jet-black and not white. The mask also portrays a golden 'A' on the upper left side. But what really stands him out from the rest is the unique priest vest over his chest. That alone lets me know he must be the leader of the bunch. A playing card, the Ace of Spades, sticks out of his breast pocket. It's got the same cyan and black color scheme as the card in my jacket. Wait…the cards aren't fashion trends; they're identity markers! *Take me to the big boy's game*, Lisa had said. Whoever owns this suit is the guy that's supposed to be in here. Should I continue to play along? What are my chances the real guy shows, after all? I doubt they'll take it lightly if they find out I'm an imposter. Still … the potential for a huge payoff is too tempting to resist.

Ace steps into the hallway and extends his hand to me.

"Nice to finally meet you, Jack. I'm Ace. Heard so much about you."

What am I doing? There's no way I can pull this off. I've got no clue what any of this is about. If I reveal myself now, maybe they'll let me go with no hard feelings. I touch my mask, intending to take it off, but the green eyes of the bat-like demon in the painting stop me momentarily.

"I see you have an eye for fine art," he says with so much class under tongue.

I lower my hand. Not knowing any art lingo leaves me silent in reply.

Lisa responds for me, "Yes, he does. He was just telling me about Mr. Jacques Philippe Dawid."

I lock eyes with Lisa. She offers a small smile. Her lipstick is a pale pink, muted so her eyes stand out among her soft features. She probably tastes like cotton candy. *Why would she lie for me?*

Ace puts an arm around me. He smells like a bottle of Caron's Poivre. "You are aware of the late Jacques Philippe Dawid's work? Only a rare type of person knows of his work. The man had a strong soul to live, very bright his artistic soul was. When he awoke from his coma, people thought he had dropped that light. He spent many years painting this godly brilliance on canvas. You know what he said after he unveiled it?"

My silence continues.

He doesn't hesitate. "'My soul is not contained within the limits of my body. My body is contained within the limitlessness of my soul.'"

He gazes at the painting. A few seconds go by, and I exchange a glance with Lisa. His arm is heavy across my shoulders.

After a few more seconds of his frozen stare, Ace turns to me. "You ready to step into the ring, old sport? Or is this perhaps a little too rich for you?" He laughs and slaps me on the chest. He leads us into a medium-sized room with a white, sculptured, custom-designed ceiling, recessed lighting, and walls of deep red boiserie. Other than a circular, marble table in the center of the room, there is a small, well-stocked bar in the far corner, but no bartender.

He walks Lisa and me to the table, where a dealer and three other players are sitting—one with a cyan Queen of Hearts in her jacket pocket and a matching mask, another with a cyan Ten of Hearts and mask, and a third with a cyan King of Hearts and mask.

"Our knave has arrived!" Ace announces to the group at the table and finally releases his hold on me. They all clap in excitement.

"He is also on fire tonight," Lisa says and pulls off a sexy wink at me. Maybe I can carry this charade for at least one game.

"Jack, meet the rest of the royal flush members!" Ace points to the King. "This is the King of Hearts. Tell Jack all about yourself, my King."

The king stands.

Looking at him, I can't tell much other than he is an average-sized man with a strong athletic build.

The king pulls a card from his inside jacket pocket. He reads, "My name is Charlemagne, but I am also called the 'suicide king' because on my card's portrait, my sword appears to be sticking into my head. This is a result of centuries of bad copying by English card makers where my axe head has disappeared."

Ace claps rapidly. "Just wonderful!" He points to the Queen, who is sitting on the left side of the table. "This beautiful mistress is our Queen of Hearts."

Measuring her up, I notice she is the same as the King. Average-sized woman, slender, with no sign of skin color.

The Queen takes a long puff from her cigarette holder. The smoke is then released through the lips slit in her mask. She takes out a similar card from her purse and reads, "My name is Judith. I have been known by either the biblical character or the wife of King Louis. But my favorite interpretation would be of the Red Queen in *Alice in Wonderland*. Off with the crown—and with the crown, his head!" She sniggers—a raspy, smoke-worn sound.

Ace points to the final person at the table. "And our last comrade is Ten."

This man, just like the others, has hidden his ethnicity well. But what distinguishes him from the rest is that he is smaller in size and a bit stout around the waist area.

The white-masked man gets out his card. He reads, "I am just Ten?"

A few seconds of silence follow. Everyone, including myself, stares at Ten. He breaks the silence with a short, high-pitched scream. His quirky laugh alone makes the rest of us join him with hesitant chuckles.

Ace turns to me, "You have already been cleared and can assume no one here has divulged their real story or names. The reason is, once again, to keep the privacy to an art. Being someone else for a night adds a little fun and mystery to the game at hand. And after tonight is over, our identities remain hidden, and no one is the wiser regarding who stole or won money from whom."

Ace sits and indicates the empty chair for me to claim. "Now, my young Jack of Hearts, what is your story?"

My throat constricts and my stomach tightens. I should have known this moment would come. I reach into my inner left-hand pocket, hoping the card is there. Nothing in the left pocket.

Everyone stares at me as I try the other side. I close my eyes, praying it is there. Nothing but empty silk. I sweep my hand along the fabric, searching for any other pouch it may be hiding in. Their stares seem to penetrate the hard resin of the mask. They know I'm a fake. I shouldn't have done this. I shouldn't have.

My hand hits on thin, plastic-coated paper. My eyes snap open. It's the card! I hold it in view and read the typed information. "My name is Jack La Hire. I am a French warrior who fought beside Joan of Arc in the Hundred Years' War."

I tuck the card back into my jacket pocket and sit down. The other members clap.

"Nice to have you here Jack!" Ace runs his hand through his light blond hair. It settles back with a subtle wave on one side. He looks around the table. "I will, as you've figured out, be your ace for the night. The ace originally meant the side of a die with only one mark. Since this was the lowest roll of the die, traditionally it's been considered bad luck. But as the ace is often the highest playing card, its meaning has since changed to mean 'high-quality, excellence.' And that, lady and gentlemen, is what I am offering to you tonight for the price of only ten thousand dollars! Chump change to all of you, I know. But after tonight, one of you lucky fools will leave here one hundred thousand dollars richer!"

Everyone applauds, and I join the clapping, grateful my expression is hidden behind a mask. Ten thousand is every last cent I've got—the thousand I picked up at the pawn shop on the way over, and the nine thousand I won at the roulette table. Ace continues. "Also, a special prize will be awarded to the victor of the night."

The dealer pushes several piles of neatly stacked chips in front of each of us. Could I be so lucky? The entrance fee's already been paid?

The king turns toward Lisa. "I'll have another."

She shifts to move away, but I grab her arm and pull her down close to me. "Who are you?" I whisper.

"I am the bartender," she whispers back. She smiles and heads behind the bar, where she begins making a cocktail.

The dealer is already shuffling the cards. I can't help looking back over at Lisa. With an athletic body like that, I bet she's got some stamina.

"Look boys," the Queen says. "Jack's caught the love bug."

My face burns. Thank God they can't see my blush. "Sorry, boys and girl, but sadly, I'm married." I flash my wedding ring.

The men laugh so hard they shake the table. Did I just give myself away? The King says, "That's a good one, Jack!" and the Ten yells "Bloody, classic, Jack."

Ace leans forward with a smile on his face. "Cheaters always cheat. Am I right, my fellow suits?" He lifts his hand, showing his own wedding ring, and the others do the same. They are all married. I push my chair back, stand, and walk over to the bar. *Cheaters always cheat. Cheaters always cheat.*

"You feeling lucky tonight, Jack?" Lisa asks. She leans over the bar, and her cleavage deepens as the glittery dress falls open a bit more.

I look down at my ring and back up to see Lisa smiling seductively with those cotton-candy lips.

She whispers, "Keep it on. It's more fun that way." I could get lost in those liquid gray eyes. The dealer's voice brings me back to earth.

"Break's over! Players return to their seats."

Lisa winks at me. I walk back to the table and sit down.

The dealer shuffles the cards like a magician.

The Ace sits back in his chair and says, "Gentlemen, and lady, tonight the game will be poker. Two-round buy-in. On the second round, there will be no folding of your cards. You must play to win. Now, if you win the first round, you have the right to leave or stay.

If you win the second and final round, then the pot is yours, and don't forget the special little surprise that comes with it. Lastly, to go over the rules again with all of you: First, if you are a horrible loser, not only will you be thrown out of this fine establishment never to return, but you'll be badly beaten with a blackjack by the person who wins the whole pot in the end."

Ace takes out a baton and shows it to everyone. He places it on the table and holds up a cyan and black King of Spades. "We all remember what happened to our last King David, right?"

The Ace places the King of Spades card on the table and hits it with the baton. I flinch, and everyone sits there in silence. Perhaps in a similar game, "King David" went home with some permanent injuries.

"Second, if you try to cheat, well, I really shouldn't have to repeat the penalties you've got coming. As I always say, 'Cheaters in the bed but never in your head.' Enough of that; put up the money!"

The other players pull out stacks of cash and pass them to the dealer. Not so lucky after all. I fish out the cash from my wallet. Bet big to win big. Anyway, it's not likely I can make it out of here alive at this point without putting something up.

The cards are dealt, and I sort through my hand. All the cards are colored in the same cyan and black color scheme as the cards in our pockets. The only difference is that something is sticking out around the suit and number of each card. I softly move my fingertips along the raised dots and figure it has to be Braille.

Someone must be blind at this table, but I wonder who?

Looking around the table, I can't tell, as they all appear so natural. I get my head back focused. I can't get distracted, not even for a second.

My highest card is a King of Diamonds. The Queen pushes three of her five hundred chips to the center. Everyone matches the amount. I discard a Three of Hearts and signal for another card. The dealer slides me a card facing down. I slowly pick it up: King of Clubs. There's no way I can win with a pair of Kings. Why didn't I just stay in the casino? Could I even have refused Lisa's proposal? What was I thinking, stealing this tux and figuring no one would notice? Sweat beads form above my upper lip. My fondness for the mask grows.

Two Kings. I could always bluff. But a smart man would fold, get lucky in the next round. Without thinking further, I watch myself go all in. Ten, Queen, and King immediately fold.

After a moment of tension, Ace goes all in. The blood drains from my face, and I feel light-headed. I should have known he would call my bluff. He's a thrill-seeker. Money means nothing to guys like him. Just in it for the rush, while poor guys like me fall right into his lap.

I turn my cards over and lay them on the table. "One pair," says the dealer. Ace folds. Queen curses. Ten slaps the table.

I won? I force myself to sit still as the dealer pushes more than twenty-four thousand dollars' worth of chips in front of my place. I won! This is my night. No way am I cashing out now.

The Ace lays a briefcase on the table and opens it. It's packed to the seams with neatly stacked bills like some kind of drug deal is about to happen. He lays each stack of bills one at a time on the table and looks at me.

"So what kind of person are you, old sport? A lost soul willing to risk it all? Or a soul survivor willing to settle on what he has? The decision is up to you."

The dealer exchanges the stacks for a pile of chips. The pot sits in the middle of the table, ripe for the winning. With the streak I'm on, there's not much to think about here. They stare at me, waiting for my answer.

I smile beneath the mask. Suckers. "I think I am feeling like a lost soul tonight."

Out of excitement, Ten bursts out with a short, high-pitched scream, which gets everyone chuckling again. I signal Lisa for another drink. She saunters over with a martini, leans in with that swooping neckline again, and says in a low voice, "There you go, slick." Her hair brushes the tip of my ear before she straightens and returns to the bar.

I catch the Queen eyeing me. And then the dealer deals the next hand. I fan the cards and sort them so the lowest is to my left. A Ten of Spades, Jack of Spades, Queen of Spades, Ace of Spades, and a Jack of Hearts. So close to a royal flush!

The only thing missing is the King of Spades. I resist the urge to look at my breast pocket. The card I need is only six inches from my hand! My heart beats faster. Excitement. Danger. But there's no way in hell I could get away with that. They'd all see it.

The Jack of Hearts in my hand mocks me. I'd like to rip that little plastic-coated paper head clean off him. Oh, how one simple card can ruin a man's life.

Dreams of getting my life back in order and finally finishing my book start to slip away. After this hand, I'll be ruined. If only there were some sort of diversion. Perhaps I could make the switch unnoticed. The unified color scheme of the cards might just make it possible if I partially shield my pocket with my hand. My heart pounds faster; the blood pulses through my temples.

The sound of breaking glass near the bar turns everyone's head.

Lisa rushes to gather the broken stemware from the floor.

This is it. Everyone's got their eyes on Lisa. I deftly swap the King in my pocket for the Jack monarch in my hand.

"Our bartender appears to be having a little too much fun, am I right?" says Ace. He turns his head back and locks eyes with me. His seem to hold only good humor. My fanned-out hand is blocking his view of my pocket. So far, so good.

One more round of dealing goes by, and I decline any more cards. Ten goes all in, followed by Queen and King. Ace looks up at me, down at his own cards, then back at me. "Well, Jack, this is it. All or nothing time." His eyes reveal a grin beneath his mask. He pushes all his chips in.

Well, I can't turn back now. I push all of my chips to the center of the table, adding to the mound.

The dealer says, "Call!"

The King lays down.

"Flush!" says the dealer.

The Ten flips up.

"High card!" the dealer says.

The Queen turns each card one at a time.

"Four of a kind!"

Ace finally lays down, staring at me unwaveringly as he presents each card.

"Straight flush!"

All heads turn toward me. No one had the King of Spades. There's no reason to think anyone will be the wiser. I slowly lay out the Ten of Spades, reaching far enough in front of me to keep the focus away from my jacket pocket. Next, the Jack of Spades, Queen of Spades, King of Spades, and finally, the Ace of Spades.

"A royal flush!" shouts the dealer.

There's a corporate gasp, and even Lisa's jaw drops open.

Adrenaline is coursing through my body now, and it's all I can do to keep my hands from shaking as I fold them together and hold them under my chin. My forearm should block any sight of the Jack. Ace watches me but says nothing. The dealer slides all the chips over to me.

Ace pushes his chair back, steps toward me, and slaps me on the back. "Good hand, old sport! Good hand! All's fair in games of chance!" He walks toward Lisa as though he's going to order another drink. How can he be so cavalier about this? All that money must've been pocket change to a guy like him.

My King of Spades card is lying by the dealer. I reach to grab it, just as the dealer picks it up. He puts it back in the stack with the others. Heat rushes to my face. What if he counts the cards and realizes there's one extra in the deck? They'll figure out its the King of Spades, and they'll know it was me! I've got to get out of here.

The dealer hands me Ace's briefcase. "That is one hundred thousand dollars for the winner. Bring this man our finest whisky!" I hold the briefcase in my lap, making sure it's high enough to cover my breast pocket. I've got to shield this Jack of Hearts until I make to the hallway.

Lisa walks over with a bottle of Macallan whisky and places it beside me.

She steps over to me and puts her hand on my shoulder.

"Good game, all, but I am now taking the winner away for my own amusement purposes." Her own amusement? Conjured images parade in my mind of the slinky, sparkly dress sliding from her shoulders and a wet tongue on my ear. Does the gown button or zip in the back? My ring glints from where my left hand holds the briefcase.

Lisa lifts my bottle off the table, and I stand.

"Jack promised me a dance, and that's a promise he'd better keep!" Everyone laughs.

King reaches into his jacket pocket and pulls out a room key with the number six on it. He tosses it to me. I catch it midair with one hand, leaving the other to shield the deadly card.

"Jack, you're room six. Word is, the stereo system is astounding, especially from inside the bedroom."

Ace walks over to me as I begin to panic. I look down at the Jack card peaking out of my jacket pocket. I don't have time to push it down. He is going to know.

He stops in front of me and stands there in silence.

He knows.

Lisa steps in front of me and tucks the card down deeper into my pocket.

Lisa kisses the lips of my mask.

She then turns and faces Ace. "I hope you don't mind him keeping the mask for a few hours. I will be sure to bring it back," she says with a wink.

Ace doesn't move nor talk. His silence speaks volumes. He must have seen what Lisa did. There's no way out now. What am I going to tell Madi? That's if I live through this.

Ace clears his thought, "And the card?"

Lisa's face goes white. "The card?"

It's over.

My whole body feels as if it was covered in sweat.

Lisa pats my chest pocket where the hidden card lies.

"Oh! This card. Don't you worry. I'll make sure the only thing he loses tonight is his pants."

The players chuckle, and Ace says, "You are a diamond in the rough. Take care of her, Jack."

She takes my hand, and we head back toward the sliding wooden doors.

She pulls me one-handed through the hall, looks back and winks, and says, "You owe me a drink, Jack."

"My name is actually—"

I take my mask off and she places a finger on my lips. She looks into my eyes and smiles.

Her smile alone is enough to weaken me.

Then, still facing me, she slides the door open, leans close to my ear, and says, "Tonight it's Jack! Tonight you become someone you're not. Tonight you can be whomever you want to be." She backs through the curtains into the main gaming room, pulling me with her. "So...be Jack. And what does Jack like to drink?"

I can't help but feel dangerous as we step up to the bar. She uncorks the bottle and pours two full glasses. I straddle a bar stool and bring Lisa to stand between my legs. My right hand rests just above her hip, feeling the ripple of her athletic torso.

"This may very well be the best whisky you will ever taste," she says, running her hand over mine and smiling.

Her hoop earrings swing with the slightest movement of her head. Her moist lips reflect the dazzling lights of the casino.

The briefcase weighs heavy in my left hand. One hundred thousand dollars. My life is finally taking off. This is what I was meant to do. I finger my wedding ring with my left thumb. Tonight,

I'm Jack. I pull Lisa in close and nuzzle her hair behind her ear. "Tonight is going to be one lucky night!"

She cocks her head with pleasure and turns toward me. We clink our glasses together and throw back our drinks. I plunk my glass down on the bar.

Lisa's amber hair sways back and forth. Her steel gray eyes swim among those long, thick lashes, and her features blur together. I've never felt so euphoric. This is going to be a night like I've never known before.

I try to stand, but the room is spinning, and now there's an incessant beeping in the distance. The beeping gets louder, and my vision goes black.

*T*here's something wet all over my face. I open my eyes, and my surroundings slowly come into focus. My watch is still beeping, but I can't move my arms. I'm tied to a wooden chair, my arms and legs strapped down. *What the...?* The beeping finally stops.

My watch indicates 25:05.

My body is shaking. Either it's freezing in here, or I'm in shock. Where is *here*? And how in the heck did I get here? The walls of this room are a metallic light gray. Metal tracks run across the ceiling, and there's a metal door in front of me with a thick, circular glass window about head-high. To my right are dozens of empty meat hooks. To my left, a stainless-steel sink. Frost and condensation cover everything.

A meat locker? Ace and the others must've figured me out. The glint of one of the meat hooks threatens me. How long could I live with one of those in my back? A bead of something thick and warm makes its way down my cheek and drips off my jaw. A bright red splotch soaks into my designer pants.

Images of the park and Michael and the dead tree spring to mind. Wait! This isn't Ace's doing. It's something else. And I'm not where I need to be. Those skeletal creatures are going to be coming for me! I struggle to free my legs and arms.

Something slaps my right cheek hard. Searing pain shoots through my cheek, neck, and torso. Through my now spinning vision, a man in an all-black getup with a brilliant black skinny tie begins to take shape. *Michael*. If only my arms weren't tied to this chair.

"That's what ya get for almost gettin' us reaped. You better be glad I got ya out on time before the tree could spit ya out and land you where you don't belong!" Michael slaps me again, on the left cheek this time, just a little bit harder. Blood spews from my mouth and splatters an empty chair a few feet away. I want to scream at him, but I can't make my mouth move. Not even a sound comes out.

I reluctantly get calm, noticing Michaels King of Clubs stuck inside his vest pocket.

It takes me back to the members of the Labyrinth and how each one of them wore a specific card that showed their membership into this prestigious club.

Come to think of it, each playing card I have seen in this place were all cards that I had played while participating in the game.

I get it now. The purpose of the playing cards and the reason why we all wear them. They are my scarlet letter. Just another torture device like everything else in this place.

I smirk at the fact that I am finally understanding this place.

"Someone looks to have found some insight," Michael says, smiling. "Maybe going in early might have been a way to do it all along. I guess we won't truly know until the end." Michael removes his inverted cyan playing card from his vest pocket and wipes the blood around my face.

"Let's get back on track, yeah? Now, where were we?"

Michael takes out something small from his jacket pocket. "I would've gotten ya out sooner, but I had to go back for this baby." He shows me a Polaroid of my office window. The man's lost his mind. I look down at my watch again; twenty-six minutes. My panic builds.

"Don't worry, they can't sense ya when your body drops below a certain temperature. Y'see, reapers have those heat-sensor eyes, all predator-like. We'll be grand in here for the time bein'. We can ride out the clock till we are back on time before they catch wind of where we are. Reapers might act like idjits, but there's a brain in that skull of theirs. No matter how small it may be."

Michael scoots a chair over to me.

"I know what you're gonna think, so don't bother thinkin' it. Cheatin' for money at a card game isn't the source of your pain. The mental pain aspect comes from yer sins. All humans have a certain amount of sins bound to their soul. It takes a lot of self-knowledge to find those sins that are bound to ya, because a sin is just another name for a demon. It gets in real deep-like and doesn't ever want to let go."

Michael whispers in my ear, "Have ya ever wondered what happens when ya leave the sink on in this place?"

He kicks the empty chair across the room and slams my face up against the sink. He yells, "We're not playin' around here!" The thick layer of frost on the sink sears the open wound on my face, and my exposed skin sticks to the surface like a magnet. Michael turns on the faucet.

The pipes clunk and groan, and a clattering sounds through the nose of the faucet. Michael plugs the drain, and the sink fills with brown, lumpy pus.

So it's not just my apartment water. *What is this filth?*

The murky liquid rises while Michael holds my head to the sink. My eyes are nearing the brown pus.

"This, my soul brother, is a metaphor for your whole existence.

Wanting to be pure, but your sinful nature always leaving ya dark and chunky. Have a smell."

Michael rips my face away from the frozen sink, leaving a gruesome layer of skin attached, and dunks my head into the pool of contaminated slop. The sensation is excruciating on my raw flesh. The chunky fluid fills my mouth and esophagus as my body gasps for air. Michael lifts my head, and I cough, then vomit.

"That's good. Keep bottlin' up that anger. The reapers may have erased your memories and forced your emotions deep down inside ya, but they're still in there. You just need to be like a volcano and rupture them out." He retrieves the chair, scoots it over to me, and sits down.

If he'd remove these restraints, he just might get his eruption!

Michael puffs a cloud of vapor and points to it. "Other things to watch out for: once you see your breath, a reaper is not too far away from ya. When ya see snow fall, ya run. That means a reaper is within ten feet of ya."

My body shivers more violently, as if the temperature has suddenly dropped drastically.

"There'll come a time when you're faced with a whole group of these reapers. And the more there are, the colder it'll get for ya. Your body's core temperature in this world is a lot higher, due to your outer and inner layer consistin' mainly of your soul. While your soul does give off more heat, remember it can only handle so much."

Michael steps close and scoots my chair to the door.

"I bet ya are wondering now why your body feels as if it was dumped into a frozen lake?"

I peek out the door window to find that two reapers are searching through the kitchen.

"Don't worry, they can't see us. The temperature in here is keeping our bodies cool enough. Remember, reapers can read a soul's heat temperature, but once ya get your body into a much colder climate, your soul's temperature drops, makin' it harder for them to detect ya. You'd be more of a blip on their radar, so to speak. But the cold can only hide ya for so long."

Michael reaches under his chair and picks up a black baton. He looks up at me and smiles.

"As ya already know, you're invincible to a point. Only when your soul is below freezin' can it get hurt." He winds up. I struggle against my bindings, but they hold fast. Michael slams the blackjack into my shoulder, my legs, and across my face. The room reels as if I'm in a fun house. My body is in shock for a split-second before the agony registers with my brain.

His messy, dirty-blond hair and shadowed eyes come into focus. I clench my fist and fantasize about ripping one of his cross tattoos clean from his neck.

Blood and pus ooze from my gaping face and drip from my jaw. Even amongst the misery, I feel alive. It's as if my existence up to this point, my high rise, my job, the coffee shop, the subway, were part of a dream I'm waking from. I'd forgotten what this feeling was like.

Michael looks at the bloody baton.

"I'm not here to punish ya. I'm here to make ya understand. There will come a time where your body is broken and tired. They will not hesitate. Not for a second. And that's all they'll need to erase everything from ya. One measly second. To survive, ya have to keep running. Run through the pain. Run through any negative feeling ya have stored up."

The cold becomes too unbearable. The room feels like it's spinning.

A brain freeze rushes into my head, knocking me, chair and all, onto my side against the frost-covered floor.

Michael's voice drops off, and the last thing I hear him say is, "Just keep running."

My vision gets cloudy, and everything fades away.

CHAPTER
EIGHT

oung voices chatter faintly in the distance.

I rub my eyes and blink. It's bright. Somehow, I'm outside, standing on a running track, surrounded by eighteen-year-old boys wearing high school track suits. All of them, including me, stand at the starting line of a race.

I feel thinner, stronger. The skin on my hands is much younger. I must be in one of my memories again. My body is moving independently, like I'm just along for the ride. Any connection with my immediate past in the meat locker with Michael is fading. A sign hanging over the front of the officiating table reads, "Half Marathon," and the scoreboard displays the date.

1988.

I position my foot just behind the starting line and relax for a minute. No one else is in position yet. The heat from the afternoon sun warms my bare shoulders. I smile, taking a deep breath.

Within seconds, other racers line up around me. Their eyes are trained forward as they take their positions.

I look up into the bleachers and notice my parents aren't there.

I wipe my sweaty palms on my shorts and place my feet into the starting blocks like a bull preparing to break loose of its holding pen.

In my periphery, the heavyset race official makes his way from the officiating table to the starting line, holding the starting pistol loosely in his right hand. The runners lean forward a little more, poised to spring at the crack of the pistol. I inch my right foot forward, breaching the white chalk slightly. Any edge I can get, I'll take. I have a thin chain wrapped around my wrist with a golden pendant dangling from it.

Sounds flood my ears with increasing and unbearable intensity—each breath from the other racers, the roar of cars racing up and down the busy street below the stadium, the jet engines of a plane overhead.

People in the crowd tell each other to hush as the race nears its start. The bleachers squeak as their bodies settle into the seats. I position my arms, one back and one forward, crouch down a little lower, and flex my leg. I shake my head to try to regain focus.

The track stretches out in front of me. But a new sound joins the cacophony. It's similar to cascading sand and resonates from somewhere nearby.

I don't see anything around me that could be making such a noise. My stomach churns. *I've got to stop the spilling sand.* I grind my teeth and clench my eyes shut. Sweat trickles down my cheek. I'm imagining it. It can't be real. It's just a distraction to overcome.

I lift the pendant to my lips and kiss the Celtic hourglass engraved on its face.

Everything around me moves like cold molasses. At the edge of my vision, the race official draws his lips into an O and squeezes the trigger. My body tightens.

CRACK! The runners explode off the line, hitting the track hard, pumping their arms, and sprinting for position.

I stay close to the leaders for nine miles. I'm in third as the lead pack passes the starting line for the next lap. A runner from behind quickens his stride, pushing hard, and passes me on the outside. My legs feel like rubber. I've got four miles to go, but I'm not sure I've got any gas left in the tank. I can't lose this race. Father's disapproving face appears in my mind. I'm going to lose. My heart pounds out of control, and my stomach feels like its being squeezed in a tight fist-hold.

Just keep running. Just keep running.

There are four runners ahead of me now. I can't catch them.

My back foot clips my front and knocks me completely off balance. I tumble onto the grass. Skin scrapes from my knees before my momentum settles. The race clock reads 42:02.

My chest heaves, struggling to draw enough oxygen to compensate for my sudden stop. It's over. There is no way I could catch them now. Even if I got back up and finished the race dead last, I would never hear the end of it from my father. He'll be glad he once again didn't show for one of my races. Taken out by a stupid trip! Could I be any clumsier?

The last of the runners make their way past me. Blood trickles from my scrapes. Do I quit now, or do I finish the race? Why couldn't I have twisted my knee? That would have solved my problem.

It's as if someone whispered the idea to me; I could lie. I am a solid actor, thanks to the many school plays I was forced to participate in. I can finally put that talent to use.

I hold my knee and writhe, putting on the most pained face I can muster. Reaching all the way back to when my mom left, I draw tears from their ducts. Two medics make their way toward me with medical kits and a gurney.

No going back now.

They ask me a hundred questions about my knee.

I lie.

They carefully feel around my leg, and grill me about anything else feeling out of place.

I lie again.

They bandage me up while I lie there, feeling ashamed of myself. The seconds on the scoreboard tick as if each second lasts a lifetime.

They lift me to the gurney. I continue to writhe and hold my knee. Maybe I really did sprain it. The pain is killing me now.

As they wheel me away, the crowd cheers, and the winner breaks the finish line at sixty minutes flat. That was supposed to be my time.

The roar of the crowd, the echo of my coach yelling, and the seconds on the clock sound as if they are a thousand miles away. And what remains in that bizarre, muffled silence are only my thoughts.

Every instinct to the contrary has simply been a denial of the following truth: I am now, and will always be, a quitter. Hiding behind my shame, I close my eyes, wanting the day to end. My watch alarm fills my ears and drowns out the rest of the world.

I blink. Empty meat hooks are suspended horizontally across the room. Searing pain registers across my face and throughout my entire body. The icy layer covering the floor digs into the open flesh on my cheek. I have control of my thoughts and actions again. My watch stops beeping.

Thirty-five minutes.

I stand up and look out the door. No sign of any reapers. I take a breath and walk outside. A large stainless-steel island in the center of the room houses several commercial-grade kitchen ranges. Pots, skillets, and metal utensils hang from metal bars above. The walls are lined with stainless steel countertops and deep, multi-sectioned sinks. There's a double door directly across from me. I shove it open, and step onto cherry-wood floors. The gold chandelier overhead stands out against the pearl-colored ceiling. I'm surrounded by crimson walls with gold accents. And Michael sits in one of the high-backed, blood-red booths to my left, staring at me.

The same waitress stands next to Michael in her form-fitting pencil skirt, her big doe eyes watching me, as well. She sets down a bottle of wine she's apparently just finished pouring. Michael takes a picture of the tray's silver cover with the waitress holding it.

He smiles at her and nods. She takes a step back and waits. Michael motions to his empty plate and grins at me.

"I was just tellin' our beautiful waitress here to turn the thermostat up; it's a bit chilly in here, no?"

The waitress doesn't make a move. *What is her role in all of this?*

"Come 'ere! Sit!"

He's dabbing his mouth with one of the crimson napkins. I take the seat across from him, lowering myself into the booth slowly.

"Don't worry, the reapers are all gone. We are where we need to be."

The waitress turns and walks away toward the kitchen.

"Hold on!" Michael shouts, and waves for her to come back. She returns. "Are ya familiar with the five-finger filet?" She looks confused.

"Then you're in for a treat! It's a specialty of mine."

The butterfly knife is in his hand.

Michael reaches for the waitress's arm. She pulls back slightly.

"It's all right. I won't snap at ya." He smiles reassuringly.

She gingerly extends her hand. Michael places it flat on the table between us. He spreads her fingers apart and puts one hand on top of hers. While holding her hand firmly, he uses his free hand to pick up the dinner knife.

The waitress tries to pull her hand back. "Wait! No!"

He stabs the knife through the scarlet tablecloth and into the table between his and the waitress's fingers, pulls it away, and stabs again between the next two fingers. His pace speeds up a little each time he stabs. "There'll come a point where your heart'll race, your mind'll be clouded, and your back'll be up against the wall. To win, ya must keep calm under pressure. When everything in ya wants to shut down, you have to fight it.

The waitress's face contorts, and tears gather around her brilliant green eyes. Her lower lip quivers.

Michael keeps stabbing the table between their fingers, much faster now. "Do ya see how her fear overcomes her? The faster I go, the more helpless she feels. This is ya at this very moment, unless ya can prove to me otherwise."

Michael increases his speed even more. The waitress squirms and struggles to free herself, but Michael's hand holds like a vise.

The seconds tick by. I flash back to the scoreboard, watching the time tick as I lay in the grass, contemplating what to do.

The waitress quickly pulls her hand away. But as she does, her fingers slide between Michael's. His knife comes down on her exposed middle finger, slicing it cleanly off just above the first knuckle. She screams and yanks her bleeding hand back to her chest. Her continued screams echo off the high ceiling as she squeezes her other hand around the stump to stop the flow of dark blood.

Michael laughs and claps his hands. The waitress's screams have transformed to terrified sobs, and she's fallen to her knees. She catches sight of her severed finger sitting in a small pool of blood and starts screaming again. She struggles to rise but falls over and ends up half-crawling toward the kitchen as she continues to shriek and wail.

Michael shouts, "Now, that is being fearless! She looked death in the eye and gave him her middle finger. That is truth. That is findin' purpose. Thank ya for participatin'. Let the Lord rebuke thee!"

"You're a monster!" the waitress yells. She's almost to the swinging kitchen doors.

The whole scene feels more like I'm watching a movie than living my life. My mind feels so numb. Why am I just sitting here and not helping her? Why don't I care enough? What does it even mean to care?

Michael leaps to his feet, grabs her by her hair, and drags her back to the table. He pulls her head back, looks at me, and slits her throat. Blood cascades from the wound like a small waterfall.

I stand up, but there's nothing I can do for her. After only a few seconds, she stops struggling, and Michael drops her on the floor. He raises his Polaroid and snaps a photo of her lifeless body.

"No. Not a monster. I'm a believer of reason and purpose. I see right through you dirty soul. I know what your after."

Dirty soul? What does he mean by that?

Michael lines up his camera from another angle, as if he were a fashion photographer, and takes another photo.

He looks at me. "She died so that ya could find some purpose to live. D'ya understand? The moment ya stop tryin' is the moment ya stop carin'. But ya have to care so that you can try. You let her die because ya don't care enough to do anything about it."

The waitress's already pale skin has turned as white as a sheet of paper, and the light in her eyes has gone out. A small fire ignites inside me. That same feeling I felt before is slowly building up again. Michael stands next to her. He looks like he's proud of what he's done. Blood splatters the Celtic cross on his neck.

He wipes the blood with his hands and then smears it on her face and hair. He looks into her eyes and says, "Alexandre Dumas once wrote, 'I don't think man was meant to attain happiness so easily. Happiness is like those palaces in fairy tales whose gates are guarded by dragons: we must fight in order to conquer it.'" He looks back up at me. "Are ya willing to fight for it?"

I seize the knife from where it fell.

He jumps up and puts his hand on the table as if daring me to do it.

The fire inside of me has grown and is now hard for me to control. I lift the knife, flip it open and over, and stab it toward Michael's hand. He is too fast, and the knife buries itself into the table. My watch beeps.

Forty minutes.

I yank the knife out of the wood and hold it in front of me. My body has already calmed back down. Where did that outburst come from?

"Nicely done! There it is! How'd it feel? Great, yeah?"

I don't have any more time for Michael. I've got to get to the subway station, or I'll have a swarm of reapers on me. I rush for the exit.

Michael shouts after me, "Ha! There ya go! Stormin' out's just another sign of anger! Proud of ya!"

Out on the street, I run toward the subway entrance, but my leg catches on something, and I trip and fall. I push off the asphalt and look back. A manhole cover is cocked half open. I crawl over and peek down.

There is only darkness. I shiver. Where does it lead? I exhale, and my breath mushrooms in front of my face. No time! With a surge of energy, I dash to the subway and board the train as the doors are closing.

I take a window seat not far from the doors. Michael walks over to me.

He stops and leans back on his heels. "Well, it's that time again."

Time for what you wacko? Why don't you just get away from me?

"Listen. The sound of your reverie is singing to ya again."

A sharp noise reverberates in my eardrums. I raise my wrist to my face.

Forty-two minutes, two seconds.

The high-pitched squeal grows louder.

"Someone on the outside must really love ya."

The noise, now painful, drowns out Michael's voice as it gets louder and louder.

Michael takes a picture, and the flash blinds me. I close my eyes and focus like I did before.

The high-pitched sound turns into another familiar piano melody, different from the others I have heard.

I let the soft piano music play through my ears and into my head, hoping against hope that I will see her again.

TEN

The airbrakes screech loudly, and the train decelerates from the subterranean darkness into the busy station where I stand.

How am I back on the platform? Where's Michael? My watch reads 2:30 PM. Someone bumps me. There are people everywhere. I must be in one of my memories again. A man next to me is reading a newspaper. I try to inconspicuously check the date: 1992. So, it's been a year since I saw Madi at the coffee shop. Did I ever find her?

My right hand has a hold of something warm. My head looks down, moving on its own. I'm holding a piece of pizza. In my left hand, I'm gripping Madi's book.

Any sense of Michael and the train station I left behind is fading.

I take a bite of my pizza slice. The grease from it smears around my mouth. As the train doors slide open, I pause and lower Madi's book.

A single guitarist and a drummer on the subway platform play sloppy but spirited music. The strings of the guitar twang, and the melody makes me think of Christmas. I know this song, "Chestnuts Roasting on an Open Fire." A small audience of smiling commuters stand around the two musicians.

I step into the subway car and take a seat facing the band on the platform.

The guitarist taps his foot, and his head pulses with the beat. He glances into the subway car and looks straight at me. I lean back in my seat and close my eyes as the synergic sounds fill my heart.

The announcement plays: "Stand clear of the closing doors, please." I open my eyes and a catch a glimpse of a cream-colored peacoat. A woman with light brown skin and hair of soft, brown waves is placing some money in the musicians' hat.

"You have got to be kidding me!" I say, drawing a surprised look from a young boy across from me who is clinging to his mother's hand.

I smile at the boy to reassure him and lean forward so I can see her again. She hurries into the train car just before the doors close. It's Madi, all right! The train inches forward, slowly accelerating into the next section of tunnel.

Madi finds an open seat, sits down, and places her bag on her lap.

Now this is something! What is she doing here? I rise from my seat as though in a trance and walk slowly toward her.

From behind me, a man shouts in a crisp English accent, "Madi! Here I am, love!"

I turn. He has short, graying brown hair and a large, toothy grin. His white suit is nicely pressed. He makes his way down the aisle, and as he passes me, I catch a whiff of bergamot tea. He sits next to Madi, and they embrace.

I move closer to them, finding a spot between two old ladies. I only want to observe, so I turn away, making sure Madi can't see my face.

"How was your day?" he asks her.

"Over, finally."

He places his hands on one of hers.

She slips it out from under his and looks away. "And how was your day?"

Is that annoyance in her voice?

"Better now." He kisses her cheek. Her expression softens, and she turns to him and exchanges a short kiss.

I take out a pack of gum, remove a stick, and push it into my mouth. Well, it looks like she found her knight. I make my way back to my previous seat and lean back, mostly concealing myself, but still watching Madi and the man talking to each other. The man whispers something in her ear, and she laughs.

At the 96th Street station, the subway train slows and stops. Most everyone stands, and people walk past one another, disembarking and boarding. I stand and hold the handrail as I search the crowd for Madi.

After most of the people clear out, I catch sight of her peacoat moving into the next car, probably on her way to the bathroom.

The man she was sitting with is still there. I grip Madi's worn and tattered black leather book. I have been waiting for so long for the chance to return it. I went back to that coffee shop numerous times, and she never was there. Now I know why. Maybe it's finally time to let her go.

"Stand clear of the closing doors, please," the announcement sounds again.

I walk over to the man. "Excuse me."

He looks at me—"Good day"—and then back down to the suitcase in his lap.

"Your girlfriend," I say. "I think she dropped this book on her way out."

The man eyes me and takes the book. He flips through the pages and snickers. "It would have been best had you left it where it lay. I'll inform her of its return. Thank you. Good day."

"I see she is good at writing piano lyrics. Does she play?"

"Ah, you are still here?" He seems confused and shoots me a dirty look. For some reason, I find his annoyance amusing. I remove another stick of gum from inside my coat pocket, unwrap it, and pop it in my mouth.

He notices the wrapper. "Tredstones?"

"You know it?"

"Truly, I haven't seen that brand in ages."

"Here." I place the packet in his hand. He looks surprised. "Merry Christmas." I return to my handrail, and the train slows again for the next station and comes to a stop.

I step through the doors as soon as they open. But once outside, I linger, hoping for another glimpse of Madi before the train pulls away.

"Stand clear of the closing doors, please," the announcement repeats.

The man is still alone, holding the book. The doors close, and the train slowly starts off into the dark tunnel ahead.

She is gone.

It feels like I've lost her all over again. I turn and notice a strange disco ball hanging on the ceiling of the subway station. Its presence seems odd and out of place. Its mirrored surface reflects a soft ray of light straight down on to my face, blinding me.

I get underneath the ball of light and look up towards it.

I hear a snap from above me. The disco ball falls directly down and I just stand there, frozen.

I dodge out of the way just a few seconds short of a head on collision. The disco ball shatters next to me. On the ground, I look at one of the broken mirror pieces. In its reflection is the hourglass pendent around my neck. I continue to stare almost as if I was hypnotized by it. I suddenly feel trapped and disjointed by the illuminating experience. I can't seem to blink my eyes. The first thought that enters my head is of my father. I can see him now, looking down on me, disappointed at my clumsiness. Images of my father's wrath and a mother's lust plague my mind.

I focus on the hourglass to get rid of the cancer inside my thoughts. I watch as the sand comes to life and pours down the hourglass's neck. Black walls barricade my vision. In the darkness, is a long running track with a finish line up ahead of me. It's too far. I force my eyes to finally blink and when I open them everything is back to normal.

Did I just have a panic attack?

Looking around, I see people not even caring to help me back up. Everyone just playing on their phones going about their day. Like mindless drones they all are. I could've gotten seriously injured or maybe…What if I died? I almost regret now moving just to see if anyone would have even shown a bit of compassion. Like what if I never moved and died by a random disco ball? Would they care?

I stand up and look around at the soulless people walking over each other to get to their destinations.

What if this is really my hell? A world full of empty souls and regrets. The term *regrets* makes me come full circle back to thinking about Madi. I'm no better than them.

I walk up the stairs, out of the subway, and home to my hole-in-the-wall apartment building. I make my way up to my assigned unit, lighting a smoke as I go. How many people have committed suicide because they'd rather die than have to sleep another night in this hellhole?

I burn out the cigarette in the wall next to my door, adding to the art left by many others before me. I unlock it and walk in.

As I sit on my stained and torn sofa, Madi's soft features come to mind. Her lips were wet with strawberry-colored gloss, and her light brown skin looked so smooth. God, she is beautiful. Stacks of books decorate the tattered carpet. One in particular is an inch shorter today. Somehow having Madi's book there had given me a sense of hope. Along the wall are stacked, empty pizza boxes. Why didn't I talk to her? She was right there, and I just couldn't do it.

A car commercial plays on the TV.

A 1987 jet-black Ferrari Testarossa drives through the desert. My dream car. This is probably as close as I'll ever get to a car like that. The car drifts through the sand, doing a one-eighty and then a three-sixty.

The commercial ends, and a James Bond movie resumes. Bond sits at a high-risk card game. He looks at his hand and pushes all of his chips to the center.

"All in," he says. That's courage right there, betting it all, not caring about the consequences. Bond wins the hand, and piles of money start to stack in front of him. That's the way to get fast money. Bond's got the right idea. Now he can go kill the casino manager-terrorist, get the girl, and save the day. If only life were like the movies. How easy everything would be. I turn the channel and a romantic movie is playing. The lovers kiss as the romantic piano music comes on and the screen fades to black. Credits.

The music, coming from the film, is the exact same melody that played in my Purgatorium.

Just beyond the TV, my pooching stomach fills my view. Funny how fast the weight comes on.

I pick out a chocolate bar from the bowl I just recently filled with candy. The decadent, smooth confection melts on my tongue and fills cheek spaces. Desperately trying to obliterate the feeling of loss and to forget about the man sitting with Madi, I take another bite and savor the sugar rush.

My gluttonous stupor is interrupted by a knock at the door. Surely it's not the landlady. I paid my rent…fifteen days late, sure, but it's paid. I retrieve my baseball bat from beside the door before I open it. No harm having it, just in case. I open the door, keeping the bat concealed. Madi stands there, holding a red Christmas stocking with clear plastic packages of Tredstones gum sticking out of the top.

I stand there with my mouth open, half full of chocolate.

"I heard this gum was only sold in one place. I thought you could use a surprise." She smiles.

Perfect teeth. Perfect lips. Perfect nose…

I swallow the rest of the chocolate down and can only think of one thing to say. "You're late." I pretend a semblance of control. Can I freeze time? Can I make this moment last forever? Am I dreaming?

I can still hear the romantic music playing on the TV, making this moment seem more perfect if it were actually happening.

Her face starts to flush, and she looks away. This is real.

I drop the bat behind the door, step forward, and grab hold of her waist. I pull her closer to me, moving her face in next to mine. The stocking slips from her hand onto the floor, and the packages of gum spill out. She is the best surprise I could ever ask for. I can almost feel her lips on mine. Suddenly, a familiar noise is heard.

Beep…beep…beep.

ELEVEN

he subway breaks scream and blend with my watch alarm. The floor of the subway car is pressed against my cheek. I reach up and grasp the dirty, cushioned seat and pull myself up. The beeping stops.

Forty-five minutes.

The doors to the car slide open. Adrenaline hits my bloodstream, and my eyebrows raise. Is Madi here? I look around wildly, half expecting her to appear like magic.

I was so close! The music couldn't have given me just a few more seconds?

The butterfly knife is sticking straight up from the floor beside my head. Michael's camera is right next to it.

I sit up and slowly stand. The searing pain I felt in the meat locker has disappeared. Light from the station ahead streams in. I pull the knife out of the floor and pick up the camera. The train comes to a stop, the doors slide open, and I walk out.

The lights in the subway station go in and out as a crooked disco ball is oddly hanging above the ceiling. As I watch the disco slowly rotate, I see something within its mirrored surface. For a split second, a dark object appears. I blink, just once, and it's gone.

Curious, I lift the camera up and take a photo, hoping to get evidence that I'm not going crazy.

As the photo ejects out of the Polaroid, I continue to stare at the sparkly ball but nothing appears. I take out the photo, noticing the disco ball and nothing else.

I must be going out of my mind.

I get my head back on straight and walk up the stairs to the street level.

I stroll along the old traffic bridge, watching each of the shimmering lanterns hanging across the wooden beams. I get distracted by their mystical light and accidentally drop the knife.

I sigh loudly and kick the knife along the ground. I bend down to pick it up, and as I rise, Madi's billboard fills my vision through the railing. The lanterns over the bridge seem to dance around her smile. Their light beams on a silver musical note that shines over everything else on the billboard. A warm wave of happiness washes over me. She has to be real. I lift the camera and take a photo.

The photo slowly ejects. I pull it out and flap it back and forth. Madi's face begins to develop.

I tuck the photo into my wallet and walk forward, now with more purpose and determination. My apartment building is just ahead, and I quicken my pace. I step into the elevator and press the button for the roof. My watch beeps.

Fifty minutes.

The electric blue of the cross painting grips my attention. The first time I saw it, in the narrow, white hallway of that casino, there was no way to know how something so significant, so beautifully brutal, could mean so little and yet so much to the outlining of my life.

At the left side of the cross, the yellow demon is missing the golden eye of greed.

Someone must have stole it. But why?

The elevator doors open again at the rooftop.

Michael is waiting. He relaxes in one of the deck chairs while reading a book.

"So, are ya lion or lamb?" he asks without looking up.

I walk over to him and hold the knife in what I hope is a threatening manner.

Where does the music come from?

Michael looks at me, and I'm sure he can read my thoughts. "Well, it goes through your ears, into your eardrums, which then send the information to your brain." He lays the book aside and leans forward. "So, if your question is where the music is comin' from, then your answer is *everywhere!*"

Everywhere?

"Your outside body can still feel, taste, and of course hear when things are happenin' or being done around it."

That means someone must be playing music on the outside.

"Correct, sir! Don't ask me who because I don't know."

Or you do know but you won't tell me.

"Either case, it doesn't matter who's doin' it or why. All that matters is that it's helpin' you remember who you were.

How is that possible?

"There's a study that shows how music can help bring back comatose victims. Whenever memories have an emotional context to them, they tend to hold much more power in the brain and tend to be processed differently. In which case, a specific song can help trigger vivid memories if they are powerful enough. Someone on the outside it seems is trying to communicate with you."

They're my memories? That means...Madi is real. I'm curious to know who is playing the music?

Michael in anger, tosses a chair off the roof.

I look over to him confused at his sudden out break.

"You're the lucky one in all this. Thanks to the reaper, you're hearing all these songs for the first time. Do you know how many times I've heard each song?! Too many and it doesn't help that the track only has five measly songs! But the worst part is that once the track finishes, the songs cycle back to the very beginning. It never changes. It's like they have it set on some alarm system that triggers it everyday at one specific time. I can't take it!"

Michaels face turns red as if he is about to explode. He screams out at the sky, "Stop torturing me! How about just mixing it up a little? Just one song! Is that too much to ask?!"

Michael takes a deep breath and calms himself. "Sorry, the music is slowly driving me a little insane. Where was I?"

Still holding the knife, I pull the camera over my head, and toss it to him.

He catches it and, after a few moments, starts laughing. "There was a reason I left this for you. A picture is worth a thousand words, remember? Takin' a picture can tell the soul many things.

"Let me see what you're passionate about, so we can see where your hope lies. Show them to me, if ya would." Michael extends a hand.

I hand him the two pictures I took. He keeps his eyes on me. "Ya took two? Odd. Normally, ya would only take one. Ha! Ya are something else." He looks at both of them and snickers to himself. "Ya will find out tomorrow on how ironic this truly is. But let's focus on this particular one for right now. At least this hasn't changed."

He holds up the one of Madi from the billboard.

"Ya always end up taking a picture of her. Always making her your symbol of hope and look where that's gotten ya. Y'think she'll be your guidin' light out of this darkness? You're wrong."

He looks at me, crosses his arms, and waits a few moments. "I'm over this. I've helped ya too many times, and each time we run through this race, it just gets harder when it should be gettin' easier.

Maybe ya just wanna stay a walkin' mannequin. Maybe feeling anythin' is just too hard for ya to comprehend. Maybe it'd be easier for ya to stay…how'd ya put it…content."

A sharp pain sticks in my side, as if the word were a blade.

"I really don't see what Madi ever saw in a quitter like ya. Maybe she just felt sorry for ya."

Rage surges through me.

Michael turns and takes a few steps toward the elevator.

His retreating figure reminds me of being on that grassy field, watching the other runners leave me behind.

My anger overcomes me like a wildfire, and I throw the knife toward Michael.

Time seems to slow down. He continues to laugh as the knife gets ever closer to his face.

My extreme emotions consume every part of me. Any thoughts crawl into the shadows of my mind. I am blind with rage. I am no longer me. I have no control, and I like it.

I find myself running with supernatural speed, passing the knife in midair. As the blade enters Michael's mouth, I catch it, stopping it one centimeter from his uvula.

Michael doesn't even flinch. He forces a smile with the blade still inside his mouth. I take several deep breaths and can feel myself back in control.

I remove the knife, flip the blade in, and hand it to him.

What just happened? I stand there, chest heaving, glaring at Michael's deeply shadowed eyes.

"Y'feel it all now, don't ya? You've broken your emotional barrier. Ya can now start to experience your humanity again."

I do feel different. My mind is clearer, as if my thoughts are no longer enslaved. I am free.

I try to talk, but still nothing comes out. Instead, I bow my head to Michael, displaying my gratitude.

He walks over to me and lifts my head. "So then ya must know your overall purpose?"

Millions of thoughts run through my head simultaneously. It used to be just one thought or none at all. I try to sort through them. What is my purpose?

"It's grand," he says. "We can hear your thoughts. I'm sure ya must have learned that by now."

I look into Michael's verdant eyes for a few seconds.

I want to live.

"It feels good to want rather than to need." He straightens his shoulders and looks pleased with me. "Those words are worth more than gold. It takes a strong heart and a bright soul to find that revelation in oneself." He takes a step toward the ledge and sweeps his hand from one end of the horizon to the other. "Have a good hard look at the world ya live in now. Your eyes are now open. What do ya see?"

Over and beyond the ledge, the city lights seem to shine brighter than I remember, and they tear into me with their radiant hues. The northern lights dance above me. Their reds and greens shimmer in the night sky, blanketing everything with dazzling beauty. *What exactly am I supposed to be looking for?* From our fifty-story height, the streets look like a tic-tac-toe board, and the cars are the size of ants. But I can still make out the coffee shop where Madi and I met. And there is the subway station where I saw her again. The park also stretches out below, its brown expanse housing the nude statue and the giant Ferris wheel. The ghostly images I saw of a picnic with Madi come to mind.

This place is built around my memories.

I look out upon the city and visualize a map over the entire area—my apartment, the coffee shop, the park, my office, the restaurant, the subway, and all the way back here. Each location leads to the next, making one big circle back to my apartment building.

One big circle. Sixty minutes in a day. The same time in which I would have finished the half-marathon if I kept running.

This whole place is structured as if we're one big racetrack.

Michael stops me. "Bingo. One race to grant ya a one-way ticket back up to the living."

That's it? I just have to run around the whole town once and I will be set free? What are we waiting for?

"This is your trial, your second chance on life, and it's goin' to be a lot harder than ya think. This race is gonna test your body and make you work for it."

How many times have I already tried this and failed? How many times has a reaper erased my memory?

Michael laughs. "All in good time! Let the past stay the past for now." He looks at my watch and says, "I think we've enough time to celebrate!"

He walks to a table, reaches underneath, and pulls out a briefcase identical to the one that I won in the casino. He flips it around, lays it on the table, unlatches it, and flings it open.

Expecting it to be money, I'm surprised to see the two flintlock pistols from my office—one with the engraved golden lion, the other a lamb.

"I'm sure you've seen these before but never realized the importance they hold. This will be apart of your final challenge. You'll soon enough know their purpose, but until then you'll have to choose one."

The handles of the guns look smooth and worn. Elegant lines form the images of the lion and the lamb. The lion, strong, full of authority, and all-powerful; versus the lamb, weak, gentle, and merciful. Whatever I'm going to need this gun for, all-powerful, sounds like the wise decision.

The gold, shining from the lion's head, gets my attention the most. I select the lion and hold it in my left hand. It's heavy and clunky. How am I going to fire this thing?

Michael smiles and snaps the case shut.

"Lion you are."

I hold the barrel up to my eye. It doesn't appear to be loaded. And Michael doesn't seem to have anything else for me.

"Almost forgot!" Michael holds up the Polaroid and takes a photo of the ledge. He tucks it into a stack with the others. "You'll also need these for your next self-discovery." He retrieves a stack of Polaroid pictures from his pants pocket and hands it to me. "D'ya know why I don't give up on ya? Because somewhere inside ya, there's still a good soul, and I'm fightin' for it. Now I need ya to, too. You have a second chance to rerun a race you never finished, and a life you haven't yet fully lived. Don't rush the process. You only get one more chance at this. Ya hear?"

I take the pictures and shuffle through them, hoping to find some kind of inspiration, but they are only random shots that he took today.

He really is crazy. I slip them into my jacket pocket just as my watch beeps.

Fifty-five minutes.

When I look back up, Michael is gone. I walk through the open elevator doors and press the number six.

The elevator descends. Something's different in me. No longer do I feel constrained. Everything is clearer now, yet I still don't know who I am.

The electric blue cross sparks a whole new thought process. Each of the demons claws its talons into the light of the cross. They need the light to live. The light is hope. Demons feed on man's hope to survive.

The elevator stops, and the doors slide open. The stacks of gum still sit in front of my door. I take them into the living room.

Now, where to put the gun?

I sort through the kitchen drawers and come across an assortment of kitchen knives and silverware. In another drawer is an almost empty roll of duct tape.

The duct tape might come in handy if I need to secure the gun up and under something. I turn to the refrigerator and open the freezer door. Light pours over the kitchen floor and walls. This is as good a place as any for the pistol, I suppose. I place the weapon on top of the ice trays in the back right corner and crank the thermostat to its lowest setting.

I linger at the now-closed freezer. I can't believe my weapon of choice is a Revolutionary War pistol. It's hardly reliable.

Back inside my bedroom, I place the gum packaging on the bed.

I rifle through the photographs Michael gave me. There are twelve pictures, all completely useless. What could Michael possibly be trying to show me? I slide them back into my jacket chest pocket and undress.

I slide between the satin sheets and snuggle into a pillow. I take a piece of gum from the packet. Madi's beautiful form pops into my mind. I put the gum in my mouth and begin to chew. I sink deeper into the pillow, imagining the taste of Madi's lips on mine, and I take a few deep breaths. As I calm down, I drift toward unconsciousness just as the clock reaches 60:00.

Ahead is an old, narrow wooden bridge. Dim lanterns are laced around the whole outer structure. The snow is still blowing furiously. Silhouettes of trees fly by on either side of the car. The temperature in the car climbs. Every inch of my skin, from my head to my feet, perspires as if it were a sieve.

Madi sits in the passenger seat. Apparently, she has been there all along.

She puts her hand on mine where it rests on the steering wheel.

I drive over the bridge. I slow the car down as the bridge creaks, giving away its instability. A familiar sound from my childhood can be heard, coming from behind us. My pulse is racing as I look up at the rearview mirror. Nothing but darkness. I grip the wheel tighter and floor the gas pedal. The snow falls heavier as it's caught in the headlights and swirls across the windshield. Still nothing in the rearview.

An unknown vehicle suddenly comes out of the darkness, speeding closer to us. Looking in the rearview mirror again, I see bright red lights flashing from the vehicle.

In the distance, I hear an insistent, disruptive *beep, beep, beep.*

GABRIEL

MONDAY

*J*jolt straight up, my eyes wide. The alarm clock is still beeping. I turn it off and wipe sweat off my forehead. I hold my right hand in front of my face for a couple of seconds, turning it over and back. It's completely healed. Not even a scratch. My alarm clock is counting up. The Bible once again rests beside my watch. I toss it back in the drawer.

Stay in there this time.

I pick up the snow globe, lightly shake it, and stare at the gently falling flakes. My bare feet grip the smooth, cool hardwood as I make my way to the window. The whole city is covered in snow.

Yesterday it was autumn, wasn't it? I scratch my head while surveying the wintery landscape. I make my way to my bathroom. I smile at my reflection.

I pick up my straight razor and look back to the mirror.

Madi stands behind me, looking angry, holding the razor up to my neck. I startle, and my face turns white. She breaks into a smile and laughs. She puts the razor down and brushes shaving cream onto my face. She brings the razor back to my face, then hesitates and puts her hand down.

I laugh, reach down, and take her hand. With my hand on hers, I slowly guide the razor over my right cheek. On the next pass, I drop my hand and let her take over.

I relax into her sure touch. I love when she does this.

Madi takes the towel and wipes off the little leftover streaks of shaving cream.

Even though I feel myself smiling, my reflection smirks. I watch in horror as my reflection seizes the razor and slits Madi's throat.

I try to scream. I turn to help Madi, but she is gone. The mirror reflects only me now and is true to my movements.

The razor is still in my hand. I drop it into the sink and take a step back. That wasn't real. I haven't killed Madi. My hands shake with involuntary tremors. I must be going crazy.

The piano starts to play in the living room.

My watch shows three minutes, ten seconds.

The music provokes a battle of emotions within me. Pain and anger win the war.

I charge out of the bathroom and remove the hatchet from the glass case. Without hesitating, I stride to the piano, raise the hatchet above my head, and bring it down with all my strength.

The lid slams down onto the body of the piano. I hack away at the keys. Some of them fly into the air as the sound of the song mixes with the cacophony of splintering wood and ivory. Off-tune notes ring out with each impact. I slam the hatchet into the player mechanism, and the song stops. The sudden silence is followed by a slurping sound behind me.

I spin around. Gabriel, with his jaw-length, black hair parted down the middle and his dark sunglasses, sits at the table, holding a bowl up to his mouth. He's wearing the same black sports coat and light gray V-neck shirt. He continues slurping, seeming not to notice me.

A couple of seconds pass. He finally looks up, raises his eyebrows high above the rim of his glasses, and smiles. After setting his bowl down, he retrieves his already chewed gum from his napkin and pops it into his mouth. He looks at me, maintaining the smile while he smacks his gum. The cyan and black Jack of Spades still protrudes from his jacket pocket.

He wipes the napkin around his mouth and puts it back on the table.

He leans over and looks at twelve Polaroids spread across the table.

I slap my chest where I placed Michael's pictures in my jacket pocket last night, but my hand hits only cool skin. I'm still stark-naked!

"I see you've met Michael," Gabriel says as he spoons cereal into his mouth.

I cover my crotch and sidestep toward the bedroom while he rifles through the fridge. He lets out a loud giddy squeal and holds up a jar of pickles. "Eureka!"

Today is going to be one long day.

I slip through the bedroom door and rush to my bathroom.

Fully dressed, I rush through my shaving routine, nicking myself in the same spot as yesterday.

Gabriel walks into the bathroom, eating a single pickle, and stands in front of the mirror.

"Until I am measured, I am not known." He turns back and forth in front of the mirror. "Yet how you miss me, when I have flown. Today is the day we open your eyes, sunny Jim." He takes the Polaroid of the bathroom mirror from his stack, licks its back, and stamps it with his hand to the mirror. "Twelve pictures. Twelve flaws," he whispers to himself. He puts the remaining photos in his pocket. "Albert Einstein once said the only reason for time's existence is so everything doesn't happen at once. Some would also say time is only a mental construct that has no existence in real space outside of human perception. It just goes to show how far the human mind can evolve past a certain idea to a more realistic one."

I leave the bathroom and head for the front door. If I stay here much longer with this jerk, who knows what I'm liable to do to him? Too bad my gun doesn't have any ammo. My watch indicates 4:15.

I put my hand on the doorknob but can't seem to twist it.

Why? I want to leave but for some reason I can't. Why don't I have control over my body?

"Your body is still being controlled by the strings of the system. The body says stay while the mind says go. Michael got your mind back on straight. I'm here today to help get your mind and body reacting as one again. So whenever you choose to leave there will be no hesitation. But let's not get you to cut your strings quite yet."

Gabriel puts his used gum back in his mouth. He appears in front of me and looks closely at my face. He chews his gum like an addiction. I can hear his smacking noise getting louder the closer he gets.

"Your race isn't just a normal, everyday jog in the park kind of race." *Smack, smack, smack.* "There are rules you need to learn. Rules that can make or break you. It isn't all one foot over the other. Got it, cupcake?" His stomach growls, and he breaks his gaze for a moment to eye the kitchen, assumedly for cupcakes.

"Today is that opportune moment. Today, you will learn how this world is run and what it will take to win your trial. You may have chosen the scenery and this lovely wallpaper"—he scans the walls—"but a prison is still just a prison, no matter how much money you have in your closet." *Smack, smack, smack.*

He takes out the twelve remaining pictures Michael took yesterday and hands them to me. "Twelve pictures. Twelve flaws."

He'd stuck the first photo, the one of the bathroom mirror, to the mirror itself. Is there a flaw in the mirror?

Gabriel cackles and yells, "Five minutes!"

My watch beeps.

I shove the twelve photographs in my jacket pocket and force open the door. I step into the hallway and turn around. Gabriel is gone.

The door across the hall opens, and the waitress emerges. She's still alive? But how? She waves to me. Her hand has five whole fingers again.

I reach down and remove a pack of gum from one of the clear plastic stacks and offer her a stick. She accepts it, smiling. Her brow-length bangs frame her creamy skin and emerald eyes. Her cherry gloss accents her brilliant smile.

She saunters down the hall to the stairway door.

Who is she?

*A*s I'm about to cross the street, my car detonates. The surprise explosion sends me to the ground. I look back up at my now-burning vehicle with only one thought.

I'm going to kill Gabriel!

My watch beeps.

I suck in a breath and stagger to my feet. There's not another car in sight. Music plays to my left and gets louder by the second. But it isn't time to hear the music yet! Just when I think I'm finally figuring this place out...what's going on? The music gets clearer. Its melody isn't from a piano. It's a jingle that makes me think of childhood and summer days.

An ice cream truck, blaring the familiar jingle, careens around the corner and screeches to a halt in front of me. The passenger door opens, and Gabriel sits in the driver's seat with ice cream dripping from his mouth.

"Ten minutes past! Come on. Don't be angry. Ice cream?" He extends a popsicle that looks like a reaper. "I do have to warn you this one might give you a brain freeze." He giggles.

I take the popsicle and throw it in his face. There are no other options for transportation, so I get in and shut the passenger door. He puts the truck in drive and floors the gas pedal.

We lurch onto the interstate, the truck accelerating at an alarming speed. He eats one popsicle after another and throws the empty sticks out the window. After a long abnormal burp, he looks back at me.

"You see, time here is a dimension in which every move you make occurs in five-minute sequences. As you well know, a full day lasts only sixty minutes."

Gabriel sets the car to cruise control and goes back to the refrigerator. I grasp the wheel, holding us steady on the road. He comes back with ice cream sandwiches in his mouth and two popsicles in his hands. He gives me a popsicle that resembles my face. I give him my best you're-a-nut-job face.

"Now! During each five-minute interval, there is a pivotal place in which you must remain before you can proceed as you well know. I like to call these places time zones. The nasty coffee shop, your grungy office, the horrible-service restaurant, the old rickety subway train, your gloomy high-rise apartment, and this hell-driven highway full of cars that don't know how to drive!"

Gabriel honks at the car in front of us, and jerks the steering wheel to the left, crossing over multiple lanes. He yanks the wheel back right, colliding with the car that was in front of us, knocking it into another vehicle. We speed past them while Gabriel laughs as if he just gained an advantage. My side-view mirror reflects a huge car pile-up behind us. Fires ignite all across it, and smoke surges toward the sky.

Once Gabriel is calm again, he looks over to me. "Let's be friends!" He opens another popsicle. This one looks exactly like him. "Look at me! I'm eating myself!"

He takes a bite and cackles with his mouth full. Still chewing the mass of frozen sugar, he says, "You need to lighten up. It's not like you're dying today. You have at least a few days left before that happens."

I look at Gabriel incredulously.

Gabriel swerves past three cars, barely avoiding them, and accelerates dangerously, laughing maniacally. I brace myself, holding tightly to the door handle and dashboard. His dark sunglasses can't be helping.

"Pop open the glove box, if you please, and hand me my leftovers."

I open the glove box. There is a half-eaten, aged lollipop lying on top of its wrapper. I carefully touch the part of the stick that appears least stained and hand it to Gabriel. He promptly puts it in his mouth and savors it loudly.

He's still passing cars quickly and dangerously. Ahead in the right lane is a truck hauling glass windows. Gabriel pulls up alongside it and shoots several looks at my left pocket.

I retrieve the twelve pictures and rifle through them. I stop at a picture of the window glass the truck is carrying.

He nods.

Is there a reflection of something I'm supposed to see? Just like my bathroom mirror, there's nothing out of the ordinary in the glass, only a reflection of the ice cream truck.

"Look past the reflected image and see what really lies inside."

We zoom past cars left and right, and exit signs fly by. Everything is going too fast for me to be able to concentrate.

A steel black sedan with the license plate LBYRNTH pulls up alongside us. Gabriel breaks the rest of the lollipop off its stick and drops the stick onto the driver's side floor. Abruptly, he rams the yellow Maserati in front of us. The car spins out of control as Gabriel just laughs.

I clench my jaw and narrow my eyes at Gabriel. He has thrown his head back with laughter, baring his square jaw. I can't see his eyes behind the sunglasses, but I'm sure he's not watching the road. I grab the steering wheel and jerk it to the left to avoid hitting a hot pink Fiat.

The little car swerves right and is plowed down by the truck carrying the glass.

Gabriel snaps his head down, claps his hands on the wheel, and twists to see the truck's load of glass. He screams, "Is it broken?"

In my side-view mirror, the truck grows smaller, but I can still make out the unbroken windows. Gabriel pulls onto the shoulder and slams on the brakes. The car comes to a halt.

Gabriel turns to me. In a serious, dark tone, he says, "If that glass would have broken, then all that we have worked for would have been erased. Do you not understand that?"

What is he talking about?

"Did Michael not go over the two reasons why a reaper would show up?"

Let's see. Michael and I were in the hallway when we had that talk.

He said that if I leave before or far after the time I need to leave, only then will the reapers make an appearance. I don't remember him giving me a second reason.

"Well, that explains your cocky attitude toward all of this! During your trial, you can't just run into each time zone on the exact time and win. If that was the case, then you would have already won many times over!" Gabriel stomps back into the refrigerated compartment.

I stay seated and stare out the window at the passing cars. The window truck has already recovered and moves on ahead.

He comes back with two fudge bars and three blue turbo-rockets. "Had to cool myself down." He chomps half of a fudge bar and talks around the chewy morsel. "What you just did would have rang the brunch bell for the reapers to come gnaw our heads off. Now when you break more than one of those flaws the reapers will come for you. You get one mulligan. Break two and they won't stop. No going back after two. Do you understand me?"

Mulligan? So that's what Michael was referring to yesterday.

He puts the truck in drive and stomps the gas pedal, juggling the wheel and the ice cream treats in his hands.

"Let me tell you something! They don't want just you! They want anything that disturbs the balance in this place, including me! It doesn't matter if I am a lost soul. They are the timekeepers, the enforcers, the mind-erasers, the voice-takers, the alpha and the omega. Don't mess with the flaws! At least not yet."

He plucks a popsicle from the back of his seat. "Now…would you like a Madi pop?" The popsicle has Madi's face on it.

I slap it out of his hand, and it splats against the inner windshield as we make our way off the interstate and to the parking lot of the small coffee shop.

My watch beeps.

Gabriel yells, "Twenty minutes!"

abriel chomps on what looks like a biscotti. "Doesn't that beeping drive you mad? I remember the last version of you before your reaping. You knew this place like the back of your hand. Didn't even need your watch anymore. You used the flaws to guide you when you needed to go. Very soon again, you won't need that watch."

Gabriel eyes the coffee shop window, making me remember that Michael had taken a picture of it yesterday. I sift through the photographs.

Here it is, the photo of the coffee shop window.

Gabriel snatches the picture out of my hands and licks its back, then slaps it onto the coffee shop window.

So this is the third flaw, always a reflection, it seems.

"If you can't see the flaw, then breaking it would be pointless." He takes another bite of the biscotti.

Beyond Gabriel, a pure white blanket of snow covers the entire park.

He takes me by the hand and runs toward the Ferris wheel. Snow crunches under our feet. No one is manning the ride, and we traipse right on through the opening gate.

"This looks like fun!" He throws me in a passenger car and sits next to me. Our feet are soon off the ground as Gabriel chomps on another bite of his biscotti. We ascend to the top, and I can see my apartment building.

"Eternity is endless, but time is measured by a beginning and an end. No amount of time can atone for one's sins. But accepting them and moving on is another story. Once you begin to understand there is a way out, there will be."

As the ride descends, Gabriel points down to the dead tree in the center of the park.

"You know how I know that this time is going to be different? Because each time so far, it has taken you until the fifth day to walk through that door. Never have you done what you did yesterday, never. What you saw in there may not make sense to you now, but it will soon enough."

The ride ends, and we get off. We continue walking through this dazzling wonderland and stop near the nude statue. The glass box in its outstretched hand has several inches of snow topping it, like icing on a cupcake. I glance at Gabriel, and his stomach rumbles.

This glass box was in one of Michael's pictures. I take the remaining nine pictures from my pocket and sort through them.

I find it, but my attention is then swayed to the picture behind it. A picture of the tree.

The recess in the dead tree feels like it's calling me. I need to go back in.

"Well?" Gabriel motions to the statue.

I hand him the picture of the glass box. He licks the back and slaps the picture on the box.

My eyes return to the tree. Gabriel waves his hand in front of my face, but all I can think about is my sin hiding inside of that tree. How is the gun that Michael gave me going to kill my sin? Sin is a mental act of a conscious mind, not physical in form. A bullet can't stop a thought.

"Your sin is in the form of a demon," Gabriel says while finishing the last of the biscotti.

A demon? Demons aren't real.

"How did I know you were going to say that? You might want to jot down some notes on this. Things are about to get a bit wordy."

Gabriel takes a breath and begins, "The soul and the spirit are the two primary immaterial parts of your humanity. It can be confusing to attempt to discern the precise differences between the two. The soul and the spirit are connected, but separable. The word soul can refer to both the immaterial and material aspects of humanity. You still with me...? That's the spirit! Speaking of spirit. The word spirit refers only to the immaterial facet of humanity. God is a spirit. The devil is a spirit. You are spirits. Hell, demons are spirits! Beyond the essential meaning, the Bible speaks of the soul in many contexts. One of these is in relation to humanity's eagerness to sin. Human beings have a sinful nature, and our souls are tainted with sin and who feeds us these sins?"

Does he expect me to answer?

"You guessed it! Demons! So demons and sins are one and the same? How interesting, wouldn't you agree?"

I can assume now that he is having a running joke with me, knowing I can't speak. I would be pissed if I wasn't wanting to understand more.

"You see, demons are considered to be a cancer. It only takes one act of sin before it can spread throughout your central nervous system and it won't stop until they get what they desire. So what do demons desire?"

I slap Gabriel in the face to make him continue further.

"Rude! Just making sure your understanding everything correctly. I've rehearsed this speech with you a lot more times than I can count. I'm not going over this again. May I continue further?"

I raise my hand to him again and he proceeds, "Onward then! Now remember, since demon spirits take up no room, have no mass, there can actually be several demons inside a single human being. Demons are energy just like you and I. Thank God you only have to deal with one."

What does it want from me?

"It only thrives to want one thing... the original soul's physical form. Your human vessel."

Gabriel takes the tree picture from my stack and walks away from me.

So if my sin is a demon that means...

Gabriel nods, "Means you will be forced to challenge with it to win back your freedom. And the only way it can escape and go back up to the soul's physical reality is if it either wins in the souls final challenge or if the soul gives up. Once a demon wins, the soul's Purgatorium collapses, leaving the soul to become a lost soul. A soul that is completely detached from its vessel and stuck inside the comaverse. Like me!"

So what you're initially saying is that my last trial comes down to either me or my demon taking my life back? But if I'm still here that means I haven't challenged my demon yet.

I follow Gabriel to where he has stopped in front of the tree. His voice drones on as I stare at the dark, angelic war carved into the door of the tree. The tiny square mirror at its core draws me closer to it.

"The closest you ever came to actually challenging your demon was the last version of you. You just had one flaw left to break before facing it. Sucks."

Gabriel licks the photograph and covers the mirror with it.

How would I even beat my demon?

"A duel to the death! Both challengers will have a pistol of their choosing with one bullet loaded in each. If the person with the loaded weapon misses, you both will have to hurry and quickly reload your weapon. You both will share one case holding five bullets inside. Five bullets, five attempts."

That explains Michael giving me a pistol last night. Though I don't even know how to fire an old revolutionary war pistol. I panic at the thought.

I step around Gabriel and approach the shadowed recess. The answers to what sin binds me here is in there. It will also help me understand more about my past, especially about Madi and me.

"If you go now, you won't see her again," says Gabriel. "You got lucky last time, but you can't handle the truth about your past just yet. We must stick to the recipe and continue cooking."

I reach for the handle.

"Your demon is waiting for you in there. He is fast, strong, and can hear your thoughts like we can! If you let your thoughts slip and reveal that your last day of living is just a few days from now, do you really think he is going to go easy on you? You don't want to tick him off this early in the game, do you?"

I can take it.

"And he can take your meat suit if you're not careful."

What is he going on about now?

"Like I tried to tell you before. A demon has the ability to go back up instead of you. It waits till you complete your trial and targets the exit door. That is why it is important for you to wait till you're mentally prepared."

But I thought you said I had a choice?

"In the end, you do. You can choose to let your demon take your second chance or you can fight it and take back your life for yourself."

That's what happened to you? You let it win?

Gabriel looks over to me as serious as I ever seen him.

"I didn't let it beat me. I was just too weak to face it. A demon in this place is the embodiment of a person's own sin. It knows how to pull the right strings and I wasn't ready."

He turns away and starts walking to my office building. "Live or die. It's up to you."

My watch beeps.

Gabriel yells, "Twenty-five minutes!"

I drop my hand, not wanting to risk it.

I run up next to him as he proceeds, a smirk on his face.

I want to know more.

"Now demons don't have the ability to manifest into human form. And because of that, they desire to experience a physical reality. I know what you're thinking, demons no more exist than the tooth fairy. You're a man that has to see it to believe it. I get it. But what if I told you that you've already seen one before and didn't even know it. That's right! I'm talking about human possession!"

Like 'The Exorcist?'

"Those are just fictional stories. Have you never heard the stories of surviving coma victims? A seven-year-old boy, Tommy Wauls, lived in Georgia, got hit by a car and fell into a coma. A little while later, he woke up. It's a miracle! Hallelujah! But. He was different. Started smoking a pack of cigarettes a day. Sloth got a hold of that one. A month later, he left his home. Parents haven't heard from him since. Bye-bye, Tommy. An eighty-four-year-old granddad falls in a manhole, boom, coma for a month. Wakes up as a sex addict and has a heart attack at a strip club. Poor girl didn't notice he was gone till the song stopped. Rigor mortis, am I right? How lust gets the best of us."

I push his hand away and walk around him. He's got to be making this stuff up.

Gabriel catches back up to me. "Oh! How about this one? A twenty-year-old girl, Michelle Prier, Minnesota. She comes out of her coma, knocks three nurses out, breaks her doctor's arm, sets the hospital on fire, and walks across the street to a pub. Ruthless, that's probably the girl's Wrath."

To the left of the statue stands a little girl. I do a double take. Where did she come from? She looks to be the same girl I saw on the subway, skinny, wispy bangs. Her big, emerald eyes are full of tears as she looks at me. Gabriel follows my gaze. He bends over and comes up with a large, packed snowball. Taking a step forward, he lobs the snowball at the little girl. It smacks her right in the back of the head.

I turn to Gabriel, a look of displeasure on my face.

"What? She's not really a little girl. Not anymore. She's a lost soul. Remember when I was explaining the difference between lost souls and soul survivors?"

I turn back to the statue, but the little girl is gone.

"Well I forgot to mention that there are other kinds of lost souls. They aren't all willing to help like we are. Some wander around other souls' prisons either to pass the time, waiting for their own death or to keep souls, like you, from ever going back home. The waitress and that little girl have dirty souls. Seen them in a few of our earlier jobs. Their mission till the day their human body dies in the outside world is too stop soul survivors from achieving their trial. They believe that their mistake in life is everyone's mistake. One of our soul purposes here is to stop dirty souls like that from trying anything foolish."

Well, that explains Michael's torment of the waitress yesterday. But what happens when the body dies? What happens to the lost soul then?

"Where else? Their soul gets sent to the place where the flames never burn out. The lake of fire. Where you will soon be heading if you don't finish this race."

Out of everything Gabriel just explained to me, that little-known fact has stuck in me the deepest. Enough to put a little pep in my step.

I quicken my pace, but not too fast, as I make my way to the office. I get the glass elevator and ride it up.

My watch beeps.

The elevator stops, and the doors slide open. "Thirty minutes!" Gabriel yells in my ear.

I push his face away and step into my office. The grandfather clock ticks loudly. My stomach feels a bit off.

Tick-tock, tick-tock, tick-tock.

Gabriel motions toward my pocket, and I pull out the rest of the pictures I have left. He chooses the photo of the wall of windows opposite my desk. He grabs a roll of duct tape from one of my desk drawers and walks to the windows. In the middle of the transparent wall, he slaps the photo up with one hand and wriggles around, using his knees and free hand to rip uneven lengths of duct tape from the roll. The haphazard frame holds the Polaroid as if it were suspended amongst the gray clouds.

Tick-tock, tick-tock, tick-tock.

Gabriel positions himself in front of the grandfather clock and stares into its ornate face. He lifts the grandfather clock like he would lift a pillow and flings it against the wall. It smashes to bits and lands in a heap on the floor. "That was getting annoying."

I wander to the wall of windows. Beyond the taped-up photo, dense wintery clouds have blocked out any evidence of the sun.

Gabriel crosses the room to the record player and leafs through the stack of records. He selects one, takes the vinyl from the sleeve, and places it on the platter.

Gabriel reaches behind his neck and retrieves his already chewed gum. I watch with disgusted fascination as he pops it in his mouth—who would have guessed lost souls would be so...human.

What was your sin?

Gabriel stops moving. With his back now facing me he says quietly, "Gluttony."

I find that not shocking in the least.

He turns around and says, "I was a fat kid growing up! Ok?! The only time I moved my feet was when the ice cream man showed up down the street. My shrink later suggested that my eating was a way to stuff down uncomfortable emotions due to my family." He turns back to the record player and in a darker tone says, "No family is perfect."

After a long silence, he changes back to his uplifting tone and turns around.

"Today, class, we will begin music therapy. It's based on the principle that to maintain our coherence as beings in the world, we must creatively improvise our identity. Creative activity, music for example, allows us to retain coherent organization, which links our soul, body, and mind. Just like what you have been hearing on the subway, for example," he says as he places the stylus on the record. The room moves as if I'm standing on the deck of a boat. I stumble to the couch and sink into its plush cushions. My eyelids feel very heavy, and it's difficult to stay upright. The muscles throughout my body relax like a cascade of dominos, and I find myself lying down.

Gabriel slowly begins to blow up a gum balloon from his mouth. He then puts his feet up on the desk, exposing his bright orange socks for the world to see.

It still seems to me like an odd fashion choice to make but the color does suit his odd behavior. Besides if I ever lose him, I will be able to spot those socks from a mile away.

I find humor in it as I display a smile.

It doesn't take long for Gabriel to realize what I'm smiling about. He takes his feet off the desk and pops his gum balloon.

"Now, before you enter that tree, you need to learn more things about yourself. The more you know, the more you can understand why you did what you did." The sound of static comes through the speakers. "Sebastian Coe once said, 'The mile is just the right length: beginning, middle, end, a story unfolding. Find that mile, your mile—the mile that leads to your story.' Music is the guide to your soul. Feel it out. Let it in. Remember what made this mean something to you. What life change did you come across when you first heard it?"

Half-delirious, I close my eyes and imagine running toward a light.

"That's it," says Gabriel.

A stupor comes over me, half-awake, half-asleep, a trance induced by the music. The music and I become indistinguishable.

FIFTEEN

A small cloud of vapor rises inches from my eyes. There's a window in front of me, reflecting my over weight six-year-old self wearing a thick coat and a pair of headphones. The same music from my office is playing in my ears. Giant flakes of snow fall all around me like miniature doilies in the twilight. I flutter my eyelids to clear the icy powder accumulating on my lashes.

Behind me is a driveway with an old beat-up station wagon. Beyond that is a forest of leafless trees with a few conifers here and there. To the right, the front porch light shines over the door. Control of my body and mind are slipping away. Memories of my soul-prison are fading fast. My six-year-old mind takes over. I blink. What was I just thinking?

I look over to see my mom getting out of an unfamiliar car. A man approaches her from the driver's side. He lights her cigarette for her. After a few seconds of talking, I see them kiss one another. She stops when she notices me watching. The man runs back into the car and drives off. She puts out her cigarette and tries to pretend like nothing has happened. She walks inside as I stand there, not really knowing what I just saw. The pain in my knee becomes too great for me to stand. I make my way inside.

I step to the right and quietly open the storm door. Just as I'm about to step inside, a scraping sound above and to my left stops me. I take a step back and lean around the corner of the house, toward the garage. Father is standing catlike on the downward slope of the roof, leaning over a telescope. His gray beard is caked with snow. I smile. Father looks like Santa Claus!

As if the heavens are at his command, the snow stops, and a clear, cold black replaces the overcast wash that blanketed the sky most of the walk home. I step a few feet closer, and the snow crunches under my boots. Father's posture goes rigid, and he stops moving. Without looking at me, he scowls.

"You're late. Dinner's in the fridge."

I pull my pants leg up, exposing my swollen, bloody ankle. He'll understand when he sees it.

"Get inside, son!" he barks. "You're going to catch cold, and neither of us can afford to stay home with a sick kid."

I can smell the alcohol on his breath from here. I notice the empty beer cans laid out beside him and know this isn't the time to get him upset.

I turn and limp toward the door, my pants leg still hiked up, tears gathering in my eyes.

He glances my way.

The tears overflow, streaking down my cheeks.

Father shakes his head and turns back to the telescope. As I near the door, everything becomes a blur. There's a distant sound of static, then a loud beeping.

A light flashes and momentarily blinds me.

I blink several times. I'm back in my office, alone. Through the windowed wall, the day has turned into night. The record is skipping. My breath escapes as thick steam. I look at my watch, almost waiting for Gabriel to peek around me at any moment and scream out, *Thirty-five minutes!*

But no sign of Gabriel can be found. I take out the photos, remembering a picture Michael had shown me before. I flip through them, only to find one taken of another window. I shoot up.

A shrieking echoes far away, slowly getting louder. I grab my coat, searching the windows for some sign of the clue while I shove my arms through the sleeves. There's nothing but my own transparent reflection. I drop the picture to the floor and spin toward the elevator. I hit the button several times before the doors slide open.

By the time I reach the ground floor, I'm shivering. I sprint through the front doors and down the street toward the Lighthouse

Restaurant.

I pull the door open just as snow begins to fall and slam it closed behind me.

That was a close one.

I walk into the dining area and notice Gabriel sitting at my table, the waitress by his side.

"So? What did you learn?" Gabriel smiles widely.

Does he ever take those sunglasses off?

The waitress sets a plate of apple pie in front of Gabriel. He puts a hand over his stomach and looks pained as he stares at a stack of dirty plates on the table in front of him. I sit down and register what I just remembered. I revisit the recollection of my parents.

Was my mom actually cheating on my father? I wish I had more answers than questions, but that never seems to be the case.

Gabriel takes a bite of pie, spits it out, and yells at the waitress. "Yuck! Are you serious with this pie right now? What's in this, anyway? I dare you to say 'apple'! I dare you!"

Her eyes go wide, and she works her hands over. "It *is* apple."

"Well, now I can start to understand how you got into a coma. Your husband must have thought it was the only way to make you stop your horrible cooking. The picture is clear, darling. I am going to need a lot of whipped cream to dilute the horrific taste in my mouth. Bring me a big tub full."

She stands with her mouth pursed, looking back and forth from Gabriel to the kitchen as if she's not sure if he's serious.

"Do the words that I am saying to you sound anything like a joke? I need something to drown out the flavor of your homemade dog-crap pie. Thank you, succubus!"

He kicks her in the butt, and she stumbles toward the kitchen.

Even if she is a dirty lost soul, she doesn't deserve this.

Gabriel whips his head around to face me.

"Continue. You were thinking about your whore of a mother and your alcoholic father? Correct?"

What did he just say?

The waitress comes back through the kitchen door, carrying a plate covered with a silver dome in her right hand and a silver bowl of whipped cream in her left. She puts the covered plate down in front of us. I gaze at my slightly droopy eyes and soft jaw reflected in its surface.

I take the last six pictures out of my pocket. Here's the one Michael took of the silver dome on the table.

Gabriel looks at the picture with recognition in his eyes. He glances up at me with his eyebrows raised. I still don't see anything out of the ordinary in the photograph. He sighs deeply before whisking the picture away and sticking it to the dome.

I raise my head a few inches and straighten my shoulders. There's nothing there to see. He's crazy.

The waitress removes the dome with a trembling hand, dips a serving spoon into the whipped cream, and turns to Gabriel. "How much do you want, sir?"

"Till I can't taste a single crumb, please." She puts five heaping spoonfuls on top of his pie. He plunges his fork into the pie, lifts a piece covered in two inches of white cream, and chews it with a wide, open smile.

"More, please." he says, with his mouth still full. The waitress looks down at the plate, then back up at Gabriel. She slaps another heaping spoonful on top of the creamy mass.

"More, please." She adds two more spoonfuls. There is no longer any trace of the pie underneath the whipped mountain.

"This is another lesson for you. Putting too much on your plate is a no-no. You need to separate your past from the now. Only learn from your past; don't let it consume your thoughts." Gabriel nods toward the silver dome. "Focus and clear it."

I stare at the silver dome and try to focus, but still see nothing.

He turns back to the waitress and yells, "More!"

The waitress takes the bowl, tips it on its side, and scoops the rest of the cream onto his plate. Some of it spills onto Gabriel's lap, and some of it runs off the plate and onto the floor.

Gabriel doesn't seem to mind his lap full of confection. He reaches inside his jacket, takes out a gum wrapper, and unfolds it.

The wrapper is empty, and he looks panicked. He pats down his jacket and his pants pockets. He stands up and inspects his chair and the floor. He sighs loudly and looks up at the waitress.

He says calmly, "Well now, look what you did. You made a mess."

Gabriel darts behind the waitress, grabs her by the neck, and forces her face into the pie. Her screams are muffled in the thick pile of cream. She kicks and flails her arms for what seems to be an eternity.

I blanch, glued to my seat. I continue to concentrate on the silver dome as everything around me fades. I now see an hourglass in the silver dome. My eyes grow wide. "You see the flaw! Well done." The waitress's flailing weakens, and she slumps. Gabriel feels her neck, and then looks up at me.

"She'll be back again tomorrow. I kill her two or three times a week. It's a hobby. Like decoupage. Everyone needs a hobby."

I look at her dead body and back at Gabriel, not understanding him.

He lets go of her head, and her body slides to the floor in a heap.

The waitress's dead body lies motionless on the floor. Gabriel uses his index finger to scoop some cream off her face. He pops it in his mouth, swallows, and makes a disgusted expression.

"Hmm. That actually doesn't taste that bad."

He throws down the napkin and walks toward the exit. He yells, "Forty minutes!" and then steps out the door.

My watch beeps.

My reflection in the dome stops me. What kind of man am I, that I could just sit there and watch him do that to a woman? Something isn't right. My reflection smirks, acting on its own. I jerk my head away from the dome and stare at the table. In my periphery, the waitress's body remains in a heap. Her wavy, dark hair has been ripped from its pins and is coated in white cream. I leap to my feet and sweep my arms across the table, sending the glasses, plates, and cutlery crashing onto the floor. My breathing is heavy, and clouds of vapor pour from my lungs. I've got to get to the subway.

I charge out the door and toward the subway, almost falling into the open manhole in the middle of the street.

I race down the stairs and jump over the gate. Ahead, the subway car is stopped with its doors open. I slide through the doorway just as I start to shiver.

Instantly, my breath returns to normal, and the temperature is comfortable once more. I make my way to a booth.

The window across from me is the one Michael photographed. I look at the remaining three photos and find the one of the subway car window. Between the photo and the window in front of me, I see the hourglass.

The piano music begins to play. Another new melody.

My watch hands point to 42:02.

The sounds of the subway fade away. Everything breaks into puzzle pieces that fall away, leaving nothing but black.

SEVENTEEN

y eyes adjust to the dimly lit restaurant. A small fire burns in the fireplace to the left of the back windows, where patrons stand with drinks, talking and looking out over the expansive bay. To the right of the front windows is a black grand piano. It reminds me of the player piano in my apartment. I fight to hold onto the world I just left, determined not to allow this one to control me. A man dressed in a tailcoat jacket is seated at the piano bench. He stretches his hands out, adjusts his position on the bench, and begins to play. It's the same music I heard on the subway.

The walls are crimson, accented with elegant gold patterns. High-backed booths, also a deep red, line the edges of the room. The Lighthouse Restaurant. This is the restaurant of my soul-prison. Madi sits across from me. Her silky, white dress fits like a glove, enhancing her feminine curves. She stands out like a pearl in a red-mouthed clam. We're seated at a table in the middle of the room, exquisitely set with crystal and fine porcelain.

She looks especially stunning tonight. I'm guessing she's in her early twenties, which means I am, too. I try to tell her how beautiful she is, but I find once again that I can't move my mouth. The memories of the soul-world are fading. I'm losing myself to the piano music and can't seem to stop it.

My mind shifts into auto pilot. "Happy one-year anniversary, pretty girl!" I raise my glass to hers. The glasses, half-full with red wine, make a clinking sound. Both of us take a sip.

Madi looks to the piano, recognizing the song. Her smile grows. She sings quietly, almost whispering, along with the music.

I smile. "You really should pursue singing."

Madi frowns.

"I know I tell you that all the time, but I'm serious. Your piano skill level is off the charts! Your singing combined with that will make you a super star! You know you have a terrific voice. Don't hide it."

She dons a Russian accent. "When I am ready, dear, I will be ready. You know this." She smiles and takes another sip of wine.

"You know I'm not just telling you that to be nice."

She returns to her normal voice. "I don't know. Maybe you are." She gives me a coy look, but shifts uncomfortably in her seat.

She never could take a compliment about her voice. "Hiding away talent like yours is like slapping God in the face."

"Is that so?" she says, a hint of sarcasm in her voice.

I nod.

"Well, I'm going to slap you in the face if you don't pick out what you want to eat."

She draws out a laugh and looks at the menu. The brilliance of her diamond necklace is almost blinding in the low lights of the chandelier. I could've bought her a knockoff to commemorate the anniversary, but beauty like hers should only be adorned by the genuine artifact. I hope to God she never finds out I stole it.

I finger the tag that's fallen into my palm from my jacket sleeve and turn it over in my hand. $1,599.99. I tuck it back up and out of sight. How many other girls would role-play with me as a couple of fat cats for entertainment? Tomorrow, we'll drive to the next city and return our apparel, get our money back. But tonight...tonight, money is no object.

A quiet voice whispers into my mind. *She doesn't care if she could help financially. She wants you to drown in your debts.*

"Fine. Let's not be rich then," I say. "Keep your talent hidden, and we can keep pretending, just for kicks."

"You know my priorities." She looks up at me over her menu. "Let's not talk about this now, okay?"

"Right, I do. Because living in a cramped loft on the east side of town is an ideal, safe environment. A car that only stalls out half of the time is reliable enough. And, oh, yeah, Dollar Tree is the best place to pick up the finest steaks."

"Oh, please, keep going." Madi scoffs.

"Oh, I can keep going, all right."

"How about this?" Her voice is a little cold. "I will promise to do something about my tragically withheld pianist career just as soon you finish the bestseller you've been working on for...how many years is it?"

I roll my eyes while sloshing my wine around in my glass. Like I haven't heard that one before.

"Well?" She looks at me as if she's just called checkmate.

"I happen to have gotten some really good stuff down on paper lately."

"Is that so?" She arches her eyebrow.

"Yes, and once my book finally gets published, you're going to wish you never made that promise."

"We'll see," she says softly.

"We will! You and I will be bathing in money!" I bury myself in my menu, hoping she'll close the door on the subject.

"Money can't buy you love." She lingers on the last word, in that maddening way she always does when she wants to make a point.

I lower my menu and sigh. "Let's not start this again. Look, you know how strongly I care about you. Can we drop this?"

Madi crosses her arms and leans back. "You're going to end up exactly like your father, aren't you?"

I reach into my jacket pocket, pull out a cigarette pack, flip open the lid, and remove a smoke. While feeling around for my lighter, I mutter, "I am not at all like my father." I must've left my lighter in the fitting room. Well, it's history now. There's no way I'm showing my face back there after lifting Madi's necklace this afternoon.

A waiter pushes through the kitchen door and swaggers toward us. He's a black man, looks to be in his late forties. His close-cut hair, well-kept goatee, and bulging muscles boast of a man who takes care of himself.

He stops at our table, looks at the cigarette in my mouth, looks at Madi, and says with a polite tone, "Are you ready to order?"

The man's sculpted muscles put my flab to shame. He could probably break me in half. There's no way he could know Madi's necklace is hot, could he? Before he or Madi can say anything more, I blurt out, "Do you happen to have any matchbooks…maybe at the bar?"

The waiter looks from me to Madi and back. "I am quite sorry, sir. But we do not allow smoking anywhere in the restaurant."

I drop the cigarette on the table beside my empty plate and raise my voice a couple of notches. "Who said anything about smoking? Can't a guy just want a matchbook to remember the great service he had on this fine night?"

The waiter shifts his weight back, appearing stunned. "Pardon me, sir?" He offers what looks like a forced smile.

"What is your problem?" Madi asks, shooting an embarrassed look at me. She looks up to the waiter. "Everything is fine here. We'll have the veal medallions in raspberry truffle sauce. That comes with the sea scallops and puréed artichoke hearts, is that right?"

"Yes, ma'am, that's right."

"Give us a double order, thanks."

"Very well." He stiffly gathers our menus and starts back to the kitchen.

"I think I have a matchbook in my purse," she says quietly to me, still red-faced. She searches her purse, and after a few moments, slides a matchbook across the table to me. It is elegant— silver filigree against a gold backdrop. "I grabbed it when I was in the ladies' powder room." She takes on an annoyed tone. "So I could remember this wonderful moment we are sharing." Her voice becomes genuine again. "I was serious, though. What's wrong?"

"What do you mean?" I clutch the matchbook.

"You've been getting so stressed out lately."

"So?"

"So? I don't know what to do."

"Who said you have to do anything, Madi? I gave you a nice necklace. What else do you want?"

"Only you would think that buying me something expensive would keep me happy. I'm trying to get you to open up." She reaches behind her neck, unclasps the necklace, and places it in front of me beside the matchbook.

"When are you finally going to open up to me and tell me what's going on?" She leans in and places a hand over mine.

I breathe out heavily and slowly. Shifting in my seat, I try to keep my stress level under control.

"I mean, we've been together for a year, and you still haven't told me a thing about your past, except that you don't like your dad."

I sneer. "Look who's talking! What about you? You clam up all the time. Like when we're on the highway and drive past rest-stop signs. You freak out. And then, when I ask you what's wrong, you go completely quiet."

"Don't drag me into this."

"Why not? You're more than willing to interrogate me!" I drop the matchbook, slide my hand out from under hers, and grip the table edge with both hands.

The waiter approaches, carrying two silver dome-covered plates. "Pardon me. Your meal is ready." He places the covered plates in front of us. As he pulls back the silver lids, the image of dark, wavy hair immersed in a cloud of cream flashes in my mind. I stand, knocking my chair over.

"Is there a problem, sir?"

I remember. My current thoughts override the memory as I rally my strength and will power.

"Where are you going?" Madi asks, half-rising from her chair.

I step back and spin away. The sound of cascading sand grows louder and louder. *Don't even think about changing anything while you're inside there, or it will come for you.* I gasp. Michael's warning stops me in my tracks.

"Talk to me!" Madi is at my elbow now, purse in hand.

I step back to the table, grab the wine bottle, and chug two mouthfuls. The heat in the cool liquid calms me slightly. I put the bottle down, loosen my collar, and pull out the golden coin pendant I'm wearing. The memory drowns my independent thoughts, and I let the reins go.

"We'll be right back," I tell the waiter. I pocket the matchbook and pick up the cigarette. With Madi's arm in mine, I lead her up a set of stairs to an outside balcony. My hands tremble as I light my cigarette. A set of black, metallic stairs leads from the balcony up the side of the circular building. I nod toward them, and Madi gives a small smile in consent. We ascend the wrap-around staircase. The breeze ruffles Madi's silky white hem and sweeps her soft bangs out of her face. I take a long drag of my smoke. The nicotine calms my mind.

Above us, the glow of white light flashes intermittently. It really is a lighthouse. After reaching the top, I tug Madi to the railing.

The full moon shines bright over the bay, releasing a certain calm inside of me. I take another drag and pull her hips close into mine. I nuzzle her ear and then use my nose to turn our faces toward the shoreline. She tightens her grip on my forearms, and the water glitters with reflected moonlight.

"Are you okay?" Madi asks softly.

I lean away a few inches and lift my pendant between us. "I don't remember much of my father before my mom left." The golden celtic hourglass glimmers, the wings in the background full of shadowed contrasts. "He was the ultimate man's man, always fixing stuff around the house. He never asked anyone for help. My old man wanted to do everything by himself." I drop the pendant and remove myself from Madi's arms. Taking another drag from my cigarette, I turn toward the water and rest my elbows on the rail.

"My father never once said, 'I love you.'" I blow a cloud of smoke into the clear night air. "Not to me, at least. As a child, my mom would tell me it was because of his bipolar condition. That the medicine he took wiped away his emotions. I knew better though. He was nothing like my mom. She told me she loved me at least fifty times a day. Sometimes I thought she was trying to make up for the affection missing from him." I clear my throat. "I guess that's why they never really suited each other. I remember my mother's kindness and love. She loved to dance." I smile. Air currents from the water hint of salt and fish. "She taught me everything from the waltz to the mashed potato. She loved singing. She sang me to sleep almost every night. She had an old record player and tons of albums. Her favorite, though, her absolute favorite, was 'Running on Empty' by Jackson Browne. I still remember her singing it to me as clearly as if it were last night. Best song ever. Especially when my mom sang it to me. It was probably the main reason I started running."

In the corner of my eye, Madi nods and looks at me. She is probably hoping I'll give her a kind look in return. The waves crash gently on the rocks below.

"I love that song," she says, almost whispering.

"When times got hard, though, my father sold all her records, even her favorites." I take another drag from my cigarette. "My mother also loved taking pictures. She had one of those old Polaroid cameras. Growing up, that thing was like her third arm. She always took pictures, pictures of everything. I have a box full of those old pictures. But there's not a single photo of her in there. She was behind the lens, never in front of it."

I pause a moment, remembering the images, ordering them into a coherent chronology. "My father kept his feelings to himself, which drove her crazy. Then she cheated on him, and not long after, she told him about it. He was furious that night. I could hear everything through my bedroom door. It got so bad, she came into my room and hugged me goodbye. Little did I know, that was going to be the last time I ever saw her. She didn't even come back to get her things."

"I'm sorry," Madi responds quietly, still watching my face.

"After she left, he shut down. He rarely came home. Always working or drinking. Never went to any of my races. When I turned eighteen, I left. I couldn't stand the sight of him any longer. He became a drunk who took his problems out on me one too many nights. The only time I hear from him is when I get a card on my birthday. Always says something simple, and till this day he never ends it with I love you." I steel myself, fighting back my anger.

The cigarette in my hand has burnt down to nothing. I pull the pack and the matchbook from my pocket and put another in my mouth.

"I found out she got into an accident a few years later. Put her in a coma. Been that way ever since. There are days I want to go and see her but I just can't."

Madi wraps her fingers around my hand and steadies my shaking. She slides them across my palm and takes the matchbook, strikes a match across the sulfur, and holds it to the cigarette. Her eyes are wet.

"She's been in that coma for two years now. Two years. If it were up to me, I would have pulled that plug a long time ago. End her suffering."

"If you want, we can go visit her? You won't have to do it alone."

I take a couple puffs and say, "I don't want to see her like that. Her laying in a bed so helpless. I just can't see her be so weak. I like to remember this one time at the beach with my family. My mom was wearing a green and pale blue sundress, taking pictures of me and my father as we dug moats and made sand castles. Everything was tactical for him. He measured every angle, made sure everything was just right."

I exhale deeply. As hard as it is, I was going to have to tell her about all this sooner or later. "That was just like my father, though. No room for error. Mom first taught me how to dance, right there in that sand. She was always a great dancer. Could have made something of herself, I guess, maybe gone professional." I give Madi a look that I hope says, *Like you.* "I wish those days could have gone on forever."

Madi locks her eyes on the black horizon and remains silent.

"I bet you had a lot of great family moments," I say.

Madi covers her face with her hand and weeps quietly.

"What's wrong?" I pull her into my arms and gently kiss her forehead.

"I have been so afraid to tell you this," she says between sobs. "I always thought you would think less of me or something when you found out."

"I would never think badly of you, Madi, not ever. Why are you crying?" I lift her face, but she avoids eye contact, so I kiss her nose instead. "Something about your mom?"

"No, my mom was…"

"You can tell me." I slide my hands down her arms and squeeze her fingers.

"When my dad died, my mom was scared and alone. But she was a mother, and she believed in that ideal. She took care of me as well as she knew how, but when I turned six, there was this guy my mom started dating. There had been others before, but this guy… his name was Jacob."

My heart seems to drop to my feet. Anger beats against my calm facade like a caged beast, threatening to unleash its destruction at Madi's next revelation. "What about Jacob, Madi?"

"My mother only knew Jacob for about two months before she married him." Madi laughs despairingly. "He seemed like a fun guy. He even took our last name, Jacob Persail. It seemed like a kind gesture, but as it turned out, he only did it to hide from the drug dealers he owed money to. He used to play games with me. He loved to hear me play. I didn't really understand at the time the kind of pleasure it gave him. He also had a game called Candy Town that he never let me win. We played it all the time. But his favorite game was his own special version of Red Rover...."

Madi grips my hands tightly, crying harder.

"It's okay. I am right here," I say softly.

"I didn't know it at first, but my mom was doing drugs, too. Not just on the weekends, either. She was using heavily. They gave her an escape, a convenient avenue to forget about her life...forget what my father's leaving had done to her."

Two strangers join us from the stairway and plant themselves about ten feet away. They hold each other closely, kissing and whispering. A shaft of light from the lighthouse sweeps across the bay, interrupting the moon's reflection.

"She never really saw the man she truly married...the real Jacob. I think she ignored all the signs; she wanted to be with someone so badly." She lets out a long sigh, pauses until the beam makes another pass, and continues.

"With the drugs slowly taking over, my mom was a mess. She started job-hopping. She ended up with one that required her to commute far away. Every day, Jacob would drive her to and from work. He would pick me up from piano lessons when she didn't have time or was too strung out. He loved to hear me play. He always would be staring at me as I played. Every note I got wrong he would get angry at me. He liked to smack me in the back of the head until I got it right. I went through eight piano teachers that summer. He made me hate playing the piano, knowing it got him off."

I can guess what Madi will say next. But I need to hear it from her. I need to know it's true.

"There was a rest stop." Her face screws up, and she struggles to keep the tears back. More composed, she says each word slowly, taking a breath between each phrase. "This abandoned old rest stop along the highway where we would stop every time." She loses it again, her shoulders shaking with each sob. Her voice becomes high-pitched, and she brings it to almost a whisper. I lean in close, our cheeks touching, her body trembling. "He told me to get into the backseat. He got in on the other side. Then, he'd say he wanted to play a different game than the ones we played at home. He called it Red Rover. He kept whispering those words to me, over and over, 'Red Rover, Red Rover, send Madi right over.' He told me I had to play the game; it's what good little girls did. He said I had to come over to his side of the seat when he said, 'Send Madi right over.' So I did, not knowing what he was going to do next."

Madi hyperventilates a little. In my periphery, the two strangers continue to make out, oblivious to our presence. She breathes in deeply, grips my hands firmly, and calms herself. Still trembling, she continues.

"Jacob told me never to say anything to my mom because it was our secret, and my mom might not understand. But he also said that if I did say something, he might have to hurt me." She gets a faraway look in her eyes, seeing something beyond the moonlit waters and the night sky. "So I said nothing. And every day after my piano lessons for the whole summer, we pulled into the rest stop, until I eventually told my mom. Long story short? Jacob was thrown in jail." Madi is breathing more steadily now. "There are nights I can still see him in my dreams. Always waiting for me to mess up on my piano. Always repeating, 'Red Rover.'" She lets go of my hands and covers her face. "I'm so sorry. I'm so sorry."

"Don't do this to yourself." I wrap my arms around her, and she rests her head on my chest.

"I couldn't make him stop. I'm so sorry. I couldn't make him. I wanted to—for it to stop."

I squeeze her tightly and whisper to her, "It's not your fault, Madi. Surely you know that. It's not your fault." I stroke her hair, caressing her soft waves, and bury my nose in the silky strands. I'll kill him. I don't know how or where. But if I ever get my hands on him, Jacob's a dead man. "I promise, I will never let anyone hurt you again."

Her body relaxes into mine, and after several minutes, her quivering settles.

"I mean it. I'll always protect you." I pull a handkerchief from my jacket pocket and wipe her face and hand it to her.

She looks at me and gives a small smile, blows her nose gently. She studies at my chest and picks at my shirt buttons. "I thought you'd never speak to me again after that."

I raise her chin and look into her glistening chestnut eyes. I drop my hands to her waist and envelop her, pulling her lips into mine. Hers are soft and warm and full of desire. The lighthouse beacon cuts a swath across the bay, and, though closed, my eyes are filled with bright light. The sounds of Madi's breathing and the crashing waves fade away.

EIGHTEEN

ease out of the elevator and onto the rooftop. I look up at the night sky, trying to distill all my negative thoughts into something positive.

There is someone up there who knows me well enough to play music that reaches to the core of my soul. Who but Madi would know something like that?

The hourglass on the roof's edge steadily empties sand into its bulbous lower half.

My watch beeps.

"Fifty minutes!" A slow, light clapping begins. I turn around, and Gabriel is standing just a few feet in front of me, smiling sarcastically and antagonistically. He holds up four pictures.

I feel around in my pocket and notice the rest of my pictures are missing. I guess it doesn't really matter. It comes easy now. Leaving the train, I saw the ninth hourglass reflecting off the disco ball. The tenth was even simpler. Saw it from over the bridge, reflecting off a shiny musical note on Madi's billboard.

I look at the odd hourglass on the edge of the roof. The only one that isn't reflecting off anything. Number eleven.

He tosses three of the photos.

"Heard you loud and clear! Just making sure we are still on the same page."

He takes the last photograph and sticks it in my pocket.

"For luck," he says. "And now for your final lesson. The flaws are the order of things in this place, which means they must be broken for you to escape. To win the race, you must destroy each flaw in the exact order of the day and within a certain amount of time. For example..." Gabriel points across the roof to the hourglass.

"At this moment in time, you have to leave here at fifty-five minutes, right? Well, any time before fifty-five, you're golden. Once it's past fifty-five, though? Breaking it will do no good. You will lose."

Gabriel turns and walks to the table, still set with an open bottle of red wine and two glasses. He sits down and fills the wine glasses halfway. I wander over to the telescope. Gabriel is still sitting, watching me. This is the first time I haven't seen him stuffing his face or smacking that piece of gum. Maybe he is finally full.

The view through the telescope still reveals nothing but blackness. What's wrong with this thing? In my periphery, Gabriel is suddenly standing next to me, holding out a wineglass. I yank the glass from his grip and hurl it over the ledge.

"Probably best. Even though you can't taste it, you still can feel the side effects. It hits you a lot faster, and the hangover is a lot stronger."

As I narrow my eyes at Gabriel, light glints off of a golden pendant hanging around his neck. The Celtic hourglass stands in contrast to the wings behind it. *Was he wearing that earlier?* I don't think so.

Its glimmering golden shine reminds me of the eye of greed.

Why was it missing in the painting? Could the two be related some how? What does it even have to do with me?

Before I can think about it any further, Gabriel moves his head closer to my watch. 3:30 "Don't hang too close to that time piece. If something were to happen to it, you'd soon be fighting off frostbite. Instead, learn to count every second of every minute. Have it ticking away in the back of your mind at all times. If you lose track of the seconds, study the flaws. It will help you to find how much time you have left."

Gabriel sits tall, hands on knees. "Once you start the race and you begin to notice inside the hourglass, the sand turning to snow, that means there's no going back. That usually happens after you have broken two of them. Now, when all twelve flaws are broken, the reapers will be put on pause; they won't pursue you any longer. The flaws are connected within this world, holding everything together. Once they are all destroyed, the barriers around this place shatters. Everything will freeze over and start to fall apart. Buildings will collapse into a black void of nothingness." Gabriel points to the elevator.

"Once the barrier is down, your finish line will be right there."

I look at the elevator, hardly believing it's going to take me up into my body.

"But you will need a key to ride back up."

A key?

He must be referring to what he had said earlier. The key being the second challenge. Something that involved using my mind.

Gabriel rises, walks to the telescope, and runs his hand over it.

"The key was created along with the flaws to this place. It doesn't even look like a key. It's a physical object that has a certain meaning to why you are here. Once fully attained it will help clear your mind of who you once were. Not even I know what it is. Your past self found it initially but told no one what it was. Apparently, he didn't trust anyone but himself with the secret." Gabriel shrugs. "He did give us one clue, though. The clue was that *the key was never an object given to you.*"

The hourglass on the edge of the roof steadily empties its sand.

I wonder what my key could be?

"Once the key is found and the flaws are all broken you will be left with your final challenge."

Killing my demon in return cleansing my soul.

Gabriel nods, "Just remember this is your last attempt. By accepting your demons challenge you are initially going all in. All the chips are on the table and the wager is your life. If you lose then you will give it the right to take your place. If you don't accept the challenge then everything will restart back to the beginning. Where you will eventually have to wait till they pull your plug on the outside. If you choose this path, you understand where you will go after death?"

I understand. I also understand that my demon won't be running around the outside world in my own body if I don't accept. It's a gamble any way you play it.

The northern lights dance overhead, promising hope, if not success. When I raise my head, Gabriel is gone. My watch beeps as the last grain of sand falls through the neck of the hourglass.

Fifty-five minutes.

I step into the elevator and press the button. It hums and begins its descent. I stare beyond its doors and tense up.

I slow my breathing back down. I turn to face the painting.

Each demon displays a unique facial expression. While they are all fixated on the light, they seem to have different motives toward it. One looks as though it would like to eat the light, another as if it would undress and abuse it. Still others look as though they envy it or may want to kill it. They hug the light like a child hugging his mother.

A picture of my mom soon enters my head.

Thinking back to that last memory, I remember me saying that my mother fell into a coma, too. I wonder if she had to suffer the same type of trial as I am. I wish she could be here right now.

The elevator dings.

I make my way back to my apartment door. The waitress's door is closed. A vision of her lifeless head buried in cream flashes before my eyes. My heart sinks.

Should I feel remorse? She is a lost soul, after all. I shouldn't feel any kind of remorse toward her. But I still can't fight the sensation of sorrow for her. I push through my door, closing any thoughts I have of her until tomorrow.

I put my hands in my pockets and take out my keys and wallet. My fingers touch something thin and flimsy. I pull it out, and it's the picture that Gabriel left for luck. I turn it over and see that it's of my bedroom window.

Twelve flaws.

As I gaze at the image, I wander back into the bedroom and stop at my window.

The green-tinted aurora borealis flickers in a soft arc across the sky. I ignore the dancing lights outside and focus on the surface of the glass. A steady stream of sand cascades through the neck of the hourglass.

I finish undressing and climb into bed.

My eyelids feel weighted, and I struggle to keep them open.

My clock counts up: 59:14 . . . 59:15 . . . 59:16.

My eyes grow even heavier. I take a deep breath and try to force them to stay open. At the same time, I know that this is unavoidable. I watch as the hourglass reflecting in the window drops its last sand particle to the bottom, and my eyes close.

♣ ♠ ♦ ♥

I swerve the steering wheel to the left as the van speeds past us on the right.

A bottle of half-empty Macallan rolls around at my feet.

Madi and I both take a look and see that it's an ice cream van. We sigh with relief.

We get to the end of the bridge and continue to drive forward through the blizzard.

Madi reaches her hand over and places it on mine. Her skin is so soft, so warm. With her other hand, she cups the golden pendant hanging from the rearview mirror.

"When are you going to tell me what this means?"

The necklace looks cold and hard compared to Madi's gentle touch. She smiles at me.

"Family," I say.

"Ha, that's what you always say."

She drops her hand and rests it against her torso. "Honey?" She's looking ahead through the windshield, her forehead wrinkled with concern.

The sign beside the road reads, "Dead End 1/4 Mile. Last Entrance to Interstate." The last ramp to the interstate is just ahead.

I grip the steering wheel and turn into the on ramp.

Beep…beep…beep …

RAPHAEL

TUESDAY

NINETEEN

*slam my hand down on the alarm clock, and the beeping stops. My eyes slowly adjust to the light. I sit up and reach for my watch. The leather bound Bible once again rests beside it.

What is your deal?

I ignore it's existence and let it be. Maybe it will do the opposite and be inside the drawer tomorrow. I slide my feet to the cool, wood floor and run my hands over my face. My chin and cheeks are rough with overgrown stubble. I run my hand through my hair, at least a centimeter longer than yesterday. *Why is my hair getting longer every day?*

I walk over to the window. Outside, it looks to be spring weather, not winter anymore.

To my left, the sound of a match being lit startles me. A small flame appears in the hand of a black man seated on the brown leather chaise. The tiny light flickers off the Ten of Spades protruding from the pocket of his dark violet suit jacket.

Raphael.

He lights a cigarette hanging from his mouth and speaks in a low, gravelly voice. "Springtime brings with it ideas of regrowth, rejuvenation, renewal, resurrection, and most of all, rebirth."

He leans back into the soft curves of the expensive leather chair, and puffs on the cigarette. The edges of the brow paper glow with the heat. Tilting his head back, he blows a stream of smoke into the air. Then he smiles, exposing his white teeth in stark contrast with his dark skin and black goatee, and takes a few hard puffs of his cigarette.

The piano starts playing in the living room. It must be 3:10. I'm growing accustomed to not looking at my watch.

Raphael stares at me, dragging on his cigarette. "We find out today how strong your soul really is." He rises with unexpected elegance. The thick fabric of his suit ripples over his bulging muscles.

He laughs as he draws on the cigarette and exhales the vapor into my eyes.

The smoke blinds me. I wave it away, and when it clears, Raphael is gone.

Finally. I pass the hatchet in its glass case and walk into the bathroom. In the mirror, the hourglass's ghostly image steadily empties sand through its neck. I reach my fingers toward the surface of the mirror. At less than a centimeter away, I jerk my hand back. I can't risk it.

I lift my razor to my neck and shave upward, slowly. No mistakes this time. My feet slip, and I crash face-first into the mirror. Glass shards spray across the countertop and floor. The hourglass is nowhere to be seen.

What have I done? I grip the marble edge of the counter. The blood-covered razor blade rests in the sink, surrounded by glass particles. I touch my neck and raise my head. The mirror is whole again, the hourglass unbroken. The fragments of glass that had covered the sink and floor are nowhere to be seen.

My reflection reveals a small nick on my neck in the same place it was last time. My mind is playing games on me again. It's feeling more real. Soon I won't be able to tell reality from fantasy. Maybe this has something to do with my body on the outside. Or the reapers have erased my mind so many times that it's all messed up.

A sensation moves through my body as if a cancer is spreading and it's just a matter of time before it eats me alive. I rattle my head. *Think happy thoughts. Think happy thoughts.* Madi's silky, fragrant hair against my nose...the warm curves of her body in my hands—*I promise, I will never let anyone hurt you again.* I straighten up and walk to my closet.

In my closet, I take out the same designer suit, the one Madi bought for me, intending to return it to its sister store the next day. For as little as money actually meant to her, she was always willing to indulge my dreams of grandeur.

Her perfume wafts from the lapel as if I'd just been holding her against me. I remove the suit from the rack and commence my morning routine.

As I slide my arms through the jacket sleeves, the cyan and black Jack of Hearts flashes in the mirror.

I need to know what else happened that night. But am I ready to enter the tree again? What if my demon attacks me while inside?

I go over to the refrigerator, open the freezer, and pull out the pistol Michael gave to me.

I know it's not loaded but if my demon is in that tree then the bullets have to be inside as well.

I stick it in the back of my pants and tuck my jacket over it, hiding it away from anyone to see.

I stare at the watch on the kitchen table, wondering if I should take the gamble of not bringing it today. I get nervous, thinking of all the things that could go wrong. I place my watch around my wrist and clamp it tight. I turn toward the bedroom door. Madi stands there, holding a plate of eggs and sausage. She's wearing a red silk robe over her long, smooth, bare legs. Her waves are pinned out of her face, but still spill over her shoulders. The sensation of death spreads through my body again. She is not real.

"Oh, I was hoping to catch you before you left," she says, smiling. "I made breakfast."

It's not her. It can't be her.

She approaches and puts a finger on my mouth. "Don't say anything." Her fingers are long and elegant, and end in perfectly manicured French tips. "This is your big promotion day. I know you hate kind gestures, but I got you something, anyway. This is a momentous occasion. I was going to surprise you, but I couldn't wait. I hope you like it!"

Madi leaves the plate in my hands, walks through the bathroom to the closet, and looks around. "I hid it last night, hoping you would find it in the stars." She turns to me with a coy smile. "Poo. I know it's around here somewhere. I'm sure I'll find it when you're gone. Just pretend I didn't say anything, okay?"

In the bathroom mirror, my reflection smiles at me and winks. It turns, yells at Madi, and pushes her to the floor. I spin from the mirror, but Madi is gone. When I turn back, the hourglass overlays my true reflection. It flips over just as my watch rings out.

Five minutes.

I rush out of the bathroom.

The hatchet is oddly missing from its glass case. Suddenly, a cloud of vapor exits my mouth. I dash across the living room and fling open my front door. At my feet are three clear plastic stacks of gum packaged in silver and white wrappers labeled, "Tredstones."

The door across the hall opens, and the waitress steps out, turns, and locks up. There's no trace of her tragic, whipped-cream demise. I want to apologize, but I know nothing will come out. She gently touches her hand to my mouth and offers a small smile. Her brilliant green doe eyes seem to harbor nothing but compassion.

We exchange a look that says we are both okay.

She nods her head and walks to the stairway door.

I head toward the elevator and press the button.

In my periphery, Raphael appears. "So…?"

I recoil.

"You just gonna let her walk away?" He struts around me, eyeing me up and down. "Only one chick in this whole place, and he doubts himself. Typical white boy…"

He shoves me into the elevator and walks in behind me. The painting's electric blue life being smothered by the hungry, twisted demons haunts me to my core. I can almost feel my own demon clinging to me, as the canvas suggests.

Staring at the painting, he says, "That a misinterpretation piece, right there. Someone done took a lot of pride and not much else, developing this monstrosity of fine craftsmanship."

Does that mean he loves it or hates it? Raphael looks at me and then at the panel of buttons. What exactly does he want from me?

"You know who I am?" Raphael asks, pausing for me to respond. I remain silent. "And again the Lord said to Raphael: 'Bind Azazel hand and foot, and cast him into the darkness, and make an opening in the desert and cast him therein. And place upon him rough and jagged rocks, and cover him with darkness, and let him abide there forever, and cover his face that he may not see light. And on the day of the great judgment he shall be cast into the fire.' Meaning you best be pushing that button, before I makes you press it. Got it, cracker?"

I think he literally thinks he is The archangel, Raphael.

I press the L button, and the elevator doors close. Today is going to be another long day.

He turns toward me and nods at the nick on my neck. "Never once while you been here did you ever cut yourself. I noticed it when I saw you a few days ago."

He puts a meaty hand around my neck and presses his thumb against the shaving scab.

"You got the gift to regenerate yourself. Bet you didn't know that, either. But it's true. That what I'mma teach you today. That cut can be gone in an instant."

He releases my neck, and I stumble back. I rub the nick softly.

Raphael chuckles, puts a cigarette in his mouth, holds a match to the end of it, and inhales deeply. He expels a smoke trail and starts humming "Man in the Mirror."

He sings the first line loudly and slightly off-key.

The elevator finally stops, and the doors open. Smoke wafts from the compartment into the lobby. Raphael flicks his cigarette onto the marble floor and performs a poor imitation of Michael Jackson, still humming the song.

I follow Raphael at a distance.

He moonwalks into the revolving front doors. I step into the slot behind him. We move slowly, keeping pace with the doors.

Raphael steps out and waits for my section to reach the opening. As I exit, he pushes my shoulder back, forcing my right arm into the approaching jamb. The door's momentum drives it into my arm, lodging me in place.

Raphael raises my missing hatchet and slices my arm clean off. It falls to the floor just behind the glass door. The arm hits the ground, shattering instantly into electric color puzzle pieces. I reel from the door and stumble with the sudden change to my center of gravity. There's no blood spilling from my shoulder, just bright, electric blue sparks falling to the sidewalk. I prop myself up against the building, groping the rough brick with my remaining hand.

"Matthew five-thirty: 'And if thy right hand offend thee, cut it off, and cast it from thee: for it is profitable for thee that one of thy members should perish, and not that thy whole body should be cast into hell.' Today we going to cut away at your soul, piece by piece, cleaning away your doubt and reforming you back to new."

He pulls a cigarette from an inner jacket pocket, strikes a match, and lights the end before moonwalking around the corner.

I lean against the building, breathing hard. The temperature falls, and each breath becomes thick vapor. I push off the wall and rush toward my parking spot.

Out of nowhere, my car gets run over by a monster truck.

You've got to be kidding me!

The driver's door automatically opens, and I bite my tongue, knowing it doesn't even matter. My watch beeps.

Ten minutes.

I slide onto the torn and stained upholstery. Raphael sits in the passenger seat with a wide smile on his face.

My shoulder has stopped shooting sparks, and I lean away from Raphael, hoping the extra inches might protect the gaping wound somehow. As I floor the gas pedal, the monster truck goes from zero to ninety in a matter of seconds. I careen onto the interstate, driving over cars as I go. It sure would be nice if I had both arms. Driving with one arm is not what I call helping out my situation.

I bore into Raphael, hoping he heard me. Instead of reacting, he calmly stares out the window with that infuriating grin. He's got the same close-cut hair and well-kept goatee and the same haughty hold to his jaw. But where's his cigarette? Where are his snappy comebacks? I swerve to avoid a sedan. The momentum causes a necklace to slide into view between his open collar. It's the golden pendant I've seen the other lost souls wearing at times. It's the same pendant hanging from my rearview in my nightmares. What is its significance?

Still nothing from Raphael. As we continue to race across the asphalt, I give him a look that I hope conveys disdain.

I recoil, expecting a sudden display of violence. He just sits there like it didn't even faze him. What is going on?

"Would you sell your eyes for one million dollars?" Raphael says, still looking out the window. "How about both of 'em for twenty million?" He looks at me. "Your eyes are priceless, yet they merely the windows of your soul. Your eyes are worth nothing compared to the value of your soul. Mark nine, forty-seven say, 'And if thine eye offend thee, pluck it out: it is better for thee to enter into the kingdom of God with one eye, than having two eyes to be cast into hell fire.'"

My jaw goes slack. *Is he about to pluck out my eye?*

I cover my right eye with my one arm, leaving the steering wheel free.

The monster truck slams into something. The sound of twisting metal fills the car. The steering wheel spins out of control. I put my arm back on it, hoping to get it back on track. The car whips around and around. We are about to collide with the off ramp.

Raphael hasn't made a peep. He's still got that silly grin on his face as if we were on a carnival ride.

The truck carrying the glass windows is just passing. My one arm isn't strong enough to hold us steady. As we lurch toward the hourglass reflection, Raphael clamps his hand on the wheel. He steers the car back to the right, barely missing the glass.

The monster truck straightens out onto the exit, and Raphael removes his hand.

The truck proceeds down the interstate, the hourglass still pouring sand, letting me know I'm more early than late. I sigh deeply and slow way down. I stare straight ahead, afraid to see Raphael's reaction to my near blunder.

Up ahead and to the right is the coffee shop. Raphael reaches across the cab and pulls the emergency break. The car jolts, and my face slams into the steering wheel. We come to a complete stop. *What's going on?*

Raphael leans behind me and locks my door.

He turns my chin so I'm looking straight into his jade eyes and says, "I got to tell you something."

His expression is peaceful and strangely compassionate.

"This something you need to know. We waited till now to tell you 'cause you ready to hear it."

I stare at him and firmly shake my head.

My watch beeps.

Fifteen minutes.

"Being content is a self-revelation on what you deem pure to your own soul. But as you well know, you can be deceived on being content. A demon's whisper can play tricks on you. It clouds your reasoning on what you *think* content really is."

He points at the tree in the park over yonder.

"The spawn to your ultimate sin."

From here, I can just make out the shape of its dead form across the park.

I don't know if I'm really ready to face my demon now.

"Your demon ain't inside that tree. It's out here. In the open. And it could possibly be posing as any one of us for all I know. So ease up."

I raise my eyebrows and face Raphael.

My demon is free?! And it could be anyone?

Michael's angry eyes and quick, Irish chatter flash through my mind, then Gabriel's jaw-length, symmetrically parted hair and dark sunglasses.

"I knew it was good for you to learn this while with me. I can already see you're ready to pee yourself. Just knowing I could very well be your demon. It could be any one of us. Have your suspicions. But remember, a demon's only weapon is its mouth. Its sinful words alone can make an honest man lie. A civil man murder. A strong man suicidal. All you got to do is just not listen. Don't be pushing away the people trying to help you recover. To help you learn to survive. To help you one day live a long life. You may not remember your childhood, but that don't mean I have to reteach you the fundamentals of right and wrong. You already know that 'cause you ain't no fool that believes you don't have a choice. You got the choice, and you can prove it to me and yourself right now by choosing to go it alone or not. But I pray you realize you ain't never alone."

Raphael puts his hand on my gaping shoulder. "No matter how crazy we all may seem, just know we all want the same thing. For you to finish this race. Use our help for your gain. "Besides even if one of us is a demon it won't do anything until the end of the trial. It needs you to succeed too. That's the only way it can be free. Just be smart about looking over your shoulder when passing through that finish line." He unlocks the doors and steps out of the car.

I never would have guessed Raphael would say something like that. My adrenaline spikes. I shove the door open and hit the pavement at a dead run. Breathing heavily, I burst through the coffee shop doors and stumble to my normal table.

The hourglass in the window trickles sand, slowly filling up its lower half. I have only one shot at this and only one arm. Thank God he didn't chop off my leg instead. God. *Am I really thanking God?* With the upper bulb almost empty, I rise and exit the coffee shop. My watch beeps.

Twenty minutes.

Despite the overcast sky, the park is glorious. Bright red and yellow tulips dot the gently rolling hills, and the trees are clothed in pink and purple blooms. Birdsongs travel on the breeze and fill the air.

Raphael is still nowhere to be seen. The Ferris wheel projects above the newly-awakened spring beauty. Today would be a perfect day to take a ride up. I run up the hill and slide into one of the cabs. The monstrous machine gently lifts me to the top. As I ascend, a radiant field of sunflowers comes into view. And the gaping, dead tree is no longer dead, but rather covered in white blossoms and full of life.

If Raphael is right, then I am going to have to start being extra cautious when finding my key. I now understand why I never told anyone what it was before. I wonder if any of the other versions of myself knew who my demon really was? The sad truth of it all is that it could literally be any one of them.

The uneasy feeling stays with me as I make my way back down to the start of the ride where Raphael is waiting for me.

"Move it along, one armed Nancy!"

His neck is bare, the golden pendant now gone. My watch beeps.

Twenty five Minutes.

I put everything from the mystery necklace to Raphael having a mental split personality breakdown to the back of my head. I can't let him know anything until I am sure that he is not my demon. I must continue to act natural.

I follow behind Raphael, making sure he is in front of me at all times. He looks over to me and holds his hand out, stopping me where I stood. He waves me over and I slowly walk to him, almost afraid he heard what I was thinking again. He takes hold of my tie and yanks me to him. Fear overtakes me as he places his finger to his lips, telling me to be quiet. I kinda felt this was uncalled for since I couldn't speak anyway. He turns his head over yonder to the oak tree as I do mine.

I see the little girl standing beside the tree again. She sees my face and her smile lights up. But when she sees Raphael, her smile turns to a look of sheer terror and she runs behind the tree.

Raphael takes out a pistol case and starts setting up the powder, the lead shots, and the ramrod. Looking at him carefully, and thinking about his erratic behavior, I wonder if Raphael really could be my demon. Remembering the pistol tucked into my pants, I reach behind my back and cock the hammer back.

"We need to get you ready for your third challenge."

Raphael looks almost sad saying it. He goes back to the pistol case, making loud noises from whatever he is doing with it.

Raphael reaches into his pocket and takes out some lead spoons. He looks behind him, stands up, and gathers some twigs, making them into a miniature teepee. Finding some larger fallen branches, he breaks them apart and builds a tiny log cabin structure around the tiny teepee. Finally, Raphael throws some twigs into the center, pulls a cigarette and matchbook out of his inner jacket pocket, lights the cigarette, and then uses it to light the twigs.

He and I sit together silently, watching the flames grow until all the wood is engulfed and coals are starting to form. Raphael takes the lead spoons and places them on top of a silver tray of metal with small molding bullet-shaped and sized indents. He places the tray on top of the coals. The spoons slowly begin to melt and gather in the indented molds.

"Might not kill a demon, but it will do for practice firing. You know, back in the Revolutionary War, the fastest soldier could fire six shots in one minute. A demon can do it a lot faster so best pay attention."

Now melted into the mold, Raphael picks up the tray by the handles and quickly places it on the bench between him and me. He waits for it to cool, turns it over, and taps it against the bench. Five balls fall out onto the bench. He lifts his hand toward me, waiting for me to give him the pistol. I don't move, not trusting Raphael.

He reaches around behind me and takes my pistol out. He knocks the end of it against my head.

"How were you going to shoot me without bullets? You jackass! Now, let me teach you something you already know but have once again forgotten. Gather your primer, black powder, ball, patch, flint, and ramrod. The patch should be made of linen or cotton. Load the flint into the cock. With the cock half-cocked, load the prescribed amount of black powder down the muzzle and tamp down. Wrap the ball in a patch and put in the muzzle. Tap down the powder and ball with the ramrod. Prime the flash pan with a small amount of the primer, usually less than a third of a pan. Got it?"

What did he just say?

He finishes loading it. "Now, wasn't that easy?" says Raphael. "Okay, not as easy as something more modern. But it was *your* weapon of choice. Life's battles don't always go to the strongest or fastest man. Sooner or later, the man who wins is the fellow who thinks he can. That's the truth you need to embrace. What if I told you that the previous you was able to get off eight shots in a minute?"

I take the pistol. I look at the golden lion on its side. Raphael points to the little girl. "Now shoot it."

I look at the pistol and then at the little girl. I hesitate.

"Now, when a brotha asks a strange white boy, you, to shoot at something, by God you better pull that trigga. She isn't going to die. She won't feel a thing. Go on now!"

I look at Raphael for a moment, then hold the pistol steady and aim.

"Well, what are you waiting for?"

I nervously look at Raphael, then at the little girl in the clearing. I hold the pistol up, aim, and pull the trigger. Crack! The gun sounds and echoes in the park. The little girl runs off.

I smile, knowing I missed her on purpose. I look down and notice that my arm is back!

An overjoyed Raphael shouts, "My brotha! Horrible accuracy but we will get you there. Now hand it back over."

I hold on to the pistol, not trusting Raphael. In a blink of a second he grabs my arm, swings the hatchet down swiftly, cutting my arm off once again. My arm and pistol hit the ground, breaking apart like puzzle pieces. Raphael reaches down and picks the pistol up.

"That's what you get for missing on purpose. Now as we were," he says with a joyous look splashed across his face.

He turns, walking his way toward the office building while leaving me crippled once again.

I think I hate him the most.

he doors open, and I step into my office, noticing first thing that a cloud of smoke is coming from behind my office chair. His purple sports jacket can be easily noticeable through the white smog.

"Thirty minutes on the dot! How's that arm looking?"

Raphael swirls the chair around to face me, laughing at my disfigurement. He takes away the cigarette from his mouth and flicks it to where my arm should be.

"Still with the one arm? I guess I should have taught you the trick first, huh?"

I see Raphael has taken the other flintlock out from the glass case. He has laid out the hardware necessary to load the pistol on my desk and drops two lead balls next to the gun.

"The fastest time you have ever reloaded was ten seconds. Your demon can do it in half that. So, if your wanting to breathe fresh air again I would suggest you sit."

I sit down across from Raphael, who shows me how to load again. I attempt to load my pistol only using one arm. I fumble the bullet and it falls off the table, making Raphael wait until he scoops it back up.

"There's no turning back for you this time. You hear me? By the end of this you are going to have to face your demon. No more running away. So best be getting serious about this."

I only have one hand!

Raphael slams his fist down on the desk. "By the time you reach the final challenge you might not have any hands! Stop making excuses."

I copy Raphael's actions, but much more slowly. I fumble and drop the flint. Raphael sighs and lights up another cigarette. He looks at me and raises his eyebrows.

"Maybe I should just put you out of your misery right now. Save you the trouble."

Raphael picks up his now loaded pistol, points it at me, and pulls the trigger. The pistol misfires. I look at him, terrified.

"These pistols can only kill demons. Such an idiot." Raphael drops the pistol on the desk, laughing.

"We might just need to pray that the first shot you fire counts."

I turn and walk to the office kitchen, not wanting to speak to him.

Dishes clatter, and the refrigerator door closes. The smell of pancakes meets me as I step onto the yellow vinyl floor of the seventies-style kitchenette.

Raphael sits on a teal chair pulled up to a round dinette table, smoking, with a stack of pancakes in front of him. Syrup oozes over the edges of the stack, and a large pat of butter melts on top. "You need to lighten up. Stress is not going to fix that nub of yours."

He shoves his cigarette in my mouth. "Just take a few puffs and don't be a baby about it."

I try to spit it out, but he won't have it. "Don't make me cut off the other one!"

I stop fighting and take a few puffs. "Now, that's better."

Raphael pushes the plate toward me.

"Pancakes make me happy. They make you happy? You see, happiness or really any kind of wildly aggressive feeling of emotion is the key to healing. The feeling of happiness, though, heals you up a lot quicker. It cleanses you. Make you feel all warm and fuzzy inside. You like feeling fuzzy now, don't you?"

I push the plate away and fantasize about shoving the pancakes down Raphael's throat until he chokes and suffocates.

"What you gonna to do, one-armed Willy?" Raphael narrows his eyes at me. "Nub me to death?" He guffaws, pushes the plate back toward me, and places a fork beside it.

"You want your arm back, don't you?"

I look at the meal in front of me, giving in to his little game.

He yanks back his cigarette and takes a long draw before blowing smoke on the buttery pancakes in front of me.

"Now give it time to sink on in, and we can begin."

Sink on in? What does he mean by that?

He shows me his cigarette, "You didn't think inside it was tobacco, right? Heavens, no! You, my brother, are about to go on a trip! Hopefully a very happy trip. Hopefully."

I begin to panic as my senses start to feel more heightened. I can actually now smell the delicious syrup coming off the buttery pancakes.

"Good, the bloodshot in your eyes are telling me you're ready for the ride! Now, try to imagine coming down the stairs and your mom making pancakes."

He stops, looking out into a daze. "Sorry. Just started thinking about my own mother."

It's hard to think Raphael had a mother at one time in his life. It's finally good to see there's still a soul left in him.

"She was a cheating cow."

Anger emerges from his face, letting me know his mother and him must have not ended on good terms. He takes up the fork and holds it out in front of me.

"Now...she hands you a fork. Remember the feeling when you touched the fork—anticipation, excitement, hunger, love from a mother..."

I touch the fork, and I can actually feel its metallic surface against my skin. This feels amazing!

"You heal your arm back right, I might reward you with a surprise gift."

I close my eyes, take a small bite, and put it in my mouth. My taste buds go instantly crazy as this quickly sparks a memory in me.

TWENTY-ONE

irdsongs and the chopping of wood drift through an open window over a kitchen sink. My hands are small and youthful and covered in white powder. I'm seated on a teal chair over yellow vinyl flooring. In front of me is a cheap, metal and plastic dinette table with a bowl of fruit in the center. How young am I now? My short height and small frame tell me I must be around nine or ten years old. I touch my chubby belly, realizing I was one fat kid.

"Just what do you think you're doing?"

I raise my head. My mother stands next to the round dinette table with her hands sternly on her hips. I had been making a mess, sifting and funneling baking soda from the box into a volcano that I've made.

Mama's face holds love and concern, with only a touch of annoyance. Her soft, light hair frames her beautiful hazel eyes. I wish I could talk to her, but know that I can't. I try with all my might to make myself move. I succeed in falling out of the chair. Mama bends down and lifts me up. With more control now, I wrap my arms around her waist and squeeze, wanting to hold her forever. I tighten my hug as my mother hugs me back. My control is slipping. This moment will end soon. I raise my chin and take in her smile-crinkled face one more time before I get sucked away.

"Is everything okay, dear?"

"Hey, Mom." I flash her my best little-boy smirk. It always makes her smile.

"Son." She has that tone that says she knows I'm getting into mischief.

"This is my science project," I say proudly, continuing to funnel the white powder into the volcano. "It's something I got to do for school."

"Your volcano looks great! I still can't believe the ten dollars I gave you was enough to make it look that good."

I try to not look at her when I say, "I told you there was a special going on at the price club. It was a steal."

I chuckle at my hidden meaning. I've never stolen in my entire life. Not once. The idea for stealing it just popped in my head. Like someone whispered inside my ear, telling me that it was okay. It gave me such a rush at the time.

My mother folds her arms. "You know, I don't need to say it."

"So don't." I wiggle my eyebrows at her.

"Your father won't like you doing that in the house."

"Mom, please." My voice turns whiny. "I have to, Mom. Otherwise I'll get an F!"

She sighs. "Well, let's hurry before your father finishes the yard work." She picks up my instruction sheet from the table.

"Yes!" I pump my baking soda fist in the air.

Sun beams through the window, and the Mister Softee jingle rides the breeze. I hop up as the ice cream truck passes my house. My stomach growls loudly.

"Didn't you get enough to eat at lunch, baby?" Mama's always trying to feed me something.

I shrug my shoulders. "I forgot."

"You forgot to eat?"

"I was busy, Mom!"

"Well, what if I make you a quick batch of pancakes when we're done with this? As long as you eat it before your father gets in, it'll be okay. We'll have to hurry. And don't let him know."

I grin. With a little more urgency in my pace, I move the makeshift laboratory beaker to the sink, where the half-full vinegar awaits inside the volcano.

"Careful." Her head is in the cabinets, collecting the cooking utensils needed to mix up some batter.

"Here it goes!" I remove the lid from the vinegar and trickle it down through the open spout. As soon as the vinegar touches the soda, a small, popping reaction occurs, followed by gentle fizzing. "Darn!"

"What's the matter?" Mama asks, ignoring the indiscretion of my swearing. She sets the utensils on the counter.

"I don't know what I'm doing wrong."

Mama places a hand gently onto my disappointed head. The chemical reaction dissipates to nothing. "You're supposed to mix the two together?"

"Yes." I tilt the volcano model side to side, hoping for a second reaction. "They're supposed to create carbon dioxide gas."

"Are you sure?"

"Yes, Mom." I give a long, exaggerated sigh. "It's science."

"Maybe I can help?"

I keep my head trained on the failed experiment.

She walks over to her record player and places a vinyl record in it.

"How's that supposed to help?'

The music plays, and she smiles, weaving back and forth.

I step closer to her. What is she doing now? "Why are you smiling, Mom?"

It takes her a second to look back at me, as if she were in a daydream. "Because I was remembering the first time I heard this song. I was just as young as you are now. It was the first time I saw your father. The song was playing in a bowling alley."

She closes her eyes as if she were traveling back through time to that exact point. I beam. Mama is so beautiful when she is happy. Lately, she hardly ever smiles anymore or dances. A tear slides down her face, and her smile fades.

I run to her and grip her hand. "Why are you crying?"

She pats my hand and kisses my forehead. "It's nothing. I just really miss those simple times, is all."

"Did the music make you travel back in time? Because if so, I can really get an A on my science project!"

She chuckles. "For a second, I felt like I was reliving the whole night over again. So yeah, it kind of is like a time machine. Though I don't think the world, including your science teacher, is ready for this invention just yet. I was actually thinking about giving the record player to you. I think we both know how special it is."

I grip her other hand, too, and start spinning her around the room. "You will give it to me?"

"The conditions of you getting it will rely on three factors. You must never sell it, and you must never tell anybody its secret powers."

"And what's the third thing?"

She stops, lets go of my hands, and swaps the record out. Violins blend with piano notes. She returns to our dance hold and resumes our movement across the floor. "Whenever you play this song, I want you to think about this moment, right now."

"How come?"

"Because I love you. And because this is the day we got you an A on your science project. Give me just a second"—she kisses me on the forehead—"and I'll show you how this experiment was performed back when I was a child."

After disappearing into the bathroom, she returns with a bottle of toilet cleaner.

"What's that?"

"I think we can solve your problem." She opens a kitchen drawer and removes a roll of aluminum foil. "Here, take this."

"What do I do with this?"

"Rip it into tiny pieces."

I tear off a sheet of foil and shred it to tiny squares. I start bouncing on my toes. "Now what?"

Mama opens her hands. "Put the pieces in my hands and open the bottle."

I drop the aluminum squares into her hands and twist off the top of the bottle.

She funnels the shimmering stream of foil in. Once the inside surface is lined with tiny bits, she opens the toilet cleaner. "Watch this." She pours the green fluid over the aluminum.

"What do I do?" I'm bouncing faster now.

"Close it, and I'll be right back. Cover your daddy's war memorabilia so nothing bad happens to it." She runs into the living room. The doorway to the living room frames an American flag, placed behind glass and centered on the far wall.

I look at the flintlock pistol beside it and remember the story my father would always tell me when I was younger.

That my Granddad was a war hero. Shot down over Laos. Tortured and put into a prison camp. Survived fifty-two days until he found a flintlock pistol buried in the ground near his cell. Used it as a weapon to break free. He saved over a hundred and fifty-three soldiers. Father never lets me forget it.

Mama returns with the Polaroid camera. "Okay, be sure to shake it up really vigorously." She positions herself in front of me, holding the camera up.

I close my eyes and shake the mixture.

"Come on. Shake it up!"

I open my eyes. Her face is expectant, her finger on the camera shutter. "Like this?" I shake the container more forcefully.

"Yes! Only more!"

"You mean like this?" I shake it as hard as I can. My whole body is jiggling from the effort.

"Yes! Now stop."

I stop, but in the process, I lose my grip on the bottle. Grasping desperately at its awkward shape, I fumble it onto the floor. I gasp.

"Grab it!" she shouts! The bottle rebounds off the floor and spins, shaking its vigorous, frothy contents. As I scramble over to it, the bottle explodes and sprays its green fluid across the kitchen.

Mom rushes to me. "Are you okay, baby?"

I stand and hold up my arms with a big smile. "I'm not hurt."

Mama breaks into hysterical giggles, and I join her.

Through her convulsions of laughter, she manages to lift the Polaroid. "Smile!" The shutter snaps and whirs as it spits out a photograph.

I grip the countertop, stopping myself from collapsing with laughter. Between giggles, I intersperse the words, "What happened?"

"Maybe a little less tinfoil next time?" She flaps the Polaroid back and forth. "I don't know."

"I want to see! I want to see!" I rush to her side.

"I love you, baby." She squeezes me, and, for a moment, we linger in silence, mother and son huddled together as the images start to appear on the photo.

I grab my purple book from the table. On the cover of the book, it reads, *Physical Science*. I show her what's on the next page.

"If it makes you feel better, I could have chosen how to make a flare stick."

"Whoo! What fun. Maybe next time."

I close the book, laying it back down in excitement.

Mama's body stiffens. It's too quiet. The record's not playing. Mama's jaw is set, and I follow her gaze to the window. No sounds of wood cleaving.

"When did you stop hearing the chopping, baby?"

I grip her tighter.

"What was that noise?" My father's gruff voice carries through the window.

The green liquid splattered every surface in the room. Can I clean it up fast enough? How much time do we have before he completes his trip from the shed to the door?

"Nothing!" Mama shouts back, her voice trembling.

"I heard a racket!" His voice is much closer now.

My body goes numb. The back door opens and slams shut. My father's footsteps echo through the hallway. He steps into the kitchen, carrying a hatchet. His faded overalls are stained with sweat and dirt, his sandy brown hair disheveled.

He looks around the room with wide eyes and brows raised to the roof. "You look at this mess," he yells, "and you tell me nothing?"

"Everything's okay. Don't worry." Mama's hand is shaking now, too.

Father swishes his hand in front of his nose. "Gah! It stinks! What is that crap?"

"Toilet cleaner." She smiles and takes a hesitant step toward him.

He stomps past us to the sink, lays his hatchet down, and turns on the water. Without saying a word, he pulls a towel from a drawer, wets it, and holds it to his face.

Mama approaches him and puts on a cheerful facade. "Finished with the wood so soon, sweetheart?"

Father groans into the towel.

"We were just working on our son's—"

He looks over at the flag and pistol to see that it also has been in the crossfire. "What in the hell happened here?" he roars, throwing the towel into the sink and whirling toward us.

Mama steps back. Her face is tense. "Just a science project, darling. I was going to clean everything up before you came in."

"You're not cleaning. It is his mess. He cleans it. Stop babying him. He won't learn nothing if you keep babying him all the time!" Father steps toward me. "Didn't I tell you to do those science projects of yours outside?"

"Hold on!" Mama says, raising her voice a little and stepping bravely between us. "It was my fault! Not his!"

She looks through the cleaning closet and finds nothing to clean with. "I'll just need to run to the store for a quick second."

She then goes to look through her purse. But I know already there isn't any cash in there.

She takes out everything from inside her purse. "That's odd I could have sworn..."

Father snatches away the purse from her and says, "Where's the fifty dollars I gave you yesterday? Don't tell me you already spent it."

"I'm sure I just misplaced it."

"Misplaced it? That money was supposed to last us for the rest of the week. You know things are slowing down at work right now."

"Just give me a moment to find it!"

Red-faced and with veins bulging from his neck, Father turns and looks at the cooking utensils Mama set out. He charges toward them and raises a glass measuring cup. "And what is this?"

"You're being ridiculous."

"Oh, am I?"

"He was hungry when he got home so I was going to make him a snack."

"He doesn't need any snacks! Look at him! You turned our son into porky pig."

Father grabs an apple out of the fruit bowl in the middle of the table and holds it in front of her face. "This is a snack!" He points to the gathered utensils. "That is a meal!" He looks at me. "You think money grows on trees around here?"

Mama takes a small step toward him. "Look, let's be reasonable."

"You shut up!" he shouts. "I'm talking to him!" He turns toward me and pulls a long, silver butterfly knife from the front pocket of his overalls. He flips the knife open and performs a reverse twirl, a backhand opening, and an aerial. Without blinking, he slices the apple into precise quarters.

"Maybe the cash is in my jacket pocket!" Mama shouts as she walks to the other room.

Father walks toward me, and I take a small step back, my muscles taut. He puts a hand behind my head and forces a chunk of apple into my mouth. "This is a snack."

Tears stream down my cheeks as I reluctantly begin to chew.

"From now on, you're going to start helping out in the yard!"

I nod.

"You're old enough," he says, gritting his teeth. "You don't need to be babied around anymore. It will hopefully even make you lose some weight if not all of it."

He strides to the kitchen sink, picks up his hatchet, steps back to me, and places it in my hands.

Mama comes back in with her head down.

"Let me guess. The money isn't in there either?"

Father's bipolar condition is so heavy that even he can't control it half the time. He smashes whatever he sees in front of him including my model volcano.

Mama is crying, struggling to maintain composure. She takes out a cigarette and starts smoking.

Father looks down at my now broken volcano. "How much did you spend on this?"

Terrified, I can't help but stay quite.

Mama speaks up for me, "It was only ten dollars."

He looks over to me, "Is that true son?"

I should confess what happened to the money and how I stole it, but I can't force my mouth to speak the truth.

"That's correct, sir."

"Wait outside," Father says in a quiet voice. "I'll be there in a minute."

Mama cries harder. What do I do? I can't leave her alone with him. But I'm no match for his strength. I'd be totally useless if I stayed. Mama looks at me with bloodshot eyes. She nods toward the door. I slowly turn and walk out of the room, my heart pounding, tears still streaming down my face.

I push the back door open and step into the backyard.

Father shouts through the window, "There's already a log lined up! Start practicing! Remember, practice makes perfect!"

I raise the hatchet over my head. It's heavy and wobbles a little. As I swing it down toward the vertical log, a crash booms from inside the kitchen. I startle, and the hatchet falls to the ground.

"How could you be so stupid, Nora?!" Heavy furniture scrapes against the floor.

Mama screams. Something thuds against the floor. Another scream. I drop the hatchet and run toward the door. Coldness spreads through my body. I must keep running! The door is only a few feet away, when everything goes black.

TWENTY-TWO

M y eyes slowly adjust to a dim light. Pressure in my shoulder is building, and my arm slowly reforms. I look over to find that I'm in the Lighthouse Restaurant. Raphael must have dragged me here.

Raphael is sitting at my table, smoking a cigarette, with the menu draped across his lap.

"Good trip?"

I touch the fork with my right hand and can't feel it. Whatever Raphael gave me must have worn off.

"I see someone got their arm back."

I'm astonished to not have noticed that my right arm has fully grown back.

Raphael takes my hand and shakes it as if he is testing to see if it functions correctly. "Also looks like you cleared up that scar of yours."

I narrow my eyes at him. Raphael taps his cigarette on the handle of the silver dome, speckling the crimson tablecloth with glowing ashes.

I look at the silver dome and notice the shaving cut on my neck is gone.

"You see, your arm grew back 'cause you felt something. Anger from a father, love from a mother—it don't matter what, long as your feeling is powerful. The day you stop caring, feeling, be the day your demons have your soul."

My demons? I've been so preoccupied that I forgot my demon is loose somewhere. Or it could be right here in front of me.

Raphael slides a folded sheet of paper in my direction. I recognize right away it's the paper he tore out of the book he wanted me to read.

"As promised, your surprise gift."

I grasp it up, unfolding it like it was the winning ticket to the lottery. I look over the handwriting once again, knowing good and well that it was hundred percent mine. I find where I last stopped and begin to eagerly read:

One day I heard the music coming from up above. Its beautiful melody swept me up and sent me to a past memory of mine, the coffee shop where I first met Madi. When the song ended I felt something new inside me. It grew with each new song that played, like watching a love story unfold. This prison began to build on those memories, buildings began to appear through out my dark voided existence, first the coffee shop, then the subway car, the park, the Lighthouse restaurant, and then my office building, and then people. Though mindless and wondering around without a thought, it was good to see I wasn't alone anymore. It wasn't until the last song, where I found my love story had taken a dark turn.

One spring filled morning a tall dead oak tree appeared in the park, bringing my sins with it from within its hollow. Inside my greatest sinful memory had awoken from its deep slumber and I didn't need an invitation.

Raphael takes back the paper with still more left to uncover. Annoyed, I try reaching my hand for it back but Raphael is too quick. He uses his right hand to take me by the wrist and gently folds the paper back with his left.

I need to know more! Why don't you just let me read the rest of it?!

"Because you ain't ready yet."

Raphael grips my wrist tighter and quickly chops my hand clean off.

He lifts the menu to table level. "Now, what you want, brother? It's on me."

My eyes grow wide, and I can only sit there and stare at him. My anger starts to take me over until I hear something coming from the kitchen.

The waitress emerges, her curvy hips swinging smoothly, a pleasant smile on her pale face. "May I have your orders?"

I calmly try to readjust myself, not wanting Raphael to harm her in any way.

"Well, look here, the floozy from next door, the cat with unlimited lives waiting on us." Raphael looks from her to me. "This a coincidence all by itself. Ain't that right? I mean, what's the chances?" He turns to the waitress. "You know, I never got your name, honey. What, pray tell, is it?"

She parts her lips as if to speak but wrinkles her brow instead.

Raphael leans toward her. "No name tag. What your name, dear?"

She stammers.

"Well, I gonna call you Rhonda. I knew a girl named Rhonda. She was a lost, soulless witch like yourself, and she was pretty fat."

He turns to me. "Rhonda here what we like to call a soul squatter, a soul that link onto another soul's strand and just wait till the time be right. She gave up her body to her demons and now, instead of going from port to port, she drop anchor here. Just waiting for your holy exit door to open so she can slip by you without you even noticing. She then go and take your human suit for a ride, all the while leaving you down here to rot."

The waitress turns toward the kitchen, but Raphael grabs her arm.

"He got complete admiration for you," Raphael says, looking at the waitress and nodding toward me. "He done got so much admiration that he want to give you an extra tip. How grateful he be, Rhonda? Give Rhonda the extra tip, will you please?"

What's the point of this? I pull the fold of bills from my wallet.

Still holding her arm firmly, Raphael looks from the money back to the waitress. "How much that be, you think? Around two hundred? That a lot of money, wouldn't you say? You can do a lot with that money. You could spend it on clothes or get your nails done or...I don't know!" She winces. The skin around his grip is turning even whiter than the rest of her already-ivory skin. "Just get the hell out of here and move on to somewhere else. Maybe find someone else who maybe even give a crap about you. Have a couple soulless kids. Maybe pay to have your name changed. Really settle down, you feel me?"

The waitress struggles a little to free her arm, her eyes filling with tears.

"Still not gonna leave? I was expecting that. I was counting on that, actually." He jerks her closer to him and looks back at me. "I tried to do the noble thing, just keep that in mind."

With his other hand, Raphael slowly runs his fingers down the waitress's thigh and back up her inner leg. She stiffens against his touch. He reaches inside his jacket, pulls out the lamb pistol, and shoves the barrel against her stomach, angled up toward her vital organs.

"You got a beautiful smile, Rhonda. I bet a lot of guys compliment you on that smile, don't they?" He waves the gun in my direction. "Don't let my friend here infect you with his shyness. You better than that."

The waitress stares at me, her eyes pleading. "Cat got your tongue? At least nod, for Pete's sake!"

Raphael pulls the waitress to her knees and crams the pistol against her temple. Shaking, she nods her head vigorously.

"Yeah, I bet a lot of married guys like that smile, too. Rhonda, you like when married guys compliment you on your smile? Oh, I bet you do. I mean the reason you got a divorce was 'cause you cheated on him with another married guy, that so?"

"I don't know what you are talking about!" she screeches, her eyes wide, her body trembling.

"Sure you do, Rhonda! You like married men. Say it!" Raphael grins. He cocks the hammer on his pistol. The waitress sobs, her buxom chest heaving.

She takes a long deep breath and then babbles loudly, "I'm sorry! I didn't mean—"

"Oh, but you did, Rhonda! You did! Why him, though? That's what I want to know. Out of all the strands of all the souls, why latch on to my boy here? Hmm? It because my boy here sorta still married? Getting cheap thrills? Maybe someone to relate to, that it? You forming a little cheater's club? My mother never got the invite. And she would have loved to have been a part of it! I bet just like her you realized the world weren't good enough so you have to go hanging around married men in this bizarre sort of afterlife? Or you trying to get him to stay here? I bet you the reason he still here in the first place. Who wants to bet?"

"No!" Her voice has reached fever pitch. "I would never! I was only trying—"

"You were letting your demons make a fool of you, and now you trying to make a fool out of us. But 'cause I like you, Rhonda, I gonna give you a second chance."

Raphael forces her cheek onto the table, her face turned toward me. His pistol still presses against her temple.

Raphael's voice turns gravelly. "Now, tell me the reason you here!"

"He is my friend," the waitress whispers. "He took care of me. He believed heaven would accept me."

"Home wreckers don't go to heaven. I learned that from my mother," he says to her.

With one hand still on her face, Raphael replaces the hammer and lays the pistol on the table. He grins, his white teeth brilliant against the ebony of his skin. "I didn't even load it! Good one, right?" He lets out a belly laugh.

The waitress and I simultaneously relax our shoulders and exhale. Raphael lets go of her head, and she jumps to her feet. Raphael's laughter fizzles.

I relax into my chair.

Like lightning, Raphael grabs my hatchet, turns to the waitress, and downs the blade on the top of her forehead. She drops to her knees and falls onto her side.

I leap toward her, knocking his chair over. But I'm too late. Blood pools under her head, matting her hair and spreading across the cherry-wood floor. Her limbs jerk, but it's only a reflex. She's dead.

Raphael puts my hatchet back on the table. "Looks like you're getting the hang of this." He chuckles, pointing at my newly formed-again hand.

I don't bother looking as my eyes have sight of the folded paper beside Raphael.

The reflection of the hourglass in the silver dome flips over.

Forty minutes.

I quickly snatch the paper and race out the door.

In subzero temperatures and with my breath billowing like a steam engine, I sprint across the street to the subway and slip between the closing doors of the train car. The air warms as the train moves forward.

The dark walls of the subway tunnel whiz by outside my window. Ahead, the door between the cars slides open. I run in, sit at the first seat I see while unfolding the paper in my hand. I hurry to find where I stopped last and begin to read:

As each day slowly passed by, I became more aware of the sins that haunted me from within that tree. Even the music started to portray me, learning that once all five songs were played, it would then repeat again from the beginning, making me recount everything all over. Each time I found something new about myself that I despised. I was a selfish greedy little man that only thought of himself. Watching that person everyday made me realize my memories weren't some big love story but a greek tragedy. It was then I knew what this place was to me - My Hell.

I turn it over and the page is blank.

That can't be it.

Raphael walks through in his gaudy violet suit, the cyan Ten of Spades still on display in his jacket pocket. He saunters down the aisle and sits beside me.

Striking a match from the silver filigree and gold matchbook, he lights a cigarette. After a long draw, he hacks like somethings stuck in his throat. Still coughing, he turns his face toward mine. He intersperses his coughs with laughter as he sprays saliva over me.

"I told you that you weren't ready."

He takes what's left of the burning match, lights the paper in my hand, and smacks it to the ground.

He's gone too far. I leap to my feet and force him to the floor. I land a couple of hard blows on his face. He continues his coughing, infused with laughter.

I rise just enough to place some strategic kicks in his stomach and ribcage.

"Tell me. Is this because of the waitress?"

I go for another punch but he blocks. I can tell by his huge smirk that he's done playing around with me. He tosses me to the side and stands back up.

"You can't trust dirty souls like her! She will feed off your humanity. Making you think she cares for you…"

He takes a long drag from his cigarette.

Just like a mom.

He looks at me almost stunned.

"My mother cheated and I found out. No news there. I prided myself on keeping the secret from my father. Holding that one thing over her shoulder made me feel powerful. She gave me anything and everything I asked for. Just so I wouldn't tell. Then one day I asked for a pack of smokes. Just because I wanted to test my full power over her. She hated when my father smoked and just smoking in general. If she did this, I would know I had her. Anyways she left to go get them and never returned. Maybe that was the last straw."

Raphael just stands there in silence. His soft eyes alone show an emotion I never thought he could express.

The subway car fills with the sound of mashing piano keys.

It must be 42:02.

The music grows louder. Raphael clambers up and starts flailing his limbs in a clumsy dance. What is he doing?

He bumbles closer to me and flicks his cigarette into my face, blinding me.

"Heads up!" Raphael shouts.

I clear enough ashes from my eyes to make out Raphael's form. He swings my hatchet and slices it clean through my neck. Electric blue light beams from my neckline.

My head makes its way to the ground as everything around me breaks into puzzle pieces and my vision is enveloped in a blinding white flash.

TWENTY-THREE

rees sway lightly in the breeze, vibrant with twinkling icicle lights and strands of white Christmas bulbs. Despite the winter chill, hundreds of hearty souls fill the park, chatting with each other. Just past the crowds is a brightly lit, glassed-in pavilion. Inside the pavilion, people sit at rows and rows of tables elaborately set and adorned with Christmas decorations. About one hundred yards to the left of the pavilion are hundreds of seats, mostly filled, set up in front of a large stage.

I make my way through the crowds into the pavilion. I brush the lapel of my cheap tuxedo, making sure everything is absolutely perfect. A clock at the far end of the space reveals I'm running late. The guests talk and laugh as the wait staff clears dirty dishes and offers champagne flutes on dainty trays. It looks like Madi may already be done eating. She's nowhere in sight.

I turn back and exit the pavilion, stepping out under the night sky. The crowd gathered near the stage is applauding loudly.

"Bravo! Bravo!"

"Encore!"

"One more!"

My heart races, and a lump forms in my stomach. *I can't be that late, can I?*

Madi steps out from behind the curtain, the spotlight illuminating her glittery white dress. Her smooth brown skin and dark hair form a stunning contrast to the flowing gown.

A hush falls over the audience as she sits by her piano and begins to play. Madi looks out over the crowd and parts her full, red lips.

"This one's for a special someone of mine. Who taught me why I should play again."

She puts her hands on the keys and begins. The piano's melody carries through the thin winter air, sending a thrill across my skin. The crowd is silent, embracing it all in as well.

That's it, Madi, you are doing it. I walk along the rear of the crowd, but keep my eyes on the stage, watching Madi's every movement, every expression. Her music reaches deep down to my core.

I find an empty seat on the left side and lower myself into it.

The man seated next to me leans over and says, "Great girl you got there."

The man's black, jaw-length hair peeks out from under a dark green fedora. His nose is refined, and he has narrow-set eyes and a square jaw. His fur-lined leather coat and wool scarf say he comes from money.

"Thanks." Who is this guy, and how does he know Madi is my girl?

"I'm glad she finally got over her stage fright." He leans forward in his seat, resting his elbows on his knees. "Outside of church, that is."

Madi moves across the stage like she's been doing this her whole life. "Yes. Very good thing."

"I hear you had something to do with that?"

"I signed her up for this gig, to tell you the truth." The notes flow from her delicate key strokes in perfect arrangement.

"Please do."

"Actually, she hasn't really spoken to me since the week I told her about it."

The man's face has a taciturn, but sympathetic, expression.

Madi smiles as she hits the chorus. "Worth it, though," I say.

He sits up and turns toward me with an extended hand. "I'm Peter. A childhood friend of Madi's."

I shake his hand. "Always great to meet a friend of Madi's." Life must've put this guy through the ringer. His face is weathered, and I would've pegged him as bit older if I didn't know otherwise.

"I always said her voice needed to be heard. She's been truly blessed."

"Yes, she has."

Madi plays the last note, and the crowd erupts with admiration.

Peter leans in toward my ear and yells above the din, "You know I tried to sign her? You know how stubborn she is, though." He shakes his head.

I give him a polite smile and nod as Madi offers a graceful curtsey.

Peter continues, "She never talked about me?"

"No, I'm sorry. She never has."

Madi exits the stage, and the audience drops its volume to a consistent murmur of conversation.

"Yeah, I guess that makes sense. My parents moved when we were kids, and we lost touch."

"That's too bad."

He's got his full attention on me now. "So, what, may I ask, do you do?"

"Sales." Well, it *was* true. No need for a stranger to know my current state of affairs.

"Salary with commission, I hope." Peter laughs. "Times are tough. Sales isn't what it used to be."

"Isn't that the truth?" Who does this guy think he is, implying I'm broke? "I've also been working on a novel."

Peter's eyebrow arches. "Oh, yeah? For how long?"

"A year." No need for him to know it's been five times that long. "Give or take a few months."

Peter smiles wryly. "Well, you know what they say, right?" He reaches into his inner jacket pocket. "Rome wasn't built in a day. Here's my card. If you're serious about writing, give me a call. I can contact a friend of mine who'll steer you in the right direction."

I grin. "Hey, thanks!" I pocket the card without looking at it.

The crowd noise increases as people rise from their seats and gather near the front of the stage. Madi's there, smiling and shaking hands, now wearing a heavy coat over her gown.

Peter nods toward her. "She's a star and doesn't even know it."

He focuses on something far away. "There's always been something holding her back, though."

I furrow my brows at him. "Oh, yeah?"

He looks back at me and smiles. "I'm glad she's with a decent man. Maybe you'll help her get past it and she'll finally give serious thought to going on tour."

"Tour?"

"Yeah. I'm a record company executive."

Maybe I should've looked at that card.

"Madi's mom told me she was playing tonight. I came to see if she still has that special something." Peter looks just past me and waves. A waitress approaches, carrying a tray of full champagne glasses. "And she still does." Peter takes a glass, nods to the waitress, and sips at the flute.

This man could actually do something for Madi, way more than anything I could ever do. Them being old friends, they already share a positive connection. And although it looks like he's been through hell, he's not entirely unattractive. I pull his card out of my pocket.

Peter J. Cameron

"Nice ring to it, right?" Peter grins. "Moving to Los Angeles changes more than just your way of thinking."

What's that supposed to mean? I nod and slide the card back into my pocket. "I guess so."

"A whole new frame of mind."

If Madi decides to tour with this guy, I'll never get her back. I turn toward Peter and blurt out, "She won't do it!"

Peter's eyes widen. "What makes you so sure?"

"I don't know. Leaving to go on tour? For months at a time? Not up her alley."

"Well, I hope you don't mind. I came here to give it my best shot. Anything else Madi is interested in is up to her. Just know her face was meant to be on a billboard!"

I stand and extend my hand. "Nice meeting you, Mr. Cameron."

"You too. And call me Peter. You're very lucky. What was your name again?"

"I'm sorry, did I not give it? I'm bad at that. My name is—"

Peter's cell phone rings. He looks at its screen and says, "I gotta take this. Tell her I send my love." He puts the phone to his ear, turns his back to me, and walks toward the parking lot.

Probably something important, something that involves a lot of money. I sigh.

I sit down again and slump over. Taking one more look at Peter's retreating figure, I finger the card in my pocket. Is that a monster truck he's getting into? He *would* be that rich.

Madi looks to be rushing through her conversations, moving from one person to another while scanning the surrounding area. She spots me, recognition lighting up her face. After shaking one more hand, she slips around the rest of the milling public and makes a beeline for me. Behind her, the Ferris wheel towers over the park, with happy young couples riding its circuit. *How little do they know.*

"I did it!" she shrieks as she gets closer. "I did it!"

I try to force a congratulatory smile, but my affect is flat. Who do I think I am, dating a girl like Madi, when she could have someone like Peter?

A voice whispers, *Madi is better than you. You'll never be worthy of her.* I shake my head and shut my eyes tightly. *Get out of my head!*

Madi glances behind her, reaches into her jacket, and removes a steel flask. She unscrews the top, takes a quick swig, and hands it to me. "I think my lucky flask did the trick! Don't you? Let's get drunk and ride the Ferris wheel! What do you say?"

I keep the flask at waist level.

She laughs uncomfortably. "What's wrong?"

"Nothing. I guess this means you're not mad at me anymore," I mutter. "Let's go up." I hand the flask back to her.

She takes my hand, and we walk silently to the looming attraction. The line has died off, and we enter a car immediately. The wheel turns smoothly, raising us slowly to its peak.

"It looks like you need an early Christmas present," Madi says, revealing a small wrapped gift box. "I tried to surprise you! I picked this up today. So...surprise!"

"Madi, I—"

"I can't wait five more days!" She thrusts the box into my waiting hands. "I'm way too excited!"

I set the gift box on my lap and play with the wrapping. Once we reach the top, the ride stops. The park sparkles with the light of hundreds of twinkling lights. In the center of the glorious display is a large, dead tree with a gaping hole at its base. I sigh, reach inside my jacket pocket, and retrieve a cigarette and a matchbook. After lighting the smoke, I take a long drag, hopeful that the calming effect of the nicotine will take over.

"What's going on?" Madi's voice is soft but serious. "I thought you were quitting!"

The ride jolts into motion again. I exhale a trail of smoke and reach for Madi's flask. She pulls it back, holding it beyond my grasp.

"Not everyone can be like you, Madi."

"What does that mean?" Music plays through the park, swelling and abating, stringed instruments blended with woodwinds and piano. *It's the music from the subway.*

I frown, lifting my face back to the cold winter sky. A few stars reach through the thick glow of the park. "Have you ever seen the northern lights? I've only seen them once, when I was a child."

"I think so."

"They're beautiful. All of the different hues engulfing the night sky. Everything becomes one dynamic canvas with many shades of green."

"Maybe we will see them together someday?" Her voice lifts a little. She nuzzles in beside me. "That is, if you make it past the age of thirty with this terrible smoking habit. I am not going to help you kill yourself anymore."

"What does that mean?"

"It means, I guess I love you too much."

"Nobody told you to save me," I say a little too gruffly. I'm not sure how anyone could measure up to her expectations and ideals.

"What are you talking about?"

"Forget it."

"This is all because I said I love you again, isn't it?"

I throw my cigarette out into the night. "Your dreams are so big, Madi, and I've been in a rut with my writing."

"That's okay." She puts her hand on my sleeve.

"I can't think! You're suffocating me!" Gah! She's so needy. Always afraid Jacob is going to come for her. She's a grown woman, for God's sake! Grown...and talented. With her piano skills, she's going to make it big. There's no way she stays with me once she's famous.

"Where did this come from?" Madi asks.

I raise my voice. "You have to understand this, Madi. Jacob is not coming after you! You changed your name. You even changed states. You hide away from your past, trying to better yourself. You changed your whole life because of this man!"

"What has that got to do with your smoking, or your writing, or what you're feeling right now? I'm doing my best to deal with my past, which was really painful. Why are you talking about it like this?"

"You're letting him win! He is still beating you, and you can't see it!"

"Don't make this about me."

"What am I supposed to make this about, Madi?"

"You know I'm getting help," she says quietly.

"For the past four years, you have been getting help!" I roar. People in the adjacent cars crane their necks to look at us. I lower my voice. "When is all that time going to pay off?"

"I don't know."

"Because I can tell you right now, if I was paying for those sessions—"

"But you're not! I am!" Madi hisses, stilling my fury. "You have no idea how it feels to have something like that in the back of your mind. I'm sorry that it bothers you! But that's not what this is about, is it? You're afraid of what we have. Once again. This is about your fear, not mine."

"That's not true!"

"It's not?" Madi softens her face, the anger melting away. "Just because your father couldn't manage the words 'I love you' doesn't mean you can't."

I look away.

She places her soft, gloved fingers on my chin and gently turns my face back toward her. "I am so sorry. I didn't mean to say that. I just want you to talk to me. Say what you are feeling and stop closing me off all the time."

I lower my head and mumble, "Nowhere can a man find a quieter or more untroubled retreat than in his own soul."

"And who said that?" She frowns, her forehead puckered.

"Marcus Aurelius."

"That's great! Hide behind your quotes and books."

"I'm not hiding." But she's probably right.

"You abstract your feelings by quoting books! Maybe if you spent more time writing and less time memorizing quotes, you would learn to make one up for yourself, to speak for yourself for once!"

The ride begins another descent.

Madi hugs herself. "What do you want? You want to be that man up there in his hundred-thousand-dollar-a-month suite? You want to wear tailored suits, drive sports cars, and be served gourmet meals every day?"

"What's wrong with that?"

"You know where that life gets you?" Madi screams, unconcerned with the attention she is drawing. "A whole lot of money in solitude. Is that what you want?"

"I lost my job today!" I shout, and turn away, unable to face her.

Her voice becomes compassionate and confused. "Wait! What happened?"

The black cavity of the dead tree fuels the pain in my stomach.

"You were late again, weren't you?"

"Does it matter?" I turn a little farther away.

"How do you think you can be somebody if you can't even be on time for important things like work?"

"And who are you to judge?" I whip around and face her. "You sit back and avoid the opportunities laid out before you."

"What are you talking about now?"

I pull Peter's card from my pocket and place it in her hand.

"What is this?" She looks at the card, flipping it over and back. "Peter Cameron? A record producer from Los Angeles?"

"He is the guy I can never be. He says he's interested in working with you on a tour. He thinks you can be a star." I cross my arms and stare into the night.

"Don't give me that!" Madi throws the card back at me. It flutters to the floor of the car.

"Someone like you deserves a guy like that."

"I don't know where all this self-pity comes from! But don't tell me what or who I deserve! I think I know what and who I deserve!"

"Oh, yeah? What do you deserve?"

Her voice becomes hauntingly calm. "I deserve to know if you love me or not. We've been together for almost a year, and sometimes I feel like you are never going to tell me what you feel."

"This again?" I narrow my eyes at her, and my skin flushes.

"Maybe you just don't feel it with me." Tears pool in her big, brown eyes. "If you think I'm holding you back from being a better you, then I'll leave. I would do that…because I love you."

I hunch over, snatch Peter's card from the floor, and crumple it. Why does she make me so angry? Madi's my everything, but those three words feel like a cage. The ride comes to an end. We exit and walk along a concrete path that skirts the entertainment area. After almost five minutes of silence, Madi wipes the tears from her eyes and glances at a small group of people gathered near the stage.

"I guess I should say goodbye to the producer and musicians," she says, composing herself. "I guess I'll see you later." She turns and strides away.

I sit down on a bench along the path. I smooth out the business card, take out my wallet, and reluctantly slide it inside. The pain in my stomach intensifies as Madi shakes hands and hugs people on stage.

She is going to change the world someday, and she doesn't even know it. I'm still holding the gift box in my left hand. Hesitantly, I pull on the red bow, and lift off the lid. There's a silver cloth bag folded on top of whatever is underneath.

I remove it, revealing a watch with a black face and white numerals. Not too fancy, but not shabby either. I carefully lift it out of its plastic molding and turn it over. There is an inscription on the back.

I believe in you.

I try to swallow the lump that has formed in my throat. Tears balance precariously on my eyelids. I sniffle and cough to keep myself from losing it.

Madi is just finishing a conversation with a couple.

Can she feel my gaze? Is she trying to keep herself from looking back at me?

Energy floods my muscles, and the urge to run to her overcomes me. I dash down the aisle toward the stage.

As I near, I blurt out, "I love you, too!"

Madi and those around her turn toward me.

"What?" Madi says, her eyes wide.

Those in proximity smile and whisper to each other.

She closes the distance between us and whispers, "What? What did you say?" Light dances in her eyes.

"I want to be that someone who makes you feel like you are the most important person in the world, because in my world…" All inhibition has left me, and I'm raw and honest, perhaps for the first time in my life. "Because in my world, you already are, and I love you for that."

Madi beams. Her small laugh rings through the air, and tears stream down her cheeks. She embraces me tightly. We hold each other, closer than we have ever held each other before. But as I embrace her, the black, dead tree haunts me from across the park. A violent shiver wracks my body. I let her go and hold her at arm's length. "Let's ride it again."

Madi pulls the flask from her coat pocket and places it in my hand. It's inscribed with the words, *Après moi, le déluge.* The same flask I took away from my father years ago. He never could put it down. Now neither can I.

"I some how knew you would be needing this," Madi says through her tears.

I raise the flask to my lips.

"Sadly, I can't drink tonight…"

I invite the heat of the intoxicating brew, but the liquid is cool and bland. It's water. I crinkle my brows.

"Or any night for the next six months."

The flask clatters to the ground as my jaw goes slack.

"I have been trying to find a way to tell you...I'm pregnant."

Beyond her, the dark center of the tree sucks me in. My body turns cold and hollow, as if in that moment my life and soul were taken from me. A beeping sound comes to fruition, and everything goes black.

TWENTY-FOUR

luorescent lights buzz overhead. The sound mixes with an engine hum and the clacking of heavy, metal cars zooming over steel tracks. My watch stops beeping. I open my eyes to find I'm back on the subway train. I turn over to see that Raphael is gone and the hatchet is lying next to me. I feel around my head, seeing it's all there.

I hadn't imagined him chopping my head off, had I?

I lower my hatchet-wielding arm and stand up. The light from the next station floods into the car. The brakes squeal, and the train decelerates to a stop.

A chill runs through me.

But the hourglass reflecting in the window confirms I'm right on time. The doors open, and I wave off the sensation as I walk out, hatchet in one hand.

I move away from the train. The gray concrete beneath my feet serves as a backdrop to the thoughts racing across my mind. I am a father. A sudden surge of pride moves through me.

I ascend a set of stairs to exit the station. I push through the doors. Across the street is the Lighthouse Restaurant. Beyond that is the park and the interstate, and, past that, my apartment building. This is the same station at which I just boarded!

Raphael must've sped up the train somehow and circled me back to this point!

Clouds of vapor form with each breath I take. Looking back, I see that the train car has already left the station.

What do I do?! If I don't get in the right time zone fast the reapers won't think twice about erasing my memories. I can't let that happen.

I panic and run toward the park. Screeching sounds come from all sides. I could try for my car, like last time. But who am I kidding? The reapers will have me way before I ever reach it. The hatchet weighs heavy in my hands. If I could stop and think, I might find a way to survive this.

My feet pound the ground. What have I got to work with? The Ferris wheel is up ahead, but what good will that do me? About ten feet away, the inky chasm of the dead tree yawns at me. It's my only option for escape. Snow falls gently in the short gap between me and salvation.

Three reapers fly down in front of me, forcing me to adjust my direction back toward the subway. Three more reapers land near the subway entrance.

Now the Ferris wheel is the only direction still clear. Perhaps I can defend myself somehow once I'm on the ride.

I toss the hatchet into one of the passenger compartments and jump in. The monstrosity groans into motion, lifting me upward. Cold wind brushes through my hair and blows snow into my eyes. When I reach the top, the machine stops.

The reapers probably froze the engine.

The northern lights swim among the twinkling stars.

I jolt up. At the bottom of the Ferris wheel, six reapers stand, looking up at me with their laughing skull masks. They extend their bony feet to the ground. The whole park slowly freezes over, turning it into one big ice skating rink.

The reapers climb the structure, and the cars ice over.

As the deadly ice reaches my car, the lyrics to "Wheels on the Bus" play through my head. The Ferris wheel must rotate on a seventy-one-ton, forty-five-and-half-foot axle that is freezing over as I think. The only way I can make it back to the apartment is if an extreme amount of force breaks that axle, which would, hopefully, roll me back home. Hopefully.

The cast-iron spider that makes up the core of the Ferris wheel hasn't yet turned to ice. I shove the hatchet into my waistband, positioning it so it won't impale me. I leap from my seat to the nearest spoke and make my way to the core of the wheel. Once the reapers see that I am trapped in the center, surely, they'll come for me.

The reapers swarm over the structure, pushing their skeletal bodies toward the middle. With every push, they break away a little more of the wheel's axle. The whole structure teeters. *That's it, keep making your way toward me.* With a great crash, the Ferris wheel detaches and slowly begins to roll.

Picking up speed, it tumbles across the ice-covered park and onto the interstate toward my apartment. The centrifugal force presses the reapers to the circumference of the great circle. As the frame rotates along the asphalt, the reapers touch their feet to the interstate, freezing the road and enabling the wheel to continue gaining speed.

The wheel bobbles off course, exiting to the right instead of the left. If the park is on the left side of the interstate, then what was on the right again?

Just ahead, the asphalt gives way to a waterless dam. The wheel plummets over the edge. I cling to the spindly structure of the wheel as freezing air rushes across my face. The perimeter bounces and skids on the side of the dam. Each passenger car shatters against the cement wall as it hits it. The reapers take to the air.

Vibrations from the collisions with the wall fracture the spindles, and the internal structure of the wheel loses integrity. I clamor to hold onto anything still stable, but fail and plunge through the air.

The ice has completely encased the outer edge of the wheel. It forms a shape more akin to a car tire than a Ferris wheel. I land inside the frozen track. It tosses me along as the wheel spins toward the bottom of the dam.

I brace my legs, trying to right myself. My feet slide on the ice. The cleats in my shoes extend, and I dig in. In a fraction of a second, I leap up and run like a hamster in an enormous hamster wheel.

The reapers dash back and forth at me, leaving ice trails to shatter as the wheel plows through them. I dodge every known attack I can see and keep moving.

One swoops in close, its arm reaching for me. I pull the hatchet from my waistband and chop its arm off.

A sharp sting blasts through my left calf. There must've been one coming from behind! A bony hand is wrapped around my shin. My left leg freezes over, now secured to the wheel's rim.

For one rotation, I struggle to free myself from the reaper. It's futile. Instead, I swing the hatchet toward my frozen leg. It severs, and the wheel carries the reaper far down the circuit.

I somersault along the ice track. The reaper and my leg are making the round back to me. I have to repair myself!

I think about being a father, and a sudden warmth surrounds my left leg. I try to watch as my leg reforms like puzzle pieces coming together.

I did it!

I turn my head to see how much time I have left to jump out, only to realize it's already too late.

The Ferris wheel collides with the bottom of the dam. For a moment, I hover over the ground, energy building beneath me.

My head snaps backward as my body is yanked forward. The jolt throws me up like a rocket lifting off to space. I'm propelled off the wheel, icy wind raking across my face. I shut my eyes against the frigid blast. Gravity takes over, and my momentum changes direction. The sudden splat of my body against the solid surface of the dam takes my breath from my lungs.

Lying on my back, I watch as the frozen wheel casts a shadow above me. It begins to slowly tilt over in my immediate direction. Every little thing that is still left inside comes crashing down around me. I try to scramble out of its way, but I already know the outcome. I stop and close my eyes, giving into my sealing fate. I hear the ride from hell screaming from above as it makes its way down to greet me. Suddenly, a shadowed figure stands over me, the golden pendant coin shines around his necklace. The mysterious person lifts me up, making the golden coin shimmer closer to my eye site. I trace my eye's around the hourglass engraved in the pendant until everything fades to black.

TWENTY-FIVE

I open my eyes. The aurora borealis billows high above deck chairs and tables placed around the apartment rooftop. What just happened? Who was that person? Where are the reapers? After a couple of seconds, I recover enough to walk to the telescope — my father's telescope. *I still have my memories. Why didn't the reapers erase them?*

After few seconds, I feel overjoyed. I did it. I don't know how, but I survived! I'm a soul survivor!

"You see…being prideful ain't all bad."

I turn to find Raphael standing right behind me. The golden pendant isn't hanging around his neck, letting me know right away it wasn't Raphael who saved me. But if he didn't save me then who did?

He laughs, strolls over, and claps me on the back. "You awoke today as a man not sure whether or how you could win this thing, a powerless man. Now look at you! I see you, brother! I see you! It good to see that you see you, too!"

I jerk at Raphael's voice and whirl to face him. *Was this a test?*
I charge toward him.

He spreads his bulging arms open. I tackle him to the ground and punch his face. I land blow after blow. Mama's sweet smile fills my mind. I left her in that room with my father, her cries pouring through the window. I pound Raphael's face harder. Blood spews with every impact.

I'm a father, and I have no idea what my child looks like. My fists slam into his face.

Raphael takes it like he deserves it.

The Ferris wheel, the reapers—I could have had my memory erased again! *You are messing with my life!* I tire and roll off of him. Seconds go by as Raphael gets back on his feet. He spits blood from his mouth and walks to the edge of the rooftop.

He looks out over the city. In a serious voice, he says, "How it grasps onto the most influential things, like this broken old telescope. Your daddy's ole toy. Always fascinated with the stars. He was a cowboy, your father. Never was much of a twentieth-century type of man like yourself. He just loved looking into it every night. Gave him peace of mind."

My breathing calms as I lie on my back. The lights dance and sway across the sky, their beauty unmatched by anything in the world.

Raphael hands me my flintlock pistol, "Best not ever lose this."

I forgot all about it. Feeling relieved, I stick the pistol back behind my pants.

Raphael saunters over to the telescope, taking out a cigarette. "I remember you telling me how Madi got so mad at you for selling this broken piece of junk. Kind of odd, ain't it? For her to get mad at something so meaningless? So pointless."

A thick, black hand fills my vision. Raphael silently offers to help me up. I don't move a muscle.

"Who are you really angry at?"

Raphael's green eyes hold a certain glimmer of truth in them. He waits, hand extended.

I'm angry at myself for giving up back there. Just like how I did during the race. I just let myself quit.

I take his hand and get to my feet.

Raphael lifts the elegant matchbook and lights his cigarette. He draws on his cigarette, looking up at the northern lights.

The gold filigree of the matchbook glints in the flickering light.

Madi gave me that matchbook on our date to the Lighthouse Restaurant.

Other objects in this world are familiar, too. The engraved flask in my coat pocket is the one I was drinking from in the park, when she told me I was a father. The Polaroid Michael carries, that was Mama's. What does it all mean?

In a calm voice, he says, "You choose what you suffer through."

He takes out another piece of paper from his back pocket and hands it to me.

He flicks his cigarette off the ledge and offers me back my hatchet. I grasp the handle, but he doesn't let go. He holds my gaze for a second before letting it go. He nods and walks toward the elevator, then turns around and faces the panel of buttons. "You wanna come push this for me?"

I stand immobile. *Funny.*

He laughs. "That's my boy." He presses the button, and the door closes in front of him.

I quickly unfold the paper and begin to read:

But no matter how far I strayed I didn't let my demon beat me. I would risk my memories to the reaper before I would ever give in to it.

I then built the rest of my time here around reading the good book and writing the novel I never could finish in the real world. After awhile my mind felt more at peace. With that clarity I began to see the flaws to my prison where I soon then learned about my trial. One race to set me free.

I attempted the race numerous of times, always losing. If the Reapers didn't catch me my demon sure would. When my memories got erased the music would help me remember myself again and I would do it all over again. An endless cycle that constantly repeated itself for what felt like years. After awhile I began to feel like my fathers telescope. Broken with no chance of ever getting fixed. Eternity has found me but I will never give up hope. I swore an oath to God, that I would never fall prey to what I was before. That when I reach my finish line, I will choose love every time.

I wonder how many times I have read this over the scope of my time here?

Scope?

Turning my head back to the telescope, I have a curious suspicion as to why it could seem broken.

I walk over to it and unscrew the top scope. Inside the main cylinder is a small piece of dark cloth, folded in on itself. I carefully reach in and pull the cloth out.

It's wrapped around something circular and hard. I unfold it. Inside is a golden ring. It looks just like the ring I saw Uriel wear. Why is it hidden in here? I must have known I would search this scope. This could be my key! Perhaps I hid it so my demon wouldn't get its hands on it.

The golden shine from the ring oddly hypnotizes me. My thoughts become empty and my body feels weightless. Time feels as if it is standing still and yet I know it has done no such thing. My body feels like it's heating up all of a sudden.

What is this feeling? It's not a feeling of guilt or remorse? Like a raging passion of some sort. A craving of desire. Is this what love feels like? It can't be, could it? Maybe Michael was right. My humanity does feel like it's slowly starting to come back to me.

I rewrap the ring in the cloth and place it back in the scope. It's been safe here so far; better it stay that way.

My watch beeps as I screw back on the lid the hourglass on the edge of the roof has drained its last particle of sand and yet all I can think about is her.

I'm losing it. I don't really even know her but I can't help but feel this certain way. I need to calm myself back down, but I can't. I think about her warm comforting smile and my heart races, letting me know I've fallen in love with her all over again.

♣ ♠ ♦ ♥

There's a rest-stop sign up ahead. I turn on my right signal light.

"What are you doing?" Madi asks. Her knuckles turn white where she's gripping the door handle.

"Madi, it's getting way too bad out there. I have to pull off like everyone else is doing."

"We can make it; just slow down a little. We're almost there!"

"Madi, we have like forty-two minutes before we're home. We won't make it!"

Madi opens her purse, pulls out a small orange bottle of prescription anxiety medicine, and removes two pills. Tilting her head back, she hits her open palm against her mouth, throwing them back into her throat. She swallows and breathes in and out slowly and deeply.

I start to pull the car to the right.

"I can't do this!" Madi growls.

Snow blows furiously past the headlights and over the hood of the car.

I respond in a calm but firm voice, staring straight ahead of me, "Madi, stop this."

"Daddy?" asks a small voice from the backseat. I shift the rearview mirror to see my six-year-old daughter, Anna, sitting patiently behind me.

"Yes, pretty girl?"

"I'm hungry."

Madi opens the glove compartment, finds a sucker, and unwraps it. Keeping her eyes on the road ahead, she reaches back to Anna.

"Here you go," Madi says. "We won't be home for quite a while."

Anna stretches forward, trying to reach it. Her arm is too short, and she unbuckles her seatbelt.

"Got it!" she says victoriously, grasping the white stem and popping the sucker into her mouth. "Thanks, Mom!"

Madi nods. Her eyes remain fixed on the road.

"I can't," Madi says quietly to me. "I can't do this!"

"You need to calm down, Madi."

"I'm sorry."

"Listen to the music. Do what Dr. Wiser told you to do."

She breathes slowly in, narrowing her eyes.

A vehicle parallels us in the right-hand lane. It's a utility truck carrying plate glass windows.

The snow pelts harder against the window. A distant beeping grows louder and fills my ears.

URIEL

WEDNESDAY

TWENTY-SIX

jolt upright in bed to the sound of my alarm. Something's different about the back of my neck and face. I run my hand around my head. My hair's longer—it almost touches my shoulder—and I have a full beard.

A bright light shines through the curtains, muting the rest of the bedroom. The leather-bound Bible is tragically still resting on my nightstand. I shove it off.

In the periphery of my left eye, there's a body-shaped lump under the covers next to me. When I went to bed last night, I was alone, wasn't I? The only woman I've met in this place is the waitress...

I slowly pull back the blanket and sheet, exposing a long, blond ponytail; smooth, flawless, lightly-tanned skin; and a closely trimmed jawline beard. The man's eyelids pop open.

I scramble out of bed and run to the other side of the room, covering my genitals with my hands.

Uriel sits up in the bed, the sheets falling down around his bare chest. He looks at me with a shocked expression and shouts, "Ah!"

After a moment, his face calms. He gets out of the bed, completely naked. He imitates me, covering his crotch, and grins.

In his thick Australian drawl, he says, "Morning, Gucci! Today will be your awakening." He strides to the window and peeks through the curtain. "Summa is the season of lustful behaviors and lurid imaginations. Hollywood weatha! Look where you are, Gucci. Gives heaven a run for its money, doesn't it? Better hurry and see it in the light before it's too late."

The light? The sun is out! When was the last time I saw the sun? When was the last time I even thought about the sun? I never thought this place could contain anything so pure, like the nonexistent water.

I inch toward the window, keeping as much distance from Uriel as I can, still covering my crotch. As I peek my head out the window, a dark shadow obscures the sun before I can get a glimpse of it.

What just happened?

"It's an eclipse, Gucci. Every Wednesday, it comes along and blots out the light"—he inflects *ight* as *oit*—"and lets the night last for the remainder of the day."

Figures. So close, and yet…

"In hindsight, it seems fitting, since the club we are going to is called Eclipse."

Club? What club?

Uriel ignore's my question, "Now, what to wear? What to wear?"

His clothing suddenly transforms into a navy blue tuxedo. His bowtie hangs untied around his collar, and his feet are bare. Wiggling his toes, he says, "I like my feet to feel free."

How did you do that?

Uriel turns and looks at his reflection in the closet mirror. "Hmmm…something's missing." He reaches inside the tuxedo jacket, removes a cyan and black King of Diamonds, and places it halfway into his outer pocket.

He keeps his face toward the mirror. "That was called the mirroring trick."

What's the mirroring trick?

Uriel goes through several pairs of sunglasses just like magic.

"I must say, this suit is the perfect shade of blue. Not too light, not too dark. Perfect bliss."

He parades across the bathroom and back. "Your turn, Gucci. Aren't you tired of wearing the same clothes all the bloody time?" he asks. "Day in, day out? Not this time. We are going to the hottest club in town tonight, so we must dress to the nines."

I don't understand. There isn't a club in town.

"Why, sure there is! Silly! How could you miss it? It's in the park between the Ferris wheel and the sexy statue man."

I take a moment and realize he is talking about the tree.

"Bingo! And your wardrobe is tragic. It simply won't work for me. So listen up!"

I jolt with excitement. Finally, I can understand who I really am or at least what sin I have committed that led me here. This news motivates me as I begin to listen carefully.

"That's the spirit! I heard you already went on Monday with Michael. Which got me super worried at first, but I'm glad you didn't stay long enough to witness the B side! My personal fave, by the…"

The player piano fills the apartment with its opening notes. Uriel's eyes start to twitch from the music. He begins rolling his ring around his finger like a strange tick.

"This depressing music has to go." Uriel retrieves a cassette tape from his pocket.

He leaves the closet and disappears into the bedroom.

The piano melody stops, and 90's pop music blares from the living room.

With his eyes steady on me, he sets his boombox down and snatches my Jack of Hearts card from his vest pocket. He holds the card up. "Keep your eye on the card. The trick is called mirroring."

He lays my card face up on the kitchen bar. With the other hand, he takes out a deck of cards, slides them from the case, and does a smooth, one-handed shuffle.

"You, sir, may be surprised to learn that you yourself are mirroring right now."

My eyebrows shoot up. *What's he talking about?*

He turns my card facedown. Smiling, he flips it back over. The card is now the King of Clubs.

"You don't believe me? How do you know that what you see in a mirror is actually you? Perhaps you just believe that what you see is true—it can't actually be verified. Astonishing, isn't it?" He transforms the King of Clubs back into the Jack.

I touch my face. *Is what Uriel says true?* If he's right, then my appearance could be just a mask, not what I really look like. But then, what do I really look like, and how would I know myself if I saw myself?

"If you're not dead and you're not alive, then what are you?" Uriel turns the card face down again. "You are the incorporeal essence of a person. The innermost aspect of a human, that which is of greatest value, that by which you are made in God's image—a soul. It has no shape or design. You see what you want to see, but truthfully, you're not seeing anything at all. You see what you choose to see. You take up no space. You have no volume. You have no mass. You are a consciousness contained in a bit of energy. Meaning you can look however you want to look! Be whoever you want to be!"

He flips the card back over, and it's the Queen of Hearts. "It makes you wonder who the waitress claims she is." Turning it again, he changes the card back to the Jack. "Think of a soul as if it were similar to clay. You can mold, shape, and create whatever image you can imagine." Over and over, he rotates through many of the face cards, using only my card. After setting it back to my Jack, he lays three other face cards beside it. I keep an eye out for mine as he shuffles them.

"If you don't look carefully, you might just miss it." He stops the shuffle. I point to the far left one. Uriel flips it over, and it's the Jack of Clubs. He flips the far right one over, and it's mine.

Uriel is now the spitting image of me. "Told you to look carefully." He shuffles the cards back into the deck. One by one, he turns over eight Jacks of Hearts.

Uriel mimics my every move, from a silent look across the dining hall to my brooding stares. I stop moving. Uriel changes his appearance back to himself. "Any questions thus far?!"

So wait. You literally choose to have a man bun?

He moves his hands around his hair, looking now insecure.

"I like to think this style matches well with my eye's."

That's another thing I have a question over. Why does everyone have the same green eyes as mine?

"Probably, because the last person we all tried to mirror was you. It's hard remembering to change the little things sometimes."

You've all looked like me?

"I've been you many times—we all have. When you first arrived, we all thought it would be easier if we mirrored your appearance. The reapers can be fooled, but only for so long, you see. They observe us very closely because we are, in a way, disobeying the order of things. Even a demon can be seen by a reaper."

They can see my demon too?

"It's getting harder to avoid their suspensions as of late. You see, souls bring out a light. That light inside you transmits enormous amounts of energy that reapers can detect." Uriel licks his finger and thumb and turns the eight cards over.

"Now reapers can't see too well toward lost souls because our light isn't as strong as yours. You still are connected mentally with your body on the outside world. Being a lost soul means we are no longer attached. Because our demons have full control of our bodies which makes our souls light weaker."

That's a good thing! That means they can't see you.

"Reapers have a way around that problem. They have hunting dogs that can sense when we are around. If we stay with you any longer than we do, they will begin to sense something is wrong and unleash the hounds. We have it down to a science. Only one lost soul can be with you for a certain amount of time. That is why you will never see more than just one of us with you. Mirroring as you also created problems with the reapers. The reapers almost caught me one time."

He laughs. "If they ever got one of us..." He looks at me "...dare I say what would happen? That is undoubtedly why we changed our image, so the reapers would stop thinking we were you." He flips back over the eight cards. Each is a different combination of face card and suit. He places them back in the deck, then flings it into the air. The cards fall around me.

"Thank you! Thank you! I will be here all night!" He gives a halfhearted bow.

Uriel looks at me top to bottom.

"No time to waste; it's time for a self-help makeover!"

Uriel skips to the next track on his boombox and plays, "I'm so excited," by The Pointer Sisters.

"Now let's start off small. Imagine wearing different clothes. Watch me."

Uriel suddenly is sporting a beach look.

"I even added a six pack to my abs! Just because I can! Now just imagine any style of clothing. Listen to the music, mate! Let it bring you inspiration."

I can't think of anything.

Uriel twists his ring, incessantly, "You are the hidden sixth singer to the Backstreet Boys, go! Unless NSYNC was more your style. No shame, mate."

I close my eyes and follow along with the music.

Uriel makes a high pitched scream, "Looking pretty fly, Gucci!"

I open my eyes back up to find I have on a 90s pop idol outfit. Baggy pants and all.

"Don't stop there Sugar Ray!" He begins to sing, "Come on Barbie, let's go Barbie."

One by one, I try on different suits: ranging from silly to outrageously bad.

For once, I'm actually having fun.

"Now you're getting into it. Let's go more James Bond."

I mirror my clothing into in a black tuxedo and fix my bowtie as best I can.

Uriel screams like a mom on prom night. "Gucci… I love it! A man that knows style."

As I leave the living room, the bathroom mirror reflects my brown, shoulder-length hair. What with the slight droop of my eyes and my soft jawline, I look like a bum who's ripped off a formal-wear joint. I push my hair back, off the shoulder of my tuxedo jacket.

Uriel steps in behind me. "Yuck. You need to fix all that, mate."

I close my eyes. I imagine my face without the beard and long hair. I open them now to see Uriel staring back at me with a questionable gaze.

"You're thinking about it too much. Try mirroring me."

I close my eyes and try to focus on looking like Uriel. I open them and look at the bathroom mirror. Nothing changed.

"Remember, you're just a soul. Souls do not have shapes or dimensions. You are only projecting an image to yourself because it's the only thing you know how to be. But your image is a choice. Just choose to be someone else. Watch."

Uriel transforms into Prince and sings off a few lyrics of "Purple rain"

I close my eyes and try again while Uriel transforms back.

I can do this. I can do this.

I open my eyes, waiting for Uriel's hopeful response.

"You still look like a tool, I'm afraid."

I turn to the mirror to see that it didn't work again.

He reaches for the Brylcreem, puts some in my hair, and combs it back. In a soft tone, he says, "If you don't love yourself first, then all you'll have is y'self."

Once done with my facial hair, he pulls a hair tie from my tuxedo pocket and secures my hair into a bun. "I've done all I can."

In the mirror, Uriel and I now look almost exactly alike.

Uriel places the Jack of Hearts card to stick out of my breast pocket. He twists the ring on his left hand with small, quick movements.

The ring is identical to the one in the telescope.

He flashes me a grin and whirls around, headed to the bedroom.

"Don't get mad, but I didn't want to roll up at the club with that 1980's cliché."

I run to the window and look out to see that my car has been crushed into a cube.

My car!

I want to yell Uriel's name at the top of my lungs.

He calls from the other room, "You're going to like what I picked up! Don't you worry your sweet face about it!"

I stare up as the darkness of the solar eclipse serves as a metaphor of my whole life.

Anything that brings a little bit of light is instantly covered in darkness.

He returns, holding up a sparkly, off-the-shoulder red dress, gliding across the floor as if he were in heels. "Do you think this dress makes me look fat?"

Is he being serious? The image of his naked body lying in bed next to me flashes in my mind. I gag. This lost soul seems to be on the loosey-goosey side. My watch beeps.

Five minutes.

"I kid," Uriel says to me, laughing. Still holding the dress, he opens the front door and exits. I follow.

He walks directly across to the waitress's door and knocks six times.

"I don't feel like getting a popsicle stuck up my bunghole today." Uriel laughs. "I'm still recovering from last time. Remember that night?"

What is he talking about? Whatever it is, I probably don't want to know.

"Hey, I barely remember it, either. Don't worry. It can be our little secret." He winks at me. "That's a joke. I kid. But not really."

With overwhelming joy in his voice, Uriel screams, "Your makeup's terrible!"

Her mouth drops in absolute shock.

Uriel throws the dress in her face. "You are going to look so much better. I swear to you." He pushes her back inside, the dress still half covering her face. "Don't wait up, Gucci, I have to fix this catastrophe. See you at the party!"

He slams the door.

I stand there for a few moments. *What exactly just happened?* Since there's not much I can do, I head for the elevator. It automatically opens, and I step inside. As the sliding doors close me in, a thought comes into my head.

Wait. I don't even have a car.

TWENTY-SEVEN

round me, men and women dressed to the nines laugh and chat amidst a haze of cigarette smoke. The cavernous room is filled with gaming machines that flash bright, electric colors. In a corner of the room is a set of burgundy curtains.

The casino.

I'm back.

I turn around. A thin, athletic woman walks through the crowd toward me. Her hair is cut in a chin-length bob, and her hoop earrings add to the glamour of her look. With each sway of her hips, her off-the-shoulder dress glitters as if it's made of rubies.

Lisa.

And her dress—the same dress Uriel threw at the waitress.

She hands me a drink. I take the glass, my body switching into auto-drive. The band in the corner begins to play classical music. It makes me think of my mother and how this style of music made her feel young again. I down my head, fondling over all the times

240

when she was teaching me how to dance in our small childhood kitchen home.

"So…how about that dance?" She smiles seductively and holds out her hand.

I down my drink and set the glass aside. Hand in hand, we maneuver through the crowd to a mostly open, hardwood dance floor. A few couples are waltzing around on the gleaming surface.

How great can this possibly get? The one dance I know.

I pull her into a confident hold, my right hand firmly placed between her shoulder blades, and extend my left hand. She relaxes into my frame, and we begin to dance.

Lisa leans in close to my ear. "You dance well. Who taught you?"

I stop to think. *Who taught me?*

Lisa's hands slowly transform into the hands of my mother. As we continue to glide across the floor, the room spins. My drink has taken its toll, wrapping my mind with delusions. I am now dancing with Mama. Youthful energy courses through me as my height shrinks and her height grows. We laugh and whirl around the whole place.

I rattle my head. After a few blinks, I whisper, "Mama?" perhaps to Lisa, perhaps to the memory of my mother. It doesn't matter. My younger self matures and expands to the man I am today. Still in my arms, Mama's smile crinkles her skin into stress-worn wrinkles I'd never noticed as a child. Her brilliant, laughing eyes that always made things better hold a glimmer of sorrow. She gazes at me with pride beaming from her pores. I stop our momentum, tuck her body in close, bend my knees, and gently lower her into an elegant dip.

Abrupt beeping rips through the moment. I know this sound from somewhere. It's a watch alarm. As I lift her out of the dip, Mama has changed back into Lisa.

Fake snow falls from the balcony as the next song plays. We continue to dance as the snow drifts around us. The flakes accumulate on her amber hair, and I press the bridge of my nose to her forehead. She smells delicious. Lisa giggles, and I pull her closer, stepping off of the dance floor and letting my hands slide to her hips.

Laser lights shoot across the dance floor and throughout the club. A eurodance track replaces the orchestral music, and men and women filter on and off the floor, gyrating and bumping to the beat. Bar waitresses carry trays of shots through the surrounding crowd.

Lisa slides her hands up my neck and behind my head. Her eyes glisten with desire. My hands glide across her tight abs and up the sides of her ribcage. I bring her lips close to mine. She puts her finger to them. "Shh…" Holding up a key with the number six on it, she motions to a set of elevators. She winks and whispers, "I'll be waiting." She hands me the key, swivels, and weaves her way through the crowd.

I grip the key, my heartbeat racing out of control. I can almost feel her bare, supple skin in my hands, my tongue tasting her pale pink lip gloss. Forcing my breathing to slow, I head to the elevator, attempting a casual stroll. The doors open, and I step in.

By the time I reach Lisa's floor, my inner thoughts have regained control of my body. In front of me is a hallway full of doors. This is where Michael stopped me last time I was here. He didn't want me to see what was behind door six.

The key disappears from my hand. Do I really want to know what's behind the door? As I get closer, the skinny little girl in the pale blue dress appears.

"You don't want to go in there," she says in a sweet, tiny voice.

I move past her, giving her a pleading look. "I have to." I grab the doorknob, turn it, and push through.

The room is extravagant, with high ceilings. Floor-to-ceiling bookcases line the walls. A brocade settee marks the sitting area, and a Yamaha Grand Disklavier occupies the corner. I don't have to look in the kitchen or the bedroom to know what's there. I've woken up in this place every day since I've been in my soul prison.

The number six key is now lying on the table next to the door. A wall clock above the piano moves from 3:09 to 3:10 AM.

Three-ten. The piano. It's somehow all connected to this specific moment. My head starts to hurt. The glittery red dress lies in a heap next to a pair of high heels. A tuxedo jacket, white shirt, and dress pants are strewn across the floor, as well. The pain in my head gets worse. Moans of passion penetrate the bedroom walls.

I sneak to the open bedroom door. Two people are entangled together within the bed sheets, their limbs writhing like snakes. I move closer to see that one of them is me!

In a blink of a second, I have become him. I'm lying down, weighted by a warm, undulating body. Amber hair is brushing up against my face. I lift my head to find Lisa looking back at me. I look around and see that we're alone. I face her again and smile before being overwhelmed by desire. I can't stop myself—she doesn't want me to stop.

A beeping sound rings in my ear.

I stagger backward. What have I done? I squeeze my eyelids shut and wring my hair with both hands.

TWENTY-EIGHT

y watch beeps.

Thirty-five minutes.

The lighting is dim and the air frigid. The walls are metallic, encased in a layer of frost. The meat locker? The red dress underneath me comes into focus. I push the body off and roll away. Instead of Lisa's slim form in the sparkling red dress, it's the waitress's voluptuous figure. Her exposed shoulder is covered in bruises that continue down to her elbow. She cowers, looking at me through dark waves of hair.

I point to her arm, questioning if I did that to her. She nods and shifts her gaze to the floor.

Behind me, Uriel sings Boyz II Men's "I'll Make Love to You," swapping out his Australian accent and mimicking the quartet.

I whirl around. Uriel stands by the door, holding a boom box on one shoulder and bobbing his head to his mix tape.

As he walks toward me, he dons his diphthongal speech again. "Gucci! You almost had her!" He slaps me on the back and laughs heartily. "Well, I lost the bet…again."

The waitress picks herself up and inches her way toward the door.

Uriel ejects the tape and turns it over. "What are you, an A-side or B-side type of guy?"

I narrow my eyes at him and scrunch my brows.

"A side or B side, eh? The two sides of a record. The hit songs or the secondary recordings that aren't played as much."

He presses play, and a upbeat song I don't recognize fills the meat locker.

"Me personally, I love the B side betta. Gives talent the ability to go off the rails. It's the surprise factor! Everything you thought you knew changes."

Uriel laughs again, while stepping back to intercept the waitress. He yanks her arm, shoves the door open, and pulls her through. "When you're done being a sook, meet us out here," he calls back.

Now that I'm alone my mind can only picture Lisa's naked body around mine. My heart feels guilt beyond repair.

I cheated. How could have done that to Madi? How?!

I seize the boom box and punt it into the wall. It shatters. I leave through the kitchen and push open the door to the restaurant. On one of the middle tables, another boom box plays a waltz. In the space between tables, Uriel dances with the waitress.

"Always carry a back-up, Gucci!"

I charge forward, about to smash the extra boom box. Blood runs down the waitress's leg, and I pull up.

"Hey, Gucci, did you know that divorce rate in America is fifty percent?" Uriel sweeps the waitress across the floor. She looks miserable but doesn't seem to resist.

"Twenty- to twenty-four-year-olds have the highest percentage of marriages that end in divorce. Don't beat yourself up about it. It's not worth it! She's not worth it. In this day and age, it's everyone for themselves. There are new rules to live by now. Whoever said marriage is foreya, they lied to you. Every man and woman cheats! Physically or mentally, it doesn't matter!"

No! He's wrong.

"I know what you're going through, Gucci. How do you think I ended up here? Sexual desire is in our blood. We can't control it. I even cheated. Though I would have taken different actions if I knew I was going to end up here. But the worst part is I never got the chance to tell her. I mean, how could I? She was pregnant with my second unborn child. It would have ruined her. Maybe that had something to do with me choosing to be a lost soul. I try not to think about it."

Uriel twists his ring while clutching the waitress closer to him. "I've heard the chatter from other lost souls. Soon there will be dating technology so advanced that marriage will be non-existent. You've started to notice the rise of technology before you even fell into your coma. Pagers turning into cell phones. Cassette tapes turning into CD's. The world is ever changing! Do you remember how you imagined all the people here, playing on their cell phones? How ironic to know that you just reimagined the future of the human race! Your brain is already thinking two steps ahead of you! Might as well catch up and get with the times. Why be with only one woman when you can be with an infinity! You could even try new things. Try a hotdog without a bun. I'm referencing a hotdog to a male penis. If you didn't catch the reference."

Uriel stops dancing. "Thank you for the dance, sweetheart." He kisses the waitress's hand and lets her go. The music comes to a stop.

Then he lifts a knife from a nearby table and jabs it into the waitress's eye. She doubles over and releases a blood-curdling scream, which is soon reduced to short, repetitive screeching. Holding her hands to her face, she stumbles around the tables, bumping into chairs while blood and eye fluid seep through her fingers.

Uriel turns to me. "Lust is blind. Get it? Some people can't see the truth until it's too late."

I stand motionless, my mouth agape. The silver dome reveals that the bottom half of the hourglass is almost full. I narrow my eyes at Uriel. He must be my demon.

"Don't look at me like that. I'm not your demon. I'm a realist. I'm looking toward the future not hiding away from it like you are."

Uriel laughs, watching the waitress continue to stumble and scream until she falls to the floor. I walk over to see that she had fallen head-first onto the hard floor. I quickly take the knife out just to find her dead.

I was too late again to help her.

"Do you think I personally wanted to kill the only chick in town? No, you did this to her."

I turn to face Uriel with my hand gripping the knife toward him.

"Deep down she reminds you of yourself. A weak and pitiful soul that is consumed by their past. A scared dingo of a baby, waiting for mama to come and make it all better."

You take that back!

"Do you ever wonder why you're still here? You choose to be. Maybe you're afraid of what's changed out there. Maybe you feel like you won't be smart enough to adapt. You had a hard time adapting to change before the coma. Why would this be any different? You keep finding ways to quit on yourself."

Surreptitiously, I reach down and turn off the notification sound to my watch.

"I'm not your demon, Gucci. I'm just a lost soul trying to open your eyes to the possible future that awaits you on the other side. It ain't going to be easy but it's a whole lot better than being a lost soul, I can tell you that much for certain."

He shudders. As his breath hangs in the air, his expression changes. I race to the kitchen, past the stainless-steel countertops and the commercial-sized sinks.

His voice booms from behind me. "What've you done?"

I slip inside the meat locker, lift the lever on the door, and slam it tight. Securely locked inside, I plant myself in front of the thick glass window in the door. Uriel bursts through the swinging doors into the kitchen. He spots me and runs to the door. He yanks on it, but the door holds fast.

"What're you doing?" he shouts. "What, you think I'm your demon? Really?" Uriel continues to pull on the door.

My watch displays forty-one minutes.

"The thermostat inside the meat locker quits cooling at forty-five minutes. What do you think happens after that?"

My hopeful plan has now backfired, leaving me afraid of what I should do next.

Uriel, still grinning like an idiot, yells, "I can only hold them off for so long!" and slaps his mix tape against the glass.

Frost spreads over the dining room doors. He shoves the tape in his boom box, presses play, and sets the player on the floor. He cracks his neck from side to side as Kenny Loggins's "Footloose" blares through the speakers.

He crosses the kitchen and takes up a defensive position away from the meat locker.

Maybe he isn't my demon, after all. I push the meat locker door open a couple of inches as Uriel runs back into the dining hall. He yells out, "Like the great Kevin Bacon once said, 'I thought this was a party? Let's dance!'" The chorus blasts through the kitchen door.

I slide out of the meat locker and out the back door.

I run down into the subway station, still hearing the music playing in the distance.

My watch shows 42:02. Breathing heavily, I sprint as fast as I can and leap through the closing doors of the subway car, landing splat on my face. The piano music carries me away as everything around me—the doors, the seats, the subway car—rips away into puzzle pieces.

TWENTY-NINE

A cold breeze blows across my face. Everything around me is dark, but a brilliantly lit city spreads out beyond a ledge twenty feet away. I'm up high—the rooftop of a building. It resembles the same rooftop as the one in my prison world. The ghoulish shapes of outdoor furniture dot the area. The tuxedo I'm wearing is a slightly different style from the one I wore in the casino, cheap but clean. A single sunflower is pinned to my lapel.

The bank tower clock across the street ticks down. Only fifteen minutes until midnight and the dawn of a new year.

My stomach flips and gurgles. I rush to the ledge and empty my stomach into the alley below. The clock shows fourteen minutes to midnight.

The elevator dings. I turn toward it. As the doors open, a man with a long, dirty-blond ponytail and a closely-trimmed jawline beard steps out. He's wearing a tux as well, still buttoning his jacket. It's Chris.

My body doesn't respond to my efforts to move. Here it goes again. My thoughts scramble as my memory-mind takes over.

"Chris! I'm over here!" I yell.

He stops buttoning long enough for a brief wave. "Nineteen-ninety-four is going to be the year of a new chapter in your life, mate!"

"You're late," I say weakly. My stomach somersaults again, and I lean over, resting my hands on my knees.

"Where are you? I can barely see up here."

"Over here!" I shout more forcefully.

Chris walks toward the sound of my voice. Within ten feet of me, he stops cold. A smug look washes over his face. "Hey." He snickers. "You party animal. What a great way to end the old year?"

I groan. "Yeah, real great."

"You okay?"

"I'll be fine." I straighten slowly. "Where is everyone?"

Chris points his thumb toward the elevator. "They're all down in the lobby." He steps closer and nudges me in the ribs. "And they'll be up in five."

I jerk. "In five? We're running out of time. Get the switch!"

This is what I get for being a procrastinator. Madi would have already set this whole thing up a month in advance and timed out everything perfectly. That's just another reason why I need her in my life. She helps me stay on time.

Chris disappears behind the elevator housing. His voice travels around the corner, almost drowned out by the wind. "That's the way!"

Nothing happens.

He reappears from behind the elevator. "That's not good. The lights should be on!"

The elevator dings again, and the doors open. The bridesmaid, April, is inside. She's slender and dressed in a sky-blue, sleeveless mermaid-style dress. In the light of the elevator, the dress sets off her light blonde hair and striking blue eyes. She wraps her arms tightly around her torso as another cold breeze hits the rooftop.

I rub the back of my neck vigorously and shout to Chris, "Check it again!"

Chris strolls past the open doors and leans into them ever so slightly. "I've never seen an angel in an elevator before."

April frowns. "In your dreams," she hisses and walks out onto the rooftop. The elevator doors close, and it moves down the shaft again.

April steps closer to me, her face in shadows. "Why is it so dark out here?"

I squeeze my hands together against the cold. "Where is she?"

"I can barely see you!" She squints her eyes. "I tried to stall her by kicking her out."

"But?"

"But she's not buying it."

Chris returns, still in darkness. "It must have shorted or something."

"What about the fireworks?" My voice has a frantic edge to it now.

"It was wired to the same switch." Chris shrugs. "I don't know, buddy. You shouldn't have done this last minute."

I raise my voice. "Gah! You think? Get the record player on!"

He strides over to a record player on one of the tables. Orchestral music flows through its speakers and rides the chilly air across the roof.

"April!" I shout. "Get to the elevator!" I drag Chris to the opposite end of the roof and take position. We all three stand, shivering in the cold, eyes on the elevator doors. The record stops.

I run to the record player and jiggle the platter. It won't budge. "The batteries are dead."

"I told you not to bring that old piece of junk! You best be glad I'm your best man." Chris runs to a duffle bag he stashed on one of the chairs.

"I can't believe I forgot to switch out the batteries." I hurry toward him.

From the bag, he produces a boom box. "No worries. Now get back in position!"

I rush back to the far end of the roof, and the initial strains of "Auld Lang Syne" fill the air. He joins me again, and I shoot him my best *what the hell?* look.

He shrugs again. "I was saving the song for the end. You know, because it'd be midnight and all. It's the only thing I had time to bring."

I stagger, still feeling ill. What kind of man am I that I can't pull together a simple wedding?

The elevator dings, and the doors open.

"Is that Madi?" I shout. "Baby, follow the music."

April starts down the aisle. Several feet behind her, Madi steps out of the elevator. Her brilliant white dress drapes elegantly over her four-months-pregnant belly. The cheerful bouquet of sunflowers in her hands brings out her smooth, earthy skin. Even from across the roof, her brown eyes sparkle and her smile warms my cheeks. She's like an angel who just stepped out of heaven, instead of a girl from an elevator.

April nears and moves to take her place across from me. "Where's the priest?" I whisper as she passes.

Madi answers in her own whisper. "He's behind me." She steps aside so I can see the elderly, white-clad priest bringing up the rear.

I raise my voice to the priest. "Where have you been? I told you to be here at eleven."

He yells back, "New York traffic on New Year's Eve; that is where I have been!"

"Come this way. Run!"

The priest hurries past Madi, but trips on the gravel before he reaches me and falls into a heap.

"What is happening?" Madi looks around the rooftop, squinting her eyes in the darkness.

The breeze gusts into a howling wind, drowning out Chris's boom box. This is all ruined. The bank tower shows it's just a few minutes till midnight. Maybe we should just cancel and somehow...

Madi's clear, virtuous voice rings out with the chorus of "Auld Lang Syne." April and Chris join in as she closes the distance between us and settles in beside me. The warmth of her breath washes over my neckline. Her eyes tell me she doesn't care that there's no electricity, no music, no lights.

She finishes the last line of the song, with April and Chris closing the harmonies.

The rooftop falls silent.

Her lips are so soft and inviting, and I can't help but return her smile.

The priest launches into his prepared speech. Madi's eyes glisten, and her smile gleams. April reaches over to her, her hand trembling in the winter air, and offers her a gold band. Madi takes it and turns to me. She slides it onto my ring finger and looks up expectantly.

I turn to my "best" man.

He whispers, "You didn't trust me with it so you took it away from me, remember?"

He shrugs and shoots an apologetic look past me to Madi.

He's right! I think I had it on me last night.

Chris scoots away and then runs back behind the elevator. He's probably looking inside my pants that I wore last night. I already know it isn't in there.

I don't even try looking through my pocket, knowing it isn't there either.

I shut my eyes. How can I face her in this moment? I want to say I'm sorry but no words will ever be enough.

The sky suddenly fills with a barrage of bright colors and loud bursting fireworks.

Chris runs out of the back and shouts in the distance, "I got it working! You're welcome!"

Madi squeezes my hand. I turn back toward her and I can see Madi's face clearly now. I then notice her tears rolling down her cheeks.

Her mouth open and ready to speak she softly says, "You remembered?"

She surprisingly pulls me into a tight embrace and she brings her lips to mine. She raises her jaw and leans in, lips slightly parted, warm and full.

Lights explode around us as our lips meet, her tongue soft and wet.

Best moment ever.

The crowd from the streets below yells, "Five…four…three… two…one! Happy New Year!"

The sounds of the wind, the fireworks, the crowd, and the priest fade. I squeeze Madi's body into mine, but it yields. And in the silence, I'm left with nothing.

he elevator car stops, and the doors slide open. Uriel is at the far end of the roof, barefoot, with the cyan King of Diamonds protruding from his charcoal suit pocket. He stands there, his eyebrows raised, twisting the gold band on his finger.

"Here comes the groom! Congrats, Gucci! I know its odd saying this after you married the girl and cheated on her all in the same day."

What's wrong with me?

"What d'you want me to say? Blame your upbringing if you want someone to blame. Trust went out the door with you a long time ago. An abusive fatha and a cheating motha. Those are your role models right there, sweetheart. Sometimes love only exists in fairy tales, Gucci."

I look out across the roof at the billboard of Madi. Sadness consumes every bit of my soul, knowing Uriel might be right.

"You don't get it, do you? I'm not the enemy here. It's human nature. In today's society, people are bored! They're bored with their life, their routine, and their grasp on the natural way of things. They desire what's new—excitement, danger, the unexpected, the unknown! You wanted more, and she was bringing you down. That's why you cheated. You didn't need me to tell you that."

Uriel plucks my wallet from my pocket. His face is twisted with anger. He pulls out the photo of Madi I took when I was with Michael. He holds it in front of my face.

"You keep making the same mistakes over and over! You never learn! And that mistake is using Madi as your crutch. You can't win if you are doing this for her. Madi's probably moved on by now. Found a better man. One that will love her like she always wanted! How's that truth for ya? Does that truth hit home?"

Liar! My muscles coil, ready to spring into action.

"It's time for you to grow up. Stop running away from your past but instead run past it. When you do wake up, Madi might not be yours anymore. That's the hard truth I've been trying to spoon feed you today. You don't know what the future holds. Expect the worst and learn to deal. Because at the end of the day, you still got you and that's not such a bad thing."

I relax a bit, the energy draining from me. *He's right.* After what I did, there's no way Madi would stay with me. It makes sense now. All those versions of me that chose to fail and stay here were afraid of what awaits on the outside. Being alone.

Uriel's gold band encircles his ring finger just below the photo. That's my ring. The ring Madi gave to me. He has no right to be wearing my ring. *No right!*

I snatch the photo from Uriel with one hand and try to work the ring off his finger with the other. He twists his hand out of my grasp and kicks me down.

I fall on the telescope, and the top pops off it. Madi's ring rolls out.

I reach out my hand to pick it up, but Uriel is already on top of it.

"I can't wait till you realize why you never loved her. It wasn't because you cheated. Any man in love can fall victim to a proper woman. No, you went and sold the telescope. Even you should have guessed it by now. I mean, did you really think selling that junk from your basement and your daddy's telescope got you that five grand to spend at the casino? Give yourself more credit than that!"

The ring was hidden inside of it. That's what Madi was looking to give me. She must have found it and put the ring in the telescope without my knowing, but why?

Uriel steps between me and the telescope. "To surprise you. So you could make that romantic grand gesture you kept promising her you would."

I must have sold it without knowing.

Uriel laughs heartily and claps me on the back. "The pawn shop dealer did his full inspection on the telescope and found this special ring in the process. While you were still there. And guess what you did? You sold it, anyway!"

He chuckles, putting the ring back in the scope and screwing the cap back on.

"Just in case you were wondering, the ring isn't your key."

My eyes sting as I fight back tears.

"I know it's hard. You being in a coma and selling your wife's ring pretty much makes this a dog-day afternoon. But look on the bright side. I got you another mix tape!" He forces another cassette into my pocket. "So long, Gucci!"

I look up from my pocket, and Uriel is gone. My eyes well up.

I sold her ring.

Furious, I kick the telescope and it breaks on impact.

As a tear rolls down my face, it turns into ice on my cheek. My body shudders.

I stare at the half-filled Hourglass.

I don't understand. My five minutes isn't up yet.

The reapers are in the distance, coming straight toward me.

You're not suppose to be here! I'm where I need to be! Can you hear what I'm thinking?! I did nothing wrong!

Hanging on those last words cuts me deep. Who am I to say something like that?

Everything around me blurs. I fall to my knees and drop the photo of Madi. The elevator doors open. Large flakes of snow swirl around me.

An obscured, dark-hooded figure stands before me.

I am defeated, and it doesn't matter what I do. I will always end up right back here just like the other versions of me. This is my punishment, and there is nothing I can do to change that.

The cloaked figure reaches for me. I close my eyes. This will all be over, and I can forget about Madi, forget about what I've done. Instead of a searing brain freeze, my body is whisked into the air by strong arms. I open my eyes. The stranger's hold is warm and calming.

Who are you?

The unknown stranger jostles me toward the elevator. From the hooded creature's neck, on a silver chain, dangles the hourglass pendant. The golden shimmer of the engraved time piece stares back at me. A godlike gold. My eye's feel heavy and drained.

The deep glossy gold draws me in and holds me in a trance, dragging me into an abyss of nothingness where I am utterly alone. Gold consumes my vision then fades to black.

♣ ♠ ♦ ♥

Ahead is a sign for a rest stop. To my left is the truck carrying glass.

Madi stares at the approaching rest-stop sign, her body rigid. Her knuckles are white from gripping the dashboard and the door. Madi jerks and grabs for the steering wheel.

"What are you doing, Madi?" I scream. "Let go!"

I push her back toward the passenger seat, but it's too late. The car skids out of control in the snow. We fishtail, run over the rest-stop sign, and plow headlong into the truck. Shards of plate-glass windows fly through the air, glimmering in the moonlit sky. The car launches from the roadway and flips midair. Above the noise of twisting metal, an alarm clock beeps.

THIRTY-ONE

I jolt upright, drenched in sweat. My hair drapes over my shoulder and down my back. I push the damp strands out of my eyes and slap my hand on the alarm, ceasing its insistent blaring. My watch lies on my nightstand next to the leather-bound Bible. I strap the watch to my wrist. My head pounds. Wait. I'm back in my room. How do I still remember?

I thought I was done for! Flashes of Madi, Lisa, April, and the car crash roll through my mind like a movie reel.

The alarm clock steadily continues to count up the time. 00:03...00:04...00:05. I yank it out of the wall socket.

It still counts up. 00:06...00:07...00:08. I throw it across the room. It smashes against the wall, breaking apart. I seize the Bible and throw it through the window.

How do I still remember? How?

I put my head in my hands. The pendant. Maybe it wasn't a reaper at all. One of the lost souls? Something else?

Thunder peals outside the window. I walk over and push open the curtains. There is no rain, but the sky is dark. Lightning stretches across the sky, flashing briefly over the city.

I turn from the window to the snow globe, once again resting on my desk. What kind of cruel joke is this place playing on me? I snag it from the desk and shake it. The snow swirls around the tiny town like a tornado wreaking havoc.

Who is this stranger and why does it hide away its face? Could it be my demon? It would make sense. It needs me to finish the race so that it can challenge me. But what if I kill it before it gets the chance to? The stranger always shows up right when I'm in danger. I wonder...

My focus shifts to the surface of the window and the hourglass's distorted reflection.

I raise the silly child's toy above me and hesitate.

What if I'm wrong? What if it isn't my demon? But I have to know for sure. Besides I technically haven't left my time zone. It's a risk but if I know anything about myself thus far its that I'm a gambling man.

My muscles are primed to smash the window right along with the hourglass it holds within it.

Knock! Knock!

I look toward the living room and lay the snow globe down.

Knock! Knock!

I stride toward the bedroom door, glancing at the bathroom. No time to get dressed. Let's just deal with this and get it over with.

Knock! Knock!

Once in the living room, I approach the front door, waiting silently for another knock.

Nothing comes before I reach it. With muscles tensed, I place my ear on the cool wood.

Knock! Knock!

The piano starts to play, and I jolt against the door. It must be 3:10.

I go over to the piano, flip the music switch off, and head back to the door.

Knock! Knock!

I heave an exaggerated sigh, unlock the door, and throw it open. A thin man with graying brown hair, dressed in a stylish white suit with green vest, smiles a large, toothy grin. Sealtiel. The cyan Ace of Spades still peeks out of his jacket pocket, and his horn-rimmed glasses once again reflect an ominous glare. No sign of a golden pendent around his neck. A briefcase stands next to his leg, and he's again languidly sipping a cup of tea.

"Knock, knock. May I come in?" he says crisply.

Sealtiel gazes at the watch on my wrist for a few seconds. "Time is ever—"

I slam the door in his angelic face and lock it.

That makes me feel a little better. I turn and walk toward the kitchen. Sealtiel is at the kitchen table, holding his cup and saucer, his briefcase on the table in front of him. He sets the teacup in its saucer and places it beside the briefcase. In his intolerable English accent, he says, "Have a look at yourself. You are in the thick of it now, aren't you, old fellow? I am not referring to your barnet, either."

I touch my face and hair, matted and unkempt. Did he have something to do with the reaper last night? Is he even a lost soul, or is he ...?

He smacks his lips and nods toward me, one eyebrow cocked. "I am not your demon, sir. Consider me more of a personal accountant of sorts. I remind you to cross the T's and dot the I's. Checks and balances of time spent to time lost. Of all the fine qualities that I possess, being a demon is not one of them."

Fancy talk and suits don't mean anything in this place.

"Right. For proof on the matter of my innocence, share with me your valuable time, would you?"

He gestures for me to join him. Why do I get the feeling I'm in the presence of a lawyer? I don't move.

"How about we make a deal, you and I? You're a bit of a gambling man, are you not? That gives me a rush indeed. But the deal is simple. Accept the contents of this case, and in return, I shall leave you be for the rest of the day. Have we a deal?"

The thunder outside roars as if I was making a deal with the devil.

I nod.

He twists the briefcase so the locks face him.

"You have requested two things from me."

Snap! Snap!

He unlocks the briefcase and removes a black, worn leather-encased book.

That's the same book that Madi had left at the coffee shop.

"Firstly, you personally entrusted this to me and fixed this day to return it to you." He lays the book on the table. The leather has a couple of latches of some kind on the front cover. He slides it slowly over to me. Might as well find out what this is about. I lower myself into one of the open chairs.

"So then, it seems we have a deal! Feels good, eh? The word you liked to call it was your logbook. It's brimming with notes you wrote to yourself."

What could I have written to myself?

"Your exact words were, 'These pages are the guide to finding the light within my soul.'"

No way did I write something like that. It doesn't even sound like me. Funny, I really don't know what I truly sound like.

"As you can see, there are two locks on the outside. Both are rotary dial locks. Both take a five-letter combination to release them. He, or you rather, did not, unfortunately, give me the code for either of them. Afraid of it falling into the wrong hands and what have you."

Five letters? Great! Just another thing to add to the list. I can stick it between finding my key and discovering who my demon is.

"Secondly, you left a single clue to help you solve the code, a question rather." He looks deep into my eyes and says, "What do you desire?"

What have I desired? Why would I have spoken in past tense? I don't even know what my favorite kind of food was, let alone what I desired.

I bang a fist on the table.

Sealtiel shifts in his chair. "Desire is probably a play on words. It could mean many different things to many different kinds of people. It could either be positive or negative, depending on how you choose to calculate it."

I don't know what I annoys me worst about him. His English accent or the green vest he wears that doesn't clash with the rest of his outfit.

I pick up the book. It doesn't feel familiar to me in the least. Why would it? I don't remember writing in it. But if Sealtiel's telling the truth, what's in this book could tell me everything I need to know. It might give me the key I need to discover the important things. Who my demon is. Who I am, even. I need to know what's in this book.

"Right. So sort that out, and Bob's your uncle." He shuts the briefcase. "This concludes our meeting. A deal is, after all, a deal. Good luck to you, old chap, in your endeavors." With a refined hand, he lifts his teacup and saucer and places them in the briefcase.

Emotionless, he locks the briefcase and stands up.

Thunder crashes outside. The electricity cuts out and back in.

Sealtiel has mysteriously vanished after the first switch.

I don't need his help anyway. I just need to think of five letters that describe something I used to desire.

The only thing I'm really sure of is how I feel about Madi. *Madi.* My shoulders slump. Her name has only four letters.

I leave the book at the table and walk to my closet. I put on my suit, jacket, and cross-fit shoes. The cyan and black Jack of Hearts peeks out from my handkerchief pocket. *Jack.* No, that only has four letters, too. The Jack's one eye seems to accuse me. All it took was one night for my life to end. My hand bumps the flask in my jacket pocket. I remove it, and the steel glistens in the bathroom light. I set the flask on the counter and walk into the bedroom.

Five letters. Does anything in here have five letters?

I look around the living room and shuffle through some of the books. My watch beeps.

Five minutes.

I grab the logbook off the table and open the door, thinking randomly of the waitress across the way.

At least with Sealtiel gone, she won't be hurt in any kind of...

I open the door to find the waitress's lifeless body hanging feet above the floor, neck tied with a noose, attached to a chandelier above me.

The booming rumble of the thunder vibrates the whole building. The lights in the hallway go on and off, making the waitress's hanging corpse that much horrific to look at.

I mourn for her until I hear snickering coming from down the hall. I turn my head and see Sealtiel standing inside the elevator

"To make things easier for you, you should know that she"— Sealtiel points at the lifeless waitress—"was there when you were reaped the last time. It's kind of odd how she made it out with her memories still intact." He gives a smug grin just as the doors conceal him.

I really can't trust anyone in this place. For all I know he could be lying or she could be my demon. That would kinda make sense come to think of it. Maybe that's the real reason why the lost souls keep killing her. They aren't allowed to tell me who my demon is but they can secretly try to show me. Maybe she's the one wearing the golden pendant.

I look for any kind of necklace around her neck. Nothing.

I look at my watch to see that I need to hurry and leave. I tuck the logbook into my jacket and decide to take the stairs for a change.

After running out of the stairwell, I exit the building right on time. Sealtiel stands to my left, just outside the revolving doors.

Well, that didn't last long.

The golden pendent hangs from his neck and dangles in the strong wind.

There it is again!

I gaze at it's color and how it strangely reminds me of the golden eye that is missing in the demon painting. What if they are one and the same?

Thunder booms overhead and distracts Sealtiel's attention. I grab for the necklace, but he turns back, and I retract my hand. He steps past me and picks up something from the ground. "Looks like you dropped something."

He lifts up the black leather Bible I threw out the window.

"Maybe this could be a clue to opening that lock."

A clue? I spin the first rotary dial on the logbook in my hand and spell out B-I-B-L-E.

Nothing.

My shoulders droop as I brace against the wind.

Tell me what the coin means? Is it my key? Is it?!

He acts like he doesn't even hear what I'm thinking.

Instead he says, "We all have our foibles." Sealtiel pats the book. "That's not down to God, but down to you. You choose your own path. You can either listen to the angel on your left shoulder or the demon on your right." He flips through the book.

Why, all of a sudden, does he want to start preaching at me?

Sealtiel's green eyes hold an immense calm in them. Fearless and strong. Not a worry in the world can break that steady gaze he has on me. Why is it that when I see that golden pendant they always seem different from before?

My watch beeps.

Ten minutes.

"There are no more shortcuts. You must face what you did and learn from it. That is life. Things a father teaches his daughter."

Daughter? I turn from Sealtiel. That word sounds so...

Daddy? I'm hungry. The scene from my nightmare, with my precious Anna in the backseat, strikes me like a bolt of lightning from the storm above.

I can't let her down.

The air takes on an unnatural chill, and a cloud forms when I exhale. I need to know what that coin means to me. I whirl around, and Sealtiel is now gone. Across the street where my car should be is a pink bicycle with a basket.

Oh! Come on!

I look around for another vehicle I could jump into and don't see any. I can't believe I'm doing this.

I grab the bicycle, sit my butt in the seat, and pedal my way toward the interstate.

THIRTY-TWO

hunder echoes in the night sky. I make my way up the hill. Seated on the park bench where I saw him the very first time is Sealtiel, teacup in hand. I sit down next to him, watching the lightning flash. His pendant is no longer around his neck.

Typical. Just typical.

Without looking at me, he says, "Calming, isn't it? Even in a place like this, you can find solitude." He sips his tea, gazing out at the vast park. "I am pleased to see you have ascertained a new perspective on life."

Strikes of lightning illuminate the storm clouds. Thunder rolls over the park. Sealtiel eyes my watch. We've got plenty of time. I remove the logbook from my jacket and fool around with the rotary dial. *What other words have five letters and are somehow related to my desire?* For kicks and giggles, I put in J-E-S-U-S. Nothing happens. Maybe it's my daughter. But *Anna* is spelled with only four letters. What would be another word to describe my child?

Another grumble of thunder reverberates in the air. *Child*. I enter C-H-I-L-D. Nothing happens. Okay, I need to really think here.

Sealtiel said that desire could be either good or bad. If my desire was bad, then it could somehow be related to my sin. Does remembering my sin somehow unlock this book? *Lust* is four letters, not five, so that can't be it.

I try D-E-M-O-N in the top rotary dial. Clack! The first lock is open. I hold my breath. Sealtiel doesn't seem to have noticed. I slowly replace the logbook in my jacket, hoping to avoid Sealtiel's wandering eyes.

Sealtiel turns to me. "Have you decided what you are going to do about the 42:02 problem yet? I mean, you're simply far too pedestrian, plebeian even, to resist the music just yet."

42:02 problem?

"I mean, you are still new to this. You still use your watch to help you track the seconds here. The old you would already be proficient at counting the seconds. And look how far he got. I mean, you got. I mean…well, you know what I mean."

What is he going on about?

He turns to face me, "Gabriel didn't go over that with you? Figures. Probably too busy filling his gut to ever…."

He coughs, not finishing his sentence, and points across the park at the stairs leading down to the subway.

"The 42:02 problem will be the greatest challenge you face in your race. The music coming from the outside will always play at 42:02, and you will fall prey to it every time. Let's say the day of the race you fall prey to it once again. Reapers flying by the seat of your pants and suddenly, WHAM! The music takes a hold of you. What do you think will happen once your mind comes back to reality or whatever this is?"

I've never thought about it before.

"You will be welcomed by many reapers, happily willing to suck every memory you just gained out of existence. Unless you learn how to beat the clock. Though we've tried before to teach you the trick, and you never could grasp onto it. I was supposed to teach you today, but since you made that deal, my arms are tied."

Beat the clock? I need to know. Can we make another deal?

Sealtiel's ears turn red, hearing my thoughts. "Go on." He looks at my watch and smirks.

I take off the watch and place it on his lap. Sealtiel eyes it suspiciously and scratches his chin for a moment.

"You are willing to part with something so precious and unique for something you never were able to learn?"

It's just a watch.

"Just a watch? Never have I seen you bargain with this before. Particularly interesting. A deal, then," he says, holding his hand out to me. His grip is heavy against mine. He lets go and picks up the watch. He looks at me with lowered brows as he latches the watch buckle around his wrist. Apparently satisfied, he relaxes and smiles as he models it to himself.

"I suppose that does change things now, doesn't it?" Sealtiel holds his ear out and a mischievous looking smile runs across his face. He stands and walks to the tree. I guess that's his way of telling me to follow him.

"To beat the 42:02 problem, you must complete the race before the music ever starts."

So your best advice to me is break all twelve hourglasses in perfect sequence while being chased down by over a hundred reapers, keep a watchful eye out for dirty lost souls and a demon, and do all of this in under forty-two minutes and two seconds? Plus "finding a key" somewhere in that sentence too.

He leans forward with a sour expression on his face. "That's more or less an accurate assumption. Yes."

He bows his head, taking another sip of his tea. He says softly, "I bet you are wishing now that whoever is playing the music out there would just shut it off already, yes?"

I push off the bench and tramp toward my publishing office. These lost souls are literally going to be the death of me. Some distance behind me, I can hear my watch alarm going off. This might have been a mistake.

THIRTY-THREE

I look at the glass elevator and decide to take another route for a change.

Inside the building, I step into the lobby elevator. There's no way I'll finish the race by 42:02. It's impossible. I press the button for my office floor and hear a rattling sound coming from above me. I turn around and look up to see a latch allowing access to the top of the elevator. The noise stops.

The doors start to slide closed behind me, but it catches on something. I whirl around. A reaper stands in the doorway, its inky black robe blocking me from any escape I could make. I stumble backward. Not again! There's no coldness in the air. How did it sneak up on me? I'm in my correct time zone. It shouldn't be here! Maybe I'm doing something wrong?

I lift my arm in front of my face and close my eyes.

I slowly open my eyes and stand. The reaper hasn't moved. I take a step closer. Still nothing. As I reach out to touch the reaper's skull mask, it transforms into Sealtiel.

He pushes me to the floor. "I am very disappointed in you. Didn't even put up a fight." He steps inside, turns, and presses the button for the office once again. The elevator doors close us in.

I lie on the floor, eyes wide and mouth open.

I need to find my equilibrium. We had a deal.

He keeps his face toward the doors. "You need to start looking for the key. That's time well spent."

Maybe instead of blocking the sound out I could trick the reapers into thinking I was someone else.

I jump up.

I could try mirroring to look like a reaper!

"Didn't work. Already tried and failed."

I need to try something! I cannot fail this time.

"Ha! You're already failing, friend. Look at yourself. How can you mirror a reaper if you can't even keep your appearance in check?"

I look in the shiny metallic reflection in the door to see my bearded face.

"You're losing sight of who you are. How can you gain your equilibrium if you can't even remember what you look like anymore?"

I feel around my scruffy beard, understanding its purpose now. Have I lost sight of myself?

"You look like a pitiful shaggy dog. Okay, fine, I will try and teach you again. First, we start with body."

Why not mind first?

Sealtiel glances to my book, "Solve the lock and you'll gain access to the mind. Are you sure you want to keep going? I've run the numbers and the odds of you attaining your equilibrium is a thousand to one."

I puff out my chest and stand straight in ready position.

We start with body. What must I know?

"You must learn who you are in terms of who you want to be."

Who do I want to be? Is it based upon the man that I was?

"No, not who you were, but who you want to be. Let me tell you a small fact about who you were. A writer with no ambition. A book you have worked on for many years that you never truly wanted to finish. You were a shell of a man."

I turn from him and his blunt honesty. As we continue to ascend, I focus on the surface of the walls. Who do I want to be? Apparently, I wanted to be a writer at one point. Throughout my time here, I've had an enormous amount of writer's block, never once writing a single sentence. Am I even good at writing?

"Writing is one of the ways you free yourself from concern, a way to stop the world through total mental, spiritual, and physical involvement. Your past selves were always writing who-knows-what in that logbook you're carrying. Maybe writing will help you with the situation you are in now. It may make you think more clearly about who you want to be."

The elevator doors open. Sealtiel's watch beeps.

Thirty minutes.

He becomes giddy at the sound.

I approach my elaborate mahogany desk, at which I spent a countless amount of time trying to write the perfect story. Nothing ever came out right. Nothing ever came out at all. The grandfather clock ticks steadily beside it. No matter how many times it gets destroyed, it always seems to come back a bit louder than the day before. Maybe before all this happened, it was the only soothing noise I was accustomed to. Now it just haunts my soul.

He turns and walks down the hall toward the kitchen. I sit at the desk and pull out my logbook for guidance. Maybe who I want to be is in these pages.

DEMON is still displayed on the top rotary dial.

Out the window, lightning leaps from cloud to cloud. What is the second passcode? My strongest desire has to do with my demon, my biggest sin. But if that's the case, why wouldn't lust be the answer? That is my biggest sin, isn't it?

Footsteps sound from down the hall. I slip the logbook back into my jacket. Sealtiel walks in with a tea set and puts it on the desk. He sits down in a chair opposite me and slides a blank sheet of paper across the desk.

"The only way to truly know is to try," he says, and places a pen in my hand.

Just like many times before, the white paper fills my vision. Where to begin? I shift in my seat and tap the end of my pen on the surface of the desk. I press the pen to the paper, holding it steady. The ink glides over the paper and forms a meaningless mark as always. I advance to the window as the lightning dances amongst the clouds. On the surface of the glass, the object of time releases a stream of sand from one half to the other. I touch the reflection. After a few seconds, I sit back down to start again.

He pours murky liquid from the teapot into his tiny cup. Steam rises above the rim, forcing him to blow across the top to cool it down. He takes a sugar cube off the tray and drops it into his teacup, repeating the action six more times. Clinking his spoon in his cup, he stirs the tea counterclockwise. The sound carries along with the ticking of the old grandfather clock. The two in tandem could drive a person mad.

He is doing this to distract me. I steady my wrist and touch the pen to the paper. Tick-tock. Clink. Tick-tock. Clink. Tick-tock. Clink.

Sealtiel stops. He takes a sip from his teacup. "You are ahead of the game. You already know you are a writer. That peace, that peace that you're after, lies somewhere beyond personality, beyond the perception of others, beyond invention and disguise, even beyond effort itself. Don't let anything distract you from the light that shines through your soul to the words you write."

I add some pressure to the tip of the pen.

"You cannot write based on the assumption that you can write. Write for yourself, not for anyone else. Let your heart bleed onto the paper, not caring for one second who reads it. Find that self-peace, hold it deep in your mind, and push through that writer's block inside your head that's telling you that you're not good enough."

Sealtiel resumes his stirring. Tick-tock. Clink. Tick-tock. Clink. Tick-tock. Clink. "Listen for it." Tick-tock. Clink. Tick-tock. Clink. Tick-tock. Clink.

What's he trying to tell me?

I slowly move the pen to the right. Tick-tock. Clink. Tick-tock. Clink. Tick-tock. Clink. The only thing still fresh in my mind is the 42:02 problem.

That's it! The music!

I hum one of the songs from the outside music to the beats of the clanking spoon and the ticking clock. The rhythm of the music moves through my body, and my hand flows freely.

The music that comes from above is always manufacturing scenarios that try to keep me trapped in the multiplex of my own mind. My eyes are not only viewers, but also projectors that are running a second story over the picture I see in front of me. My memories are writing that script, and the working title is, "Providence."

The words unravel all at once. The walls that once blocked my imagination are being torn down. Sealtiel clinks his spoon harder against his cup, cheering me on. Words of passion flow from my heart, through my lungs, and into my head.

Who am I? I am an unknown soul lost in a world that leaves me with no voice or memories. I have come to understand that what I lack in memory, I gain in discipline. I am formed through pure, absolute light. A light that my soul perceives to be good and, at times, bad. When that shift happens, the battle between my inner demons and my free will converge. I take arms to defend against its unsavory motives. My white paper becomes the shield that blocks the evil force of fear and doubt. My pen is the sword that strikes down despair and stress with the words I lay down. There's no story the mind could create that will be as compelling as facing one's sins with the outcome always being in the mind of the believer.

I lay the pen down, shoulders back and chest swelled. I fold up the paper, now filled with words, and place it in my jacket. The clanking of the spoon stops.

Sealtiel slurps his tea. "Well, that will do just fine."

A crack of thunder shakes the building. The power goes out. Darkness falls over my world, with the only light coming from the intermittent lightning bolts. Sealtiel is now gone.

A bolt strikes just a few feet from the window, blinding me. The thunderstorm seems to be getting fiercer. I rub my eyes and blink several times.

The hourglass reflection steadily trickles sand through its neck, giving me a clue.

The coin. The hourglass in the coin. It had to have been carved from the eye of greed. It has to be my key. It explains so much.

The thunder crackling across the sky urges me forward. I rush into the elevator. As I descend, the coin is all I can think about. How did I originally get it?

I close my eyes. A calm breeze wafts over my cheek. Water crashes nearby. My feet rub against granules of sand. Radiant heat warms my face. My toes strike something small and hard. I open my eyes. The sun is high and bright over turquoise waters, and white sand stretches as far as I can see.

A flat, shiny disk is lodged between my toes. It looks like a golden coin of some kind. From a little way down the beach, my father runs toward me. Light reflects off the coin and obscures my vision.

I blink.

The beach is gone, and I am back inside the elevator, the storm raging outside. The elevator car descends a few floors. Was that a memory I just had? It must've been. The elevator doors open, and I walk out. Taking the paper from my jacket, I read what I just wrote. I smile. For the first time, it feels genuine.

I make my way through the blowing wind, across the street, and into the Lighthouse Restaurant.

Sealtiel stands behind the bar. I take a seat on a stool halfway down. He picks up a bottle from the cabinet behind him. "You want to know what heaven is like? This is it, a fifty-year-old Macallan whisky. Puts hair on a lost soul's chest." He laughs as he pours two glasses and slides one to me. The amber liquid sloshes. Since I still can't taste, there's no point in drinking it. I push it aside.

Sealtiel takes a sip of his. "Hmm, it's missing something." He flips open a butterfly knife, retrieves half an orange from a mini fridge below the bar, and slices a wedge from it. He squeezes the wedge over his glass and then stirs it with his finger.

"I should tell you about the time Uriel had to chase you down the street, an ice shard up his bum. I actually thought I heard a reaper chuckle at the sight." He laughs.

I smile as I picture Uriel in his dark navy suit and bare feet running down the street with an ice wedgie.

He stares at his wrist where my watch is attached, his eyes glazed over. He takes a gulp of his drink and looks at me.

Why not mirror Madi? Wouldn't she have been a good person to use on me?

"I was wondering when you were going to ask me that. You made us promise never to mirror Madi. You said that the promise of false hopes is a far worse punishment than anything else you could ever face in this place."

My mind journeys to that night at the casino. I understand what my past self meant by false hopes. To think that Madi forgave me and then realize it wasn't true would be soul-crushing, to say the least. Besides, it's taunting to even entertain the idea she would ever forgive me for what I've done.

The Macallan I pushed away now draws me in. Who cares that I can't taste it?

As long as I can feel the side effects, it will be worth the drink. I lift the glass to my lips.

"I know loss, regret, and confusion reign in your mind; however, it is important to leave the past where it belongs. If you cannot, then mirroring will be useless. Controlling who you are and how you see yourself is crucial. Knowing that you want to be a writer shows focus toward yourself. When you look at yourself now, you can see a man who knows who he wants to be. That is a man willing to change. It's really that easy."

I stop myself from drinking. If it were that easy, then why have I never been able to do it?

"Your progress stopped because of your attachment to your pain. You hid yourself in the things you know. You are still afraid to accept the things you do not want to know. Ergo, why you forced your sins inside a tree, and why what truly scares you is locked inside your dreams every night. What you don't know makes you stronger, was your belief. But really, the saying goes, 'What you don't know just makes you stupid.'"

I bottled up my sin in a tree and my fear in my dreams. Can't say I didn't try to make it work. Do they all know what I dream, too?

Sealtiel gives me a reassuring look. "Oh, we all know. Once those dreams kick in, we are all watching the show along with you. We are all of one mind in this place."

He clinks my glass and drinks the rest of his.

Now how do I attain the soul?

"The one thing you never could get. You have to ask yourself, why do you even listen to the music in the first place? You're searching for something."

I'm searching to find myself.

Sealtiel walks around to my side of the bar and sits on the stool beside me. His graying brown hair gives an impression of trustworthy maturity that doesn't match his goofy grin.

"You're halfway there," he says, taking one more shot before my watch on his wrist beeps.

He whistles and skips gleefully out of the restaurant.

I race after Sealtiel, sprinting past the oddly opened manhole, and into the subway station. I slip into the subway car, and the doors slide closed behind me.

I sit, watching the hourglass reflection in the subway window. Sealtiel walks in from another car with a bottle of Macallan in his hand. He sets the bottle on the seat across from me. I slump down in my seat.

"Do you understand why this watch is so important?" he says. "Why it is something to be desired? It is another thing I haven't the ability to emotionally understand. A gift given out of love. That is a hidden treasure in itself. A treasure I shall forever envy."

He removes my watch from his wrist and shows me the back engraving.

I believe in you.

"It was a statement of love and understanding. An understanding that through all your hardships and abuse, she would be there for you. That is courage and strength beyond compare. She shows you her value. The funny thing is, you don't know your own worth anymore."

Maybe I'm not worth much of anything.

"My worth is how I choose to see myself. That is my self-worth. That is belief in myself. Took me awhile to figure that out. On the outside, I remember being jealous of everyone I saw that found love. Seeing couples playing in the park to holding hands down the street. I wanted that so badly. Went as far as online dating. Nothing. I was stuck in a world where nobody wanted me and then I settled on someone that didn't quite fully complete me. I began to lose myself and the thought of love to me then was merely nothing more than a Valentines card once a year. I changed once I arrived at a place like this. I started to believe in myself again and only took me being a lost soul to finally see it. Don't let that be the case for you. I believe in you. Now why don't you?"

How can I believe in myself if I don't even know who I am? I don't even know my name!

"That's a crutch. That's a lie to make you feel helpless. Another word for that is lazy. You doing nothing is lazy. You giving up in the middle of a race is lazy. You cheating on your wife is lazy! You being too afraid to do what you love is lazy! If you make yourself out to be worthless, then that is all you will ever be. Worthless!"

He lifts the bottle of whisky. "Let's have another toast." He twists the cork out and raises the bottle to me. "To the man with no self-worth."

I knock the bottle from his hands, almost hitting the hourglass window. Shock crosses Sealtiel's face.

He yells, "When will you realize that your life out there is close to perfect? Anyone would be grateful to have it! Your self-worth is something to desire. Even to remember a name is worth more than you know. To my dissatisfaction, you plainly do not see it!"

My name is something to desire? Is Sealtiel giving me a hint that it's my name? Could that be the answer to unlocking my book?

I hurry to take the logbook out of my jacket pocket.

Piano music floods the car.

Not now! Not now!

Sealtiel screams, "I'll see you in there!"

Wait! What do you mean by that?!

I cover my ears with my hands, shutting my eyes tightly, trying to concentrate. My heart pounds, and I struggle to get enough oxygen. The emergency exit is at the end of the subway car. I jump up, run to it, pull it open, and leap out. While in midair—the music now deafening—with only the tracks below me, everything breaks into puzzle pieces, and I relapse back into my reverie.

THIRTY-FOUR

I'm seated behind a large mahogany desk facing a wall of windows. To my left is a full bar and a treadmill. To my right is an expensive-looking leather sofa. There is a Christmas tree in the corner, decorated and lit with red, green, and white lights. The wall behind me is full of framed publishing awards. I work for a publishing company? Maybe I finally did achieve my goal. A calendar posted on the wall shows 1999. That's the most recent year yet.

Outside, it's dark and the snow is coming down hard. The parking lot far below is mostly empty and covered in inches of snow. Everyone must have left the office except for me.

On the far edge of the desk is the back of a nameplate. Finally! I can find out who I am. I spin the nameplate around.

President Mike Donald

Mike Donald? That doesn't sound familiar at all.

Next to a printer on the desk, a coffee cup displays #1 Dad.

The door opens. I jump up. A man steps in, looking surprised. He appears to be in his mid-thirties, not much older than I, lanky with close-cropped hair. His prominent nose and ears give him a bit of awkward charm.

"What are you doing in my chair?" He sounds serious but not angry.

I find myself unable to move. "The printer is broken. I had to use yours, Mr. Donald." My body moves on its own, and I stand up and pick up some sheets of paper from the print tray.

Mr. Donald gives me a strange look. "All right. Make sure you're at the meeting tomorrow—bright and early this time! I can't always cover for your lateness. You did finish the outline I asked for, right?"

My anxiety mounts. "I was going to, but you see—"

"Always an excuse!"

I lower my eyes.

In my periphery, Mr. Donald shakes his head and takes his coat off the rack. He turns back toward me. "You know something?"

I raise my head.

"I see greatness in you, and it's just sad that you don't take the time to realize it in yourself. We've talked about this many times before. So, don't bother coming in tomorrow or the day after."

"Sir? Mr. Donald?"

"I'm letting you go, son. I will leave the light on for you, so you can pack your belongings," Mr. Donald says. "Just remember to shut it off when you leave."

He walks into the hall, leaving the door open for me. Moments later, the lights in his office go out. The Christmas tree glows, casting shadows of branches around the room. My head pounds as I trudge down the hall to my cubicle, still lit as Mr. Donald had promised.

Mysteriously, an unopened bottle of fifty-year-old Macallan whisky adorned with a red bow is sitting on my desk. The very same bottle given to me that night. In an instant, I freak. My mind races with thoughts of hows, whys, and whens.

This can't be a coincidence, can it?

My work phone lights up and rings, snapping me back to reality. The caller ID displays Madi Hayes.

Great. What am I going to tell her? I have to find some excuse to buy me time to think.

I step away from the desk and pace between the cubicles until the phone stops ringing. A few seconds later, it starts again. I walk into the darkened hallway. The phone's ring echoes through the silent office building. In the sitting area beside the elevator, the Christmas tree is still lit with white lights. The ornaments are of various shapes and sizes, but they all swirl with designs of red and white.

The phone rings again. There's no escaping it. I rush back to the desk and scoop up the receiver. "Hey! I am going to be late again."

After a moment of silence, she replies, her voice flat, "It's Christmas Eve."

"I know. I will try to make it back as soon as possible." Silence. "Tell Anna I love her."

"Tell her yourself." Madi switches the phone to speaker mode, and she and Anna sing the opening lyrics to "Chestnuts Roasting on an Open Fire," while accompanying music plays faintly in the background.

The sound pulls on my heartstrings.

The elevator dings in the hallway. Mr. Donald? The faint accompanying music drifts in so I'm hearing it in stereo now. Madi walks through the doorway holding a small portable record player in her right hand and Anna's hand in her left. The phone dangles in my hand. As they near my cubicle, the song ends and another begins. I quickly stash away the Macallan bottle in my drawer.

"Here's a song I wrote for you," Madi says and her recorded voice joins the soft piano music.

"Now I'm fighting for my life and I'm fighting to survive. Without your love I am nothing. Without your love I am nothing. I need more time with you. I need more time."

I am mesmerized by the lyrics as I listen to her beautiful voice. Anna runs forward and wraps her arms around my legs.

"What are you two doing here?" I bend over and pick up my daughter. As the song ends, I kiss Anna on the cheek.

Madi sets the record player on my desk and leans into me, her lips inches from mine. "You are that December morning, and now you're finally here." She kisses me firmly on the lips. From her bag, she pulls out a large, thin, square package wrapped in shiny red paper.

Anna kisses me on the cheek. "You can't be alone on Christmas Eve!"

I force myself to keep smiling. With wide eyes, I say, "I think there's a surprise from Santa Claus for you, Anna." She looks at me and bounces in my arms. "I think he left it in my coat. You want to check for me?"

"He remembered this year!" she shouts to Madi.

I set her down gently. A pain strikes my stomach, remembering how I hadn't gotten them presents last year because I gambled our money away.

Anna runs past me into the cubicle and retrieves a wrapped box from my coat. She's already pulling the bow off when Madi says, "Should we wait for Daddy to open his?"

Anna smiles brightly. "Can I go first?" Her voice is sweet and hopeful.

I sit in my chair and roll it next to Anna. "I think I will be okay going second this one time."

"You can share mine!" she says, beaming. I help her crawl up onto my lap. She tears the rest of the wrapping away, revealing a small, plain, white box. Anna pulls the lid off and looks inside, her eyes wide with anticipation. She puts her little hand in and, making a small grunting sound, pulls out a snow globe. She smiles uncertainly and looks at me. I take the orb and shake it, sending white particles swirling throughout the miniature city. Her eyes light up as I hand it back to her.

"Your mommy had something just like this a long time ago that she got from her mommy."

Anna winds up the bottom, and a familiar piano melody begins to play.

Anna runs her finger along the snow globe base. With a click, the city slowly separates into two separate halves inside the globe, revealing a photo of Madi and little baby Anna.

I smile at my sweet child. It's like it was yesterday she was that tiny newborn. "Mommy's mama always put a photo of her and your mommy inside hers. She used to call your mom her 'little hidden treasure.'"

"Was this the first picture you took of me? I was so small."

"You're still small." I tickle her.

Anna laughs. "Does this mean I'm your hidden treasure, too?"

"Always, little girl."

Madi swipes tears from her eyes.

Anna smiles and giggles as she throws her arms around me and squeezes me with all her little-girl might. "Merry Christmas Eve, Daddy!" She holds the snow globe up to Madi.

"That's beautiful." Madi runs her hand over Anna's soft brown hair.

"Can I give him mine now, Mommy?"

Madi nods. Anna rushes to Madi's side and digs in her purse. She pulls out a small package shaped like a book and runs it over to me.

The red and green wrapping crinkles as I tear it back. It's Madi's black leather-bound book.

"It's mommy's book!" Anna screams with excitement.

Madi touches her shoulder. "We thought since it started giving you ideas when you first started your novel that it could work again to help you finish it."

Anna looks with wide eyes from me to Madi. "Can you read me the story once you're finished, Daddy?"

"Yes, of course. I will even put you in it. How does that sound?"

She jumps back into my lap. "Really? Can you make me a princess?"

"I wouldn't imagine it any other way, little girl." I kiss her nose. "Thank you for this." Her childlike laugh pulls at my heartstrings. She hugs me again. The black leather of the book is soft and inviting, the locks intricate.

Madi bends down and balances on the balls of her feet. She kisses Anna and me on our cheeks. Over the top of Anna's head, I mouth, *Thank you*. She nods and puts a shiny red package in my hand.

"My turn. I hope you like it."

I give Anna a silly look with my mouth open and brows high as I rip the wrapping away. Madi's beautiful soft smile and windswept bangs adorn the front cover of a music album. Her piercing brown eyes jar me. The photo from the billboard! The backside of the record reads:

Produced by Madi

"How did you...?" I can't seem to move or hardly breathe.

"I had the church music director help record me as I played." She stands and takes the record from me. After swapping it for the record that was playing when they came in, she turns up the volume.

It's the same song Madi was singing to me earlier.

Over the music, she says, "This is the last song on the track, but it won't be the last song that reminds me of us." She tears up again. "Each song is from an important moment we've shared together."

Anna shouts, "Mommy took the songs and she learned how to play all of them on the piano!"

This is it. This is the record someone's been playing for me from the outside world. That's how I keep getting these flashbacks.

"How did you remember every song?"

Madi picks up the black leather book. She flips to the inside of the back cover. In delicate script is a list of dates next to a specific song title. She points to the very first song.

"When I saw you come into the coffee shop, the day we met for the first time, I wrote down the song that was playing. I thought that if you were the one, it could be our first song."

I pull out my wallet. "I've got something for you, too." After thumbing through my collection of business cards, I hand her Peter's.

She gasps. "You still have it?"

I nod. "This calls for a celebration!" I retrieve the Macallan from my drawer. I grab a couple of glasses off the desk. I uncork the bottle and fill two glasses to the rim. I slide Madi one as I shoot mine down. The alcohol warms me from my throat to my stomach. I relax a little. She's still studying the card.

"Don't call him for me, though. Do this for yourself." I hand her the glass.

She sighs and puts her glass on my desk. "I'm sorry. I have all that I need in life right here." She puts her arms around my neck and kisses me softly on the lips. "Nothing more, nothing less."

Angry voices whisper again in my head. *She thinks she's better than you. She feels pity toward you. She feels like you are holding her back. She thinks you're a failure.* I try to make the voices disappear, but they only get louder. I can't hold it in any longer.

"Stop being stupid with your life!" I explode. "If you don't do this, I'll always feel like I kept you from being someone great!"

"I'm not going through this again with you," she says calmly. "Not in front of Anna."

Her calmness only fuels my fire. "You're hurting her most of all!" I roar. "You're teaching her not to strive for something, not to be anybody! Is that what you want?"

Madi takes Anna's hand. "Go wait by the Christmas tree. I'll be there soon."

Anna clings to her snow globe and wanders toward the Christmas tree, looking back behind her every few steps.

Madi lowers her voice even more. "Why don't you understand I'm fine where we are?"

I bring mine down to an angry whisper. "Fine? How can you be fine? We can't even rub two pennies together! We are barely making rent. We shop at the dollar market to get by. You can't get a job because we can't afford a babysitter! And guess what? I just lost my job! So now, we are even more in debt! We are always in debt! And the one thing you could possibly do to get us out of this hellhole, you don't even do!"

"It's always about the money, isn't it?" Madi raises her voice a little. "I don't think it's me you're mad at for not following a path that will lead to bigger and better things! It's yourself!"

My palms are sweating, my heart pounding. She's right. And I hate it. She turns to gather up the presents. I can barely restrain my taut muscles from slapping her. Whispers enter my head again. *She deserves it.* They scream at me, *Do it!* Shaking, I raise my hand.

"Mommy?" Anna peeks her head around my cubicle opening. What was I thinking? I drop my hand.

Madi looks up. "What is it?"

Anna smiles. "Daddy's car looks like a snow cone!"

"Let's go look!" Madi returns her wide grin. She takes Anna's hand and turns back to me. "Come, let's look. For her."

I drink down Madi's glass and follow them to a window. My car is completely covered in a thick blanket of snow.

"Is Daddy going to ride with us?" Anna tugs at Madi's hand.

Madi looks at me.

Does she know I almost tried to hit her?

I pick Anna up. "Of course, honey!" I turn to Madi. "You two head down, and Anna can look at the big Christmas tree in the lobby! There are even some candy canes on the lower branches"—I nudge Anna's cheek with my nose—"but don't take too many!"

I put Anna down, and she grabs Madi's hand. Madi carefully picks up the still-playing record player and walks toward the elevator. I follow. They step in, and I smile as the doors close.

If I just keep drinking, I'll make it through this. Images of myself on top of Lisa, her red dress on the floor, flash through my mind. I take another long swig of the whisky.

I put the bottle inside the bag, walk back to my desk, and quickly throw my belongings into a cardboard box. With the box under one arm and the whisky in my hand, I board the elevator. As the car descends, I chug the fiery liquid.

I look over and Sealtiel is standing inside the elevator with me.

"Don't worry, only you can see me. Your memory self just keeps drinking the rest of the ride down, mumbling to himself. So I thought it best to come aboard the stage for a little."

How is this possible? How are you in my memories?

"Silly rabbit. You still think this is all one big flashback to your past."

What is this place then?

"We are still in your Purgatorium. All of this is just window dressing that you've created inside your mind. Everything you see before you is based on the memory that is attached to the song that is currently playing. Under the curtains you'll see we haven't even left the subway car."

I try to move my hand but as I do, the other side of me takes over and pours another shot of whisky down my throat.

Then why can't I move?

"Think of your brain as a VHS player. The song playing is a VHS tape. A homemade movie, being your memory, is recorded on this particular tape. Mentally, you force yourself to watch this tape play out. What you don't realize is that your consciousness is the controller. You have the ability to press the stop button to all of this."

To not listen to the music.

"Exactly! But the rules here are tweaked. If you try to change anything major that wasn't true to this specific memory then the reapers will come for you. So let's not do anything foolish, friend."

I can't move let alone speak. So I think I'll be alright in that department.

I listen as words are suddenly forced out of my mouth. "I can't believe I got fired," I say, chuckling to myself. My eyes are being forced away from Sealtiel and focus on the elevator's layout. I see that it is surrounded by mirrors. Just like the elevator to my office in the coma world. I look at my reflection and spit on it.

Sealtiel jumps back into my eyesight. "Try gaining control of your body."

He leans over and whispers in my ear, "Give me a low five."

Sealtiel brings his hand out, palm up. I look at my hand and try to force it up. It is moving at a snail's pace as Sealtiel starts to get irritated. "Come on, Thelma! Get your old raggedy bones up. Remember what you've learned today. What kind of a man were you?"

A nonbeliever.

He leans over and yells in my ear, "Who do you believe in now?!"

Myself.

"What was that again?!"

I believe in myself!

I force my hand higher. My hand goes straight in the air almost like a Nazi salute.

"Okay, Hitler, now bring down the heat and smoke this skin."

The elevator suddenly stops on another floor. Sealtiel is gone. The doors open. A man appears standing there in shock as he looks at me with my Nazi hand sign still raised in the air.

I try and make my hand go back down. By the way he's glaring at me, he must be thinking I have some kind of mental disorder or part of a Nazi cult.

He nervously nods to me and gets in, pressing the lobby button. I look over and see Sealtiel is back right beside me.

"Don't worry. Remember he can't see me. I'm still waiting," Sealtiel says to me, extending his hand out towards me again. The struggle is real as I slowly force my hand to Sealtiel's palm. I watch the man inside the elevator looking over, confused. I finally

make it to the edge of Sealtiel's palm.

Sealtiel takes his hand back, laughing. "I would say too slow but it's pretty obvious."

I see the elevator is nearing the lobby floor. "You're doing great. Now remember your name. Open that mouth and scream it!"

What's my name? Why can't I remember it? Why does this have to be so difficult?!

I force my mouth open. My unknown elevator passenger looks over at me with my mouth still opened wide and gives me a *What is the matter with you?* look. I turn my head, exposing my wide mouth to him. Feeling uncomfortable he says, "Are you okay?"

Sealtiel gets in his face, "What are you looking at? Turn your Jheri curl butt around."

The man, not seeing or hearing Sealtiel, continues to look at me. I try again but instead of words I accidentally pass gas instead. The man scoots slowly over away from me.

Sealtiel, ashamed, looks over to me. "We need to hurry this up before the reapers start catching a whiff of what you just did to this poor man."

My name is…

I instead make a gargling noise come out of my mouth.

The man, feeling extremely uncomfortable, moves a step up in front of me.

Sealtiel looks at me strangely and says, "Time's up."

Suddenly, the elevator stops at the lobby and he is gone. I force my thoughts back inside and let go of the controls.

Out of the haze, I strangely gaze at the man in front of me.

When did he get on?

I raise the almost empty bottle to my lips when the elevator doors slide open. I've had enough for tonight. I step out, tuck the bottle out of sight behind me, and shout to Madi and Anna across the lobby, "I'll bring the car around!" I wave to the security guard and make my way through the rotating doors.

The cold weather hits me like a sledgehammer, and I brace myself as I trudge to Madi's car. With the bottle still in my hand, I stop and pop open the trunk. To my surprise, inside is a pink bicycle with a pink wicker basket. I drop the bottle next to it, settle my box inside, and slam the trunk. It must've been a gift Madi put in there for Anna from me. She thought I would forget to give her something like I did last Christmas. Well, don't I feel lucky having a wife to pick up after me? I slide the top of my tongue against my front teeth with distaste.

The wind nearly knocks me over as I get into the driver's seat and close the door. Snow pelts the windshield. I turn the key. The other side of the street is barely visible. I accelerate slowly into a U-turn and stop in front of my office building. Madi and Anna run out the front doors and across the sidewalk to the car. They hurry into a shower of thick snowflakes as I finger the golden coin pendant at my neck.

I remove it and hang it on the rearview mirror. The rear passenger-side door opens, and Anna climbs in. Madi closes it behind her and gets into the front passenger seat.

This was never just a nightmare. It was all real.

Madi pulls the door shut. I put the keys in the ignition and stop. I need to warn them! But how? I can't talk.

My eyes move forward toward the foggy window.

I can try and write a message! That's nothing major.

I force my hand up, stick out my finger, and press it up against the glass.

What should I write? It will have to be short enough to not cause any major red flags for a reaper to show.

Madi looks over my shoulder, "What are you doing? We need to hurry before the weather gets worse."

I curve my finger and write each letter as fast as I can.

S-T-A-Y.

From behind my seat Anna yells out, "Stay!"

A reaper's unbearable screech is heard in the distance. I turn my head as Madi and Anna don't seem to have heard anything unusual.

Madi looks at me and says in a serious voice, "Start the car." She says it almost like she knows what's going to happen. She gets closer. "Start the car right now."

I turn the key, put the car in drive, and turn up the headlights. The lights flash upon a darkened figure standing in front of the car.

No. No. No.

I become terrified as the reaper sways back and forth, getting closer to the hood of the car. It reaches his skeletal hand to the glass, cracking it instantly.

I quickly stomp the gas and my memory of this moment fades along with the reaper.

orty-five minutes.

I open my eyes. Surrounding me is the metal structure of the subway car. Sealtiel is nowhere to be seen. The bottle of Macallan rests in front of me. The electronic message board at the front of the car indicates the train is nearing my stop. The overhead lights blink on and off, and the doors open. I push myself up and walk out, reaching for my logbook in my jacket. It's gone.

Sealtiel must have taken it from me. What kind of good-for-nothing lost soul is he? I look back through the doors at the bottle, still lying on the floor. I shouldn't take it with me. It's one of the reasons I'm here. If I hadn't been drinking that night, I would've been more cautious. What difference does it make? I retrieve the whiskey and slide out of the subway car just before the doors close.

The amber liquid sloshes around in its glass prison. I'm not man enough to abandon it.

I walk up the stairs and out of the subway station in silence. As I cross the bridge, lightning illuminates Madi's doe eyes on the billboard. I stop. Did I kill her? Is she even still out there somewhere? I'm not sure if this idea hurts worse than the idea that she's moved on. Neither prospect is worth living for. I swirl the whisky around in the bottle, imagining a small demon swimming around inside. Memories of my idleness run through my head—years upon years of heavy drinking mixed with poor decisions.

I guess I am truly my father's son. If he could see me now.

This was my desire.

I raise the bottle to my lips. Another brilliant bolt hits the ground some distance behind the billboard. Thunder crackles through the air, so loud I can feel it.

Anna.

Somebody out there knows about the special record Madi made. Somebody is playing it for me. Maybe Anna is there. Maybe it's not time to give up just yet. I'm not alone. And Anna thinks I'm worth it. I raise the bottle, muscles poised to hurl it against the iron of the bridge. Something stops me. The hard liquor sloshes from side to side. I slide it into my jacket pocket for reasons I don't understand.

I can't wallow in self-pity anymore. That isn't going to help me get out of here. I move on, making my way toward my apartment. Once inside the elevator, I press the button for the roof. With no other sounds but the low humming of the elevator engine, I ascend the six levels of the skyscraper.

As I walk out of the elevator and onto the rooftop, thunder rolls through the atmosphere once again. Sealtiel is bent over the telescope lens. Lightning flashes, illuminating the city. I wince.

Sealtiel's crisp British accent adds to the cacophony. "Love looks through a telescope, and envy, through a microscope." He moves the telescope so it is pointed at me. "Don't beat yourself up over it. You've never learned to master your equilibrium."

I pull my shoulders back and stand to my full height. Holding out my hand, I stride over to him—no longer a man with no value but, instead, a man who knows the value of a daughter's love.

He looks at me as if he were solving a puzzle. "Have you discovered your desire?"

I nod.

He smirks, reaches into his jacket, and pulls out the logbook.

I think back to the whole lazy speech Sealtiel had given me before.

He was right. The first demon I ever let in.

I rotate the dial, entering S-L-O-T-H. The latch pops open.

Soon after that, my mind became a vacancy to all things demon.

Sealtiel covers the latch with a refined hand and snaps it back with great resolve. "In your own time." He looks deeply into my eyes, his green irises smoldering with hope.

"You've only got to remember your name and you'll attain full equilibrium. Just don't beat yourself up over it if you can't remember by race day."

As I place the logbook back in my jacket, my watch, still around Sealtiel's wrist, gives me pause.

"Perhaps you can't remember your name because you choose not to remember. Maybe, deep down, you're afraid to leave this place. Madi and Anna could be alive still. And I get it—you would have them remember you as a good man, not as a cheater."

Sealtiel stumbles over to the elevator and presses the button. "But consider this, were you ever a good man to begin with?"

Lightning strikes overhead as the elevator doors open. Sealtiel walks in. "I hope the book will give you what you are looking for." He grins broadly, revealing his prominent teeth, and the doors close, shutting him in.

There are only three days left. My key could be the coin or Madi's ring. Gabriel's gum-smacking voice runs through my head. It was never an object given to you. Never an object. It could be either one of them.

The hourglass's belly is full, and I head back to the elevator.

As the elevator slows, the impish demons of the painting seem as though they are leering at me. My anger builds and releases all at once. I slam my fist into the painting and pull my arm back. The painting didn't even move, not even an inch. I chuckle. That was not unlike my current situation. No matter how many punches I throw, it will never be enough. I am going to have to find a way to slow my demon down if I'm ever going to win this. The elevator arrives at my stop.

I head back to my apartment.

Outside my living-room window, lightning dances across the sky as thunder sounds in a mad roar.

I strut over to the kitchen and plant the bottle of whiskey on the counter. The trashcan is only a few feet away at the end of the row of cabinets. I step to it, open the lid, and raise the bottle. Ready to release it from my fingers, I stop myself. I can't seem to do it.

Instead, I set it back on the counter.

I'll throw it away tomorrow.

I walk into the bedroom, past the framed American flag on the wall above the bed.

As the thunder outside gets louder, Madi's singing brings tranquility in the midst of the chaos. I spin around. She stands in the doorway in a silky cobalt-blue robe, holding a birthday cupcake with a single lit candle. Singing the birthday song, she approaches until she is holding the cupcake near my mouth. How could I have betrayed her trust? My heart breaks apart. I wish I could take it all back.

"Happy birthday, Mr. Author. Make a wish."

I blow out the candle, and she is gone again. Sadness overwhelms me. She said, "Mr. Author." Did I ever finish the book? I still have yet to read the logbook I wrote myself.

Lightning strikes, and the room momentarily pulses with brilliance. I sit on the bed, grab the logbook from my jacket, and flip to the first page.

Providence.

I peruse the pages. It is filled with my own penmanship. But my name is nowhere to be found. I slump into the decorative pillows behind me. Nevertheless, I did it. I actually finished a book. Eager to start reading, I turn back to the first chapter.

New Year's Eve is like every other night; there is no pause in the march of the universe, no breathless moment of silence among created things, by which the passage of another twelve months may be noted. And yet, no man or woman has quite the same thoughts this evening that come with the encroaching darkness of other nights. This one eve comes with newfound hope; it revolves around second chances and regrets. Let the end of days speak swiftly to every hard heart, so that the New Year will bring to each no doubts but simple clarity.

Reading each successive page, I plumb the depths of my soul. My alarm clock reads 58:01. I've got to find the part about my key. I flip to the very end. On the last page, there is only one thing that my past self wrote me:

Trust Stephanie

Who's Stephanie?

The final seconds flip over on the alarm clock, ticking away to my indelible vulnerability.

59:58…59:59…60:00.

♣ ♠ ♦ ♥

Inside the car, I can barely move. "Anna? Madi? Are you okay?"

Anna wails from the backseat.

In the passenger seat, Madi sobs, clinging to the seatbelt strap across her chest. "I'm so sorry. I'm so sorry. I don't know what came over me!"

The rearview mirror reveals that Anna is still wearing her seatbelt, her eyes tightly closed.

"Everything is going to be okay, little girl. Are you hurt?" She shakes her head and brings her cries down to a whimper. "That's my strong girl. Can you look at me?"

She slowly raises her little head and opens her eyes. She shows me the snow globe in her hands, unbroken.

"That's my girl!"

"Is mommy okay?"

"She's just sleeping. Here's an idea. Why don't you play a song for her so she can hear it and wake right back up?"

Anna turns the bottom dial of the snow globe and music develops out from under it.

A set of headlights flashes through the window behind her, blinding me. The lights get larger and brighter.

Slam!

Little Anna flies toward me, still strapped to the backseat. The snow globe flies past my head. Simultaneously, my body absorbs the momentum of my seat and is pushed toward the dashboard. Our car ricochets into the guardrail, breaking through. It grinds to a halt and teeters on the edge.

A barely playing song trickles out of the snow globe from outside.

I open my eyes to see tiny sprinkles of blood on the snow leading to the broken snow globe.

I turn toward Madi. Her brown eyes stare back at me from the passenger seat, the spark of life gone from them.

Everything blurs while the sound of an alarm clock blares into the carnage.

Beep. Beep. Beep.

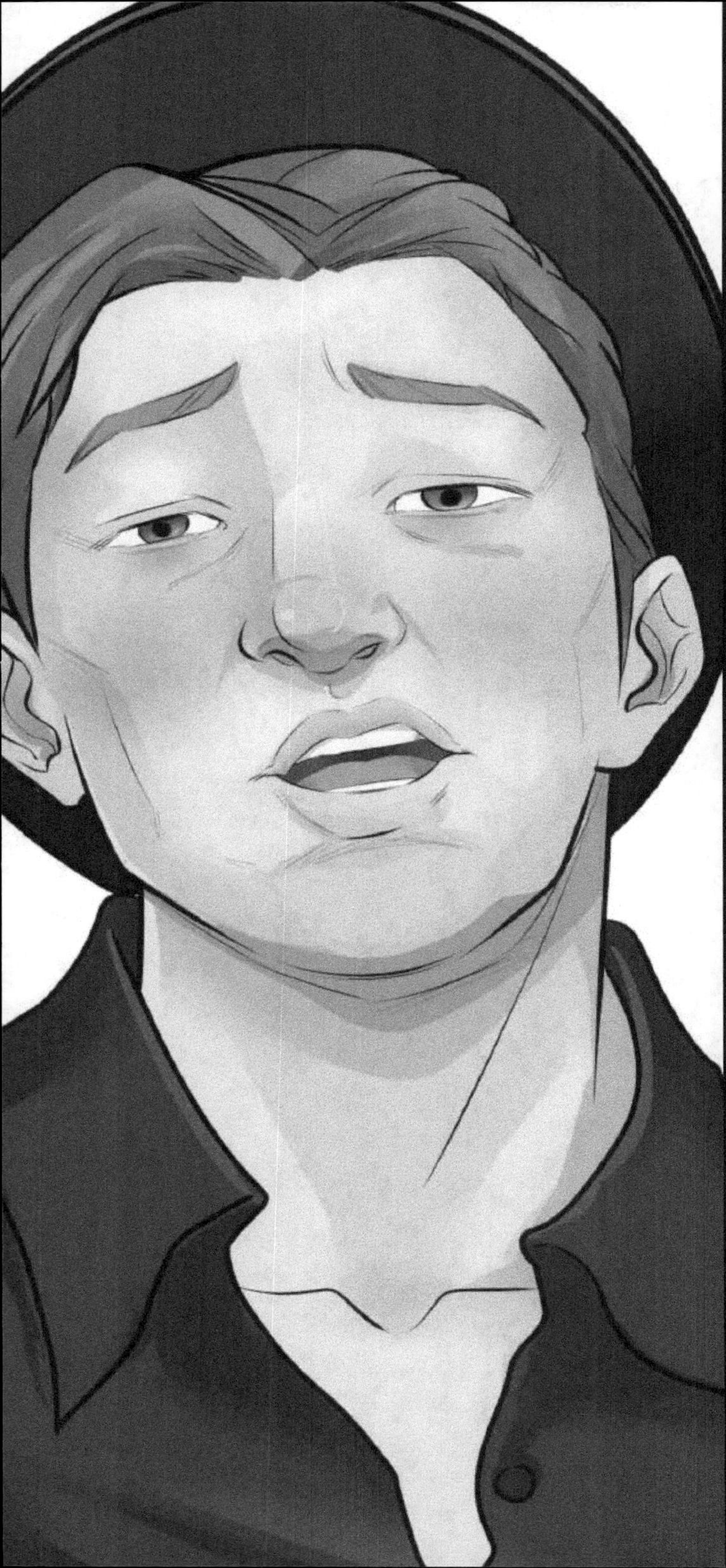

THIRTY-SIX

y eyes feel swollen and bloodshot. I reach my hand over and stop the ringing alarm clock. Long hair drapes over my shoulders and onto my chest. A full beard brushes against my sternum. I cup my face in my hands, the images of Madi's lifeless eyes and Anna's ragdoll body blasting through my mind. They're both dead. They're both dead because of me. Anna's not waiting on me. Madi hasn't moved on. They're just …gone.

The Bible rests again on my nightstand, mocking me in dark hues. I browse the contents of the drawer and come up with a matchbook. After striking a match, I seize the book and hold the flame to its pages. It flickers and then flares as it consumes the black leather and delicate pages.

Here's to you, Mother, for teaching me all about cheating.

I hurl it into the trash can by my bed. The American flag hangs on the wall above the bed, a tribute to everything evil I inherited from my father. I surge to a standing position and smash its frame on the floor. I yank out the flag, flinging the broken pieces of glass around the room.

Here's to you, Father, for telling me consistently how worthless I am.

I throw the flag into the trash. The flames leap to embrace its stars and stripes. Ashes float up and out of the trash can, flying softly in front of me.

Inches from my hand, the snow globe rests on the nightstand. I lift it to eye level. The snow swirls around the tiny city. On the surface, barely visible, are tiny fingerprints. Anna. My fingers whiten as I grip the globe more tightly, replaying the whole incident in my head. I wander to the window, the hourglass reflecting in the pane.

After a few moments, I drop the snow globe to the floor with a thud and push the curtains farther apart. The sky is like something I would see in a painting. Shades of pink and blue daub the otherwise creamy clouds. Plum blossoms cover the ground, and the trees are in brilliant bloom as far as I can see. So painfully beautiful.

I shut the curtains, not wanting to see any more. I retrieve a plush robe from my closet, put it on, and drag my feet to the kitchen. Covering my eyes, I slowly adjust from the darkness to the kitchen's bright white.

I'm surprised to see that the half-drunk bottle of Macallan rests on the kitchen counter right where I left it last night.

It's strange. Usually things go back to the way they were before the next day. Maybe God wants me to drink it. I'm going to go with that assumption.

Like a madman, I run over, unscrew the cap, and tilt it back. The hot liquid warms my throat. Even though I still can't taste anything, it completely satisfies to the last drop. The empty bottle leaves me thirsting for more. I have a feeling the alcoholic in me has fully risen to the surface. On the small chance that I can get another drop, I hold the bottle upside-down over my mouth. Nothing. I search the cabinets for more liquor but have no success.

Ah! There's a flask in my jacket pocket. I run back to the closet, also bathed in purple light, pull the steel flask from my jacket, and take a swig. I spew clear fluid across the floor. Water! Why would anyone put water in a flask? Why?

My finger hits the inscription on the back. I flip it over. Après moi, le déluge. The moment when Madi announced her big news hits me like a knife in the gut. I had a chance to let her go, to save her from me. If I hadn't told her I loved her, none of this would have happened. She would be alive and happy, and I wouldn't be stuck here!

I stumble into the bathroom, fall against the wall, and slide to the floor. The lost souls were right all along. I shouldn't have put all my hopes on them.

The hourglass in the mirror trickles sand through its neck, grain by grain. Maybe I'll shatter it. Then I could finally reach my eternal destination. Finally free my worldly body from another breath and escape from this prison into the place where souls like me belong.

The flask rolls from my limp hand and clatters across the marble floor.

With a sudden surge of energy, I leap toward the mirror and smash my head into the center of the hourglass. Cracks spider web from the epicenter of my impact. There are no noises, only silence now. My head seems to hurt more mentally than physically. The room rocks. Blood spots the broken glass and the sink.

I slam my head into the mirror again and again. The room spins, and I can't stay upright. I fall to the floor in front of the sink.

The piano plays in the living room.

My breath hangs in the air as the temperature drops. The screeching of reapers comes from the hallway. I close my eyes and spread my arms wide, sprawled on the bathroom floor.

The door bursts open. Time to end the pain.

But instead of a cold, bony grip, a soft hand grasps mine. I open my eyelids. Shockingly, the waitress is standing over me.

"Get up!" she shouts. "They're coming! Get up!"

She pulls me into the living room and looks around frantically. The cold air hovers between the two of us.

She looks at the cracked mirror. "Good. You must have not broken the hourglass all the way. " She shakes her head.

I stare through her. I don't care what she says, I'm not going anywhere. "You've been drinking."

My body goes weak and numb. She slides her arms under my shoulders and strains to lift my weight.

"You are too heavy to lift. Looks like I am dragging your drunk butt."

She pulls me through the living room and into the hallway. Muffled screeching is followed by the smashing of a living room window. She drops me and slams the door shut.

She drags me, an unknown force driving her down the hallway toward the elevator.

"You are in dire need of some warmth," she says while heaving me into the elevator.

She props me up against the elevator wall, presses 5, and the doors close.

Why would she risk her life for me? After everything she's been through! She's risking her memories to protect mine? It doesn't make sense but she also could be my demon trying to protect her ride out of this place. I'm too drunk to care either way.

There is nothing left for me anymore.

"You can't give up, not when we have come so close. I know you may not believe me when I say this, but I am your friend. My name is Stephanie."

My eyebrows shoot up, and her creamy skin, wavy dark hair, and cherry-red lips come into focus.

"What they say about me isn't true. I'm not a dirty soul. I'm here to help you."

She is Stephanie? The Stephanie I'm supposed to trust? How is she here to help me? All she has ever done is get herself killed over and over again. I shiver more violently. A new batch of reapers must be on their way.

"I have a lot to explain, I know. If you're not going to do this for me, then how about for the person still playing your music on the outside? Don't you want to know who it is?"

The music on the outside—I'd completely forgotten about it. Someone must still be alive! But who? I slowly nod and force my body to stir. I'm going to have to trust her for now.

My entire body feels like it's freezing over. Have I ever gone this long without getting to the next time zone? How long was my piano playing that song for?

She puts a soft hand on my cheek. Warmth emanates from her hand and expands throughout my body.

"So what are the chances your car is still in the parking lot?"

I smile at her attempt at a joke.

THIRTY-SEVEN

*I*n the coffee shop, Stephanie is sitting at my table, staring at the window. The sand from the hourglass falls silently, filling the lower half. She's probably counting each grain.

I pull out the chair across from her and sit.

"I still can't believe Jehudiel drove your car into a pole. What are the odds? He is one drunken mess of a lost soul. Do pretty much anything to wet his whistle. You two would get along famously."

Stephanie's long, wavy hair is wild and fierce from the harrowing motorcycle ride we just took, her bangs blown to tangles over her large, innocent eyes. The untamed mane only makes her look more beautiful. I was totally wrong about her. She isn't weak at all. Has it all been an act? But why? A few seconds go by as I wait for her to offer some answers.

"I didn't sell you out to the reapers if that's what you're thinking. I was there trying to protect you that night, if you can believe that."

Huh? What night?

Oh, yes. Sealtiel had said that she was there when I last had my mind erased.

"You will get your answers soon enough, I promise." She stands. "Time to leave." She strides to the door with me close behind. She steps outside.

The reflection of the hourglass turns over.

I step through the door, almost running into Stephanie.

The park is lush and green. Plum blossoms float through the air. The breeze combs Stephanie's messy locks. She closes her eyes, her face full of pleasure.

We stop at the bench and sit down. I turn my head toward the tree, now fully alive and covered in cherry blossoms. Beneath its boughs sits the skinny little brown-haired girl. She looks to be playing with something in the grass. I approach her and sit down cross-legged next to her. Stephanie joins us.

"Her name is Lily." Stephanie nods at the little girl.

Lily lifts her tiny head to look at me. Her light brown skin looks soft as silk. Her green eyes hold a mix of sorrow and hope. She glances at the flowering branches and says in a tiny voice, "It's beautiful."

Lily stands and twirls around as the wind brushes cherry blossoms from the tree, leaving them to drift around her. Her childlike laugh echoes through the park, bringing with it a certain calm.

"You know, you helped me," Stephanie says.

I turn to her.

"My whole world came crashing down. I couldn't even die. I tried so many times. I started moving from one person's self-made prison to another. I was alone. No one heard my screams, not even me. But you did somehow. You saved me as best you could. You even read to me every day."

The Ferris wheel towers over the park as if guarding the celebration of life below.

"I truly am here to help you. I'm sorry I haven't come and talked to you about this before, but you gave me strict instructions to approach you on this day. I'm here to help you find the key you hid. You never showed me what it was or where you hid it. I bet you wished you did now." She elbows me softly and smiles.

I relax into the plush turf and smile back.

"First off, your past self told me to tell you that it wasn't the ring."

I look at her, eyes wide. How did she know about the ring?

"And what was the other thing again?"

Leaning forward, she slaps her hands together. "The second thing you told me was a clue! You said to me, 'It's something that can never be taken away, only given.'"

Gabriel's gum-smacking voice plays through my head again. *The key was never an object given to you.*

Barachiel had said that the first morning in the elevator. My name. It was given to me by my parents. No one can give it away. No one can buy it. Jehudiel said he knew my name. He wanted something called a silver? His silver, I think it was. Isn't this supposed to be his day? The colorful park shows no signs of him.

Stephanie turns toward the tree. The little girl is gone. She hops up. In a shaky voice, she says, "I have to go. I'll meet with you later. If they knew I was helping you…well, you know what would happen."

I wonder whom they refers to. The reapers or the lost souls? I stand and turn after her, but she's already on her motorcycle, speeding off toward the interstate.

What scared her off? I pick up my flask and approach the tree, where the little girl had been playing. What does the child have to do with any of this? I stop. What if she isn't just a little girl? What if she is my demon, mirroring a little girl to seem more innocent? It would be a very clever thing to do—trying to tug at my heartstrings, making me think of Anna. Just waiting for the right moment to get itself out of here and into my human body. I shudder. The sky darkens.

I turn back and pass the statue. The hourglass reflected on its box is nearly empty.

I stop briefly at the tree, so different from what it's been all week. With the park now full of shadows, cherry blossoms bounce and dance around me in the wind. What I wouldn't give to have Madi beside me right now and Anna in my arms. It's possible one of them could still be alive, could've survived the accident. A question teeters at the edge of my mind. Who would I rather have alive? What an awful thought—one I cannot now unthink. Guilt weighs in my belly. I can't think like that. A blossom flits near my face and lands on the flask in my hand. The steel glistens. Silver! I raise the flask.

I need to find Jehudiel.

THIRTY-EIGHT

*T*he Christmas tree glows in the corner. The desk is bathed in shadows, but the red and green lights illuminate its mahogany surface. I look around my pristine office, hating how everything is so organized and well-kept. There's not even dust around the lampshade to give it some kind of flaw.

As I turn toward the windows, I exhale a cloud of vapor. The sand in the hourglass pours from the top bulb and turns to snow as it exits the neck.

I check my wrist, remembering my watch is not there.

Did I let the time slip by me?

Beyond the pane, snow falls just like it did in my memories of that night.

The elevator doors open. Stephanie stands inside, holding hands with the little girl.

I run inside the elevator with them and repeatedly pound the Lobby button. "You're late."

Those words alone remind me of when Madi had once said them to me. The best surprise I've ever gotten was in that short moment.

My depression comes over me again.

"We were worried about you." The doors slide closed, and the elevator descends.

"What is going on?" Stephanie asks.

I look down at the little girl. She's just a wisp of a thing. What are her true motives toward me? Her green eyes have a slight droop to them but reveal none of her secrets. Her skin is like smooth cinnamon, a sweet complement to the brown hair flowing a few inches below her soft jaw.

She turns and throws her arms around Stephanie's leg. A puff of thick air leaves my mouth and snaps me back to the reality of the situation. Stephanie waits with a concerned expression.

My body shivers, but they both don't even acknowledge that it's cold. How do they not feel it?

Stephanie rests her hand on the girl's shoulder. "She's not a demon. She's a lost soul, yes. But she isn't here to cause you any harm."

The elevator stops, and the doors open to the lobby.

As we dash out of the building, a loud screeching sounds from the top floor.

We race through the heavy snow toward the road, staying in a tight little group.

An unfamiliar howling resounds from the top floor. We stop. Stephanie and the little girl go completely white.

Stephanie's eyes are locked on the roof of the skyscraper. "They know." Her voice drops to a whisper. "Razors." She snaps her head toward me. "Run! Run as fast as you can." She takes the little girl's hand and darts past me. The shrill howling of the beasts rings out once again. I bolt after them.

As we cross the street, Stephanie slows, trying to flag a car. "We need to separate ourselves! It's the only way you can come out of this with your memories still intact!"

A car slows enough for Stephanie to yank the door open and hop in. She stomps her foot on the brake. The little girl scrambles into the backseat.

The snow obscures my view. Through the white curtain, their forms look just like Madi and Anna on that night of the crash.

"They're here! Run!" Stephanie screams.

Through the sky, a dark creature engulfed in flames flies toward us. It's on a collision course with the car.

From the backseat, the little girl waves for me to get inside. I have two options: save myself or save someone else. Everything slows down as I struggle to decide. I don't even know this girl. She could be my demon trying to trick me. If a reaper gets hold of me, then I might as well be dead. But…the girl makes me think of Anna.

I can't let this happen again. At lightning speed, I throw open the back door, pull her out, and bound toward the Lighthouse Restaurant. Her bare arms are frigid against the skin on my neck. I adjust her weight, so she won't slip.

From behind, an explosion pushes a blast of freezing air into me, adding to my forward momentum. I hold the girl tighter as we shoot toward the doors ahead. The cold atmosphere takes over my whole body. I slow and loosen my grip on the child.

Stephanie runs past me. Somehow, she must have survived! She opens the door to the restaurant and turns back toward us. The little girl begins to slip from my grasp.

A couple yards ahead, the dark creature steps out of the shadows. It walks on four legs, flames licking its pointed ears. Its head bears a canine resemblance. I envelop the girl in my jacket, shielding her from its view.

The fiery creature stops inches from my face. Its devilish eyes are black, except for a red-hot flame glistening deep within its pupils. It snorts cold air across my face and sniffs at me. Focusing its attention beyond me, it raises its head calmly. Apparently, it's not interested in me.

As the creature stands immobile, the flames surrounding its body ice over. The fire turns to icicles that stick out like toothpicks across its exterior.

The beast lowers its snout to my jacket. It sniffs and growls. Chains jangle behind it, and it's forced backward at its neck. Its collar is the size of a body builder's belt. Several yards past the creature, a reaper pulls on the chains and screeches.

The razor fights against the chains. I slowly back away. The beast growls, and sand pours from its mouth like foam. It caught the little girl's scent…why not mine?

Stephanie still holds the open door, gripping its handle with a look of horror on her face. I turn back as the hellhound lunges. While I stumble backward, the little girl forces her way out of my grip.

She seizes one of the icicles at the razor's shoulder, breaks it off, and stabs it into the beast's eye. It recoils, yelping and whimpering. She's tougher than she appears.

I swoop up the little girl again and run for the door.

As I get closer, Stephanie slips into the restaurant. I squeeze the little girl tighter and dive through the open door.

I slide on my back across the restaurant's frozen floor with the little girl clinging to my front side. Stephanie slams the door, but the razor breaks through, shattering the door to icy splinters.

Though the temperature is normal in the restaurant, snow still falls outside the window.

We're in the right time zone. How can they still be advancing? Using one of the dining chairs, I heave myself up.

The creature hurdles its way toward Stephanie.

Stephanie is not dying today.

I rush over and get in between the both of them. Shielding her with my body, I patiently wait for the pain to join in.

A familiar jingle comes from over the hill. The reaper with the chains is caught in bright headlights. An ice cream truck speeds across the road, plows through the cloaked figure, and zooms away. The reaper skids across the icy pavement, jerking the chains back with it. The razor is yanked sideways. It scrambles to hold its ground. But it slips and is dragged out of the restaurant.

The reaper rights itself, shrieks, and turns in the direction of the children's jingle blazing out of the ice cream truck's loud speaker. The razor fights against its master as the chains retract. The hellhound stumbles backward, landing a foot or two in front of the reaper. The reaper grabs its collar. The hound implodes into sand. After wrapping the collar around its waist, the reaper leaps into the air and flies after the car, leaving a trail of ice behind.

Was that Gabriel?

Stephanie looks at me. "We should be fine for now. The razor has to follow its master."

What in the hell was that? The little girl's tight grip eases, and her stranglehold turns into a warm hug. I hold her tightly for a few seconds. If only I could've held Anna like this after the accident, told her it was all okay…that we were all safe.

Stephanie smiles, her face soft and happy. "Thank you."

The girl releases the hug, resting her hands gently on my biceps, and lifts her head. "Thank you."

Stephanie whispers silently to the little girl.

The little girl nods and steps away. She turns back and kisses me on the cheek. Her lips are cold, and I shiver. She then runs off out the back.

I cross to the broken door. Her brown hair bounces around as she runs through the snow toward the park, her heels kicking up under her thin, pale blue dress.

Stephanie slides next to me. "I can see worry in your eyes. Don't. She'll be fine. She has been doing this just as long, if not longer, than the both of us. She is a lost soul that never stood a chance."

I turn to her.

"She was in her mother's womb when she fell into a coma. I found her alone, searching. We never found her mama. I've been taking care of her ever since. Well, I guess we have. It's kind of weird to say, but we are the only family she's got."

I turn back to the gaping doorway. She's gone. How could I not remember her? I wish I could conjure up the times we've had together.

As we cross the room, I turn my head to the door a couple times. How was that thing able to enter this time zone? Why was it after Stephanie and the girl?

"Those were razors. As you well know, reapers are the time-keepers, but their watchdogs are lost soul hunters. Like Lily and myself."

So those must be the hounds I've been hearing about. What was the reason why they couldn't see lost souls again?

We reach the bar, and she extends her hand. "Touch me."

I'm a little thrown off guard. I blush. She then holds out her hand and I realize what she really meant.

I wrap my fingers around her wrist. It's like taking hold of a snowball.

"Cold to the touch, don't you think?"

I release my fingers, and the coldness in my hand turns back to the typical numbness.

"Reapers are attracted to heat signatures like yourself. Since your human body hasn't been claimed, your soul is still pure, like a hot match with a strong flame. With lost souls, the match is black. Not even a spark."

That's right! Now I remember. I can't imagine being cold all the time. It must be hard to keep warm.

She walks around the bar counter. "You just get used to it after a while." Her tone turns sad. "Let's hope you don't have to." She pours golden liquid into a glass.

The fluid settles and reflects the light from the chandelier.

"No more drinking for you, mister."

She's probably right. I shouldn't be here.

I push away from the bar and walk out onto the balcony. On a single table in the back is a book.

I recognize right away that it's my logbook.

I caress the worn leather of the book. It's in perfect condition. Not a single burn mark from when I torched it this morning.

I flip through the pages and everything is still as it was.

How did this get here?

Stephanie steps out with the silver-domed tray and sets it next to me.

Did she put it here?

"Looks like a good book you're reading there." She sits across from me. The light wind picks up strands of her dark hair and tosses them into her face. She isn't just the waitress or a lost soul anymore; she's become a person I can trust.

"You let me read it once or twice." She blushes.

I close the book and place it on the table.

Stephanie's eyes glisten. "My husband was a lot like who you were. He always wanted something better—better car, better house, better life, and, I guess, a better wife. Every night, he would come home drunk and beat me. It just made him feel better about his life, and I just took it." Her face pales. "One day, we went to the park. We were laughing, and for a second, I actually thought maybe he'd changed. I told him I was one month pregnant. I told him that I'd hid it from him because his job had been stressing him out for the last few months. I didn't want to put more stress on him. But he didn't see it that way. He hit me, and I fell."

Her big, round eyes tear up. "My stomach collided with the top of a railing. That's when I knew I lost the baby." Sobs wrack her body.

I reach across the table and grasp her hand.

"She was going to be called Ally. It was too early to tell officially, but somehow I knew deep down that I was going to have a baby girl." She clings to my hand, letting the sorrow pour from her eyes. "Then one night, he came home drunk. This time, he hit a little bit too hard. Bada-bing, bada-boom. I wake back up, and I'm stuck in a place like this. There were voices that whispered to me all the time about Ally and how she was still alive. They also spoke about all the things they would do if they saw my husband again. I won't lie when I say that I liked every scenario they played out for me about torturing him. It kept me sane, thinking of all the ways to bring him pain. Then they told me they were a part of me and that they could bring him to justice. So…I let them take up residence in my body, and I became a lost soul. I searched for Ally a long time. Going in and out of other people's prisons got me to realize about the demons. I put two and two together, knowing they were not voices at all. To be honest with myself, I knew deep down the voices were something evil, but I just didn't care. I wanted to see my daughter. I wanted to tell her I was sorry. I wanted her to know…"

Stephanie takes a moment to breathe.

The reflection in the silver dome shows the hourglass is almost empty.

I stand, sympathetically squeezing her hand one last time before letting go.

"It's a great book you wrote! She would be very proud of you."

I pause, trying to control my emotions.

I need to know who is playing the record on the outside. I pick up the book, almost as if I am praying for an answer.

I raise my head to find that Stephanie is gone. The hourglass flips over.

There's no time to waste. Holding the book, I jog down the stairs and move toward the subway. Once inside the station, I pass a man lying on one of the benches. A black fedora covers his face, the Queen of Spades sticking out of its band. His white dress shirt, once crisp, is now wrinkled under his light blue suspenders. There's an empty bottle lying on the ground next to his limp hand.

It's Jehudiel! I run to him and shove him off of the bench.

He hits the ground with a thud and stumbles to his feet, twitching every which way. He looks at me with glazed eyes. He plays with his sky blue colored suspenders as if trying to remember something. "Wait! What's my name again? Je…Jegcial …Jesusal…

wait. I'm going to get it. Jehudiel! That's it!" He raises a finger. "Hey! Alice! Come for the tea party? You just missed the man in white. He loves tea."

Jehudiel downs another swig of liquor. The flask in my pocket! I take it out and present it to him. He gazes at it, his eyes lighting up. "You've come back to me, silver!" He reaches for the flask, but I quickly put it behind my back.

"How rude!" he says, slurring his words. "Someone told me that you were a scholar and a gentleman; apparently, they were mistaken on both accounts!" He lifts the bottle to his mouth and chugs.

Maybe this job of saving souls has gotten to him more than the others. I wave the flask over his head. He stops drinking.

He stares for a few seconds with a bewildered expression.

"Ahhh! Your name! That's right! I wish I could remember my name. A name is a very important thing. You can lose yourself by not knowing."

Is that what happened to him and the rest of the lost souls? By not knowing their names did it have some psychological effect in the way they see things. Maybe being a lost soul for so long doesn't help the matter either. That could be the reason as to why they think Stephanie and Lily are dirty souls. They survive by giving themselves purpose. They make new names for themselves and leave their past behind hoping to forget. Seeing other lost souls like themselves must make them realize the truth. That they let their demons win.

Jehudiel gets close to my face and says, "Do you know my name?"

I shake my head.

"But you do. I know you do. And also, don't you have some place to be?" He points over his shoulder.

Behind him, the subway car doors have closed. I race toward the car, but I'm too late! I bury my hands in my hair and squeeze them into fists. What am I going to do?

"Class dismissed! Or class is canceled, might be another term for it. What was I supposed to teach you again?" He leans against the bench until he regains his balance. "Ah, yes! The art of mirroring. That was it! No, that wasn't it. Why couldn't I have been responsible for teaching you how to…wait…what was I saying?" He falls back across the bench and starts whispering to himself.

I'm screwed.

His breath turns to a cloud of vapor. The earth-shattering screams of reapers echo through the subway terminal. I grab Jehudiel by his sky-blue suspenders and lift his face to mine.

What is my name?! I need to know!

"Lost souls don't drink, do they? And since I am a lost soul, then that is what I don't do. But if I were to, which I never proclaimed I did, then I would probably have said unto you…" He holds out his hand. "What is worth more to you, I wonder? Remembering your Christian name?" He points over my shoulder. "Or remembering anything at all?"

I don't need to turn around, knowing what is waiting for me if I do.

Frigid air envelops us. Jehudiel places his hands on either side of my head and whispers into my ear, "I will meet you in Wonderland. Back inside the rabbit hole you go, Alice." He twirls a finger in the air, totters, and falls back onto the bench, whispering to himself again.

What is he talking about? Inside the rabbit hole? In the story of *Alice in Wonderland*, Alice climbed down a hole. Wait! No, a rabbit hole. He must be talking about the dead tree in the park!

I hustle up the stairs and out of the subway, leaving Jehudiel with his crazy thoughts. From a distance, a familiar melody reaches my ears. It's 42:02! I have only seconds left. Pumping my legs as fast as they can go, I tear down the grassy field. The cold air leaves my mouth dry. The arctic winds rake against my cheeks and freeze my hair.

I keep my eyes locked on the tree as my eyelashes ice over. My salvation is just a few feet away. The reapers' loud screeching is drowned out by the mounting music. Almost there. The tree has been completely iced over. The polar temperature weighs on me as if I were running underwater. My soul burns away any strength I have left for this last push. I dig deep, bursting through the airy blockade and hurtling my body toward the frozen door. The sound of the music from above grows louder, cascading over the whole park. The edges of my vision break apart like puzzle pieces as I smash through the glacial exterior.

THIRTY-NINE

ilence. I open my eyes. I'm lying on a bed, naked. My head feels like I've been hit by a truck. Probably hungover. I turn to one side. I'm back in my extravagant apartment. The bedroom door is open. How did I get back here? On the floor is a set of pants and a shirt I've never worn. My mind retreats, and I find I'm observing myself again, not in control.

On the nightstand is a black leather Bible and a clock that reads 5:45 AM.

I roll to the edge of the bed. My head pounds as I pull on the pants and shirt.

I stand up, but my knees shake and my head spins. I fall back onto the nightstand, knocking the Bible to the floor. My stomach contracts violently, and I throw up on the bedspread. After a few more heaves, I steady myself and stand back up. That's better.

I reach into my pants pockets—my wallet and keys are gone. Better call reception for a taxi. I turn toward the phone, but a lacy black bra on the bed stops me. Visions of Lisa, breathing hard, her weight on top of me, run through my head like a movie reel.

I yell out, "Lisa?"

She's not in the bathroom. The kitchen and living room are empty, too.

Back in the bedroom, I find a suitcase resting on the brown leather chaise. I unsnap the latches. The money's gone. It's been replaced with a half-empty bottle of Macallan. A note is stuck to the side of the liquor bottle: *Thank you.*

She used me to get to my winnings. I look at the hotel phone on the desk.

Madi! She must be worried sick that I didn't come home.

What am I going to tell her? The truth? How is she ever going to forgive me? I fall to the floor and lean my head against the chaise. I uncork the bottle of whisky and guzzle half of it. I reach for the hotel phone and rest it in my lap. I pick up the receiver and look at the numbers, not knowing what to say.

Whispers dance at the edge of my consciousness. I regain control of my mind and try to keep the evil thoughts at bay. The voices break through.

Lie.

That hushed murmur is my demon. It has been hiding from me in plain sight all this time. Whispering to me, making me say or do things. I won't let it get to me, not now, not ever again!

Lie.

My eyesight blurs, and the room feels like its spinning. The alcohol has taken effect. My drunken haze begins sending my thoughts and vision into the pitch-black void of nothingness.

Lie.

I open my eyes and sit up. The room spins; everything blurs. An empty bottle lies next to me, a bed beyond that. I'm still in the bedroom, now wearing my designer suit. I clamber up and lean against the bed until I have a sense of balance. I stumble through the living room to the door and open it. Directly across the hall, another door displays the number 6. I turn to the front side of my door. It is marked 5. I'm in Stephanie's room. No longer am I in my memory or inside the tree.

Did Stephanie carry me all this way? I took her strength for granted.

Confused, I turn back to the room—gleaming hardwood floors, floor-to-ceiling bookcases, a Yamaha Grand Disklavier in the corner, a brocade settee. It's an exact replica of my apartment!

Are all the rooms the same as mine?

I stumble back to the bedroom. I've got to check the time. I look at the alarm clock beside Stephanie's bed.

Forty-five minutes.

I have five minutes to make it to the roof. My head is still spinning, walking back through the apartment is like wading through mud. Once I'm in the hallway, the Japanese flower design on the rug stretches and twists as if it were growing toward the ceiling. I lean against the wall until the dizzy spell dissipates. I gradually stagger to the elevator and fall in.

I'm not sure how long it's been, but the sand is falling somewhere, and I've got to get to the roof. I pull myself together enough to crawl to my knees and reach the panel of buttons. I tap the one for the roof. Just above it is a three-inch slot. As the elevator whirs and moves upward, I finger the opening. It makes me remember the card slot to get into the private casino room.

The painting of the cross reflects in the doors, its electric blue brilliant even on the metallic surface.

I whirl to the painting and gaze at where the eye of greed would go in the painting.

What if this was the lock and the golden eye was actually the key?

But the only thing that is of gold in this place is that coin necklace that magically appears and disappears around people's necks.

My head begins to hurt as if my brain is trying hard not to let me remember.

I let the bright colors of the demons on the painting distract me to calm my head. Orange, purple, red, green, navy, sky blue, and yellow. It's not until just now that I begin to realize the resemblance of the colors shown here is the same colors I've seen on each of the lost souls clothing. Barachiel's yellow pocket square. Michael's red tie. Gabriel's orange socks. Raphael's purple sports jacket. Uriel's navy tuxedo. Sealtiel's green vest and Judicial's sky blue suspenders. This can't mean what I think it means.

Tremors overcome my limbs, and my heart palpitates.

I fall against the wall and slide back down to the floor, my head in a massive amount of pain. A clamor rattles above me. The ceiling tiles are pulled away, and Jehudiel falls through. "What in the H. E.

double hockey sticks are you doing? So, this is where you went off to!" he says with a slur. He looks around the small space, apparently confused by what just went down.

"Now where is my silver, my dear Alice?" He roughly searches my coat pockets and removes the flask. He shakes it, gleefully smiling. He plops down in the corner opposite me and passionately twists the top off. He smirks and holds it a little longer, as if savoring the moment. Jehudiel tilts the flask back and swallows heartily.

His eyes widen, and his chest convulses. "What did you put in this?" He looks at the flask and drops it between us. His voice is loud and angry. He struggles to move. His face shifts to look like me as his body steams, the water struggling to free itself from what's hidden within. His expression turns beastly as horns begin to grow on top of his forehead and his teeth become razor-sharp.

It's true. I'm not guilty of just one of the deadly sins. I'm guilty of all of them. There never were any lost souls trying to help me escape. They've been trying to help me finish the race so they could get a chance to challenge me for my vessel.

He reverts to his original form with close-cut hair, black fedora, and light blue suspenders. I slowly stand and press the button for the elevator to continue.

"Glad to finally make your acquaintance!" Jehudiel screams with excitement. "I hated faking. Too much to keep up with! Never knew what to say. They even gave me the hardest name to learn. Jehudiel? Who would want a name like that? I mean, really?" He bends down next to me. "But any-who, I am so glad to hear that you loved my work. Don't get me wrong; without you, there would be no me." He gets closer, whispering, "But let's keep this a secret between you and me. Let's not bring the others' attention to your new findings. They have been working really hard. Let's not spoil it. Okay?"

I open my mouth to yell at him, but my voice still hasn't come back.

"Look, we are on the same side as of right now. We both want the same thing. You need to finish the race, and we want you to finish it."

His green eyes are the same color as mine. It's disgusting that we share that small resemblance. Why should I listen to him? He's only trying to fulfill his own needs. I don't need his help.

You did this. You're the reason I'm here.

Jehudiel produces a resounding laugh. "Me? Little ol' me? No, no, no. You, Alice. You are the one in charge of your own destiny. You are being quite the selfish one. The blame game is a nice card to play. My personal favorite. Well, that and a single white lie. For some reason, even the littlest of lies still has a grand outcome if you use it correctly, of course. Still, you got that from me." Jehudiel smiles mischievously. "Don't you get it? We are all apart of you."

I ball my fist up.

You're not going to take my life away from me! You hear me?!

Jehudiel sputters and coughs. "You don't understand, do you, Alice? I don't want your life like the rest of them do. You see, I like it here. I want you to stay. I always wanted you to stay. We are one and the same, you and me. Like soul brothers, we are! When we become lost souls, there will be no more rules. No more reapers. Just you and I to roam free and visit other people's prisons. All that needs to happen is for you to finish the race and choose one of your demons to take your place in the outside world. That's all."

This isn't happening. The walls feel like they're closing in on me. I can't breath.

Jehudiel pulls out a Queen of Hearts mask from inside his vest. He puts it on over his contorted face. "What do you say? Can I be the queen to your king?"

The elevator stops, and the doors slide open. I turn to leave, but Barachiel stands in front of me. He grabs my arm and pulls me out onto the rooftop.

Behind me, Jehudiel screams, "What kind of lost soul"—Barachiel steps around me with the flintlock pistol in his hand—"do you think—"

Barachiel presses the pistol to the mouth of the mask and pulls the Queen of Hearts card from Jehudiel's fedora. With the gun still held in place, he reaches down and scoops up the flask.

I step in, groping for the gun, wanting to be the one to make the kill. Barachiel fights me for the weapon and fumbles the card to the floor.

The elevator doors slide toward each other. Barachiel snatches the card off the floor and pulls me back from the compartment, where Barachiel proceeds to fire through the two-inch slit, hitting the mask near its lips. The doors meet, sealing Jehudiel in.

"Don't ever stand in my way again!" Barachiel shouts in my face, breathing heavily. He pounds a fist on the closed door. "I can already assume by Jehudiel's actions that you have come to know the truth."

The hourglass on the far edge of the roof pours sand.

I look at his priest attire and shake my head towards him.

This get up won't fool me. I know you're one of my demons, if you can even hear what I'm thinking. I should have known there were never any lost souls, that this was just a dog race between a bunch of demons.

He turns back to me. "Listen to me, old sport. I can't read your mind. I have no inkling what you are thinking right now. Only your demons can do that. I'm no demon nor a dirty soul. I'm actually a real lost soul. Believe me or don't believe me; that is your own decision."

He sets the lamb gun on a table and backs away. "Nearly three minutes remain. Let us not waste time on inconsequential debates." He throws me the flask.

I catch it and turn away.

Barachiel's cultured voice comes from behind. "Nowhere can man find a quieter or more untroubled retreat than in his own soul."

I release my hand, and the stainless steel clatters on the ground.

Looking at the yellow handkerchief in his breast pocket immediately brings me back into focus with all that I just discovered.

Barachiel closes the distance between us, reaches into his suit jacket, and pulls out a book.

I recognize right away that it's the same Bible from my nightstand.

He hands it to me.

I caress the worn leather of the book. It's in perfect condition. Not a single burn mark from when I torched it this morning.

What's the point in this?

He is trying to confuse me. He is only acting the part of an angelic priest. The jig is up. I'm done playing their games.

I toss the book toward his feet and stand straight to see what he has to say about that.

He casually walks over, picks the book off the ground, and begins to walk over to me. His eyes are locked in on mine.

I should have thought about my actions more carefully.

I begin to tense up and close my eyes.

This is it. This is how it all ends. By a demon dressed up in a priest suit.

After a few seconds, I open them back up and notice Barachiel heading toward one of the tables.

I step up onto the roof ledge.

Barachiel walks back to where I am standing with two chairs in his hands. "You can trust me." He sets the chairs down and sits in one of them. "I am a real lost soul. I know what you are feeling right now. I have been where you are. The only difference is that I took what I thought was the easy road and gave up. You still have a choice, old sport. You already met my partner."

Partner?

Stephanie walks through the open doorway from the stairwell. She's in on it, too? She strides across the roof and stops at the nearest table. "So the secret's out. And let me guess, you don't trust us being lost souls now. Somehow, I knew you wouldn't, which is why I brought this." Stephanie takes out a rectangular case and places it on the table. She opens it, revealing an empty depression the size of my pistol, a flask of black powder, five lead shots, and a ramrod.

There are two empty bullet slots next to the five lead balls.

"You gave this to me in trust."

She lays the flintlock pistol down on the table. On the golden butt of the gun is the lion.

"Next time, don't hide something that could kill a demon inside your fridge."

Pistol in hand, she walks toward me.

What is she planning to do with it? Shoot me?

She walks toward me with the muzzle pointed up at my chest. She stops a couple of feet in front of me, twirls the gun around, and lifts the butt toward my hand.

"A lead ball is already loaded into each pistol. Since you have chosen the lion you will not be able to shoot from the lamb. Only demons and lost souls can pull that trigger. Got it?"

I grab it and point it at her, my thumb on the hammer.

She lifts her hands. "If you fire, then you lose another bullet, and that means you are left with only five. If you do the math, then you will know there are more than five demons out there. So keep that in mind before you waste one." She drops her hand.

Barachiel steps in front of her. "You have trusted her up to now. There is no reason not to trust her now. If you are going to aim that at someone, let it be me."

I hold the gun to Barachiel's face.

"You have to shoot up inside my mouth. The bullet must hit the center of the brain. If it doesn't, the demon will not die. That bullet can only hurt demons. It will not hurt lost souls like Stephanie and I. Now, if you believe me to be a demon, shoot me. Please, just don't miss."

He is bluffing. I know it.

"I was where you are right now. I know what your feeling. I trusted someone and they proved to be my demon in the end. He caught me by surprise and shot me. The challenge was won in his favor. I think about what my demon is doing inside my body everyday. I have a daughter and I don't know if she is alive or dead." Barachiel's eyes begin to tear up. "All because I listened to someone that I thought had my best intentions. But that's what demons do. Fill your head with sin and blacken the soul. Everyday the world gets more and more corrupted by the demons we unleash. Their sin drowns human kind with chaos and destruction. If I could just save one soul from giving into them then that's one less evil in the world." He then looks dead into my eyes and says, "We can't let them win. We can't."

I step down from the ledge and thrust the gun inside Barachiel's mouth.

I don't know who to trust anymore. How do I even know if he is telling the truth?

Stephanie walks closer to me, "He never remembered his name before he became a lost soul. His alias name you gave him is Barachiel. He was the first one that trained you on how to fire your gun. Which helped you kill one of your demons. After Lily showed up and told you that your life support was ending you came up with a plan. You made your demons believe that Barachiel was the demon you initially killed. Plan A was having Barachiel distract your demons while you ran the race. But unfortunately, something happened toward the end and a reaper got a hold of you. After that Barachiel and I initiated Plan B. We got your demons on board to help move your memory process faster. Pretending to be lost souls, the archangel names, all this just so we could speed you up on the details. Let's just say what you usually learn in a month we got you there in nearly a week."

Stephanie steps around him and places her hand on my arm.

"You're not going to end up like her."

I turn my eyes toward Stephanie.

"Your mom."

I begin shaking the pistol, not wanting to hear it.

"Your past self told me things. Things that he struggled with even before he got his memory back. He always felt an unknown pain inside of him."

I hold the gun steady, not wanting to believe her.

"You are stronger than her. You told me your father may not have been a saint, but neither was he all sinner. He loved your mother. Loved her enough that when she left, a part of him left with her. He drowned in his sorrow and you were the only one there to pick up the pieces. She left, and you stayed. Why? Because you have a good soul, and just like any good soul it can get corrupted from time to time. But second chances do exist. We are sorry that we couldn't keep you in the loop and that trusting us won't come easy now. But I'm asking you to trust us. I'm asking you for a second chance."

Barachiel stands immobile, the barrel of the gun halfway in his open mouth. The hourglass pendant hangs around his neck. The golden engraved wings spread out behind the Celtic timepiece. I rip it off his neck and look at the stunning yellowish glow coming off of it. I hold it out for him to see and take the gun out of his mouth.

I'm going home.

I walk inside the opened elevator and place the coin in the yellow demons right eye. I twist it to the right and it locks into place.

After a few seconds, nothing happens.

"You can't leave without finishing the race."

I stubbornly continue to wait, realizing he is right. I take the coin out and leave the elevator.

Hopelessly, I stare at the golden coin, tracing my finger around the hourglass.

Barachiel steps closer to me. "I kept it safe for you."

I bring my finger back to the trigger.

Lies.

"You gave it to me, hoping it would be enough to trust me again. I have another way for you to make sure I'm not a demon."

I give him five seconds to make his case. I ease off the trigger.

"Demons are fast but they do have a weakness. Water. It slows them down. Just long enough to eat a bullet. Literally. Do you still have the flask?"

That's right! Jehudiel's face changed once he drank the water.

I hand him over the flask. He sips. Nothing happens. I'm still uncertain, but slowly lay my gun down. Everyone relaxes.

Looking at the pendent, I realize Barachiel must have been the one who's been helping me all this time. I take the gun and lay it on the table. I sit down in one of the chairs.

Stephanie puts the gun back in the case. "Good choice. By the way he was the one that got you up to my room on time. I surely couldn't have carried your fat butt back."

Barachiel crosses his arms and leans against the table. "In two days, your heart will stop. Tomorrow, they are expecting me to help you find your key. That will not be the case. Instead tomorrow will be your Exodus."

Stephanie steps closer. "We want you to run it tomorrow."

I raise my eyebrows and pace.

"It is the perfect time to do it. We could catch each of your demons off-guard." She looks at Barachiel. "It would give us enough time to slow them down, so they won't interfere in any way."

Barachiel's face is confident as he reaches around his back and pulls out the other flintlock pistol. "Once they get wind of what your doing they will be coming for their pistol and I will surely let them all get a taste of it before I fall."

Stephanie picks up the pistol from the table. "I promise I will keep yours safe till the duel is initiated."

They're both insane. I don't even have my key yet. I turn away from them, hoping they get the picture.

Cold air envelops me.

Stephanie hands me back my logbook and flask. "We were lost souls until we met you. You showed us how to find our grace again. There is a return. You said that."

Something as wise as that coming from me seems so off, like it was another man who said those words. But how do I become that man again? I tuck the book into one of my empty jacket pockets along with the flask.

Stephanie looks into my eyes. "Listen to me when I say that tomorrow is our only chance in getting you home."

With his hand cupping the back of my hand he closes my fingers around the coin.

"Now you have no reason to say no."

So this really is my key.

The night air is arctic.

Stephanie runs to my side, grasps my bicep, and escorts me to my escape. Her green eyes bore into mine.

The elevator doors slide open. Jehudiel's body is gone. All that's left is the mask, swimming in a puddle of water on the elevator rug.

The mask oddly exhibits a spider web of cracks from a tiny hole on the right cheek.

Stephanie peeks in and picks the mask up. "That's one down."

I walk in as the doors close behind me.

The elevator hums to life, and I turn to face the painting. The snarls of the demons threaten the brilliance of the cross. The intensity of it sinks into my spirit.

I look away and stare at the elevator panel. The card slot, sitting above it, takes up the rest of my attention.

I take the playing card out of my pocket and place it in the card slot.

Beep!

Inside the slot flashes a red color.

The color makes me remember Lisa's red dress and how it wrapped around me in the elevator that night.

I let Lisa push me inside this elevator. Just like how I've been letting my demons push me to the finish line.

I look around at the canvas and get lost in it. Gazing at each of the demons, pushing and pulling on the cross.

It's not a portrait. It's a self image.

My warm breath turns into a cloud of vapor, obscuring my vision. I blink. How long have I been standing here? I whirl. The elevator doors stand open to my floor. Why is it cold? Am I not in the right time zone? My body shivers violently.

I scamper to my door and push it open.

The whole room is a wintery wonderland. Everything, from the chandelier to the piano, is covered in ice. Snow particles drift from the ceiling, making their way down to greet me. I move silently on the iced-over ground. Framed in the living room windows is the inky night sky, speckled with points of dazzling lights.

In my bedroom, everything has also been frozen. Through a layer of ice, my alarm clock reads: 58:52. I'm in the right time zone. The temperature should be normal.

The heavy window drapes shudder, and a stiff gust travels the room, swirling the falling snowflakes. Below the sill, fragments of glass litter the hardwood, and the pane itself is marred, with only long, jagged edges of its reflective surface left. Someone broke the hourglass! I need to get on the bed right now!

I swivel back toward my bed. A reaper floats on the far side. I flinch, and my muscles coil, ready to jump for it. The reaper's skull mask shields all but its cruel dark eyes. Its black cloak seems a portal to an abyss. The bed is my safe zone, but it's still several feet away. The reaper's legs extend to the floor, radiating another layer of ice across the hardwood. Before I can dive into bed, the reaper heaves the mattress at me. I leap out of the way as the innerspring crashes through what's left of the window. A pen clatters to the floor from the nightstand, and I snatch it. I jump toward the reaper, yank its hood down, and stab the pen into its skull. The reaper drops to the floor, melting the ice below.

More reapers appear at the window. With the bed dismantled, my only option is to mask my heat signature. I skate toward the kitchen, slamming the bedroom door as I go through. That's only going to buy me a couple of seconds

I stumble and slip my way to the refrigerator, knock the inner shelves off-track, and crawl inside. After setting the thermostat as low as it will go, I pull the door closed. Curled up in a ball in pitch darkness, I breathe shallowly, careful not to make any noise. The tight seal of the fridge muffles shrieking, banging, and clattering from the room outside. The temperature plunges further than the thermostat could take it. They're probably freezing over the entire kitchen. The crackle of forming ice runs along the seam of the door.

Finally, the sounds disappear.

I put my shoulder against the door and push. It doesn't budge. I muster all my strength and push again. Nothing. How much time do I have left? What happens if I'm not in the final time zone before the clock runs out? I try pushing again. A quiet cracking sound runs along the seal. A tiny bit of light shines through a millimeter-wide gap. I give it another thrust, but it still won't open.

The sliver of light disappears, and I'm plunged back into darkness.

♣ ♠ ♦ ♥

A cracked, bloody snow globe lies in the snow, nearing the end of its broken tune. I am sprawled in the snow. The flurries have stopped, for the moment. My body is numb with shock. Beside me, the car rests upside-down, its headlights askew from the collision. The beams shine in bent and twisted angles. I slowly turn my aching head. Above is a billboard with a pop singer's face. Not far from that are the metal girders of the bridge. I turn my head back toward the car. Madi is inside, pressed against the roof. Her eyes are open, looking at me. A tear streaks through the blood on her face. Just past her, Anna's still body protrudes through the windshield.

My weak voice calls, "Madi? Madi? Please, Madi, hold on."

I grope the ground, trying to get a handle to continue my forward momentum. But my hand lands on something hard and spherical. I lift it enough to make out the shape. Anna's snow globe. It's broken on one side, and the fluid is gone. The music from the snow globe comes to an end leaving a deathly silence in the air. Tears pour like a flood, running across my temple and dripping from my ear.

My head is too heavy to lift any longer. I rest it on the ground and close my eyes as sobs wrack my body. When I open my eyes again, my vision is blurred and hazy. The asphalt crunches behind me as a black sedan drives up. It pulls into my line of sight and stops. Though hazy, its front end shows damage.

That's the car that hit us. Masculine laughter spills from the car and is joined by the merriment of a woman's voice.

The world spins, and I close my eyes for a few seconds. I slit my eyelids enough to watch the black vehicle drive away. My vision is blurred as I try to read the license plate.

Slowly, my vision sharpens: LBYRNTH.

The pain is starting to register now. With a great effort, I turn my head back toward Madi. My vision fades, and I slip into unconsciousness. In the darkness, a small voice calls out. "Daddy?"

Beep. Beep. Beep.

GAMBIT

SATURDAY

FORTY-ONE

I wake up. Silky sheets and a warm comforter cocoon me in my oversized bed. I reach over and stop the alarm from singing. I look over at the snow globe on my nightstand. In its reflection, I see my bearded face and long hair. Even my face looks skinnier. I've become unrecognizable, even to myself.

I prop myself up on my elbows. The coin necklace still rests around my neck. The Bible is back on my nightstand. I pick it up, slam it at my door, and lie there, not wanting to move. I stare at the ceiling, wondering if this was why I never could finish the race. I failed my wife. I made her a promise.

Tears develop, and my brain can't conjure up enough words to finish the thought.

The alarm clock counts up the seconds as time passes.

From the living room, the piano starts to play, letting me know its 3:10.

3:10?

I think back to what Jehudiel had told me before.

3:10 is where your name lies.

Staring at the piano, I realize it was right under my nose all along. I must have set the piano to play this specific music and time, knowing or hoping it would get my attention.

At first, I stumble, dizzy from getting up too fast, and then I walk over to the piano.

I search everywhere, from the outside to the inside, and find nothing. Taking a step back, I wait till the last key plays. I feel around the last key and find that it's loose.

This must be it!

I gently pull the key out and right underneath it lies nothing. Absolutely nothing.

I saunter my way over to the snow globe on my desk.

What good is a name, really? A name can't turn back time. A name can't save the people you love from death. A name is just a name. It holds no importance to me anymore.

I drop the key, take hold of the snow globe, and run my fingers over the smooth glass.

I shake it and watch the flakes fall around the snow-covered city. The light glances off tiny fingerprints on the surface of the glass.

Anna. That's a name that means something.

I suddenly remember her screaming out to me in my nightmare.

The time of the accident was 3:10. Maybe that's what my past self is trying to tell me.

Anna is still alive. She must be the one on the outside playing the music. That's it!

Joyful tears run down my cheeks. I wipe them away.

I kiss the snow globe, sit up, and extend my feet to the floor.

I may not fully trust Barachiel, but my past self trusted Stephanie. Maybe that's enough. It has to be enough.

I walk over to the window. Dead trees and grass, gloomy sky, like an apocalypse.

My reflection stares back at me. My beard is no more, my hair is clean-cut, and my body is back in perfect condition.

I put down the snow globe and see that Uriel's music cassette tape is on my desk. The label reads: Side B.

The music still plays on the piano. It's time to change this depressing tune. I walk back to the mix tape. In the living room, I shut off the piano, stick the tape into my stereo, and press play. I turn the volume to its highest level.

"Carol of the Bells" blasts through the speakers. I head into my closet to dress. I pick out the same suit and begin putting it on with a sense of calm urgency. I button my suit vest, leaving the jacket on the hook, knowing it will only add more weight. Facing the mirror, I knot my tie, making every swoop and pulling it tight around my neck. I pull out a drawer and retrieve some leather gloves and a pair of platinum cufflinks. Topping off my ensemble is my pair of cleats.

I tuck my Jack of Hearts card into my upper vest pocket, adjusting it to display the top half. I pause. Looking at the playing card makes me remember the black sedan and the car tag spelling out LBYRNTH.

The accident was no mere accident.

They must have found out that I cheated.

I head into the kitchen and search the drawers for knives. I lift my slacks and duct-tape one blade around each of my legs, careful to position the weapons so they don't impale me. My shoulders bear the next set, and finally, I conceal two more across my chest and back.

I hurry back to the bedroom, open the glass case, and pull the hatchet out. The blade's edge is in perfect condition, and the hammer head on the other side makes for a fierce bludgeoning. I grip the handle hard in my right hand. With the leftover duct tape, I wrap it around my right hand, tightly securing the weapon. I do a couple of swings in the air. The tape will hold.

I take up the butterfly knife Michael gave me from the kitchen counter.

I dash into the bathroom. The sand is almost through the hourglass. I snatch my razor from the side of the sink, fold the blade in, and one-handedly tape it around my ankle. I place my left hand on the mirror and bow my head. For me and for my family. I squeeze my hand into a fist. I watch the hourglass as I assume the minutes I have left before it turns. I count the seconds in the back of my mind. One…two…three…four…

Bass tones reverberate through the bathroom as the chorus of "Carol of the Bells" blasts through the apartment. I pull my right arm back and slingshot my fist into the mirror, smashing it, along with the hourglass.

Reapers shriek from a distance as I stride into the living room. I jog to the front door and pull it open. The music echoes through the hallway.

Stephanie opens her door and looks at me with confident eyes. She steps out and holds up the Jack of Hearts mask.

"Blessed are you, Who, like me, is saved by the Lord, who will wear the mask as a shield of hope. So, your demons will cringe before you, while you are treading upon their high places." She puts the mask over my head. "Show them you can wear your sin proudly. That you are not afraid of them anymore."

I take off the coin pendent around my neck and hand it to her, knowing it will be safe in her hands in the meantime.

"I guess this means you trust us," she says with a wink.

Ice creeps along the floor and slowly covers the elevator. I tighten my grip on the hatchet. There is a loud shriek from the stairwell. I flip the butterfly knife around in my left hand and coil my muscles.

Stephanie steps back into her room, nods to me, and shuts the door.

I stalk down the hallway. Four reapers burst through the stairwell door, at the end of the hallway, and fly toward me. I flip the knife in and out to reassure myself, raise the hatchet, and exhale a thick billow of air.

Showtime.

My heart pounds erratically with every step I take. Coldness rakes my skin. My body shakes with icy tremors. I puff out my chest. They won't have the satisfaction of getting the best of me so soon.

A rush of energy courses throughout my body. My soul feels like it's engulfed in flames, unlocking an undiscovered strength within me. The music fades as I sprint toward the reapers. Everything around me seems to have slowed almost to a standstill. Frost now covers the walls and the doors. I leap to the wall on my right, push off, and lunge at the closest reaper.

I yank its hood back with the edge of my hatchet and jab my knife in and out of its head. As it falls, I rip off the next reaper's hood and bring my hatchet down through its skull. Two left. I jump up, turning 180 degrees, and backhand my knife into the skull of one. Still spinning, I swing the hatchet into the face of the other.

Another reaper appears from the stairwell, shrieking violently. I step up on the left wall, whirl around, and whip the hatchet through its neck. Its head spins across the icy floor.

The elevator dings, and the doors strain to open against the ice. More dark creatures churn against the growing fissure. I turn away and dart back to my apartment. After pushing through the door, I barrel toward one of the iced-over windows, jump up, and, slamming my hatchet through the glass, burst through to the outside air.

4:57…4:58….4:59… Five minutes.

I plunge through the falling snow as the flurries get thicker and heavier.

Reapers fly up at me, their screams muffled by the deluge of water crystals. I reach out and grab hold of a reaper's hood. A wide, frozen trail flows out from under the reaper's cloak. I drop the hood and touch my feet to the icy slide.

The slick surface absorbs my momentum as I slip along. Spikes extend from my shoes. I dig my cleats in and slow myself down. The reaper turns and flies down toward the street. I hold on for dear life as my cleats tear through the top of the ice trail.

The reaper slows. The frozen slide breaks apart and plummets toward the ground. Just before my section crumbles, I push off, jumping at the reaper below. It stretches a bony hand toward me. I wield the hatchet and slice its arm off. Its screech rattles my eardrums. I kick my foot into its skull. The kick propels me into the ice trail of another reaper. This reaper screams at me. It flips over twice, making two icy loops. It stops at the bottom of the second loop and waits.

I catch my footing and sprint up and down the two loops. I pick up speed and vault at the reaper head-on. I yank its hood down as my body boomerangs behind it. Whirling, I lodge the butterfly knife halfway into its skull. The reaper careens away with the handle sticking out of its head, and I topple from the frozen trail.

I land hard on the street below. Seeing my Ferrari parked in its spot makes me wonder if I should even bother. More reapers descend upon me. I bolt toward the vehicle, knowing it's my only escape.

I notice no boot on any of the wheels. I jerk open the door and hop in. I haven't exploded yet. That's a good sign. Looking around, I see no ice cream or monster truck coming to crash into me. I become hopeful as I turn the key, but the engine doesn't start.

I should have known.

The reapers are now merely inches behind me. I take a breath and turn the key again, and the engine roars to life. I jam my foot on the gas pedal, making my tires squeal, and speed away. Reapers land on the asphalt behind the car. The street freezes over. Cars all around me lose their grip, sliding and smashing into each other.

I jerk the wheel right and then left, barely missing a pickup truck. I bounce up the on ramp and onto the interstate. A reaper catches the rear end of my car. Ice races over the upholstery. The car spins out of control. My left hand freezes over. Frostbite spreads up my arm. Ahead of me, a semitrailer screeches to a halt. The layer of ice on the truck tractor rips from the rig, creating a perfect ice mold careening into my lane.

My driver-side door is completely frozen over now. A reapers hand shatters through the ice! I lean away as far as possible to escape the creature's grasp. The skeletal fingers inch toward me, and I'm out of places to go. I look around, confused, then, WHAM, an ice cream truck slams into the creature!

I turn to see who it is. From the driver's seat of the ice cream vehicle, Stephanie gives me a big, exaggerated wave, a little happy dance, and then guns her engine. A hoard of reapers follow her down the interstate.

I can't help but smile, but I'm quickly ripped back to reality when I notice the ice mold from the tractor right in front of me.

I drive head first into it, ice chunks explode across my windshield.

9:56....9:57....9:58....9:59.... Ten minutes.

The impact changes my trajectory, and I slam into the truck hauling window glass. The hourglass reflection bursts into thousands of tiny pieces. My left arm shatters as I'm thrown through the front windshield and over the side of the interstate.

The impact carries me past the coffee shop. I land as far away as the park bench. A block of ice hurtles toward me. I dive out of the way. It collides with the bench and breaks apart. With only one arm, I tumble awkwardly. The thought of Anna's sweet smile and her strong will to live send a jolt of warmth through my chest. I will my arm back, and it reforms within seconds.

A shrill cry grates on my ears. Reapers pour from the interstate and fly straight toward me. The third hourglass reflecting in the coffee shop window seems miles away. I sigh, taking only a second to recover and re-strategize. In order to keep moving forward, I must go back and smash it. I remove the knife strapped to my left leg. After pushing myself up, I sprint toward the coffee shop. The cold winds scrape my face.

I close the final few feet to the hourglass. Inside the hourglass the sand is turning into snow.

This is what Gabriel had said would happen once I break two of the hourglasses. That means there's no turning back now. I have to finish this to the end.

With my hatchet raised at the window, I stop. Across from one of the window booths is a frozen body. Having no time to think, I slam the weapon into the hourglass. It breaks into a million shards.

Across the park, the fourth hourglass is at least two hundred yards away. Several dark cloaks block my vision as they accelerate toward me. I run at the oncoming reapers, bashing one in the skull with my hatchet. With the knife in my other hand, I drive the blade into its face. The knife sticks fast. More reapers glide toward me.

I zigzag to evade them and charge toward the park. After retrieving the knife concealed at my chest, I cut through the tape around my right hand. Sprinting past the Ferris wheel, I approach the tree and quickly fling the knife straight into the heart of the tree. Cracking the tiny mirror in two. A yard ahead of me lies the statue and its glass box. Without stopping, I throw my hatchet at it. The heavy blade shatters the hourglass and sticks into the frosted lawn a few feet beyond. I adjust my trajectory, pick it up, and smash it into another reaper's skull.

My feet pound the frozen grass as I close the distance to my office. Any reapers that get in my way kiss the sharp edge of my hatchet. Snow flurries dust my eyes as I hurtle through the door into the lobby. The time at the front desk reads eleven minutes. I whirl and set the deadbolt. That might slow them for a moment.

I run to the elevators, sticking the handle of my hatchet through a belt loop, and bang the call buttons for the interior elevators. The first elevator opens, and Stephanie comes out. I look more closely to see that she is wearing a scandalous nun outfit. Her hair is pulled into an elegant French twist, which is covered by a sheer black veil. Her bangs are draped over the Queen of Hearts mask.

"I had the reapers distracted for at least a minute."

I look at her scandalous outfit, smirking at what she meant by that.

"Hey! Eyes up here. I put a flare inside every gas tank in the parking lot. Get your mind out of the gutter."

Immediately, I hear many explosions going on outside the building. Shocked, I turn back to her.

"Stop looking at me and get your butt on top of the elevator now!" she yells.

I step in. She offers me a knee through a slit in the dress and hoists me into an open elevator-ceiling tile. I scramble up and replace the tile as she steps away.

Muffled conversation comes from outside the doors. Stephanie's voice is joined by Uriel's. My blood pressure increases. It's a trap! Next to me is a flintlock pistol. The glimmering light shines on the golden lion head carved into the butt of the gun.

Maybe it's not a set-up. Maybe this is part of the plan. I take hold of it, preparing myself for any signal she will throw at me.

Stephanie and Uriel rush into the car below me.

Uriel takes her by the waist, "I am loving the mask! I knew you were not like the rest of them! You kinky, and me likey!"

He goes in for a kiss as Stephanie quickly gets out from under him and slaps his face. "It's time to take you to church. You've been a very bad demon," she says in her erotic voice. Her watch beeps.

Uriel looks over at the time. "You got some place to be sweetie cakes?"

"At eleven thirty? Just here, baby. Let's ride this to the top!"

She beats the button for the top floor. The elevator whirs into motion, and the cables creak around me. Stephanie turns to Uriel, puts her hands behind his neck and head, and kisses his jaw, cheekbone, forehead, lips.

"Make me a believer! Send me to church on time! Hallelujah!"

I continue counting up the seconds from the start of the day.

Uriel raises his face toward me, and after a few seconds, he pushes her away. "Gucci, I am very, very disappointed in you." He takes hold of Stephanie's neck and brings her face inches from his. "So, you do have some balls underneath that skirt of yours."

Stephanie lifts her mask and spits straight into Uriel's mouth. He takes a few seconds to register what just happened before he lets out a high-pitched scream. She follows it up by a kick in his groin and a swift hand-chop to the throat. It sends him slumping back against the wall, sputtering.

"More balls than you will ever have."

I move the ceiling tile and drop down, smiling at Uriel's pain. Stephanie steps behind me as I raise the pistol to his face. The King of Diamonds is still nestled nice and straight in his charcoal jacket pocket.

"Trying to start the race off a little earlier than expected, I see. But I have to ask, was my acting on point or what? You see, that third-grade theater teacher was right about us, Gucci. We are natural-born liars, and that makes for some good entertainment! Now, if you would be so kind as to let me finish finding the Holy Spirit with our dear nun there."

With a jolt, he goes for my gun. I fumble it and wrestle him to the wall.

The elevator stops and opens to my office.

Uriel pulls a knife and holds the blade to my groin. "Feels good, doesn't it?" He looks over my shoulder and says in a calmer voice, "Are you finally ready to take me to church, darling?" His smile turns into something sinister.

Stephanie's watch beeps. I look at the watch on her wrist to see that it reads twelve minutes.

Bang! A bullet flies past me, straight through Uriel's teeth and out the back of his head. Stephanie holds the smoking pistol in her hand. She pulls the mask up. "No demons allowed, pervert."

Uriel's body goes limp, transfigures into a resemblance of me, and freezes over. It falls stiffly to the elevator floor and turns to sand. His ring and the King of Diamonds lie on the pile of grains.

Stephanie takes out two flare sticks from under her skirt and sparks them up. "I'll distract the reapers as long as I can." Before I can stop her, she is already out the window.

What a woman.

As I step out of the elevator, a man comes out of the other interior elevator. He's wearing a King of Hearts mask, a priest vest, and brown polished shoes. In his jacket pocket is the King of Spades. Barachiel?

He holds up what appears to be my watch.

How did he get that?

He tosses it to me.

Beyond him, another frozen dead body lies in the open elevator. The carpet looks saturated with liquid.

Did he kill one of my demons too?

That has to be Barachiel. What is he up to? Judging by the melted corpse in his elevator, he maybe actually be telling the truth.

I look back to see he is now in my elevator. He picks up Uriel's playing card and puts it in a stack with others he has collected.

What is he doing?

He takes out a pistol with a silver lamb engraved on the side of it and the elevator closes him in.

I guess that means there's no time for chitchat.

I run to my office while my watch beeps in my hand.

Fifteen minutes.

I latch my watch around my wrist.

My office chair is turned at an odd angle. It looks like there's something in it. I cross the room and rotate the chair. A man wearing a Ten of Hearts mask sits frozen, dead, and reduced to ice. I take off the mask to find it to be a demonic representation of Raphael's former image. I shudder and step back. I see that Barachiel has taken Raphael's card, too. There's no time to process this information. I spin to the window and bang it with the butt of my gun. The hourglass reflection shatters. The reapers swarming the bottom of the building look up. Screeches blare through the sky as the creatures fly toward me.

One reaper, larger than the others, touches the building. Ice races up the skyscraper. As each level freezes, it shatters and collapses, the rest of the structure slamming down to the ground.

I roll the office chair to the window and push Raphael's dead body out. Maybe that will distract them. The office trembles as the next level falls. I run through the hallway to the kitchenette on the other end. As I reach the far window, I throw myself through it. The floor drops out from beneath me.

I fall several yards and land in the bushes. The reapers haven't seen me yet. I roll to a standing position and dash across the street to the Lighthouse Restaurant. Once inside, I sprint to the kitchen. The silver dome sits on one of the counters. I snatch it up and charge my way to the meat locker. The kitchen floor instantly freezes over. My foot slips, and my arms fly into the air, releasing my steady grip on the dome. I slide my way into the meat locker, turning my head to the doorway. I notice the dome has fallen back in the kitchen. I quickly scramble up, only to find reapers coming through the restaurant doors. I slam the door quickly and look out the window at the silver dome lying on the frozen ground just a couple feet in front of me.

Someone grabs my lion pistol out of my pants.

"I guess our secret is out."

Michael.

I turn around and the first thing I notice is that red tie of his.

"Guessing that's why you've started the race a day early. What did ya think was going to happen? That I was just going to sit at home? Tsk. Tsk. It's my night, and don't ya go and ruin it for me."

He holds up the Queen of Hearts mask. "I'm really loving the masks. Can I be apart of y'all's private club, too?"

Michael steps aside. Against the far wall, Stephanie sits, beaten and bruised. Blood stains her black dress, and her hair hangs in disheveled clumps around her head. She whispers, "I'm sorry."

He tosses the mask at her face. "The first thing ya learn as a card player is: Don't play the hand in which ya were dealt if ya don't even know what ya have. This is what we call common sense, which is something ya apparently do not have." He spits in her face.

I narrow my eyes at him.

"You're actin' like a lion now, aren't ya, lad? I'd feed ya to the reapers for your insubordination, but what can I say? I need ya."

He stoops next to Stephanie and runs his hand over her loose tendrils of hair. "D'ya even understand what this day was for? Barachiel was supposed to help ya find your key. Now, since ya made this courageous effort to start off the race one day early, we're all in a pickle. The good news is that Miss Lost Soul over here knows where it's at." He smiles. "Don't ya, petal?"

I stand paralyzed—blanking my mind of everything.

Michael bends down and sticks his hand in her pocket. She screams in shock as he slowly pulls out a green marble bag. He peaks inside and sounds off a quirky giggle.

"It may not be the key but it will do."

What's inside it?

He rolls out of the bag two lead balls into his palm. He loads one inside the pistol and places the other in his back pocket.

Michael holds the pistol to her face. "You've been a thorn in my side ever since ya arrived. You've been gettin' in good with our lad here. Gainin' his trust just so ya can stab him in the back when the time comes. Isn't that it?" He looks back at me. "Y'still think she's on your side, don't ya?" He glances back at Stephanie. "How sweet is that? Oh, how all of us've been misled this evenin'." My watch beeps.

"Must be twenty minutes now, I suppose."

Michael paces in front of her, like a wolf about to attack his prey. "Best be telling me where that key is, petal. Or would ya like my blackjack to do all the talkin'?"

He holds up his beating stick. The bottom of the handle is lassoed around his wrist, allowing him to twirl the baton around and around.

She tries to speak, but Michael hits her across the head with the blackjack. She falls over, her skull smacking against the floor.

You leave her alone!

He points to Stephanie. "Who do ya think broke your window last night boyo?"

She squeaks out, "Don't! Please!"

That can't be true.

"Y'still think that I'm lyin'? They really did do a number on ya, didn't they? I suppose that's what happens after a reaper fries your memories for the billionth time. Ya get less smart about things. They are playin ya for fool. That's what these types of lost souls do. They want you to lose and be stuck here. Gives them purpose and maybe a little bit of joy from it too."

Michael can't be right. He is just a demon trying to manipulate me. I trust Stephanie.

"Trust you say? Let me show ya what trust really gives ya."

Michael grabs Stephanie's arm and drags her to the door. She screams, clawing at the meat locker floor. "It's time you start rememberin' or else I'm feeding you to the wolves."

Stephanie spits blood at him. "The reapers can't sense lost souls, remember?"

"Oh, that I do remember. That's why I see out this window here that the reapers brought their lost-soul-thirsty razor hounds out to play."

Michael snickers.

"You know what happens when they get hold of ya? Y'have heard the stories, yeah?"

Stephanie silently says, "The prism."

Did she say prism? What is that?

Michael nods, "The prism. A prison where bad lost souls go that try to intervene with a soul's trial in any way. You'll be stuck inside till your body gives way upstairs. I've heard some lost souls say that the prism is even worse than hell itself. I'll let you be the judge."

The door shakes with the impact of a razor, his snout scraping thick mucus across the window.

Stephanie yells, "You won't do it! The reapers would grab you before you can even close back the door."

Michael smiles and mirrors into a reaper. "They will have to see me first."

Michael shows his face through the cowl.

Stephanie's eyes go wide, and her face pales even more. She screams, "Don't! I'm begging you! Please!"

"One....two..."

She shrills, "Barachiel knows! He never told me, I swear!"

"Three!"

She takes out the coin necklace from around her neck. "Here!" she shouts. She avoids eye contact with me.

Stephanie, how could she?

"So that's the key. How could I've been so blind? Of course it is."

Michael takes the coin necklace and kicks Stephanie in the stomach.

He turns to me and says, "If ya can't trust a lost soul, who can ya trust? What did I tell ya?"

Michael yanks open the door and throws her out into the hoard of reapers. He slams and locks it before any of them can get inside.

"Now that the trash is taken out, we can conclude our business. Once I leave out of here, I will find a way to distract the reapers. When you see them flooding on out, ya leave. Comprende?"

He turns back and hands me the loaded pistol.

"You'll be needing this for our duel later."

Confused, I quickly aim the gun at his head.

You're dead.

"We both know you're not goin' to make it out of here without my help."

My watch beeps.

Twenty-five minutes.

I take a few seconds and realize he's right. I slowly lower my weapon.

"You always were the smart one. See you at the finish line." Michael transfigures his face to look like a reaper again, opens the door, and walks out. He shuts the door behind him.

I tuck the gun into my waistband.

Through the window, more reapers than I have ever seen at once fill the kitchen, and Michael could be any one of them. There's no sign of Stephanie or any razors. I turn to the silver food dome still lying on the ground, surrounded by a hoard of reapers. It's now covered in a thin layer of ice. The hourglass reflection still funnels sand through its neck and into snow.

If I don't destroy that cover by 35:00, all of this will have been for nothing.

What is taking Michael so long?

Maybe he doesn't need me anymore. He has the key. If he mirrors me and breaks the rest of the hourglasses, would that suffice? Sealtiel did say a reaper can't really tell the difference between a demon that looks like me and the real me.

I bang on the wall, angry at the fact that Michael tricked me.

I'm going to have to try to mirror a reaper. I sit down and close my eyes, concentrating on their inky cowls and cloaks, their bony fingers, the white skull masks they wear.

The hourglass continues to empty.

I'm almost out of time. This isn't working. The only thing left is to fight my way out. New screams echo from the kitchen. I rip off the two knives from my shoulders, cross to the door, and throw it open.

As I brandish the knives, the kitchen sprinklers kick in. The reapers screech and try to scatter. The water spreads like a virus, freezing them instantly. I wait in the doorway until the sprinklers turn off.

I run across the ice-covered kitchen, stepping on frozen reaper corpses. I scoop up the hourglass reflection and hurtle it against the far wall. The silver collides with the steel wall and shatters. I continue to run through the frozen dining area, and out the front door. Avoiding the open manhole, I run across the street toward the subway. From far away, reapers screech, no doubt regrouping. An orange glow burns from the park area. I slow down and squint my eyes. The tree is on fire! Without the hollowed-out tree, I've got no other way to escape the 42:02 problem.

I watch as a flood of reapers gathers around the fire.

They're attracted to the heat! Of course! This could buy me some time.

My watch beeps.

Thirty minutes.

I race down the subway stairs and across the station. Coldness buries itself deep into my bones.

The train pulls in and slows to a stop. The doors open, and I dart in. The subway moves slowly over the frozen rails below.

All the windows are getting foggy from the cold. I raise my head up, watching the ice slowly cover all eight windows of the subway car and panic, not remembering exactly which one had the hourglass reflected in it. I'm going to have to break them all. I go through each one, breaking them with my hatchet. I get through four and make my way to the other side.

A loud thud comes from the roof at the far end of the subway car. I pull the gun from my pants and raise it. The windows around me turn frosty. The entrance doors are starting to frost over.

A door slams at the tail end of the train. I turn my head. The man in the priest vest and the King of Hearts mask walks toward me. He holds the other flintlock pistol in his hand. I swing my gun, aiming it at him. His takes off his mask.

It's Barachiel. Tension builds in my extremities.

Maybe Michael wasn't manipulating me.

Barachiel, still holding the gun at me, walks closer and I hesitantly pull the trigger. Crack! The impact sends him back through the doors and off the train.

What have I done?

From out of nowhere, a flood of reapers bursts through the bottom of the car. The nearest one carries a scythe. I swap my pistol for my hatchet and drive it into the reaper's skull. Its scythe falls from its hand. I grab it in midair and swing it around, decapitating two more reapers.

I run across the right side, smashing three more windows with my hatchet. Only one left.

Ahead is the next station—my stop. I slide past one of the reapers, cutting it in half with my scythe. I jump to the closest window opening and swing myself up onto the roof. Reapers fly after me. I turn as a scythe-wielding reaper cuts off my arm. It freezes as it falls, still gripping its weapon of choice, and deflects off the roof of the train.

The subway car enters the station. I search from above, looking for the last window on the side of the subway. A couple feet below me, I see the chilled-over window.

I bend down, eyeing the target below me I raise my hatchet. Surprisingly enough, the window bursts from the force of a reaper flying out of it.

Four hourglasses left.

I look ahead and notice the disco ball hanging crooked on the ceiling. Hourglass number four.

Leaning on my remaining fist, still holding the hatchet, I jump off the train toward the platform. The reaper from below slices me clean in half. As I fall, I repair my lower body and arm instantaneously. I land on my feet on the platform and throw my hatchet toward the disco ball. The weapon successfully connects with its target but gets stuck in the process. I quickly jolt up off my feet, take hold of the handle, and jerk it back down with me. The ball shatters, clearing away any reflection from hourglass number four. Once my feet hit the floor, I continue my stride and head up the stairs. My watch beeps.

Thirty-five minutes.

I have seven minutes to smash the last three hourglasses. Through heavy snow and gust of wind, I sprint to the bridge. My body shivers uncontrollably. Even my hair is freezing over.

Behind me, a swarm of reapers charges after me.

Suddenly, a glacier sprouts from below and breaks through the bridge.

I dart from side to side, evading each tower of ice bursting through the asphalt. The bridge creaks and twists. I'm only about twenty-five feet away from the end of the bridge. The snow thickens, and each step is harder to take.

Frostbite creeps up my left leg as another glacier tears through my path.

I leap onto the top of the iceberg. The bridge falls away as the ice climbs higher. Searing pain shoots through my brain as my leg feels as if it was being frozen over. The billboard is up ahead but sadly it is frozen over.

How am I going to find the hourglass if I can't see it?

I squint my eyes tight at the icy barricade surrounding the surface of the billboard. Frosty shards of sleet enters my eyes, blinding me. I rub my eyes quickly trying to gain back my vision. For a blink of a second, I find a small shimmer of something that could be the glossy silver of the musical note on the billboard or it could be my eyes tricking me.

Without thinking, I fling my last knife straight to the glimmering silver. The bladed weapon flies over the billboard and into the dark forest, missing it entirely.

Well that was a mistake. Now I have only my hatchet and my vision is almost shot to hell.

I guess my only option is to just run right into it and hope for the best the billboard is soft enough to handle the impact.

I brace for collision when suddenly, I hear something falling through the trees behind the billboard. A random lamp post falls from out of the shadows and lands directly on top of the frozen structure.

I can't even take a moment to celebrate the miracle of what just happened.

The fray of reapers changes course to follow me. The nearest cowl has an unusual point sticking out from beneath it.

Could it be?

I grab hold of the reaper's sleeve and jerk it toward me. The cowl falls away, exposing my butterfly knife. An icy slide forms under its cloak. I grip the handle of the knife, slipping over the ice trail as the reaper careens through the sky.

I turn the knife to the right. The reaper turns to the right. I tilt it back, steering the reaper up toward my apartment rooftop. The flood of reapers is hot on my tail. As we near, the hourglass on the rooftop ledge grows bigger.

My right eye is icing over as the snow buries my face. The wind becomes chaotic, and I lose balance. Every hair on my body is completely frozen. My left leg has third-degree frostbite. Each memory I have of Anna and Madi play over and over in my mind, reminding me what all this is for.

I breathe in deeply, and, in the midst of the fiercest fight I have ever waged in my whole life, I feel somehow at peace. As we top the ledge, I pull the knife from the reaper's skull and topple off onto the icy trail behind it. The reaper lands on the roof with a thud. Gravity pulls me down the slippery slope, away from the roof and the hourglass.

My surroundings unfold in slow motion. I see myself as an eighteen-year-old, running that last lap in the race. The finish line is ahead. The crowd is on their feet, cheering.

The flapping cloaks of converging reapers wrench me back to the present. My left leg is slowly icing over. Any more pressure on it, and it's gone. The hourglass grows farther away with every moment.

I'm not going to make it!

A reapers hands peer around the corner of my vision. The reaper's white pale mask is now clearly visible.

This is it! I'm done for.

Suddenly, something shoots through the night sky, hitting the reaper straight in the face.

The air has a tincture of gunpowder, a smell that takes me back to the night of my wedding, watching the blue flames lick up the reapers mask I realize what it is.

Fireworks!

They begin exploding all around me, vivid colors to ignite upon impact of each reaper that gets in its way. A breathtaking spectacle of blues, greens, reds, whites, and purple sparkling lights erupting around me.

A darkened figure is seen up ahead on the roof shooting them off. I can barely see who it is due to the vivacious colors bursting into my retinas.

The fireworks burn with impatience, everything at the speed of a camera flash. Every colorful streak bares a curve of sorts, brilliant lines with a living feel, organic in the way they grow. They send hot sparks into the black flood, giving me more room to run.

The suspended ice trail cracks apart. I hurl my hatchet at the hourglass on the ledge and push off toward the final hourglass reflected in my apartment window. My iced over left leg shatters from my leap. The sharp winds carry me, almost as if I were flying. The fireworks continue to burst above me, searing their brilliant light as I make my way farther down.

I miss my bedroom window by a hair and instead crash through my living room window. I somersault across the floor. My gun slides from my waistband and clatters across the smooth floor.

The fireworks have now stopped, leaving me no time to think.

I need to grow back my leg fast and get to my bedroom! But it's too cold for me to concentrate.

Jehudiel is suddenly standing over me, smirking at my fate. "Looks like you need some help!" He drags my body to the bedroom. There, he stands me up, making me hobble on my one good leg, and says, "Like I always say, slow and steady wins the race."

He lifts me up to meet him, causing my flask to drop out of my pocket. "Just stand straight. We will get to the last flaw in a second. The cold atmosphere in this room can only hide us here for maybe a minute."

Jehudiel turns his head toward my bedroom window, where a crowd of reapers is hovering at a standstill outside the sacred glass.

They all look straight up at once and quickly jolt in that immediate direction.

"Gee! I wonder what has gotten their attention? If I were to assume, I would say Michael must have taken care of the real hourglass number eleven."

The real hourglass number eleven?

"What do all the flaws have in common? Better yet, which flaw wasn't the same as the others?"

It must be the hourglass on the roof. It never reflected off anything like the others did.

It was a fake?

"That it was! Michael made it himself. I watched of course. The real flaw was actually the glass lens in the telescope. You would have known that if you ever bothered to take out that dusty forgotten ring and look through it every once in a while."

That explains why the reapers came for me that night on the roof a couple days ago. I broke the telescope. I knew I was in the right time zone. How could I have been so stupid? I should have known something was odd about that hourglass on the roof.

Staring down at the flask, partially screwed open, I pretend to be agitated, moving my leg just enough to kick the flask cap open. He tries talking to me. I don't listen, instead looking away from him to the bedroom window, not yet broken.

I look at how clear the reflection of the hourglass is, thanks to the moonlight coming from the outside.

Jehudiel slaps me back to the reality of the situation. "Are you listening? I was saving you the trouble, last night. This could have been a lot less hard on you. How coincidental that I will be once again breaking this window two days in a row."

He was the one who broke my bedroom window last night.

Why?

"I was making it easier for you. That's all I've been trying to do for you. Making your life easier. After I break this here window, Michael will be free and we will begin our simple life together. Oh! What fun we will have!"

That's it! Michael is probably in the elevator with my key in hand. He is just standing in there, waiting for Jehudiel to break the last flaw which would bring down the barrier around this place. There won't be anyone to stop him from going up. I understand their plan now.

I immediately look down as the water from the flask reaches Jehudiel's foot.

From the proximity of the reapers, I can tell the water will soon turn into ice if I don't hurry.

A screeching sound comes from outside.

"They're back."

I look down to see the water has turned to ice, leaving me with one other option.

Jehudiel brings my head back up. "You are going to love being a lost soul."

I steady my body. With my good leg, I swiftly grind the edge of my shoe over the now-frozen water, causing my cleats to retract. With all the force I can muster, I raise my knee and quickly plunge it straight down, stomping the spikes into Jehudiel's foot. I twist my foot, letting the cleats dig in deeper.

His high-pitched yell gets the reapers' attention. I take my foot out and lunge it into his chest. The force of the kick sends me out of his grasp and back to the bedroom floor.

The screams of reapers follow close behind. I roll back and bang my head on the bed frame. As he falls backward, he breaks through the last hourglass and out the window. Simultaneously, a sea of reapers swoops in on both sides. The room reels as a reaper extends a long, bony finger toward me. I squeeze my eyes shut. The icy pain of the reaper's touch never comes. Silence surrounds me.

I open my eyes. The flood of reapers has receded, and the nearest one retracts its hand and floats toward the open window. My watch beeps.

Forty minutes.

Using the bed to steady myself, I stand and hop across the room on my good leg. The snow outside the window hangs suspended in midair. The reapers have moved up and away and now hover as if they are waiting for something.

The room gets warmer. The layer of ice clinging to my body thaws. The vision returns to my right eye, going from black to fuzzy to clear. I lean against the windowsill, basking in the moment. I did it. I'm getting out of here, after all.

My left leg reforms.

From the living room, the sound of a single person clapping travels through the bedroom doorway. A man walks in, still applauding, wearing an Ace mask. His hair is stylishly combed back, and he wears a black vest over a black dress shirt with a red tie.

Michael?

He stills his hands, pulls a blackjack from his belt, and whirls it around.

"Bravo! I'd say that was a rush."

The ice on the floor has melted, and water trickles toward Michael's feet.

I get it now. You're here to challenge me.

The water surrounds Michael's shoe.

"Not exactly."

I won't let him get the chance.

He looks at his feet, and as he brings his head back up, I'm already on top of him. I pin him down, take the baton out of his hand, and pound him. I pour my frustration and anger into his face and torso. The mask flies from his face. Blood gushes from open wounds, and bruises form across his skin.

He finally manages to kick me off.

I roll over, pick up the lion pistol, aim it at him, and cock the hammer back.

He laughs while wiping blood from his jawline. "What're ya gonna do now, lad? Shoot me? Go ahead!"

I point the pistol at his mouth, grinning. I've won.

"Though I don't know what good this thing is now, since you've used your bullet on what's-his-name again?" He lowers his brows. "Barachiel! That's it! Just like I hoped ya would."

What is he saying? I pull the trigger, and nothing happens. He's right.

He yanks the pistol out of my hand and takes out the lead ball that he had stashed away. "Here my boy, is the last bullet. Take a good look."

His raving is interspersed with mad laughter. "Thanks to you, I've already won the challenge"

How could he have won?

From far away, the music begins.

I know this melody. This is the piano music from the coffee shop memory.

The alarm clock on my nightstand reads 42:02. I turn back to Michael. My time has run out. I get down on my knees and cover my ears. I won't listen! Michael walks over and kneels down next to me. He picks up the mask off the drenched floor and puts it back on.

You can't do this! You have to challenge me in order to be free from this place! Those are the rules!

"That is correct! Rules are rules but the thing about that is… a demon can't challenge another demon."

What are you talking about?

He pulls out his Polaroid camera, bends down, and takes a photo of me. Click!

The soft melody of the familiar music streams loudly above me. I pull myself into a cannonball position. I'm not getting dragged back in this time.

The photo whirs out, and Michael blows on it while waving it back and forth.

"Silly boy. I can't challenge you…"

Still waiting for the photo to develop, Michael puts it in my hand.

The image comes into focus. My body is lying on the ground in my expensive, tattered suit, but in place of my face is the contorted, impish snarl of a demon.

"...because you're one of us."

I don't believe you! This is just a trick. Just another one of your games!

He holds the coin necklace out for me to see. The gold off the coin catches my eye instantly.

"You think the mystery of this coin is why you are drawn to it? How about the golden lion on the butt of the pistol? You didn't think you chose that one because the lion seemed cooler, did you? How about Madi's golden ring? You acted more like golem holding it than a failed husband."

What are you trying to say? I'm infatuated with gold?

"Now you're getting it."

The golden pendant shimmers in a yellowish glow.

Yellow. The sin color for greed.

I panic.

"We all have our colors," he says while rubbing along his red tie. He gives me one last devilish smirk before he makes his grand farewell. The music grows even louder, and all I can do is stare at the picture. I look at the glaring reflection of myself.

I can't be a demon.

"Why? Because you look like the real deal?"

Michael changes his appearance to look like me.

"It's not hard to mirror our creator since it's our original packaging. This appearance comes natural even after a reaper tries to erase everything. But the one thing we can't change are the eye's to the soul."

He transforms back into his own image of himself. I look into Michaels green eyes. My eyes.

Michael and my bedroom get lost in the pieces of the coffee shop as I lay there horrified of who I really am.

FORTY-TWO

*T*hrough the window, I can see Madi waiting by the jukebox. The sight of her alone makes me fully give in to the melody. I enter, struggling to pull myself together.

I try to will my hand up. I raise it to my face and wiggle my fingers, knowing that it's getting easier for me. I move my legs now and make my way toward Madi.

"Did you bring it?" she asks me.

She must be talking about the sunflowers. I feel the sinful cancer creeping itself inside my head. It feels like fire burning my skin. I yell, screaming loud, but still with no sound coming out.

Everything starts to spin as I feel whatever conscience I actually have, slip away from me. Suddenly, words are coming together in my head, spelling out a name. My name.

Almost as if the whole puzzle has finally been put together in my head, a surge of burning pain enters my throat and I say, "My name is… David."

I spoke! I found my equilibrium!

She gives me a confused look and after a few seconds she responds, "That's not what you're supposed to say."

What did she just say?

"You're not supposed to say that," she says, packing her things.

Getting carried away, she fumbles her books to the ground. I look down to see her book by my feet. I quickly reach down and grip my fingers around it. Looking back up, I see her standing over me. I hold out the book as she reaches over, her fingers brushing up against mine. We both are holding onto the book as Madi looks at me like she somehow knows who I am.

Is my consciousness playing games with me?

"You know me. How is that possible?"

I hold the book tighter as she tries to pull it away. Madi bends down and whispers in my ear, "You're not supposed to remember."

She lets go of the book and runs out of the shop. I place the book on the table and stand up, looking out the window.

Should I run after her? No, she isn't mine. None of this was ever mine.

I scream inside, when a sound forces itself from my larynx, through my mouth, and out into the atmosphere.

My carnivorous scream echoes throughout the memory landscape I've built.

The piano's sound reverberates off the structures inside my head pertaining to every layer of the coffee shop memory. Everything from the coffee shop to the people inside start breaking apart like puzzle pieces. I then become lost in the pitch-black darkness of my thoughts. The piano music still plays in the background, but I am now void of any thoughts about its significance. I continue to push through the darkness, forcing myself forward, making my way back, and all the while knowing what insufferable pain I will inflict on the person who made me forget who I really was. I close my eyes as all my memories consume back into me. I take it all in.

I can hear the music still playing above me. I open my eyelids back up. A snow globe lies beside me on a soft blanket of white. I stare at it for a couple of seconds, then reach over and wrap my fingers around it.

I whistle along with the melody, knowing it can't suck me in anymore. The reflection of my face is distorted by the curved surface. My smile goes from ear to ear. I'm back. I look at my watch. It reads 43:05.

I move my focus beyond the sphere and stand. I'm on the rooftop of my apartment building. Snow hovers in midair. Straight above me, reapers fill the sky, drifting in the foreground of the dancing green lights, from the elevator's closed doors to the far ledge where the hourglass used to sit. The tail end of the aurora borealis leaves my sight.

I notice the lion pistol is resting halfway outside of the front of my pants. I take it out and look around to find no one around.

I make my way to the elevator, with the snow globe in hand.

The elevator doors open and to my surprise the golden pendant is lying on the floor.

I hunch my back forward and extend my arm to grab for it.

I quickly stop myself, noticing the rug is soaking wet. I lean back up just as the elevator closes back shut.

I clear my throat and say, "You almost had me."

The sound of a pistol hammer cocks behind me. I twitch and spin around. A few feet in front of me stands a man in a priest vest and brown polished shoes. He's still wearing the King of Hearts mask and is pointing the flintlock straight at my head.

The gun shot wound in his right shoulder is enough to give me pause.

"Looks like I missed. I can guarantee you, I won't miss this time."

I lift the lion pistol up to greet him.

He stands silent.

"This is deja vu at its best. Wouldn't you agree, old friend?" I say. Snow lingers in the air between us.

He doesn't speak.

"You remember; I feel like it was just yesterday when you shot me and left me here for the reapers." I raise the snow globe in front of him. "You could have won that night. You were so close to freedom but you chose to stay and I want to to know why."

Silence.

"If it wasn't clear already, this is me challenging you. Also, you can go ahead and take off that mask now. No need to hide from me anymore."

His free hand pulls the mask from his face. Barachiel's bright green eyes pierce my existence. His brows are furrowed in concentration. He never once loses his steady aim. He isn't playing around anymore.

I smirk at his poor attempt to fool me. "I thought I told you. No need for masks…David."

BARACHIEL

SATURDAY

FORTY-THREE

I wake up, sweat coating my skin despite the chilly temperature. I've dreamed that nightmare more times than I can possibly count. In the back of my head, the seconds tick....00:01...00:02...00:03. Saturday. The day I have long waited for.

I rise, grab a small mirror, and hold it to my face. I am David. I am David. I am David. My mind clears.

I lay the mirror aside and prepare to get dressed. I unfold my black clergy black vest and place it over me, tightening it around my waist. Looking in the mirror, I straighten my clerical collar around my neck. The metallic walls of the ice cream truck surround me. I smile softly and sigh. Thankfully, the air conditioning in this ice cream truck has lasted the full week. A sealed compartment blocking my view out the front traps the cold air inside and keeps me off the reapers' radar.

I breathe out, and the warm carbon dioxide forms a thick cloud in the freezing air. I've grown accustomed to the cold for too long. Numbness is all that's left.

The thermometer next to me reads 34°F. Not enough to hide my full heat signature, but enough that, if I don't move, the reapers will think nothing of it. I raise the mirror and look one last time at my brown hair, slightly droopy eyes, long nose, and soft jaw. Not a mirrored image of a man I hardly knew. Just me.

I transform, shortening my nose, rounding my face, affixing a dimple to my chin, adding a subtle wave to and lightening my hair.

I am Barachiel.

It wasn't until two weeks ago, where Lily magically appeared in one of my music memories. Her unknown presence spooked me right out of what I thought was inescapable. When I realized I was back in my prison world, I saw her with me yet again. I remember her saying the music in the sky was a link from her prison world to my own. She said the music was coming from the outside world and that someone up there was playing it for me. She also said that I wasn't dead, and this wasn't hell. But most importantly she said that I had a choice. That it would be the hardest choice I would ever have to make. It was after that day, I began to plan my escape.

I learned to master the mirroring technique. Also, controlling my mind to no longer let the music sink me into my past, healing myself, and studying my demon's weaknesses. These were necessary for my survival, but I had to push myself further. I had to find patience. From putting everything into motion to watching everything play out, took a lot of time. But if today ends in my favor then it was all well worth the wait.

I lift the lid of a cooler next to me and take out a rectangular case. I pop the latches. Inside is my lamb pistol lying beside a cartridge box and four lead balls. My fingers stroke the dark-stained stock and the engraved silver lamb on the butt plate. Plastering the walls are scriptures I've written on fancy stationery.

I unroll a rag with the loading tools on the floor beside me. I quickly load one of the lead balls inside my pistol.

From one of my compartments, I pull out a dark green marble bag. I dump two lead balls inside of it and pocket the bag.

I insert the ramrod into the muzzle and ram the wadding, bullet, and powder down to the breech of the barrel.

I tuck the gun into the back of my waistband and put the rest of the cartridges in my jacket pocket. With care, I straighten the King of Spades tucked halfway into the pocket and comb my hair to the side.

With three fingers on my right hand, I touch my shoulders right to left, kiss my right hand, and draw it down. I close my eyes, clouding my thoughts and building a wall over my mind to keep my demons from coming in.

It's time. I grasp the exit lever on the sealed compartment.

Behind me, a feminine voice whispers, "Stay."

I hesitate. But there's no point in turning around. She would only be gone again if I did.

It's not her. It's not Anna.

I twist the lever and push through the exit. The run-down coffee shop is just ahead.

Outside, Stephanie licks a popsicle, leaning up against the ice cream truck. The popsicle she's devouring looks exactly like the Jack of Hearts mask. "Our little Gambit is actually doing it!" She smiles broadly and throws the empty popsicle stick into the air.

She knows I hate it when she calls my greed demon Gambit. She considers him more like a pet in that sense, but I guess it is easier than saying greed demon.

"This is so exciting!" she says around a mouthful of frozen ice cream.

"Did you bring them?"

She takes out my logbook and Bible from behind her back. "As you requested, Mr. Hayes."

As I near, she picks up a suitcase from the ground and hands it to me. I open it to find that the King of Hearts mask is lying inside.

"I thought it would be fitting."

I take the books first, putting them in my upper jacket pockets for safe keeping and then I take the mask from the case.

She gives a gentle smile.

With my thumb, I trace the heart around the left eye of the mask. Regret dances through my head, along with images of Lisa's bare skin and Madi's crushed heart. I will use this mask as a symbol. To show my demons that I have come for my retribution.

I put on the mask and turn to Stephanie giving me the thumbs up.

"Also!" Stephanie turns around and removes something from her bag. "I got a mask, too!" She faces me, wearing the Queen of Hearts mask. "We are kind of like Bonnie and Clyde now. But more on the righteous path than the wrong one."

She also takes out the coin pendent necklace from her bag and hands it to me. "For being so smart he sure is dumb. Now where's my sack of balls?"

I take out my green marble bag and switch with her. She nods, understanding her role. Through the fabric, she fingers the two lead balls. "Thought they would be bigger."

I put the coin in my pocket, turn to the pink neon-lit sign, and take my walk.

Stephanie yells from behind me, "I'll go see if he needs any help!"

In the window, the half-filled hourglass confirms the time count in my head.

I walk inside and sit at one of the booths. I pull the coin pendant from my pocket. It sways in front of my eyes. I slip it from the chain. It drops onto the shiny wooden table and spins.

From the kitchen area, Gabriel emerges carrying a pizza in one hand and a napkin in the other. His dark glasses hide his eyes. His black, jaw-length hair swings with each step. He walks to my booth and sits across from me.

"You rang?" he says. His nose crinkles as if he's not sure what's going on. He picks up a piece of pizza and takes two bites.

I say nothing. My coin spins in the haphazard way that warns that it's about to topple over. I snatch it before it lands, and set it spinning again. Its speedy revolutions form a soothing backdrop to my silence.

"Jesus! You're just as bad as Jehudiel. Shouldn't you be somewhere else? I don't know, maybe searching for the key with our mutual friend?" He takes another bite of his pizza as sauce drips onto his expensive tailored pants down to his orange socks.

I wait, patiently silent, continuing to spin my coin. Gabriel's sunglasses give off a glare. He's trying to enter my mind, but I won't let him. I keep my wall high and my thoughts safe.

I lick my lips, clear my throat, and say nothing.

A sour look crosses Gabriel's face. He leans in toward me and laughs.

I take out a napkin and unfold it, revealing Gabriel's used gum inside. I place the open napkin next to him.

He plucks the gum off the napkin, tearing bits of paper with it, and puts it in his mouth. As he wipes tomato sauce off his lips, he smacks loudly. "I was looking all over for this."

The coin is about to topple again. I reset it, and the metallic hum continues.

Gabriel laughs. "Playing hooky to your self-made plan; that's as selfish as it gets, bro. But I expect nothing less from you."

I pick up the coin and set it to spinning again. As it revolves across the polished wood, I glance toward the reflection in the window. The sand begins to fall through the neck of the hourglass and turns to snow. The drifting flakes makes its way to the empty bottom.

It has started.

Gabriel's eyes are locked on the spinning coin and takes a few seconds before he grins.

Gabriel's smile alone leads me to believe he has taken the bait.

"When he nears the end tomorrow, all bets are off. You know that none of us will commit to the rules when that soul finishes the race?

As you well know, only one of us can take up residence in his body and I'm challenging him first. So, did you keep your half of the deal?"

I pull my lamb pistol from my waistband and lay it down on the table in front of me.

"That's the wrong one! The lion is the one he chose this time, not the lamb! I thought you were supposed to be the smart one? Now the rest of them will be able to challenge him. When it could have just been between the two of us! And don't give me 'it's not part of the rules' crap!"

Gabriel's face reddens. He stares at the spinning coin and smacks the gum in his mouth as if he were trying to calm himself down.

As Gabriel watches the whirling coin, a troubled expression crosses his face. He glances out the coffee shop window. We both watch as the hourglass's sand begins to turn to snow.

"What is going on here?!"

He slams his hand down on the golden disk. He raises his hand, the coin stuck to the skin on his palm. After leaning in to inspect the coin, his eyes cloud with confusion. He snaps his head toward the hourglass reflection and the snowy granules. The smacking stops. His forehead creases as his eyes narrow. His face goes white as he jerks back to meet my eyes.

He grabs his stomach and doubles over in pain. With panic in his eyes, he tries to move, but seems unable. He sputters and chokes. The gum falls from his mouth as he attempts to speak. "W…w…wait!"

The water-soaked gum has done its job. I grab the pistol and force it into his mouth. I pull the hammer to full cock. Dropping my mirroring of Barachiel, I show Gabriel my true face.

His eyes grow big as he struggles to back away and dislodge the gun.

I remove the Jack of Spades from his jacket, peel the coin from his hand, and pull the trigger. Crack! The shot knocks his head back.

After tucking the gun back into my waistband and pocketing the card and coin, I push off of my seat and walk toward the door. I transform my face back to Barachiel's.

As I reach for the door handle, I turn my head toward Gabriel's frozen corpse. It falls to its side, slowly freezing over. Its face changes to look like my face. Its features morph as it turns to sand and its demonic form is finally seen.

I remove my necklace from my pocket, reattach the coin to the pendant, and tie it around my neck. I exit through the front door.

I signal to the car.

Stephanie starts the engine to the ice cream van, pulls up beside me, and rolls down the window.

With a happy-go-lucky smile, she says, "Care for some ice cream, mister?"

I hop in on the passenger side. Before I can close the door, she stomps on the gas. A sharp turn slams the door on its own.

"Seatbelts!" she screams.

I snap my belt in place. With the way she drives, I'm going to need it.

"Can I play the jingle?! Please! Please! Please!" she pleads with glee. "It could be our battle cry to let all the reapers know"— she raises her eyebrows and winks— "that we may not have any more ice cream sandwiches, but we have a whole lot of knuckle sandwiches! Yassss!"

I shake my head and give her a nod of approval.

An excited Stephanie plays the jingle. The childlike music blares out of the speakers. She wildly drives the van over the hill and through the park, speeding like a bat out of hell.

I grip the door with one hand.

She stomps on the brakes. The van skids to a halt as the seatbelt locks against my shoulder. The sinful, dead tree is right beside my window.

Stephanie pushes her door open and jumps out. She looks at the tree. "Are you sure you want to do this? What if he has no other option but to go inside?"

She hands me the half-empty bottle of Macallan.

I remove two self-made flare sticks from my pants pocket.

She looks at the bottle in my hand, saying to herself, "What a waste."

I rip the top off a flare, and nothing happens. I rip the other top off, and still no flame is produced.

"And that's why you got a D in science, and I got an A." Stephanie giggles. "I hope you got a matchbook handy because my flares are stashed in the girls' bathroom."

I look at her, confused, as she points to the office building.

"What? Like he's going to go in there. Chill, I'll go get them."

I turn toward the superstructure that houses my publishing company and lift my face to my office on the top floor.

"Whoo! I'm driving!" She drops the igniter cable and darts back to the truck. I'm barely seated when she spins the tires and accelerates toward the building.

I turn toward Stephanie.

She keeps her focus straight ahead. "I know. I know. He will be there on time, don't you worry."

She brakes hard, and the truck comes to a sudden halt by the building's entrance. Stephanie crawls into the back compartment. "No peeking!"

Without turning, I hand her a heavy, closed container from underneath my seat.

She takes it from me. "I know, I know. Pour just a little, not a lot. I got it. I got it!"

I hand Stephanie back the hourglass coin, and she hands me a black case.

I open to find the Ten of hearts mask but not the lion pistol. Where is it?

Stephanie innocently says, "Don't be mad but I woke up and the pistol was just gone. I looked everywhere for it."

I forcefully close the case, knowing one of my demons must have stolen it. The worst news is that it was already loaded with one of the lead balls inside. Even after all this planning something still has to go wrong.

From the back, Stephanie says, "Don't miss!"

I step out and slam the door behind me. Hurrying, I rush through the swinging doors of the office building and into one of the interior elevators. It whirs to life.

The metallic doors reflect my true face. The elevator doors open. I move my gun hand behind me and step into my office.

Raphael swivels in my office chair. A loud noise booms across the park. Raphael stares past me. Shielding the gun with my body, I turn to face the wall of windows. The interstate has seen better days. A car flies off the railing and smashes into the ground beside the coffee shop.

Raphael's voice shows a hint of amusement. "Look at him go!"

I turn back toward him and offer him the black case.

He lights a cigarette and puffs the smoke out on the case. He opens it up. Inside lies the Ten of Hearts mask. "Is it Halloween already?" He laughs and stamps his cigarette onto the desk. He points at the hourglass in the reflection. The sand turns to snow.

"I think he's finally gonna do it this time. We might actually end all this tonight. It was a good idea you convinced him to run a day early. No one else knows but us, right?" I nod.

"Trust between demons is gettin' slender these days. This were a smart idea you had, gambling to see who gets his human carry-on bag. Genius. You just remember that if he does make it before 42:02, I win. That was the deal."

He coughs up a lung for a few seconds and then puffs a ring of smoke from his mouth. I take out the half-empty bottle of Macallan and set it on the desk.

"Well, this does seem a bit celebratory. But who am I to waste fine liquor?"

He pours two glasses and slides one to me. The amber liquid sloshes. He lifts his drink and cheers, "May the best demon win." I pick up the glass, but wait for him to drink first. He puts it to his lips and stops.

"How about you take the first drink," he says, while putting his glass on the table.

I look at the glass in my hand, watching the amber liquid slide from one corner to the next.

"Would you like me to hold that mask for you?"

After a few seconds, I lift my mask halfway and gulp it down.

Raphael lingers over a smirk. "Just making sure. Never can be too careful when your brother is a greedy demon."

He smiles broadly, pulls a case of cigarettes from the desk, and offers me one. I decline. He puts one in his mouth and strikes a match to light it. He stops once again and looks down at the pack. "Had you going there. Tell me. Did you dip them in water? Nah, you're too clever for that. Must have been use of ejection? Made me think the whisky was diluted just to actually have poisoned me by my own smokes. You think for a second that I don't see what you're doing? I know how your mind thinks."

He puts the cigarette back in with the others and shoves it back into the desk.

He takes another out of his jacket and lights it up. He sucks hard on the cigarette and blows a huge amount of smoke toward my face.

"Now, when you going to sally up and lay that pigskin down?"

I don't move.

"How about this then. I'll show you mine if you show me yours."

He takes out the lion pistol from behind his back and lays it down in front of me.

So he was the one who stole it.

I show Raphael the pistol in my hand.

Raphael smiles almost like he knew the double cross was coming. He looks at the carving of the lamb on its butt.

"If you can't trust Greed, who can you trust?"

He takes one long puff feeling mighty proud about himself.

"So what are you planning to do with that? Shoot me? Ha! By the time you pull that trigger, I would have already twisted your tiny head right off. Take it as me being prideful, but I'm the fastest demon here and you know this. How about we make it interesting though?"

He looks at the lion on the butt of his gun. "Ah! Let's say the first one to reload and shoots wins!"

I give it a second before I nod to the terms. We unload both our pistols and place them both in the middle between us.

He tips his head back and blows smoke into the air. "The better the risk, the better the gamble," he says with a Cheshire-cat smile. He laughs and sucks some more on his cigarette. He puffs more heavily and places it in his ashtray. Raphael takes the Ten of Hearts mask from the case and puts it over his face.

"When it strikes ten."

The grandfather clock ticks loudly. We stare at each other. The clock dings.

Ten minutes.

Raphael snatches the lamb pistol leaving me with the lion.

Simultaneously, we begin loading our pistols, pouring powder down the muzzles.

I put the bullet in the muzzle of the gun. It slides down the barrel, and I stick the ramrod down after it.

After removing the ramrod, I cock the hammer. Looking back up, I already see him aiming his pistol at my mouth. "Don't look so glum. You lost before you even began to load. Remember, David chose the lion. You wouldn't have been able to pull the trigger even if you did get to shoot first! What an idiot!"

He takes his glass off the table, gulps down the drink, and pulls the trigger. Clink! It misfires.

Confused, he drops the glass on the table and looks at the butt of his gun. He confirms that he does have the lamb.

His face seems riddled with questions and confusion as I give him a half smile.

"Why didn't it fire?"

Raphael begins to wildly cough.

He looks at the empty glass beside him. He takes the glass, rotating the leftover liquor around and around. He gives a forced cough and drops the glass to the floor.

I finish loading the gun and place it on the table.

I swiftly yank his tie to the table. In one smooth motion, I remove a knife he has clipped to his belt and stab it through his tie into the mahogany desk. While wrestling his gun away, I kick the chair out from under him. He falls partly to the floor. The tie cinches around his neck like a hangman's noose.

Raphael struggles to breathe as the fabric tightens, cutting off his circulation.

I bend down to his level and pull him closer to me. I yank his mask clear off his face and take hold of the lamb pistol off the table and push it into his mouth. He fights me, but the laced drink has slowed him enough that it isn't a contest.

He looks deep into my eyes and after just a second, they go extremely wide.

Raphael's face darkens even more, and his brows crease with realization.

I pull the trigger. Crack!

The bullet shoots through Raphael's mouth. With his head still cocked back, Raphael wheezes and begins to transfigure, freezing over as he does.

I remove my mask to show him my face.

He gazes at me and breathes his last breath. A stunned look crosses his face. His image transforms into a demonic frozen sculpture. I pick up the mask and place it back over his face.

I put my own mask back on, breathing a sigh of relief. The Ten of Spades peeks out of Raphael's pocket. I snatch it, along with his matchbook, and pocket them. After tucking the lamb into the back of my waistband, I grab the lion and take the bottle of Macallan off the table.

I find a folder of empty pages lying in the center of the desk. I think about all the time I have spent at this desk, forced to sit without a thought to write about. It's only fitting.

I rip out a sheet of paper, walk out the door, and press the button for one of the interior elevators.

The second one opens, revealing Stephanie in a promiscuous nun outfit. Her hair is pulled into an elegant French twist, and her face has been all made-up.

I offer a harmless grin.

"I thought it only fitting."

She drapes a black veil over her hair, a white cap around her bangs holding the headdress in place. Stephanie gives a childish smile, putting her hands together in a praying position.

I make her look at the clock on the wall. Eleven minutes and nine seconds.

"I know. Eleven minutes and thirty seconds."

I give her the loaded lion pistol.

She takes it and hurries down the stairwell. I call the next car and step over in front of the first elevator shaft. The doors part, revealing Sealtiel with his glaring horn-rimmed glasses.

He stares at my mask and breaks into his big, toothy grin. "You know, if you didn't fancy the face you chose, you could have mirrored another one. No need to hide it away."

I remain silent, my eyes locked onto his.

He shifts from one foot to the other and drops the smile. "Has it been done?" He crosses his arms.

I nod, showing him the lion pistol. He extends his arm to invite me in. I proceed.

"Good." His voice is sharper now, and a rosy hue spreads across his face. "Once you challenge David and win that will finally be the end of all this."

I look at Sealtiel's watch. My watch.

Eleven minutes and twenty seconds.

"What are you waiting for?"

I look at the elevator panel in front of me, knowing it's not time yet. I don't move.

"Push the button."

In the back of my mind, the time counts up. 11:22...11:23...11:24...11:25.

"We don't have time for this."

He raises his hand to the panel. His finger gets close to the panel, making me quickly intervene by grasping a hold of his wrist.

"What's the matter with you?"

I hold it as tight as possible.

11:28…11:29.

"Let go."

11:30.

I release his hand and press the button for the lobby. The elevator descends.

"What was that about?"

Without much thought, I jokingly give him the finger.

He shakes his head. "I can't wait till you're gone. Have I told you that?"

He relaxes a bit. "Just four of us now, correct?"

I nod.

"As requested, the two-gallon container we collected has been moved to your specific location. It's all hooked up and ready to go. All you need to do is pull the switch."

I continue counting, 11:35…11:36…11:37.

"Just remember what we agreed on. I partnered up with you with the intent of you going up, not David. When you go up, I will finally be able to travel out of this dump and to other souls' self-made prisons. Hopefully, with souls that have a better lifestyle to which I can hijack a meat suit for myself. David is just a means to an end. A lost cause that not even I could help fix. I'd rather be someone who has more of a backbone, with a lot more wealth."

I grip my fist, trying to keep my composure.

He chuckles. "But good luck with all that. Maybe we can go get a drink sometime while on the outside?"

I turn to face him as the elevator slows and settles to a stop. From a pocket, I pull a napkin and drop it.

Sealtiel watches it drift to the floor. The napkin turns gray as it soaks up water from the carpeted floor. Sealtiel looks down and lifts his foot up. The wet floor suctions his shoe.

"What in the..."

I stay calm. 11:51...11:52...

With a click, I press the gun barrel to the back of his head. I maneuver him so he faces the left side of the elevator. He swiftly knocks the pistol out of my hand and it goes down below his feet. He bends down, taking hold of the weapon, and notices it's empty.

11:55...11:56...11:57.

I force him by the hair, pushing his face straight up against the elevator wall. I swiftly lean my head sideways and follow his hand holding the pistol. He brings it up to his face and notices the lion.

11:58...11:59.

He laughs as if thinking he has won.

Twelve minutes.

Crack!

A bullet shoots out of the wall, blows through Sealtiel's laughing mouth, and exits out the back of his head. His body sways for several seconds.

I turn him over and take off my mask. Recognition crosses his face in horror. I take off his glasses and crush them on the floor.

His face transfigures, and he slumps against the wall. His image fades into a demonic snarl as he turns to ice. He freezes over and falls to the floor. I reach down and remove the Ace of Spades from his jacket pocket and the watch off his wrist. After sliding my mask down over my face, I pick up the pistol off the wet carpet.

The doors open, and I step into my office. My other half comes out of the other car.

I toss him the watch.

Once he catches it, he looks at me with confusion.

The elevator doors by his side are about to slide shut. I gracefully slip into the elevator. I reach down and retrieve Uriel's ring, and I pocket the King of Diamonds with the rest of the cards I've collected. The doors seal me in, and I press the L button.

I exhale a cloud of vapor. They are coming.

I hit the emergency stop. The car halts, and the doors open.

I need to get out before they box me in. Sliding the ring onto my finger, I step into the hallway and run.

Halfway down the hall, reapers fly toward me from the other end, shrieking so loudly the paintings on the wall shudder. There's a bathroom on the right. I throw open the door, run in, and head straight for the sinks.

I open all the faucets completely. A blackish sludge rushes out of the taps. Behind me, ice races across the bathroom door and floors. The frozen door crackles and yields to force from the other side.

A reaper's skeletal hand wraps around the edge of the door and pushes it open the rest of the way. The accumulating ice makes its way to the running sinks. I jump into the last stall and shut the door before the reaper's cowl appears in the doorway.

I suddenly realize I'm in the women's restroom when I see a big bag of Stephanie's self-made flares lying on the toilet seat. I unscrew many of the flare tops and pour the highly flammable black sand into the bag.

Under the stall door, the sludge freezes into murky patches of ice. The doors of the other stalls bang open one at a time.

A dark shadow appears below my stall door. I kick open the door, slamming it into the reaper. It crashes against the wall, shattering a mirror over one of the sinks. I rush to the sink, break off one of the filthy icicles hanging from the faucets, and jab it into the reaper's skull. A reaper behind me shrieks. I spark a single flare in my hand, toss it in Stephanie's bag, and slide it underneath the reaper's cloak. The reaper looks at the bag for a beat as I run to the end of the bathroom and throw myself through the frosted window.

From above me, I can hear the explosion as my body continues to bullet downward through the falling snow. The cold wind stings my eyes.

I tumble across the ground and into some bushes.

An army of reapers throngs the base of the building. Some break away, flying toward the explosion I just caused. One of them stops above me and floats down in my immediate direction. The bush between us slowly freezes over.

Revealing myself would be suicide. I close my eyes, waiting for my demise.

A loud crash above me sends the reapers' attention upward. Raphael's frozen body falls from the top floor window. The reapers swarm toward it, leaving the bush unattended. I dart out of the bush, and, without slowing, I make my way back to the park.

The whole park has been frozen over, and everything is covered in snow. The cold wind rakes against my cheeks as I make a beeline to the dead tree.

I dig into the deepening snow, searching for the tail end of the fuse where Stephanie dropped it. A deafening clamor resounds from the publishing building.

I turn. The whole building caves in on itself.

I dig faster. The reapers will soon catch on to my heat signature. I brush more snow away. Three inches of a loop of wire sticks out from the white powder. I follow it till I get to the end. I take out the matchbook. The wind nearly blows it from my hand. There's no way I can strike a match in this blast.

Several feet away, the tree is iced over. I raise my knife high and bring it down on the layer encasing the hollow. It cuts through the ice after a few jabs. I take out the bottle of Macallan and ripped-up paper from my jacket pocket. I wad up the paper, jamming it half inside the bottle, and then take refuge inside the walls of bark. Turning my back to the outside, I block the wind and open the matchbook. There are four matchsticks left.

The first stick is a dud. I flick the head of the second match across the line of phosphorus. Nothing. My hand shakes a little as I pull the third match from the book. Only one more shot after this.

I lift my face to the door. The engraved war between heaven and hell draws me like a magnet. I graze the tip of the matchstick along an angel's wing.

Nice and slow David. Nice and slow.

A flame springs to life and catches the wooden match on fire. I hold it to the paper. A flame ignites, and I quickly take a step back. Looking at the bottle one last time, I register this defining moment. I arch my arm and thrust the Molotov cocktail into the tree's hollow. It bursts on impact, spreading the flames into its wooden bark like a wild fire. The tree begins to rumble and shake as the fire continues to consume it.

I sprint as far as I can from the tree. Behind me, a huge explosion knocks me to the ground. I roll over as the tree falls to its side, almost as if it were human. Flames shoot high, flooding the park with an orange glow. I push up from the ground and break into a run again. It won't be long before the fire draws many unwanted guests my way.

In a short time, I reach the Lighthouse Restaurant. The temperature inside feels like

I've landed on the far side of the moon. The round windows on the kitchen doors reveal that the room is teeming with reapers.

My warm breath mushrooms in front of me, I shiver violently, and the first phase of frostbite attacks my limbs. I fall to the floor, shaking.

Come on, David. You've trained for this moment. Your body can take it. You'll acclimate.

Once my senses are in order, I slowly rise and turn to the kitchen, crowded with dark hoods. If I had to bet, Gambit has gotten himself trapped.

I anticipated something like this was going to happen. With dwindling energy, I dash to the balcony and up the stairs to the maintenance room above the restaurant. As I enter, the lighthouse beacon flashes in my face from just above me. I descend a small set of stairs inside to the maintenance area just below. A two-gallon container of reaper H_2O sits where I left it in the corner. I deftly unscrew the water line for the sprinkler system and hook it into the container. It will take a few minutes to pressurize. But it should be ready by the time I hit the fire alarm in the kitchen.

I concentrate, transfiguring my body into the image of a reaper. With a white, bony hand, I yank open the door and hurry back down to the dining room.

Silently, I slip inside the swinging doors and blend with the other floating reapers. They don't seem to have realized Gambit is hiding in the meat locker.

I need to act fast. I clocked it in at thirty seconds tops on the last mirroring trial I conducted. Thirty seconds total to get in and out before the reapers pick up my heat signature.

I glide through the hoard of reapers. As I pass the circular window on the meat locker, I hesitate.

Michael paces in front of a collapsed Stephanie. Gambit hangs back, watching the scene. What are they doing in there? Michael and Stephanie have words, but I can't hear anything.

Michael probably wants to know the key. That's the only thing he has yet to figure out. Stephanie won't give it up. He will surely kill her for that reason alone.

I move away from the door, and the reapers begin to act differently. The hoods swing back and forth, as if they were searching for something or someone—me.

I hurry out of the kitchen, through the dining area, and out the front door with one second to spare. I transform back to my masked self and lean against the closed door. Michael could be doing anything to Stephanie at any moment. I can't take the chance of losing her. I need to get her to safety before I pull the fire alarm. Once I have her out, I may be able to manually turn on the sprinklers from the maintenance room. It may take a few moments more to locate the manual override, but I'm going to have to risk it.

What will Michael do next? He won't just kill her; that's too easy. He will want her to suffer. How can I use that to save her?

Reapers can't see lost souls. But their razors can! I focus my mind and transfigure my body to look like one of their demonic hellhounds. Now on all four flaming legs, I bound back inside and into the kitchen.

I need to get Michael's attention. I force a long howl from my throat and wrap it up with an evil snarl. Seconds pass, and Michael's face appears at the circular window. He sees me.

At fifteen seconds, the door still hasn't opened. What is taking so long? I pounce on the door and bang my snout against the window, leaving a thick line of mucous across the pane.

The steel door cracks open, and Stephanie flies out. I jump at her and sink my teeth into the skirt of her bloodied gown. She stifles a scream as I drag her body into the dining area and out onto the balcony. I lift her over the railing and release her. She falls to the snow-covered ground. I transfigure back into myself and turn toward the stairs.

As I take the stairs three at a time, she yells after me, "That was fun! Let's do it again!"

Just before I push through the door to the maintenance room, I lean over the edge. Stephanie lies in the snow, waving her arms and legs to create perfect snow angels.

Reapers pour down from the balcony toward her. She puts her mask back on and takes off, laughing like a kid in a toy store while she runs.

I need to hurry. I pull the handle and step through the door.

A reaper stands just inside, blocking my way. There's no snow in the air, no layer of ice racing across the ground.

The lighthouse beacon rotates, glancing off the wall and into my eyes, blinding me for a few seconds. I adjust my focus. Michael, dressed all in black, now stands where the reaper used to be. His hair is nicely combed back. He claps, chuckling a bit.

"Hello, David." He stalks around the room.

I just stare at him, not succumbing to his demand. He takes out an Ace of Spades mask from inside his jacket and fits it snugly over his face. "How ironic." He giggles, putting his hands up to the mask's lips. "Just like a deck of cards, the Ace outranks the King. I can play dress-up, too."

I lift my mask, showing him my true face.

"I must admit, you're a clever one."

The beacon makes another round.

Michael brushes off dust from his finely stitched black jacket. "Like the suit? I thought I would look my best for you when I take my final bow from this place. Going out with some class."

Michael waits, trying to push through my mental guard and get into my head. I don't let him.

"You learned how to block us out. I'm impressed."

He circles me like a lion circles its prey. I've been through enough days to know when a demon is about to give me a long monologue. He thinks by distracting me with his thought-provoking words it will leave me feeling defenseless in some way. Little does he know, I've grown accustomed to their deceptions. I know everything he is going to say before he even says it. After awhile, they are all predictable in their own ways. Its become more of a game to me now.

Michael is the easiest one to predict. He goes over my whole plan from top to bottom, leaving nothing out. First, on how I told them to pose as lost souls to gain 'Davids' trust. Second, lying about how 'Davids' life was ending in eight days. And finally, on how I had designed a plan to fool them into teaching 'David' how to win his challenges.

But as they were teaching him how to survive, I was teaching him how to live. Building his conscience was crucial.

Michael goes on praising me on how thorough my plan was. The little things. From giving them all angelic names to helping them mirror people that looked professionally honest just to further gain 'Davids' trust.

Michael screams, "I may not know what your thinking, but I know when I'm not being heard!"

I continue to look at him with no care in the world.

"I've been on to you from the start. I knew something was up ever since you gave that rousing speech to all of us seven days ago. Your performance was on point! You sounded just like Greed and had an idea that seemed right up Greeds alley."

He whips his chair into the air and smashes it into the beacon. The room goes black. As my eyes adjust, faint beams of moonlight shine through cracks in the walls.

Michael pulls out the coin necklace and dangles it in front of me. "Just remember when that last hourglass breaks..." He lifts his mask.

His voice becomes serious. "I'll be the only one left to challenge you."

He walks to the door and opens it. "Stay frosty." He puts his mask back over his face and steps outside.

I swiftly run down the stairs into the maintenance area. It's going to be a lot harder to find the manual override in the dark. I fumble over the gauges and switches. I stop when my fingers graze one that feels right.

I flip the switch and hightail it out of there.

Snow gently falls around me and sticks to the cold steel of the restaurant. I hop over the edge of the roof and fall to the street below. I make my way to a half-cracked manhole on the other side of the street and push the lid off. I look down the long, dark, tunneled abyss.

A light flashes inside, illuminating a long, narrow, one hundred-foot drop leading to the subway tracks. I take a ready stance. Carbon dioxide billows from my mouth.

The head of the subway car flashes across the tracks. I pull my mask down over my face. It may deflect a little of the cold wind's pressure once I land on the train.

I bury any fear I have.

Then I pencil-dive into the manhole. With my eyes shut tight, I keep my arms held in, legs straight, and feet pointed. The gush of wind gets heavier the farther I drop. My descent ends with my head colliding with the moving subway car. I bounce along the slippery hood of one of the frozen cars, trying to stabilize myself with anything I can grab onto. But the ice has wholly encased any potential handhold. Winds scrape my face at about forty miles per hour. The pressure flips me around like paper in a hurricane. At the second-to-last car, the furious winds force me down between two coaches. I slam into the closed door of the last car and drop toward the tracks. Just as my face is about to reach the rails, my leg gets caught by something, and I jerk to a stop.

Above me is a woman in the Queen of Hearts mask, her dark hair pulled into a tight bun. She's wearing a gray, single-piece uniform that hugs her curves like a thin layer of armor. With a grunt and a powerful arm, she pulls me onto the car's small platform. "I can't believe you actually did it!" She pulls off her mask, unveiling her creamy skin and cherry-red lips.

Stephanie.

I grin as my heart rate calms down.

"He is in the next subway car." She hands me the lamb pistol, smiling as if expecting a compliment.

I take the gun and stand up.

I hold out my hand for her to give me the lead ball.

"About that...."

I can already assume that Michael had taken it from her.

"Also, Michael said some things that I couldn't tell the whole truth about. Gambit might see you as a threat now. So best watch yourself."

She nods and walks into the opposite subway car.

Shrieking resounds from the tail end of the train. I hasten into the subway car where Gambit is waiting. All of the windows have shattered. He whirls, and his eyes light up with recognition.

I hold my gun out and take a step forward.

His cheeks flush, and his body tenses. He aims his gun at me.

I need to come up with something fast. Frost races over the doors behind me. The reapers are coming up behind me. I move up a couple feet.

Simultaneously, a bang comes from his gun, and concentrated pressure throws my right shoulder backward. I crash through the frozen doors, flying off the railing into the darkness that awaits me.

FORTY-FOUR

Reapers' screeching wakes me. Beside me is the metallic track, barely visible in the dim light. The subway car is long gone ahead of me, with reapers forcing themselves in. My right shoulder pounds, and searing pain radiates from my forehead.

"So, was that the signal?" Stephanie appears out of the blue. "Looks like your mask has spider-webbed."

I take off my mask. Cracks run from a small hole near the top. It's strikingly similar to the painting of the cracked mask Lisa had showed me.

I try to rise, but Stephanie holds me down. "I can't believe it. How are you still here? I thought once you got shot the whole race gets reset?"

I reach into my upper jacket pocket and pull out my Bible. The bullet is lodged in between the pages. We both say nothing of it knowing the puns would be limitless. I stash it back in my pocket. She helps me up and we walk down the tracks.

To our right is a dark set of stairs leading up and out of the subway tunnel. I pull the mask back over my face. The count continues in the back of my mind. 39:57...39:58...39:59...

Forty minutes.

Stephanie stops and looks up at the dark, narrow staircase. "He's almost there. Do you think he'll make it?"

I hurry up the stairs.

Stephanie follows close behind.

At the very top, I open the door to a snowy forest clearing. The full moon casts enough light to lightly illuminate the trees. There's not a reaper in sight. I draw my gun, wave Stephanie forward, and begin sneaking along the snowy path.

Looking at my pistol, I keep forgetting I'm empty. I lower it, knowing Michael has the last lead ball now.

We round a corner, and I stop to clear our line of sight. Still no reapers.

She bolts in front of me, forcing me to stop.

"You still have time to change your mind." Her face shows concern.

I try to move forward, but she throws her arms around me and holds on tight.

I put my arms around her. My hands slide across the delicate armor protecting her back. Her curvaceous body fits against mine like a puzzle piece. I close my eyes and return her firm embrace, tucking her chin over my shoulder.

Madi's warm, brown eyes, and silky-smooth cheeks fill my mind. I push Stephanie away with what I hope is a determined look on my face. She offers a smile, but it's small, and I can tell sorrow hides behind it.

I must keep to the plan. No time for saying our goodbyes. Not just yet.

We advance through the dark, snowy forest. Moonlight shimmers off the snow, making our way that much brighter.

Just ahead is a broken lamp post laying on top of Madi's billboard. As we get closer we find a knife at the tail end of the pole. Stephanie takes the knife out and says, "I think he might beat your time."

We stop as a gale-force wind vibrates the giant sign. The falling snow is sucked up in a whirlwind of vast proportions, almost completely obscuring our view. We grab the post of the billboard.

"Where did the bridge go?" Stephanie yells.

I squint my eyes, trying to make out the shape of the bridge through the squall. In place of the iron structure are several tall glaciers. I grip the post more tightly. The bridge must've somehow collapsed into the dam.

Suddenly, the wind calms, and the snow resumes its gentle fall through the moonlight.

Stephanie lets go of the post and straightens. "He must've just been through here. Probably followed by a ton of reapers, from the way this snowstorm was acting."

I push off from the post and lead the way through the glacial cliffs. As we trek across the precarious ledges, frozen reaper corpses mottle the way.

I reach the other side and move toward the billboard.

"Stay." Anna's soft voice dances over my ears.

No, get out of my head. You're not real.

A long crack runs across the silver musical note on the billboard, letting me know that Gambit only has two more hourglasses to go.

Stephanie points above me and yells, "There he is!"

I shift away from the sign to see a flood of reapers up in the air, making their way toward the roof of my apartment building. In the mist of all of them is my demon running on a reapers ice grid, heading toward the roof.

Stephanie stands beside me and says, "He isn't going to make it! I need to do something!"

I look over, and Stephanie is now gone from my side.

Suddenly, a loud noise reverberates through the sky.

Fireworks burst through the dark night, fiery blooms amongst the stars.

Stephanie not only is fast but also a quick thinker. She never ceases to impress.

I sprint down the street and around the corner.

The apartment windows are all broken, and glass litters the base of the building. Reapers float around the top of the skyscraper. Snowflakes, suspended in the air, glisten as if I were a fish in a bowl filled with diamonds.

I drift back to the moment just after the car crash. Me lying flat on my back, facing the sky, while the snow falls slowly around me. Almost as slowly as it is now. I turn my head, noticing Anna's body is laying above the snow in the distance.

"Stay," Anna whispers beside me.

I turn my head and I'm back in my soul prison again.

Don't break, David. Keep your head focused. You can do this. You're not going to give up anymore. Not this time.

Suddenly, I hear someone coming out of the woods.

It's Stephanie!

She stands beside me, almost out of breath. "I knew that box of fireworks would come in handy."

I impatiently wait for her to continue.

"He did it! Memories are still intact."

I let out a sigh of relief.

Stephanie slips her hand into mine. I don't shake it off. We walk down the wintery street together, free from the threat of the reapers. From somewhere above, the sound of a piano melody reaches out across the sky.

Stephanie squeezes my hand. "Something tells me the time is 42:02."

I nod, touch a hand to my head, and try to block out the sound. The edges of my vision break away. Its trying to suck me into one of my past memories but I won't allow it!

My soul's equilibrium instantly blocks the music. I'm yanked into the darkness.

I snap my eyes open. The puzzle pieces reconnect, and I'm back in my soul-realm.

Stephanie turns to me. "I will never get use to you doing that."

I take a breath, knowing it never gets easier.

"Let's split up to cover more ground," Stephanie demands. "You take the high-rise; I'll take the roof. He has to be somewhere in between those." Stephanie whirls and charges through an emergency exit in the side of the building.

I put my mask back on and race through the revolving, iced-over doors. Slipping and sliding, I cross the lobby. The elevator doors slide open before me. I get in and hit the level 6 button.

The elevator jolts into motion.

I hope I'm not too late.

After a few seconds, the elevator stops and the doors slide open. Wet ice crunches under my feet as I traverse the hallway,

The door to my apartment is sodden from the melting ice.

I run my fingers over the damp number six, remembering the casino night and the lustful affair in this dreadful room. I kick the door in, and make my way inside.

The living room is saturated from the thaw. I walk into the bedroom doorway, through the thin layer of water.

Michael creeps toward Gambit, moving slowly through the thin coating of water on the floor. He leans over Gambit, supine on the floor. He takes the last lead ball out of the green marble bag and loads it into the lion pistol.

He jumps to his feet and scans the room. He releases a barrage of curse words. With arms flailing, he tramples the room and tears everything from the walls, including: the Polaroid pictures and the framed American flag.

He screams over and over, "Where is it?"

The snow globe still rests on the nightstand.

He tips the nightstand over, sending the glass sphere into the air. I flinch, about to run over. But its trajectory takes it softly onto the bed.

Michael's rage leaves him tired, defeated, and out of breath. He picks up the torn American flag from the ground and wraps it around himself. Music plays slowly from the snow globe. He turns and snatches it off the bed. His eyes glass over.

I rush in behind him, grab a handful of hair, and yank the back of his head to his neckline, forcing him onto his knees. Bruises and open wounds riddle his skin.

"What took you so long?"

He sweeps my leg and kicks the gun out of my hand. His leg slips, and we are at a standstill. The water underneath him has slowed his movements, and he knows it.

He throws the coin necklace at my feet. "The coin isn't the key. Tell me what the key is. Right now!"

I see my chance, and, running over to Michael, I flip him to the ground, knocking away his gun. Michael jumps up, tackles me to the ground, and gets me in a chokehold.

I grab my logbook off the floor and hit him over the head. He swings and misses, and I deliver a series of punches to his face. His mask shatters, leaving Michael stunned and barely standing. I grab for his gun and try unloading the bullet within it. Michael kicks it out of my hand and connects on several punches, knocking me to the ground.

Kneeling, he picks up his pistol off the ground.

"I win. You should be happy it's going to be me. I will do what needs to be done. I can do that. Not you. Me!"

When I look up, he is already aiming at my head.

"Just tell me where it's at, and I will serve justice in her name."

Kneeling underneath him, I raise my eyes to his, showing him no resolve.

"Don't fool yourself in believing that this place has changed you. You still see her, don't you?"

Anna.

"We have wasted enough time in here already! We can't let them get away with what they did!"

Anna's innocent voice speaks to me again, "Stay with me, Daddy."

Get out of my head.

Michaels face turns red as he yells, "Fine! If I don't go up, you won't go up! I will shoot you and wait till the clock strikes sixty. We'll pick it back up tomorrow and do it all over again, and the next day, and the next day after that. I can do this forever! Can you David?!"

I straighten my back and gaze up at him, letting him know I'm not afraid.

"See you tomorrow then, David."

I hurry to push his pistol into his open mouth. His teeth grind against the metal barrel. I swing his body to the floorboard. I pull the trigger and nothing happens.

I'm dumbly reminded that I'm holding the lion-engraved pistol and not my own.

He lifts his head back, releasing the barrel out of his mouth. He laughs at my careless attempt.

I quickly try to jam it in once again but get blocked by his teeth.

I connect the muzzle of the gun to his pearly whites, force his finger around the trigger, and pull.

The flint strikes the frizzen and Michael's eye's go wide. The bullet drives down the barrel, out the muzzle, fractures his teeth into his jaw, and continues along its path through the back of Michael's head.

Michael grips the red, white, and blue fabric around his shoulders. The lion pistol drops from his lifeless fingers. His eyes turn from green to gray to white, as the ice takes its course throughout his body.

I snatch the King of Clubs card from his jacket pocket, and place it over my own card. The force sends a crack down the iced corpse. His appearance changes again to that of a demon. At the crack, his body splits in two and falls to the floor. The two halves shatter into pieces on the hardwood and send sheets of ice spreading across the room. The American flag drops gracefully, covering up most of what's left.

I pick up the coin pendant off the soaking floor and wrap it around my neck where it belongs. I grasp the lion pistol off the floor and stuff it in Gambits pants.

After retrieving the snow globe from the bed, I walk through the bathroom into my closet. On a shoulder-high shelf is a backpack. I toss in the globe. I add the logbook to my stash and zip the bag shut.

On my way out, I stop and bend over Gambit. Near his feet, the broken alarm clock lies in pieces, but still shows brilliantly lit numerals: 42:45.

Purgatorium

Out the shattered window, the greenish glow of the aurora borealis mingles with the light of the full moon.

I reach down and heave Gambit over my shoulder. With him over one shoulder, and the backpack on the other, I cross the apartment and step into the hall.

Stephanie waits there for me.

I nod. It's time to finish this.

We head down the hall in silence and board the elevator. Gently, I place Gambit down while Stephanie pushes the button to the roof. The doors slide closed.

The elevator makes its way up to the top level and opens to the roof. I place the golden pendant on the floor while Stephanie uses the water left over from the flask to pour on the rug around it.

I pull Gambit by his arms through the sparkling display of snow crystals and lay him out on the roof.

Stephanie says from behind me, "Whatever you decide to do"—I turn to face her—"know I'm always here for you."

I want to say something back, but the words don't come. As the elevator doors begin to enclose her, she gives a small wave and smiles. And then she is gone.

I turn back to Gambit and drag him further toward the middle of the roof. I drop his hand and pull the snow globe from my bag. Déjà vu overwhelms me as I leave the snow globe by his side.

Reapers hover above me, and snow floats motionless around me. The aurora seems to be moving away. I make my way around the elevator to the opposite end of the roof, following the northern lights. They dance majestically in the sky, enchanting me by their haunting beauty.

The northern lights fade into the distance, leaving me alone for the last time with just the twinkling stars. The image revolves in my mind for what feels like an eternity. I gaze up at the celestial bodies and try to imagine that each one is a place like mine. Which one would be hers?

Anna's voice speaks to me again. "Stay."

I whirl. A fading image of her turns into air, brushed out into the night sky.

It's all just one big trick, a joke, a torturous tool that doesn't have the leverage it once had on me. I'll no longer play the fool to this world's amusement.

A scuffle comes from the other side of the roof. The music is still playing; he shouldn't be awake just yet.

I head back toward the elevator. Gambit stands just around the corner. I pull my flintlock pistol out, knowing it's empty, and walk out of the shadows, pointing it toward his back.

He turns.

I hold my pistol firm and keep my eyes locked onto his.

"This is deja vu at its best. Wouldn't you agree, old friend?" he says.

Snow lingers in the air between us.

"You remember; I feel like it was just yesterday when you shot me here and left me here for the reapers."

I can't help but ignore his endless rant on the way things went down.

He raises his pistol in front of me which brings back my attention. "If it wasn't clear already, this is me challenging you. Also, you can go ahead and take off that mask now. No need to hide from me anymore."

Mirroring Barachiel, I steady the pistol at him, slowly pull off my mask, and throw it on the ground.

"I thought I told you. No need for masks…David."

I return my image to my own.

He yells with glee, "There you are, David! Now we are back to being twins. Oh, how I've hated being forced to mirror your image. The first thing I do when I get out is get a top-to-bottom makeover. Because this look you got going on is ehh."

He looks around the roof and back at me. "You know what I was just thinking?"

He laughs, "Poor choice of words. I'm forgetting you're not a demon. You really had everyone going with that act, I must say. I digress. As I was saying, or thinking rather, the reason to why you chose me instead of the other six is because…?"

He waits on my response while I continue to not think nor speak.

"We both truly know why it was me. Because I was the first. The one sinful deed you first committed. Your own selfish greed. You've always blamed me for giving you the idea to steal that money from moms purse. She gave you ten but that just wasn't enough. Till this day I still agree with our action! If it wasn't for bipolar dad ruining everything per usual. Regretfully, that was the fight that lead to mama eventually cheating. You blamed yourself after she left. Always with the same question. What if I never had stolen that money? There wouldn't have been a mess to clean, she wouldn't have had to cover up for me, and she would've never left. All because you wanted to make your volcano look cooler. Which it totally did!"

He wants me to break but I won't let him.

"Little did you know then but from that day going forward you gave me the keys to unlock the flood gates to your soul. Hell, if I didn't invite everyone to come right on in."

He takes a few seconds to clear his throat. He looks off at the city view and quietly says, "Matthew 12:43-45. 'When the unclean spirit is gone out of a man, he walketh through dry places, seeking rest, and findeth none.'"

He turns to look back at me as his voice grows louder. "'Then he saith, I will return into my house from whence I came out; and when he is come, he findeth it empty, swept, and garnished. Then goeth he, and taketh with himself seven other spirits more wicked than himself, and they enter in and dwell there: and the last state of that man is worse than the first. Even so shall it be also unto this wicked generation.'"

He takes a bow, "Do you know what that passage ultimately means?"

He looks up to me as I continue my silent gaze.

"It means sins never truly leave. As proved today, you can kill them but eventually they will return. It just takes one sin."

He coughs for a few seconds to clear his throat, "Sorry for the rant. Haven't used my voice in some time and had to stretch the olé vocal cords out." He adjusts back and looks around the roof.

"Speaking of wrath, what was Michael's reaction when he found out the coin wasn't the key? I can imagine him with a whole lot of built-up rage and aggression. He was always more brawn than brains. It took me a while, too, but I eventually figured it out. Speaking of which, you can toss the cards over now."

He stares at my gun. "Your scare tactics don't fool me. If you think you've got the upper hand by holding that pistol in front of me, then be my guest. There is only one bullet left and you don't have it. But I do. Michael made sure of that."

I lower my pistol, take the playing cards I've collected out of my pocket, and throw them on the ground.

"Good doggy."

Gambit goes to pick them up and walks over to the broken telescope where the last hourglass was kept. He pulls out the piece of cloth, unwraps it, and takes out Madi's ring. "You know, I'm not mad. I'm impressed, really. I mean, you had me locked into believing the doctors were going to pull me off life support. Life support! Ha! You are a fascinating liar!"

He shakes the snow globe and holds it between us. The miniature snowstorm swirls around the tiny city.

The time is at a pivotal point.

He fidgets and shifts from one foot to the other. Lowering the snow globe, he snaps his fingers over my face. "I see we are having a communication problem. Fine, then. I guess I do deserve a little more talk time. I've been a little quiet here as of late."

Gambit winds up the music box on the base of the glass sphere. A soft melody rings out as he follows along, whistling.

"I know the real reason why you kept wanting to get your mind erased all those times. Why you've chosen to be in here for so long. It's because of her. Anna. Knowing if you saw your wife again that you couldn't look her in the eyes. Not after what happened."

My vision gets corrupted again and I'm back in the upside down car. A barely playing song trickles out of the broken snow globe. Anna is lying almost lifeless beside it.

Everything fades and I'm back staring at Gambit. I try not to flinch. I consume the music still playing above us to find clarity. To find hope that she's still alive.

"Even now you're still not fully content with what you did."

Despite his effort to look calm, his eyelid ticks with growing anxiety.

He looks up and yells, "Will someone please turn that insufferable music off already?" He brandishes the snow globe like a weapon, shaking it violently.

"Nothing to say?"

He pushes the hammer back and aims his pistol directly to my head.

"When you watch as I ascend, just know I'm going to change your sorry excuse for a life and make it better than you could ever dream."

He doesn't notice the chamber opening from within the snow globe. Little aluminum balls roll out, followed by a lead ball. Just as I planned.

He shakes the snow globe even harder now, and his volume level reaches its peak.

"Say something, damn you!"

The snow globe fizzles inside.

He looks at the glass orb in his hand.

The clear surface explodes, propelling water and glass into his face. He screams and covers his face. The lead ball rolls to my feet.

I stop it with my foot, reach down, and pick it up. While Gambit claws at his skin, I calmly take the black powder and pour it into the muzzle of my pistol. After dropping the lead ball in after it, I jam the rod down, twisting it to make sure the bullet is properly loaded. I toss the rod to the side, raise the gun, and aim it at him. He removes his hands from his face, tilts his pistol at my direction, and pulls the trigger.

Nothing happens.

I stick the pistol in his mouth and tighten my hold on the trigger.

This is it. Everything I have put into motion has been ruined by him remembering. This is why I created this plan B in the first place and I know what I have to do. I failed and I'm going to have to live with that.

I grip the handle tighter as I continue to battle the thoughts in my head.

Think about Anna. Think about Madi. Anna. Madi. Anna. You made a promise.

I slowly remove my finger from the trigger and retract the gun from my greed's mouth.

I made a promise.

In a flash, he yanks the King of Clubs card from my jacket pocket and rushes into the elevator.

Gambit steps inside,, taking out the collection of playing cards. Each one he puts in the light blinks red. The last one he puts in is the King of Clubs card, and the light blinks red once again.

"Why isn't this working?"

He stares at the card, realizing it belonged to Michael.

"The name was only half the clue. Something that can never be taken away, only given. That's Davids name. Something that was never an object given."

I step into the elevator and strike his neck, sending him down to his knees. A sharp wheezing escapes his throat as he tries to catch his breath. I remove the watch from his wrist and put it on my own. I bend down and pick up the hourglass pendent from the soaked rug.

I then take the playing card hidden down in my jacket pocket and show it to him.

The face of the King of Spades gets his attention.

"King...David."

His eyes bulge with realization as he says, "Something that was never given."

I turn toward the button display and lift the card to the card slot above the panel. I stick it in. The slot lights up green. I stow the card back in my jacket while the elevator begins to shake.

He looks into my eyes and, with conviction in his voice, says, "You need me."

I confidently pull the cards out of his hand and place them into my back pocket.

I turn back to look at him. With no restraint in my tone, I say, "I'm content."

I step out of the elevator. I shove the pistol into my bag.

"I don't understand," he says, eyebrows high and jaw slack. "You're just going to let me take your vessel?" He leans forward. "Why?"

My watch reads 44:30.

I reach down to the broken snow globe and pick it up.

"I need to know!" He holds Madi's wedding ring out in his hand. "A trade!" He gently rolls the ring outside the elevator. "Please! I need to know!" As the doors shut him in, I can hear his pleading continue.

The rooftop rattles, and the elevator launches, breaking away from the building's structure and the cables that connected it to the shaft.

Madi's ring bounces wildly into the air. I run after it, but wind from the elevator's launching blows it over the ledge, off the roof.

The reapers above me begin to vibrate. I swan-dive over the ledge. The music is coming to an end as I reach for the ring. Cold wind rakes over my face.

Frozen remains of reapers explode all around me, sending a wave of water from the sky. I grab the ring midair and clutch it as the wave of water pursues me.

I concentrate on the melody. The flood of water touches my feet. I near the ground with only seconds remaining. My watch ticks off the last remaining seconds: 44:56…44:57…44:58. The swell engulfs me, submerging me as if in some way cleansing my soul. I close my eyes, letting faith guide me in.

My watch beeps.

45:00.

Everything fades to black.

PROVIDENCE

SUNDAY

FORTY-FIVE

little hand grasps my arm. I open my eyes. The darkened abyss of the ocean encompasses me. Lily's outline, barely visible in the deep blues and greens, pushes me upward. With every thrust, the light from the full moon beams through the water a little more brightly. I explode through the surface and raise my face to the moon's rays. I feel for my necklace, making sure the pendant's still safe.

After a few seconds, I suddenly realize I can't hear the music. Looking at my watch, I see that it seems to be frozen on the time 45:00. The hands are no longer even making the circuit around its face.

A few yards away, Lily stands on a small sandbar, her straight brown hair and light blue dress rustling in a gentle breeze. She calls out, "How do you feel?"

The water surges around my body, encasing me completely with its cool and smooth touch. I actually feel something other than cold. It takes me a second for my brain to register this new perspective on the sense of touch.

I glide my fingers across the ocean surface, and I feel everything. In excitement, I splash around in the water as if I were a little kid again. I release a resounding whoop. "I feel moist!" Lily's childlike laugh rings through the air. The water on my skin, which at first felt only a smidgen cold, has turned to full-on biting! My skin begins to sting, turning a bright red from the harsh caress of the liquid. I decide at this moment to get out. I begin to move my arms, pulling myself through the clear and frigid ocean.

Treading water, I force Madi's ring into one of my pockets. I concentrate on Lily's laughter and swim in her direction. I sink my palms into the soft sand and push myself up to standing. A few shimmering droplets still cling to my body, and steam rises from my hair.

The ocean view stretches to every horizon, clear and sparkling with moonlight. The heavenly body, hung high in the sky, is a perfect silver disk, bleaching the land into a ghost-like replica of daytime.

My body feels chilled to the core, but I don't shiver. The cold feels somehow a part of me.

The sandbar isn't just a sandbar. It's a small island with palm trees farther in. There's not a soul besides the two of us. Some ways beyond Lily is the coffee shop where I first met Madi. The pink neon sign hangs crooked, as if it might completely detach at any moment. The wooden exterior is scorched and blackened.

It appears that the small-town haberdashery has seen some better days.

Lily holds a good-as-new snow globe in her small hands as she says, "What price would you pay to free those you love? Remember when I said that to you long ago? Do you still think you made the right gamble, knowing the final consequences?"

I look out at the vast sea. I smile, knowing more than ever that I made the right choice.

"I had a promise to keep."

The gentle wind brushes over my skin. The palm trees sway, waving to the crystal-clear ocean. Light from the full moon bathes the whole scene in something like magic.

"Where are we now?"

"We are merrily in between," she says.

I furrow my brows. "In between?"

She turns to me. "The music has linked us between the two prisons. We must now wait till your prison is fully submerged before we get to the other side."

I look at her, confused.

"Think of it as a big hourglass. We are right now at its center, waiting for it to tip back over. Once the tides dry up and turn to dust, then you will be there."

"You? Don't you mean we?"

"I can't go with you any further. I was only supposed to be the messenger."

I hold her little hand in mine.

A few seconds pass. We watch as the ocean water runs up the shore to hit our naked feet. Actually feeling the water rush in between my toes is enough to make the whole experience worth it.

"We were so close," she says, looking up at me. "Why couldn't he be good like you?"

I take my Bible from my jacket pocket. Miraculously, it doesn't even appear remotely wet and the bullet hole has magically disappeared. "Because he never understood what this place was trying to show him."

I flip through the delicate pages until I get to Peter 3:10. Madi's favorite Bible verse, highlighted and underlined. I trace the verse with my finger.

Do you want to love life and see good days? Then keep your tongue from speaking evil. Turn away from evil and do good. Look for peace, and go after it.

Right beside it, I see my name written in my handwriting. David Hayes.

I close the book and finger the soft leather. "'For the love of money is the root of all kinds of evil, for which some have strayed from the faith in their greediness.' His soul could never be purified because he believed in only one thing, sweetie—greed. A demon thinks only of what benefits itself…not others. You can't force someone to find faith. You need to let them find it on their own."

I feel its leather one more time between my palms and then place the good book in my jacket pocket.

Anna horrifyingly says, "But now that he's free and remembers, aren't you worried about what he might do?"

I look at her sweet, innocent face, smooth beige skin, and familiar eyes. "Remember the most important thing I taught you?"

She nods. "All you need is faith."

I place my hand on top of her head. "That's right, smart girl." I remove my hand.

I reach into my other jacket pocket and take out my logbook. I open the cover and finger the writing. Madi.

"I've always thought of this as my logbook. Maybe calling it that made it easier to write in it. It's actually a novel I've penned during my time here. I can honestly say it's my best work, but sadly, no one will ever know it even exists." I take a moment to flip through the pages, marveling at what I thought would be my finest accomplishment, only to find out that it isn't at all.

"Maybe you can tell me if it's any good next time I see you? Would you do that for me?"

She eagerly nods, takes the book, and wraps her arms around my legs, hugging me tightly.

I run my fingers over her hair. "Thank you for everything. If it wasn't for you, I would have never known…."

She puts her lips over mine and softly says, "You don't have much time. Help her before it's too late."

I nod.

The snow globe rests in the sand near my feet. I pick it up and shake it. I close my eyes, praying for Anna, that she is still alive and safe. Hearing the ocean brings a smooth calm over me. I bask in that peaceful moment for just a few seconds. When I open my eyes, Lily is gone. Her small footprints in the sand are all that remains. The tide rolls up to the shore, washing over them, and just like that, they're gone, as if she wasn't even here. But I know better. I will see her again.

I turn and walk toward the coffee shop.

Inside, the furnishings are charred. Many of the tables and chairs have been reduced to ashes. The counters are barely standing.

I drop my bag near the door and walk through the shop.

"How about next time you make a plan, you be the one dying everyday," a feminine voice says behind me.

I whirl. Stephanie leans against the back door. She's dressed in a comfortable coral T-shirt and a pair of boot-cut jeans.

I walk over, put my back against the wall next to her, and slide down.

Several seconds go by.

"So, how does it feel being a lost soul?" she says.

"Feels cold."

"Yeah, you'll get used to it."

Stephanie slides the backpack to me. "It was smart to bring this." She drops a satchel next to it. "But you forgot a few things. Thought you might need them for the long journey ahead. It was hard collecting all of them, so you'd better appreciate me dearly for this kind gesture." She gives me a crooked smile.

I lean my head toward her. Her creamy skin and dark hair have a certain allure. The compassion in her eyes is what truly gets me. "Thank you, Stephanie."

I look in the satchel and pull out the lion pistol.

"I've always wanted to know," Stephanie says, looking at the lion's head. "Why the lion and the lamb?"

I take out the lamb pistol from my bag. "My mom always sang me a song at night when I was little called 'The Lion and the Lamb.'"

She gazes at the lamb on the butt of my pistol. "So, why choose the lamb?"

"My mom's favorite verse of the song was, 'Our God is a Lamb, the Lamb that was slain. For the sins of the world, His blood breaks the chains.' It has stuck with me ever since."

I put the pistols back in the bag and look back to Stephanie. "We really did it, didn't we?"

"No, you did." She smiles and cocks her head. "I might have helped a little, though."

I smile at her childlike sense of humor.

"Do you regret not going back?" Stephanie says.

I look resolutely at Stephanie. "No."

She pushes off the door and walks toward the fireplace. "I'll draw up a fire. Its warmth will be comforting, even if it doesn't do anything for our body temperature."

She loads the recess with wood.

"You wouldn't happen to have any matches on you, would you?" She grins.

I smile back and remove the filigreed matchbook from a pocket. "I happen to have one left. Now, we just need something the flame can catch onto." I pull out the cyan and black cards I collected from each of my demons.

With a grunt, I push all the cards below the woodpile.

I pull my King of Spades from my pocket and rotate it through my fingers as if the King is doing somersaults. Stephanie pulls me in closer and sits down beside me.

"So the card was your key?" Stephanie watches me play with it. "I thought you said your name was the key?"

"The name was only half the clue. You see, the King of Spades is known for being a certain biblical king."

She narrows her eyes as if mentally shuffling through her inventory of biblical kings. "King David!" she blurts out. "And the something that was never given meant the card that was never given to you by the dealer that night! How did I not put two and two together?!"

She takes the card from my hand and stares at it. After awhile she begins to look troubled.

"What is it?"

Continuing to endlessly gaze at the playing card she replies, "I was just thinking. Why would this place make your key be a simple playing card? But I think I understand. It's your scarlet letter." She looks back at me. "When did you know?"

I take back the card. "It was the only thing I couldn't get rid of. No matter how hard I tried. It would always show right back up the very next day in my jacket pocket. Haunting me with its presence. It was a constant reminder of what I did and who I was. It was fitting that it would be my key to get out."

"So then, what's the point of the key now?"

I look one last time at the card.

"Nothing."

I strike my last match and light the card. I turn my eyes to the fireplace and place it on top of the deck of cards. The fire catches immediately. Flames leap to life and wrap around the logs. Heat permeates the air in my general direction.

I lie down in front of the hearth. Stephanie lies down in front of me, snuggling back into my frame.

The heat blankets me but can't completely penetrate the hyperborean state of my body. Yet it is good to feel some kind of warmth. The crashing waves against the shore outside mark the passing minutes. The fire licks the bricks lining the small alcove. Oranges, yellows, and reds blend with hot white as the logs transform to coals.

"I'm sorry it didn't work out like you expected it to." Stephanie's voice is soft. "We almost had him thinking he was really you, too. Now that he is free, do you think he will hurt…"

"There was a moment on the roof when he was looking at this snow globe, and I could somehow tell …"

"Tell what?"

"I could tell he cared about someone other than himself. Even if it was just for a few seconds. I know that somewhere deep down inside, we got through to him."

"Do you really believe that?"

"That's what I have to believe."

Stephanie turns to me with tears in her eyes. "I'm going to miss you very much."

I relax my face and drop my chin a bit. "I guess you made up your mind, then?"

Tears fall down her face as she nods, not able to say the words. She wipes her eyes and puts her head in her hands, hiding her face.

I have never seen her open up like she's doing now. Not once. She's been a woman who acted more like an adventurous kid than a sensitive being. When I first met her, she was just a lost soul who didn't believe in hope, or faith, or love for anything. Just like how I was a long time ago.

She then points to my necklace. "So…are you finally going to tell me what that means?"

I wrap my hand tightly around the necklace and hold it against my chest. "I was around six." The memory fills my heart. The sun had caressed my face in the back of my father's pickup truck. "My family took me on our first real vacation, to the beach. I remember my mom always taking photos with her old Polaroid camera. I would try to build castles in the sand. My father would be trying to fix them." I laugh. "When we got to the last day of our trip, I begged my mom to let us go out to the beach just one more time. I knew that if I told my father, he would say no, but Mom had her way of talking him into things that he didn't want to do. She said she was interested in grilling fish for supper and wanted to know what brand to buy at the grocery store. My father, the man's man that he was, couldn't stand frozen food. My mom knew him all too well. My father got his fishing equipment together, and we went back out. I remember the breeze hitting my face as I ran to the water. I remember the warm sand in between my toes, and then I felt something else in between my toes. For a second, I thought a crab had gotten hold of me. I screamed out, and my father ran to me. He got on his knees, lifted my leg, and pulled this out."

I pull the coin away from me.

"I thought he was going to tear my butt up for not acting brave enough, but instead, he did something else. He took some leftover fishing line from his fishing box and made a necklace out of it. He put it around my neck, said it looked good on me."

The memories run through my mind like a slideshow. "That was the first and last vacation we ever took together."

I place the naked coin in the palm of my hand. The light from the fire brings a glimmering shine to the golden pendant.

My eyes get tired. I begin to worry what might happen if I close them. I wonder if my nightmares will return once again to haunt my soul. I had hoped that after becoming a lost soul, my torment would end.

I close my eyes, letting the sounds of the waves hitting the shore outside bring me peace and solitude despite the thought.

FORTY-SIX

A bright glow spills under my eyelids. I open them to see light coming through a window. I look around the room to find that I'm back in the coffee shop. I breath out in full relief.

I stand up, offering Stephanie my hand. She takes it, and I help her up. I heave my backpack onto my shoulders.

"Well, we'd better get going then," she says.

"We? I thought you said you weren't coming?"

She shrugs. "I just wanted to hear the story behind the necklace. I knew if I said I was leaving, you'd finally tell me." She grins. "Besides, I don't have anything better to do, friend."

She turns to me. "Come to think of it, you're my only friend."

Breathing heavily, I give her a hug.

She sighs, composes herself, and puts her arms around me.

A soft ticking begins. My watch has started back at zero.

"David." She puts a hand on my cheek and whispers, "It's time."

We walk out the door. The ocean is gone. The sky offers only a dusky glow to see by. The coffee shop is now surrounded by a white picket fence that runs adjacent to a long, straight, dusty road. There are no other buildings in sight, nothing but desert in every direction. Far ahead is a single, faded sign.

REST STOP NEXT EXIT

The American flag hangs from the porch, flapping in the wind. I think of my father and wonder what he would have done in my situation. The answer comes easily. I believe he would have gone to hell and back to save my mom.

I step to the fence gate, push it open, and walk out into the road. Stephanie follows. After a few yards, I turn back. The shop is gone.

She catches up to me. "So…any clue where we should start?"

I pat down my pockets. I've still got my wallet in my slacks. I take it out. Inside is the business card.

Peter J. Cameron, Music Producer

Stephanie looks at it. "Who is Peter J. Cameron?"

I crush the card with a tight fist.

"What's wrong?" asks Stephanie.

I grind my teeth. "His name isn't Peter J. Cameron."

Stephanie's brows bunch together.

I take the snow globe out of my bag.

"When Lily came to see me the first time, she gave me this snow globe. Inside, there was a picture."

I dig through my wallet.

Behind an inner flap is a picture of Madi, her mother, and her stepdad. He has light, close-cropped hair, but the eyes, jaw, and nose are features I recognize.

"A picture of a younger Madi, her mom"—I pause—"and the man who destroyed both their lives. The same man I met in the park that night, but he was using a different name—Peter J. Cameron."

I hold the picture in front of her face. "This man haunted Madi's memories and dreams the rest of her life. He still haunts her."

The whispers cohere into words. "Red Rover."

I spin around.

"Red Rover," the voice whispers again.

The desert around us is empty.

"His name"—I lift the photo again—"is Jacob."

An apparition of Jacob brushes beside me, leaning into my left ear and whispering, "Send David right over."

I turn my head, and he's gone. Dust pelts my face, and I close my eyes.

Stephanie is no longer by my side. Far off in the distance, she runs toward the rest-stop sign, her arms outstretched as if she were an airplane, as if this were all just one big game for her to play.

I raise my face to the gray sky, looking for any kind of answer to let me know that Madi is safe. A large sliver of light appears, like someone cut through the sky with a knife. The light moves and softens, becoming bright red and orange in color and breaking into strands. The lines of light shift through the sky like a new morning.

The undulating rows burst into multiple hues, brightening the world around me. They dance rapidly, touching and weaving and finally forming a baby-blue curtain across the sky. As quickly as they came, the lights recede into the sunrise over the horizon, leaving the sky clear and cloudless.

Without hesitation or fear, I stride forward, leaving the picture in the dust. I pick up speed, running down the long stretch of road toward the rest-stop sign—the first leg of my race to the real finish line.

Madi.

EPILOGUE

THE B·SIDE

THE B SIDE

Bright rays of light shine on my closed eyelids. The piano music skips on a record player next to me. I open my eyes. My blurry vision slowly tries to adjust. Through a window to my left, sunbeams bathe the sterile equipment that surrounds me.

I tilt my head down. I'm in a hospital bed. Anna's snow globe sits on the nightstand to my right. Beside the snow globe is a portable record player with Madi's album leaning against it.

I try to move, but I'm stiff and weak. I crack my dried lips open to try to speak, but nothing comes out. There's no water nearby. I try to talk again, but even opening my jaw brings excruciating pain. My hearing is a little off, my vision is fuzzy, and my brain feels completely numb.

The record still skips in the inside groove, repeating the last line of the song over and over again, a melody with which I am now long familiar. I rest my head back on my pillow.

A sharp white light glints to my left. Sunshine streams through a Celtic hourglass standing on a table next to the window. The bottom chamber is full of sand. It slowly flips over. Grains trickles through the thin neck into the bulb below.

I hum along with the last few keys that play from the record as I roll my head to the right. There's another bed a few feet away. The white hospital blanket covers a still, feminine form and drapes over a small bulge at her belly. I follow the form to its head. Soft brown skin, dark hair, closed eyes.

Madi.

He did it all to go and save her.

With great pleasure of finally understanding, I don a devilish smirk toward her comatose body. The music fades, replaced by the spinning vinyl of a record that has reached its end.

ACKNOWLEDGMENTS

I would like to express my gratitude to the many people who saw me through this book; to all those who provided support, talked things over, read, wrote, offered comments, allowed me to quote their remarks and assisted in the editing, proofreading and design.

Above all I want to thank God and the rest of my family, who supported and encouraged me in spite of all the time it took me away from them.

I would like to thank Travis Unangst and Alexsandar Radivojevic for helping me in the process of designing my book cover.

Last and not least: I beg forgiveness of all those who have been with me over the course of the years and whose names I have failed to mention.

ABOUT THE AUTHOR

J. H. Carnathan is from Tennessee and lives in Birmingham, Alabama for the time being. He is a fervent fan of honor, loyalty and chivalry. He loves to create worlds where men and women are emotionally broken and how they must find their way out of that darkness.

Carnathan is the author of the novel PURGATORIUM. Originally, this book was written as a screenplay, but as the story unfolded and throughout the editing process, it became clear that it was best fitted for a first novel. Ever since childhood, he has had an imagination towards story telling. That passion grew with age as he began to write short stories throughout his high school and college career. His degree in screenwriting from the University of Birmingham, Alabama gives his work a crisp, visual feel.

♣ ♠ ♦ ♥